1

GRETA

Today is the day!

I've been working at the magazine for twelve years and today marks the biggest day of my career to date: the launch of my very own online magazine. Well, not *mine* per se – technically, it's part of *Nouveau*'s new online platform – but it is very much my baby. I conceived it, designed it, staffed it, and edited it within an inch of its soon-to-be-out-in-the-world-for-all-to-see life.

Of course, it wasn't *all* me. Despite *Nouveau Life* being my vision, it wouldn't have come to fruition without the hard work of my carefully chosen team, or without the support of my boss and mentor, Anjali.

She's only in her mid-forties, but Anjali's professional accomplishments are the stuff of (my) dreams. She became editor-in-chief of *Nouveau India* when she was twenty-five; by twenty-eight, she'd moved to *Nouveau Britain*, our flagship edition; and within two years, she was appointed head of editorial.

That's when she hired me as a (lowly) staff writer straight from university. I was eager but green and she took me under her wing, teaching me practically everything I know about the magazine business – mostly how to be cutting edge and a leader in the industry, rather than just staying ahead of the curve. Her guidance – *and* her belief in me – is how I have achieved this incredible milestone at the relatively young age of thirty-five.

My phone chimes with an incoming message – it's Mum.

Viel Glück, mein Liebling. Wir lieben dich!

Mum is German and even though she's lived in the UK for forty years – *and* I was born here – she always messages me in German. I *understand* German, but beyond the basics, I'm rubbish at replying. I'm positive it's an enormous disappointment to her I'm not properly bilingual.

Still, her well wishes are always welcome, as is her telling me she loves me.

*Danke! *smiley face**

After replying, I tuck my phone into my handbag and turn to face the full-length mirror on the back of my bedroom door. When you work at a fashion magazine and don't look like Kaia Gerber (or her mum, for that matter), there are countless approaches to developing your signature work look.

While some of my colleagues are always on trend, my look is classic and chic, which works perfectly with my petite and curvy frame. As Coco Chanel said, 'Dress shabbily and they remember the dress; dress impeccably and they remember the woman.' And I want to be remembered – especially for being clever and brilliant at my job.

Today, I've chosen an empire-line shift dress in dove grey with a matching tailored jacket and my three-inch Lorenzo heels in silver (which are far more comfortable than they look). My straw-

THE ONE THAT I WANT

SANDY BARKER

Boldwood

First published in Great Britain in 2024 by Boldwood Books Ltd.

A CIP catalogue record for this book is available from the British Library.

Paperback ISBN 978-1-80549-869-8

Large Print ISBN 978-1-80549-868-1

Hardback ISBN 978-1-80549-867-4

Ebook ISBN 978-1-80549-870-4

Kindle ISBN 978-1-80549-871-1

Audio CD ISBN 978-1-80549-862-9

MP3 CD ISBN 978-1-80549-863-6

Digital audio download ISBN 978-1-80549-865-0

Boldwood Books Ltd
23 Bowerdean Street
London SW6 3TN
www.boldwoodbooks.com

To my bestie, Lindsey,
thanks for being my hilarious, loving, generous, understanding, no-
nonsense rock.

berry-blonde hair is pulled into a loose up-do that looks effortless but took me ages, and my make-up is natural-looking save for my glossy peach lips.

If I do say so myself, I look *fantastic*.

'Time to take the magazine world by storm,' I tell myself with a lifted chin.

Talking to yourself may be thought of as quirky or odd or even a sign of madness, but I consider it one of my superpowers.

* * *

When I arrive at *Nouveau*, my assistant editor, Bex, greets me with a squeal as I step out of the lift.

'Good morning, Bex.'

She bounces on the balls of her feet. 'I'm *so* excited. Isn't it just *beyond*? Your look is *fire*, by the way,' she adds before I have a chance to reply. 'Very classy.'

'Thanks. Not long to go now!' I gesture for her to walk with me towards my office and she falls into step, chattering the entire way. I barely register half of what she says – most of it about engagement on socials – because the closer we get to my office, the more surreal this begins to feel.

As we navigate the halls, my colleagues send me smiles and nods, with a couple of winks thrown in. Roger from accounting lifts a thumb into the air from across the office. *Are all accountants called Roger? Or is it that all Rogers go into accounting?* I think, my mind landing on an absurd thought.

'Greta!' Ivy Jones rushes towards me and pulls me into an awkward hug. 'So excited for the *Nouveau Life* launch,' she says when she releases me.

'Oh, thank you.' Having never really worked together, we're

cordial colleagues at best, so this exchange feels somewhat inauthentic.

'And do keep me in mind if you're looking for ideas. I have *lots* of them.' Ah, so that explains the effusive congratulations.

'Thank you, Ivy,' I say.

'That was weird,' whispers Bex as we walk off.

'Yep.'

Crossing the threshold into my office, Bex on my heels, I'm suddenly overcome by an intense roaring inside my head, something I've never experienced before.

'Er, Bex, would you mind closing the door?'

'Sure thing,' she chirrups.

I skirt around my desk, plop into my chair, and turn on my laptop. Bex remains standing by the door, an inquisitive look on her face.

'Are you all right?' she asks.

'I'm not sure,' I reply. The roaring has intensified and now my heart is racing. Is this a panic attack? I pick up a notepad from my desk and start fanning myself.

'It's going to be brill, I promise,' she says in a comforting tone.

'Oh, yes, no doubt.'

I glance her way and she's still watching me, her brows knitted together. 'Do you need anything from me? Or the others – they're already here. Actually, I've been here since seven.'

'Seven?' I ask with a jolt.

She shrugs. 'Excitement, I suppose.'

'Of course – also a big day for you, and well deserved.' She beams. 'And thank you for asking, but no, there's nothing I need.'

Ahh, that must be the reason I'm feeling like this. I'm at a loose end. The launch of *Nouveau Life*, which has consumed me for months now, has been meticulously planned right down to the tiniest detail. And with every logistical facet having been automated, the site will go live at 10 a.m. and dozens of posts will feed out to *Nouveau*'s social media accounts – all without anyone lifting a finger.

And, as I won't need to start on the weekly blog posts or next month's issue until this afternoon, for the next hour there is literally nothing for me to do (and I mean that in the *literal* sense, not ironically).

I can't remember the last time I had a full hour without a meeting or a phone call or an email to answer – *or* without an article to write or edit. I'm now positive that's the reason I'm out of sorts. I'm not *busy*. I glance at the time at the bottom of my laptop screen – ugh, still more than an hour to go.

I'd intended to spend the morning clocking the number of hits on the website, reading comments from readers, and graciously accepting congratulatory messages from my colleagues. Anjali has booked a celebratory lunch for the *Nouveau Life* team at Cicchetti, which I am very much looking forward to, but in my current state, I'm not sure I can sit here all morning simply *observing*. Especially if Bex is going to keep staring at me like that.

I slam my laptop shut and stand.

'Are you going somewhere?' she asks.

'Er, yes... coffee!' I declare as if I've suddenly remembered it exists. 'I think I'll pop down to the new coffee shop on the corner that everyone's been raving about.'

'Did you want company?' she asks. 'Or I can run out and get you something.'

'Actually, if you could stay here and man the desk, so to speak, that would be fab.'

She sends me an odd smile, confusion marring her features, and I scuttle past her, laptop under my arm and my handbag slung over my shoulder.

The ride in the lift feels like it takes an aeon, as does the walk through the lobby, but stepping outside *Nouveau*, I inhale deeply. Somehow, the smell of exhaust fumes is soothing, as is the thrum of traffic along the Strand.

I'm about to head towards the coffee shop when a silver Mercedes pulls up right in front of me. The back door opens and a long leg wearing a very high red heel stretches out, followed by the rest of Anjali. Terrible timing to execute an escape.

'Greta!' she says warmly. 'Happy launch day!'

'Thank you.'

She closes the car door and tucks her wavy, black bob behind her left ear. 'Where are you off to?' She eyes my laptop, and now I feel foolish for bringing it along.

'I was just popping out for a coffee,' I reply, as if my behaviour is perfectly normal.

'Are you all right?'

Clearly not if everyone keeps asking me that – well, so far it's only been Bex and Anjali, but still. 'Er, yes, I think so.'

'Nerves?' she asks with a tilt of her head.

'Possibly.'

'Understandable, but are you sure a double shot of espresso is the answer?' She pauses, her eyes narrowing. 'Just joking,' she adds with a laugh. 'I'm gagging for a coffee – I'll join you.' She looks in both directions. 'Any preference?'

'I was thinking about that new place on the corner,' I say, indicating the direction with a turn of my head.

'Perfect.' She heads off and I rush to catch up to her. We may both be wearing heels – she's also in Lorenzos – but she has a good nine inches on me height-wise and her strides are much longer than mine.

'Hopefully the nerves aren't all-consuming,' she says when I'm beside her again. 'I want you to *enjoy* this day; you've certainly earned it. Though I'm one to talk. If I think back on any of my professional milestones, they're all a blur and before I knew it, it was a week later, and everything was humming along.'

She's mentioned this before, how she only has vague memories of her professional 'firsts' – she's always been open with me about this type of thing – but today, her words have more meaning.

We reach the coffee shop – amusingly called 'The Daily Grind' – and she swings open the door, holding it for me.

The décor is inviting, if a little austere. It has a Scandinavian vibe – lots of blond wood, including the wall panelling, the counter, and the tables and chairs – and there are more plants than in a garden centre. The air quality in here must be excellent.

We queue up and order, then wait to the side for the baristas to work their magic on the giant espresso machine. I watch their precise, rhythmic movements as Anjali chats to me, but as with Bex earlier, I'm not taking in any of what she's saying. The roaring is back.

I smile and nod at her, hoping I'm doing a reasonable facsimile of listening, which I clearly am. 'So, what do you think?' Anjali asks, catching me unawares. 'Should we sack him?'

'What? Sack who?' Panicked, I conduct a mental roster of the several hims who report to Anjali. I can't for the life of me think who she might be talking about – they're all brilliant at their jobs.

'The tiler.'

'The ti— *Oh*, sorry.'

She angles her head – she's either confused or amused, probably a mix.

'To be honest, I haven't heard a word.' I tap on my temple. 'I have this intense noise inside my head.' Oops, I did not intend to mention that.

Though at least it's not as embarrassing as what I told her the night we were working late a couple of weeks back. I still cringe every time I think about it.

'My fault,' she says. 'I was trying to distract you by moaning about the utter *mare* of our renovations. And the noisy head – perfectly normal.'

Oh, thank god.

'And, silly me, I completely forgot...' she says. 'Gordon sends his love and says good luck for today.'

Gordon is Anjali's husband. He's a lovely man – a bit older than Anjali and more traditional in many ways, but he's always been kind to me. He also makes a mean G&T and enjoys trying new gins as much as I do.

'We'll have to have you over to celebrate properly – as soon as the sodding renovations are done.' She says the last part through gritted teeth.

'Angela, Gretal,' calls the barista. Anjali and I swap amused looks – the solidarity of those with a 'novel name' – then push through the small crowd to the counter to collect our coffees, a latte for me, extra foam, and a long black for her.

She leads the way to the window, where we slide into seats vacated by two men mere seconds ago. She brushes some pastry crumbs onto the floor and pins me with a look. The Anjali look.

I've been the recipient of this look *many* times. It can mean anything from 'I have some juicy work gossip and you mustn't tell a soul' to 'I know you've worked sixteen days straight and I'm insisting you take a mini break to Tenerife'.

'Now, Greta—'

'Ladies! I see you've discovered my new favourite haunt,' says a familiar voice.

'Hello, Luca,' says Anjali, warmly accepting a cheek kiss from our colleague. She adores Luca – most people do. And not just because he's handsome and charming, but he's also a brilliant fashion editor – *so* talented. He can make or break a designer just like that (imagine me snapping my fingers) and meets regularly with the top designers and their trend forecasters. In fact, he's considered *the* trend forecaster.

'Grets!' he exclaims, leaning down to land *two* kisses, one on each cheek. Luca may be London-born, but when he wants to be especially charming, he favours the customs of his Roman mother.

I graciously accept the kisses, mindful that not too long ago, this kind of attention from Luca would have sent shivers down my spine and set my nethers (as my mum calls them) alight.

Mine was an intense, several-year-long crush that had the power to derail everything from simple exchanges to editorial meetings to entire workdays. It came to a screeching halt the night I brought my best friend, Tiggy – a name she's been stuck with since birth, because her sister couldn't say 'Elizabeth' – to a staff function as my plus one, and Luca made a play for her.

She rebuffed him, of course – possibly the first woman ever to have turned him down – and he was so shocked, he made a big to-do about it. And just like that, it was as if a switch had been flipped and I saw him for who he really was: a talented, yet narcissistic playboy. End. Of. Crush.

'Congratulations!' he says. 'So excited for *Nouveau Life* – bound to be a smash hit.'

'It's very exciting, yes.'

It's ridiculous how intensely I use to long for him. Teens lust after Harry Styles with less fervour.

Luca, seemingly oblivious that he no longer wields any power over me, flashes a roguish grin. 'See you back at the office.'

I turn back to Anjali. 'You were saying?' I ask brightly.

'I—'

'Excuse me, Gretal?' When I look up again, a man is standing beside me – forty-ish, light-brown hair, kind smile, blue eyes. He reminds me instantly of James McAvoy – attractive in that unassuming, 'everyman' way.

'Er, yes?'

'I'm Ewan.'

Why is he telling me this? 'Hello, Ewan.' He continues smiling at me and I continue wondering why. 'Er, have we met before?'

He shakes his head.

'So how do you know my name?' I ask, returning his bemused smile. He did say 'Gretal' but close enough – I've answered to worse.

He holds up a coffee cup. 'I have your coffee.'

'Oh.' I look at the coffee cup I've been drinking from, which has 'EWAN' scrawled on the side. 'Oh! I'm so sorry. I must have picked up yours.'

'Yes,' he says, a lilt of laughter in his voice. 'Here.' He sets my coffee in front of me.

'I'm afraid I've already drunk from yours, but I'd be happy to buy you another one.'

He smiles again. 'No need – I'll sort it. Have a lovely day.' And before I can thank him, he leaves.

I turn to Anjali, about to ask her for a second time what she was going to say, when she flicks her wrist to look at her watch. 'Bollocks, we should probably go.'

'But what were you going to tell me?' I ask as we stand and gather our belongings.

'We'll chat about it later,' she says, smiling enigmatically.

We'll chat about it later. Well, thank you, Anjali, that doesn't sound ominous at all! Oh god, I hope it's nothing to do with what we talked about that night.

As we make our way back to the office, the roaring kicks into high gear.

2

POPPY

'Saffron, will you please get your bum out of my face.'

Tristan chuckles smugly from the other side of the bed.

'Fine for you. You're her favourite, so you get the good end,' I say, gently pushing her away from me.

She purrs loudly, nuzzling the crook of Tristan's neck, and he pets her with one hand. 'She loves us both equally.'

'Hah, *hardly*. And don't encourage her,' I add, snuggling into my now cat-bum-free pillow.

'Good morning, darling. How did you sleep?' he asks cheekily.

'Fine until our cat decided to join us,' I say, stifling a yawn. 'I'm not loving this newfound desire to sleep with us – especially when she has her own room.' Previously, we had a guest room with a study nook. Now we have 'Saffron's room', where she sleeps on the bed all day, only changing positions to chase the sun (when it's out).

Tristan props himself up, lifts Saffron one-handed, and puts her on the floor. 'Off you go, Saffy,' he coos.

Well, she does *not* like that. There's a disdainful 'meow' and she struts out of our room like a cat on a mission – probably to post on socials about how hard her life is.

'Not sure if I'm still her favourite after that,' he says, leaning over to kiss my cheek.

'Ah-hah! So, you admit it,' I say.

He chuckles again and gets out of bed. 'Tea?' he asks.

'Have I told you how much I love you?'

'Not today,' he says from the doorway.

'I love you!' I call out before surrendering to a yawn.

I'm usually a morning person. I'm also not one of those people who lives for the weekends. I *love* being an agent at the Ever After Agency, but after a sleepless night due to a certain feline, I could easily steal another half-hour under the duvet. Surely Saskia and Paloma, who run the agency, won't mind if I'm a *little* bit late.

'Darling, it's nearly six-thirty,' Tristan says from the kitchen.

My eyes pop open – bugger, I must have drifted off.

'Thank you!'

'And tea's ready.'

'Coming.'

I pad to the kitchen and take up a spot at the breakfast bar, where a steaming mug of tea awaits. No dainty china teacup for me this morning – Tristan has busted out the big guns. The only thing we own that's bigger than my 'World's Best Friend' mug is a bucket. He's also made me breakfast: three Weetabix and milk.

'I love you more than I did ten minutes ago,' I say before taking a sip of tea.

'Much on for the start of the week?' he asks.

'Finalising some paperwork on the reunited lovers' case—'

'The two ninety-year-olds?'

'That's the one. They are *so* sweet, Tris. Iris told me to expect a wedding invitation.'

'I'll have to dust off the tux.'

'I *suppose* you can be my plus one,' I tease, and the corners of his eyes crease over the rim of his mug.

'I also have a meeting with a new client this arvo – a school friend of Saskia and Paloma's. The agency's way of returning a massive favour she did for us back in March.'

'So, a VIP?' he asks.

'Yep.'

'Like I was.' Tristan's dark-amber eyes twinkle with mirth.

'Boy, you have tickets on yourself, Mr Fellows.'

He laughs at that, then tucks into his breakfast.

In autumn last year, *Tristan* was my client. I was tasked with finding him a wife by his thirty-fifth birthday, which was only forty days away, to ensure he inherited an eye-watering sum (thirty million pounds), meeting an archaic, but incontestable, clause in his grandad's will. It was either that, or the entire fortune would go to the Avian Wildlife Trust of the Hebrides, and no one in the family would see a penny.

Against my better judgement, professional creed, and everything a matchmaker is *supposed* to do, I fell in love with him. Fortunately, he fell right back, which we realised in time. *Just* in time.

'Meow.' At my feet, Saffron rubs up against the legs of the stool.

'Oh, hello, Saffron.' She's up there amongst the reasons I love my life, but I'll never tell her that. It'll go to her head.

'Meow.'

'Go ask Tristan to make you breakfast. He's chief cook and bottle washer this morning.'

She looks up at me disdainfully before stalking off into the kitchen. I just love her little half-black, half-orange face but she's lucky she's so cute, the little minx.

'Right,' says Tristan sometime later, 'I need to head in early this morning.'

Tristan's an investment banker, which is the main reason we

live in the financial district. Pre-me, all he did was work – all work and no play made Tristan a (rather) dull boy, according to our close friend, Jacinda – and he liked the convenience of being able to walk to work. Maybe one day we'll move but, for now, I don't mind the commute to Richmond where the agency is based.

And while I'm sitting here checking my socials with bed-hair, half-drunk tea, and very soggy bix, he's already had his breakfast, fed Saffron, and cleaned up the kitchen.

Tristan smacks a kiss on my lips. 'Bye, darling. Have a wonderful day.' He stoops to pet Saffron under the chin. 'You too, Saffy,' he says, his voice two octaves higher. We watch him leave and when the door closes behind him, Saffron looks at me, sniffs the air, and heads towards her bedroom.

Like I said, little minx.

* * *

'Thank you so much for coming in.' Anjali, a tall, slender, south-Asian woman, who looks like she just stepped off a runway, indicates for me to sit in the chair opposite her, then takes a seat behind her desk. 'So sorry you had to come all this way – I'd stupidly thought I'd be able to get out to Richmond this afternoon.'

I wave her off. 'Not a problem. Happy to be invited back to *Nouveau*.'

'That was a smashing article you wrote for us back in March.'

She's referring to the piece I 'co-wrote' as part of a case to reunite two fashion designers. And by 'co-wrote' I mean that I sent a pile of scribbles to my colleague, Freya, who gave the piece some shape, then I submitted it to a *Nouveau* editor, a woman called Bex, who turned it into an article.

It was a huge ask of *Nouveau* to publish that article, and it only came about because of Anjali's long-standing friendship with Saskia and Paloma.

'That's a generous characterisation of my contribution,' I say, and we exchange knowing smiles.

'But a successful case, I hear? I saw that Elle Bliss and Lorenzo just got engaged.'

'Yes! Absolutely thrilled for them – such a gorgeous couple. And that article was paramount to us making the match, so thank you again,' I reply. I don't bother correcting her that Lorenzo is the label, whereas the man behind the world-famous, sexy-but-comfortable shoes is called Leo.

'There's no need to thank me,' she says, 'especially as I am about to ask the agency to return the favour. Well, *ish*. It's not so much a favour from the agency as from you.'

'Me?'

'Yes – it's what I'd require of you. In addition to your work as a matchmaker, I mean.'

Intriguing.

'What did you have in mind?' I ask, keeping my expression neutral.

'Well, Sask tells me you used be a psychologist.'

'Yes, I practised for just over ten years before joining the agency.'

'And you specialised in...?'

'Predominantly positive psychology and treatment using CBT – cognitive behavioural theory.'

'Perfect.'

'So, how does this relate to the case?'

'Well, as you know, I'd be engaging you on behalf of a colleague, Greta Davies. She is brilliant, professional, hard-working, and very much has it together. But if this is going to work, I think you'll need to go undercover – *ish*.'

Anjali clearly likes couching her words with 'ish' but all she's done is confuse the matter – I still have no clue what the case is or what I'll be doing.

And the last time I went undercover was for the case Anjali mentioned earlier, where I posed as a fashion journalist. When I told Shaz about it, she couldn't stop laughing. I'd have taken offence if I didn't agree with her – it *was* laughable.

'Undercover as...?' I ask, hoping I won't be asked to pull any more fashion articles out of my bum.

'A romantic advice columnist – ish.' Wow, that's three ishes in three minutes. 'Soz, I'm doing a rubbish job of explaining this, aren't I?'

Yes, you really are.

'No, not at all,' I reply, the consummate professional.

'Put simply, I want you to help Greta find love.'

'Excellent. Then that's our starting point,' I say, glad we've finally got to the crux of things. 'And does Greta *want* to find love?'

'Yes. I *think* so.'

'It's best if you're certain. We wouldn't want to attempt to solve a problem that may not exist.'

'Right. Well, you see, I've known Greta for over a decade and I've watched her live and breathe work – these days, even more so than I do. And if she ever *does* take time for herself, it's only because I've forced her to. That said, if you'd have asked me a fortnight ago whether Greta wanted to fall in love, I would have said no. Her sole passion has always been her job. Well, for some time, she's had a rather obvious crush on our colleague, Luca, but that appears to be waning as far as I can tell.'

'So, something happened to change your mind – about Greta?' I ask, redirecting her back to the point.

'Yes, it was something she said. She was talking to herself, as she often does, only this wasn't one of her affirmations or verbal to-do lists. At first, I thought it was a throw-away comment – only, evidently, it wasn't.'

'What was it?'

'Well, Greta's just launched her own online vertical, you see, and—'

'Sorry, a vertical?' I ask, interrupting.

'It's like an imprint of a publisher – part of the whole, but also its own thing.'

Nope, still confused. 'Uh...?'

'The vertical, *Nouveau Life*, is an online magazine – but still part of *Nouveau*.'

'Ahh, got it. And Greta's at the helm.'

'Exactly. It's a massive responsibility, but she's earned it and I have no doubt it will be a smashing success. *Anyway*, she and I were working late one night – I'd stuck around to help her with an article from one of our freelancers about dating apps – and we'd just decided on a pull quote from one of the interviewees. It was something like, "I've been single so long, I have no idea what being in love even feels like any more." And Greta muttered to herself, "You and me both," in this *deeply* saddened tone.'

'Oh, that seems rather telling.'

'That's what I thought too. Now, ordinarily I would have pretended I didn't hear her, but as it was just the two of us, it was obvious that I *did* hear. And then I found myself asking her about it.'

I lean forward in anticipation. 'And?'

'And, apparently, the article had triggered a bout of introspection, and she's been thinking about it a lot lately – love. Especially now she's in her mid-thirties. Has she left it too late to find the perfect man, fall in love, and start a family? That sort of thing.'

'Well, that seems to answer my question.'

'I'd hoped as much. You know, this is the first time she's ever said *anything* like that to me – been that candid about her personal aspirations. It's stuck with me ever since. Actually, I nearly brought it up again this morning, which would have been disastrous timing. A huge distraction on her big day. I also hadn't met with you, of course, so it would have been premature. It's just... I've become a little consumed with it ever since she told me.'

'That's understandable. You obviously care about her a great deal.'

'I do. She's not just my protégé; she's also my friend. Well, *ish* – I'm still her boss.' She shakes her head, seeming lost in thought, then meets my eye. 'Perhaps this whole thing is misguided. I realise it's incredibly patronising of me, thinking I know best for someone else.'

'Although, sometimes that's the case,' I say, thinking of the times I've had to nudge Shaz in the right direction – like *not* ending her relationship with her girlfriend, Lauren, because she was afraid to commit.

'Look, I adore Greta,' Anjali continues, 'and if there's some-thing I can do to make her happy – *happier*, I should say, because she really is a cheerful person – then I want to do it. Which, of course, is where you would come in.'

'As an advice columnist for *Nouveau Life*.'

'Yes.'

This still makes no sense. 'And how exactly does that fit into your plan?' I ask, hoping to get more clarity.

She rests her elbows on the desk, her dark-brown eyes flashing with excitement. '*I* convince Greta to hire you as a contributor, writing an advice column for *Nouveau Life*, and *you* help Greta find love.'

That's it? That's the extent of her plan? While writing an advice column could be interesting, I'm failing to see the connection between that and helping Greta find love. Does Anjali want me onsite at *Nouveau* to *coach* Greta, to act as some kind of love mentor?

I couch my next question carefully, so I don't come off as rude. 'So, you're envisioning that I work here undercover to do *what* exactly?'

'Help Greta find love,' she states matter-of-factly.

Great – still as clear as mud.

'So, we'd be telling Greta who I really am? That I'm a matchmaker?'

Anjali appears horrified by the idea. 'Oh no, definitely not. Then Greta would realise that we're trying to find her a match.'

'And you don't want her to know?' This is getting more complex – and less plausible – by the second.

'Well, no. I think we only tell her about your experience as a psychologist. Surely that alone uniquely qualifies you as an advice columnist?'

I don't agree, but her assumption raises another issue.

'Aren't you concerned that Greta already knows me from the Elle Bliss/Lorenzo article? Won't she think it's odd that a fashion journalist now wants to write an advice column?'

'Oh... Interesting point,' she says, frowning. 'I hadn't thought of that.'

She huffs out an exasperated sigh, and I quickly parse what I've gleaned so far – that Anjali seems to believe my very presence will magically draw the right man to Greta – *and* prepare Greta to pursue a romantic relationship with said man. So, matchmaking by osmosis?

And then it comes to me – the missing piece.

'The advice column is an inspired idea,' I say, blatantly buttering up the client – the *VIP* client. 'Being a contributor to *Nouveau Life* would give me close proximity to Greta, allowing me to get to know her personally. It's always helpful when selecting potential matches to know as much about the client as possible. It would also be the perfect cover story for the rest of the team, so they're not confused about why I'm here.'

'Well, that's a much better way of articulating it.' She gives me a wry smile.

'*But*,' I add – and here's the clincher – 'I think we should tell Greta who I am and what I really do.'

'No, no, no…' she says, lifting both palms towards me.

'Please hear me out.'

'All right.' She sits back, regarding me intently.

'We tell Greta I'm a matchmaker because you're going to assign her an article for *Nouveau Life* – actually, make it a series of articles. I'll set her up on dates and she'll write about her experiences. Ten first dates… Dating as a career woman… I'll leave the angle up to you – or Greta – but dating will become her *assignment*. I'll provide the dates, and if I'm successful, one of them will be Greta's match. What do you think?'

That spark of excitement returns to her eyes, and she grins at me. 'I think you're a bloody genius.'

I chuckle softly. 'I'll take that.'

'And the idea of it being a writing assignment – that's *perfect*. Greta's already told me she wants to contribute at least one piece per issue – keep her hand in as a writer, as it were.'

'Great,' I reply, thrilled I came up with such a suitable solution on the spot. 'So, when should we meet with Greta?'

'Well, I wouldn't want to spring this on her immediately, what with the launch and everything, so how about the end of the week?'

'Sounds good. And one more thing…' I say, adopting a cautionary tone. Her smile falls away and she peers at me, her jaw tensing. 'I think you need to be prepared… It's quite possible that Greta will connect the assignment with your true intention – to find her a match. Maybe not right away, but she's obviously an intelligent woman.'

'So how do we prevent that?'

'Well, it might help if you come up with an angle that really *sells* the assignment. Dating is a hot topic... It will be a drawcard for new readers... That kind of thing.'

'All right. I'll mull it over and come up with something. Thank you, Poppy. There's a lot more to consider than I originally thought, but I think this is going to be brilliant.'

'I do too.' I stand and hold out my hand. 'Welcome to the Ever After Agency.'

'And welcome back to *Nouveau*,' she says, firmly shaking it.

3

GRETA

'You took the right one this time.'

It takes me a moment to realise that someone's talking to me and when I look up from my laptop, there he is, the James McAvoy lookalike – Owen. Or maybe it was Ewan?

I smile and pick up the now-empty cup. 'Ah, yes. Although, I've been here every day this week and they're still getting my name wrong.'

'So, not Gretal then?'

I shake my head. 'Nope.'

'Is it close to Gretal?'

I nod. 'Mmm-hmm. So close it's almost forgivable.'

'Only almost?'

'I've been here five times in five days. I even spelled it out this morning.'

'Well, that's less than forgivable in my book. Are you going to reveal how badly the baristas are murdering your name?'

'It's Greta. Greta Davies – German mum, Scottish dad.'

'Greta's a lovely name.'

'Thank you. I don't *love* it, but I suppose it could be worse. My poor brother got lumped with Dolph.'

His eyes widen and he breaks into a lopsided smile. 'Dolph, as in Lundgren?'

'Yes – although he's far too young to know who Dolph Lundgren even is. *And* he goes by Ru.'

'Ru?'

'Yep. He likes to pretend his real name is Rudolph, which he's shortened to Ru. We all call him that – his friends, his teachers, even my dad. Everyone except Mum.'

'She's sticking to her guns.'

'She is.'

'And how old is he? Obviously not old enough to have watched *Rocky IV*.'

'Is anyone else here that old?' I ask, casting my eyes about the coffee shop, and he laughs.

'Ouch. I'll have you know I was only two when that movie came out.'

Note to self: find out when Rocky IV *came out. Second note to self: Owen/Ewan has a lovely laugh – see if you can make him laugh again.*

'Though my friends and I watched it about a dozen times when we were twelve,' he continues.

'Well, this is a coincidence – that's Ru's age. He was a surprise – for all of us. I had just started working at *Nouveau* when he was born. I'm old enough to be his mum!'

'That was going to be my next question.'

'The age gap between me and my brother?' I quip.

'Where you work. I figured it was close by.'

'Three doors down, to be precise.'

I really want to steer the conversation back to names, as I'm now even keener to know if he's Owen or Ewan. I opt for a clumsy segue.

'Anyway, my guess is that once Ru starts drinking coffee and has to give his name to a barista, they'll spell it R-O-O, like in *Winnie the Pooh*.'

'You've given this some thought.'

'More than I realised until this precise moment.'

His mouth quirks and that lopsided smile returns.

'Well, sorry for interrupting your work. I just wanted to say hello.'

'Hello,' I say, with a winsome smile.

'Hello,' he replies, his sky-blue eyes creasing at the corners.

He holds my gaze for a moment, then looks away. I can tell he's about to leave me be, but I don't want to be left be. I quite like chatting with Owen/Ewan. Bollocks, is this one of those situations where it's now too late to ask his name?

'Greta, you're not replying to your messages.' In a feat of not-so-perfect timing, Luca has just shown up.

'Er, sorry?' I ask.

He points to my laptop. 'Anjali's been trying to get hold of you. She said if I saw you on my coffee run to ask you to pop back to the office – *pronto*.'

I look at my laptop, which is displaying the lock screen. 'Oh, bollocks.'

I've taken to working in the coffee shop for an hour most mornings, a change of scene that's helped me free up some brain space amid the busiest time of my career. But I've promised my team – and Anjali – that I'll always be reachable.

'I've kept you from your work,' says Owen/Ewan. 'Sorry 'bout that.'

'No, no,' I say as I stand and start gathering my things. 'Not your fault.'

As I'm about to leave, I catch Luca glancing at Owen/Ewan. It's obvious he's going to introduce himself, which is perfect – I'll learn

Owen/Ewan's actual name. Intrigued, I watch my former work crush hold out his hand to my... my... what? My nice-man-at-the-coffee-shop-with-the-kind-eyes-and-lopsided-smile?

'I'm Luca,' he says with his most charming smile.

They shake hands.

'Ewan.'

Ewan – right. *Ewan, Ewan, Ewan*, I chant in my head, committing his name to memory.

'And how do you know Greta?' Luca asks.

Wait, was there a bit of an edge to his question, or was that my imagination?

'Just from here. We're newly minted coffee-shop friends,' says Ewan, which I think is a perfectly lovely way to describe us.

He flashes me that smile and even though we've only had two exchanges, I get the sense that he's right – we are becoming friends. And if my daily visits to the coffee shop include a brief conversation with Ewan, all the more reason to continue.

'Right – apologies, but I must dash. Luca, thank you for passing on the message. And Ewan, nice to see you again.' I give them each a smile, then leave.

Out on the footpath, I congratulate myself for such a grown-up exit. 'Nicely done, Greta – and now you know Ewan's name.'

As I walk back to the office, it strikes me that I don't really have any male friends – colleagues, yes, but a man who is just a friend? None. That is, until today!

I was today years old when I made my first male friend.

* * *

I drop my things at my desk, then make my way to Anjali's office. She was right about the first week after the launch passing in a blur. I can't believe it's Friday already.

And I'm thrilled to say, we're a hit! Readers love us and so do *Nouveau*'s number crunchers, who are pleased with both site traffic and increased advertising revenue. When *Hello Britain* mentioned us this morning, our hits quadrupled within minutes.

These are terms I use now: hits and site traffic. Despite having a rather challenging relationship with technology – it drives me bonkers on a regular basis and I'd swear it's out to get me – I'm having to stretch myself professionally. Not only am I curator of all things editorial, including blog posts, I'm expected to master (at minimum) a foundational understanding of our behind-the-scenes success measures.

I suspect this is why Anjali has called me into her office – to go over the numbers and debrief on the week that was.

'Come in, Greta. I'd like you to meet Poppy Dean.'

Or perhaps not.

'Hi, Greta, nice to meet you.' Poppy is a dark-haired woman of medium height in her thirties, who seems vaguely familiar – or she could just have one of those faces. From her accent, I can tell she's Australian.

'Hello, Poppy,' I say, extending my hand to shake hers. We exchange smiles and when I glance in Anjali's direction, she's grinning like a proud mum.

What is this about? I wonder.

'Let's sit over here, shall we?' says Anjali, gesturing towards her sitting area.

Poppy and I settle on the sofa and Anjali sits across from us on an armchair, still wearing that odd expression. It's like the Anjali look on steroids.

I turn to Poppy. 'Have we met before?' I ask. 'It's just that you look so familiar.'

'I don't think so, but I've been into *Nouveau* before – back in March.'

Pieces of the puzzle begin to slot into place. '*Oh*, you co-wrote that piece with Bex – on Elle Bliss and Lorenzo. You're "P Dean".'

'That's right,' she says, dipping her chin modestly.

'So, are you hoping to write for *Nouveau Life*? Is that why you've come in?'

We're already staffed *and* have a stable of regular freelancers to draw from, but I'd be willing to hear Poppy's pitch.

'Umm, not exactly...' she replies right as Anjali says, 'Well, ish...'

Wonderful – this is one of Anjali's ishes! What on earth is going on?

'So, what exactly were you thinking?' I ask them, fixing what I hope is a pleasant smile on my face. Though, I suspect I look more like Pennywise the Clown.

'Actually, I'd like us to bring Poppy on as a staff writer,' Anjali replies.

I gaze at her, totally bewildered. *Nouveau Life* doesn't need a staff writer, which Anjali knows – *she* helped me build out my editorial team. I also have complete creative control over the vertical, including hiring decisions, so when Anjali says 'us', who exactly is she talking about?

'For *Nouveau*?' I ask.

'For *Nouveau Life*,' she replies, her eyebrows raising in excitement.

It takes me a moment to find my voice. When I do, all I manage is, 'Oh,' which I say with a bobbing head and that ridiculous clown smile on my face.

I don't want to be rude to either of them – highly unprofessional – but I am very confused.

'So,' I say, turning towards Poppy, 'what would you write about? We cover a little bit of fashion, but that's not our key focal point.'

Poppy and Anjali glance at each other.

'I'm not actually a fashion journalist,' she replies – which is *not* actually a reply. 'I'm a matchmaker.'

There's every chance I now resemble a goldfish – all bug eyes and gaping mouth.

'You're what?' I say, abandoning any hope of maintaining a professional façade.

'A matchmaker,' says Anjali, as though that explains everything. It doesn't. 'We thought we'd bring Poppy on as an advice columnist – you know, readers send in problems with their love life and Poppy helps solve them. Before she worked as a matchmaker, Poppy was a psychologist – so, you see, it's a match made in heaven. So to speak.'

Anjali's terrible pun aside, I don't *hate* the idea.

'Right, I can see the potential there,' I say noncommittally. 'And you're really a professional matchmaker?'

'Yes, I work at the Ever After Agency in Richmond. The article I wrote with Bex – that was for a case. I was undercover.'

Realisation dawns and my expression morphs into one of awe. 'Oh my god, *you* matched Elle Bliss and Lorenzo.'

'I did,' she says, beaming.

I press a palm to my chest. 'I'm totally starstruck. I *adore* those two. They are the most *adorable* celebrity couple. Did you know that I'm the one who coined their couple name?'

'Ellorenzo? Really, that was you?'

'That was me,' I say proudly.

Hmm. Moments ago, I was ready to execute a mutiny and overrule Anjali's decision – especially since it should have been mine to make – but now... *now*, I can envision how Poppy might fit into the team – *and* how well an advice column will play with our readers.

'So, just to be clear, you'd still be matchmaking?' I ask.

'Yep, I'd keep my job at the agency, then write for you part-time.'

'We were thinking once a month to start, so part of the regular publication cycle,' says Anjali, 'with the possibility of going weekly if Poppy builds up a significant following.' This is something else that should have been my decision – the machinations – but I'm starting to get excited about this column, so I don't say anything.

'There's a tiny catch, though,' Poppy says. With a head tilt, I invite her to expound. 'Outside of the two of you, no one can know I work for Ever After. Our agency is... well... clandestine. We don't advertise and we don't promote our services. We take on cases strictly by referral, so when I'm writing for you, I'll need a nom de plume.'

'But you wrote for us before as "P Dean".'

'I did – which was risky, but I was also writing about fashion. This will be a little closer to home, so...'

'Right, that does make sense,' I reply with a nod. 'You know, when you first started telling me about this, I wasn't convinced—'

'You don't say,' Anjali teases.

'An open book, apparently,' I tell Poppy, pointing to my face with both index fingers. She's gracious enough to wave me off. 'Anyway, so how about you come in next week?'

'Perfect.'

'In the meantime, I'll brief the team and get to work.' I stand, figuring the meeting is over, but Poppy and Anjali exchange another look and if I'm not mistaken, this one is slightly panicked.

'Er, there *is* one more thing, Greta,' says Anjali. Her eyes dart towards Poppy again.

'You might want to take a seat for this,' Poppy adds.

I look between them and slowly sit, more confused than I've been at any other time in this conversation.

And then, Poppy completely and utterly blows my mind. And not in a good way.

4

GRETA

'I am literally dying right now.'

Tiggy – best friend since nursery school, partner-in-crime, giver of tough love when needed, and frequent overnight inhabitant of my sofa after too much wine – rolls her eyes at me.

'Babes, you're too old to be using "literally" non-literally,' she replies with a smirk.

'Fair, but how would you react if your boss felt *so* sorry for you, she employed a matchmaker to set you up on dates?'

'I don't have a boss. I work for myself.' Tiggy is a (brilliant) freelance graphic designer.

'Semantics,' I retort.

'Regardless, it doesn't mean she feels sorry for you. It's just an assignment.'

'Hah! Oh look,' I say, pointing out the window, 'a flying pig.'

Tiggy chuckles.

'God, I'm *mortified*.'

'Clearly. You've necked that wine way faster than usual.' She leans across the coffee table to top me up.

'Thank you,' I say without thinking – my mind is still chewing on my dilemma. 'I was completely blindsided. It was bad enough thinking that Anjali had brought Poppy on as a staff writer without consulting me. Then they dropped the *real* bombshell. And am I really expected to believe Anjali was just wandering about Richmond and happened upon a secret matchmaking agency, then thought, "Oh, I've just had a brilliant idea for a series of articles for *Nouveau Life*"? My arse, she did.'

I gulp down more wine. Tiggy's right, I'm drinking this way too fast. Not only am I risking a monster hangover tomorrow, but it's a decent bottle and I should be savouring it. I get up, setting the glass on the coffee table, and wander over to the window to look out at Parkland Walk. No pigs, flying or otherwise, just people walking, some solo, some with dogs. There's also a handful of joggers. It occurs to me that I've never seen a jogger with a smile on their face – they're always grimacing.

I take in a deep breath and exhale so forcefully, condensation forms on the window.

When I glance back at Tiggy, she's eyeing me curiously. 'So, you *legit* have to go on dates for work?' she asks.

'Yep. I'm like Kate Hudson's character in *How to Lose a Guy*.'

'Andie,' she states matter-of-factly. Tiggy is a walking encyclopaedia of romcoms, which is ironic considering she's practically anti-love.

'Andie, exactly. And how sad is that? I may as well start writing listicles.'

'You're not going to start writing listicles. It's *Nouveau*, not *Woman's Weekly*. Besides, if it's really about the articles, isn't it something Bex could do?'

'Right? Bex is *far* better suited to this assignment than I am. She's unattached, she's twenty-six, she's not running an entire online magazine...'

'Well, why not suggest that instead?'

'Because I already did, and Anjali insisted that it be me. That's why I'm onto her,' I say, my eyes narrowing. 'I let slip how I want to fall in love, and she concocts this writing assignment. *Then* she pretends one has nothing to do with the other. She even made up some bunk about studies and news reports. "People with careers are prioritising love and relationships now more than ever, Greta. We need to do a deep dive into this important topic – our readers want to know how to navigate the dating landscape. And what a perfect follow-up to the dating apps piece." Hah! If those were the *actual* reasons, I could write it as an investigative series – *without* going on dates!'

'You do a shitty impression of her, you know.'

'*Thanks*,' I say sarcastically. My indignation starts to fizzle out and I meet Tiggy's eye. 'A bloody *matchmaker*, Tig. I just wish I hadn't opened up to her the way I did. So *stupid* of me – we don't have that type of relationship.'

'You *are* close, though. You spend more time with her than with me.'

'Yes, but that's "work close" not "real-life close". And with everything that's going on, I'd hoped she'd forgotten. Why did I *do* that? I've never told her *anything* about my love life bef—'

'You mean, your lack of love life.' She's smirking again, plainly enjoying this.

'Yes, thank you for the reminder, but I haven't had time for love. I've been too busy building my career. Then suddenly I lift my head and – bam – I'm in my mid-thirties and alone. Oh god,' I say, resting my forehead against the window, 'those are the exact words I said to Anjali! What was I *thinking*?'

'Um, I take exception to the "alone" part.'

'What?' I ask, turning towards her. 'Oh, sorry. You're right, I'm not *alone*. I'm not even lonely – I'm surrounded by wonderful people.'

I don't add that besides my immediate family and Tiggy, most of those 'wonderful people' are my colleagues.

'Present company included,' she quips before stuffing her mouth with Wotsits. You'd never know it to look at her – five-ten and nine stone – but Tiggy's diet is 50 per cent snack food. Wine and Wotsits is her version of wine and cheese.

'Well, obvs,' I say in response to her I'm-fishing-for-a-compliment comment. 'Mind if we get back to me now?'

She mumbles her agreement through her mouthful.

'I was going to say that until a few weeks ago, I'd barely thought about love at all.'

I head back to the sofa and flop onto it, then retrieve my glass and take a small sip. It really is delicious – a Tempranillo from Spain.

'So, what changed? What's the catalyst for all this angst?' she asks, digging her hand inside the Wotsits packet again.

'It's silly really.'

'Just tell me.'

I meet her gaze and she stares at me expectantly, her head cocked to one side. She knows I had an awkward conversation with Anjali that night – I told her the next day – but she doesn't know the catalyst for the conversation *or* how much it's been on my mind ever since.

'All right. So, I was editing this article for *Nouveau Life* about dating apps and there was this section about successful matches – people who'd got married after meeting online – and it got me thinking. I mean, I'm thirty-six next birthday—'

'We both are,' she interjects.

'Yes, but *you* haven't always thought you'd fall in love and have a baby.'

'Thirty-six isn't too old to have a baby.'

'Well, *no*. But even if I met someone now and had a whirlwind romance *and* got pregnant right away, I'd be at *least* thirty-seven by the time the baby came. And did you know that any pregnancy over the age of thirty-five is considered a geriatric pregnancy? *Geriatric*, Tig.'

'What about your mum? She was a lot older than that when she had Ru.'

'She was forty-eight, but—'

'See? You've got plenty of time to find a nice bloke and have a baby. Maybe even get married.'

'Ugh. Just the thought of that is exhausting – dating... finding the right person... telling each other your dreams... your secrets... letting them see all your faults... falling in *love*... If only I could have parlayed my crush on Luca into a ready-made family of three – no dating, no pregnancy, just a scrummy hubby and an adorable baby in the blink of an eye.'

Tiggy laughs at that. 'You really are a right muppet. And Luca's a cad. You'd have been a single mum before your baby's first birthday.'

'That may be true.'

'It is *definitely* true.'

'Oh, I envy you, Tig,' I say with a sigh. 'I have no idea how you do it.'

'Do what?'

'Have a love life,' I reply.

'First, it's not a love life, it's a sex life.'

'I suppose.'

'Second, *I'm* not a workaholic.'

'Well, no,' I reply, acknowledging that it's no secret I *am* one – by *choice*. It's a core part of my identity, one I am exceedingly proud of! (I know, I know, methinks the lady doth protest too much.)

'And third, there is a big difference between what you want and what I have with my...' She trails off without attaching a fitting label – Tiggy detests labels. She also detests the idea of being tied to one person. Her bedroom should have a revolving door.

'Lovers?' I ask.

She grins at me, shaking her head. 'You cow. You know I hate that word. It's *icky*. Right up there with panties and—'

'Moist!' we shout together.

We fall about laughing. Idiotic really, but we've been laughing at the word 'moist' since Food Technology in Year 8. Our teacher couldn't stop exclaiming how moist Trevor Landry's flapjacks were and by the end of the lesson, all thirty pupils were in fits. Poor thing. She could barely look at us after that.

Our laughter subsides and, in unison, we sigh one of those contented I-needed-a-good-laugh sighs.

'Right, so back to you and your assignment,' says Tiggy.

I groan, then drink a generous glug of wine. We should probably order food soon or I will *definitely* be hungover tomorrow. I reach for my phone and open the delivery app.

'Are you listening?'

'Sort of,' I admit.

'Greta, look at me,' she says in an appalling Australian accent. This is her doing Kath from *Kath and Kim*, something we were obsessed with in our final year of school. We'd recite entire scenes together, but my accent was much better than hers. Don't tell her I said that.

'All right! I'm looking at you.'

'Good.'

'Good.'

She rolls her eyes again and I stifle a laugh. This type of bestie banter is par for the course with us, especially this far into a bottle of wine. 'Do you want to hear what I think?'

'Do I have a choice?' I ask, already knowing the answer.

'No.'

'Then proceed,' I say with a flourish of my free hand. I down the rest of my wine and reach for the bottle.

'Less than a month after you have this major realisation, this *epiphany* that you aren't getting any younger and there may be more to life than work, a professional matchmaker practically lands in your lap. For *free*. You're looking a gift horse in the mouth. So, instead of moaning about it, you might as well take the assignment and see what comes of it.'

'I hate it when you make sense.'

'You're welcome,' she retorts.

'Even if it means I have homework to do over the weekend.'

'Homework?' she asks.

I point to the quarter inch-thick stack of paper sitting on the coffee table. '*That* is the client questionnaire for the matchmaking agency.'

'Good god!' She picks it up and starts thumbing through it.

'I know – and it's more evidence that they are *actually* trying to match me. Why else have me complete it?'

'There's less paperwork than this to get a mortgage,' she says, ignoring my comment about the mounting evidence. 'Haven't they heard of online forms?'

'Apparently, they get more candid responses from a paper one.'

She looks up from the ream of paper and sets it back on the table. 'Hmm. Worth it, though. And not just 'cause you're nearly past it.'

'Ouch!'

'You also spent far too long crushing on the wrong man,' she continues, undeterred.

'Double ouch.'

'Come on, how many years did you waste on Luca? He was never husband material and you know it.'

She's right. Too bad it took my nethers so long to get the memo.

But maybe it wasn't just my nethers. Maybe I crushed on Luca because pining after an unattainable man was easier than facing the terrifying prospect of being vulnerable with someone new.

Ugh. I'm too shattered to unpack that right now.

'Okay, fine, you're right,' I say instead. 'Now, can we please order food? I'm about thirty seconds away from eating the rest of your Wotsits for dinner.'

'You wouldn't dare,' she says, grabbing the bag off the table and clasping it to her chest.

* * *

Poppy

'Georgie Boy,' I say to my fellow agent as I perch on the edge of his desk. 'I have something to ask you.'

He slams his laptop shut but not without me seeing he was on *Spill the Tea*. If I ask him about it, he'll lie and say it's for a case, but the truth is that George is addicted to celebrity gossip. But as far as vices go, it's fairly innocuous.

'Hello, Poppy,' he says, propping his chin on his hand. 'What can I do for you?'

'It's about a case…'

'Mmm…?' he asks, feigning mild curiosity when I can tell his interest is fully piqued.

This is a well-practised routine of ours. Any time I've asked George to be my second on a case, I pretend I'm asking for a massive favour and he pretends to consider it. The reality: I bring my juiciest cases straight to George, because the juicier the case, the harder he works at it – and we both know that. I also adore working with him.

'First, it's *Nouveau*…'

'The magazine?' he asks, abandoning his coy pretence and sitting up ramrod straight.

'The one and only.'

He leans in closer and purses his full lips. 'Ooh, do tell.'

I paint the broad strokes of the case for him, each detail inciting an exclamation, wide-eyed wonder, or both. I conclude with, 'The client's coming this arvo with her completed questionnaire, but I'd love your help reviewing the long list of potentials. So, will you be my second on this one?'

'Poppy, if you ask anyone else, I'll never speak to you again.'

'You were my first and only choice.'

He nods with a slightly smug smile, then leans back in his chair. 'And what are your thoughts on the angle?' he asks.

'For the articles?'

'Mm-hmm.'

'I've actually left that to Anjali, and I imagine Greta will want to have a say. It's her online magazine, after all.'

'I'm thinking the articles should be anonymous, don't you?' he asks. 'Otherwise, Greta will have to inform her dates. And can you imagine? "Oh, by the way, you don't mind if I write about the size of your willy in my magazine, do you?"'

I inhale sharply. 'George, I love you, you know I do, but if you dare say anything like that to Greta, I will slap you upside the head.'

He waves off my (supposed) threat with a flap of his hand. 'Of course not.'

'Because from my brief experience with Greta, she's serious-minded and more than a little reluctant to take on this assignment.'

'I'll be gentle with her, I promise.'

'Good. Remember, the guise is that this is simply a writing assignment, but we only succeed if she gets her happily ever after.'

'Got it. So, what time is she coming in?'

'Four-thirty.'

He starts to open his laptop.

'Your calendar's free, I've already checked.'

'Right.'

'And I'll forward the long list of potentials in a moment,' I say as I head off towards my desk.

'Poppy?' he calls after me.

I turn back around.

'What were you thinking for the case name?' he asks.

Sigh – the confounding quest for the perfect case name. My colleagues seem to *love* spending time on this, whereas (much to their disappointment) I'd happily refer to cases by the client's last name or assign them a random set of alpha-numeric characters. Mainly because the name of a case has no bearing on its outcome *whatsoever*.

'Um, how about you decide?'

'What about "Handsome and Greta"?' he suggests.

I don't *hate* it, though I'd better appear more enthusiastic than that.

'Fab,' I reply with a smile and he beams. 'Ursula will love it too,' I add, referring to our colleague who names all her cases after fairy tales.

'I'll love what?' Speak of the devil. Ursula, who is anywhere between fifty and seventy – a well-kept secret due to the amount of plastic surgery she's had – sashays into the open-plan office amid a cloud of Chanel N°5.

'The new case Poppy and I are working on: Handsome and Greta,' George replies.

'*Oh?*'

I leave George to fill Ursula in and return to my desk. Right as I sit, my phone chimes with a message:

Hello darling. The cousins want to see us. Next Sunday work?

He's talking about Evie and Olivia, Tristan's first cousins on his dad's side who are in their mid-twenties. Last year, when he learnt about the terms of his grandad's will, he reconnected with them after years of little or no contact. And after he received the inheritance, he created generous trusts for each of them.

I met them just before our wedding and absolutely adore them. Having no siblings of my own, they've become like younger sisters to me.

I send a quick reply:

Perfect. Invite them for Sunday lunch?

Tristan's response comes in seconds:

You offering to cook?

I laugh out loud at that, causing several colleagues to glance over. It's funny because I don't cook – *at all*. I can assemble a lovely cheese platter and I've been known to microwave a ready meal, but I leave the culinary arts to my husband. That way, we both steer clear of A&E.

Hilarious. See you at home. Px

5

GRETA

I've always loved visiting Richmond – it's such a picturesque part of London – but today, the roaring inside my head that started the day *Nouveau Life* launched is back. I cannot believe I'm doing this.

I'm greeted at reception by a smiling woman, who introduces herself as Anita. She stands and comes around to my side of the desk. 'This way, please,' she says as she leads me across the office towards a meeting room.

When I enter, Poppy's there with a man – early thirties (my best guess), lean, with strawberry-blond hair, pale skin, and the type of handsome looks that scream 'pop-culture vampire'. He could easily be an Edward or a Lestat.

'Hi, Greta. Come on in,' says Poppy. 'This is George – he'll be working on your case with me.'

George – a good name for a vampire. My mind's doing that thing it does when I'm uncomfortable – fixating on absurd thoughts. Between that and my 'noisy head' (as Anjali calls it), I'm going to have to properly focus to get through this meeting.

George and I exchange pleasantries, then I turn down Anita's offer of a beverage, even though she mentions a fully stocked bar and it's nearly 5 p.m. I may regret that decision later.

After Anita leaves, Poppy sends a welcoming smile my way. 'So, you've brought the completed questionnaire?'

'Oh, yes, I have it right here.' I take the enormous document out of my handbag – it barely fit – and slide it across the table. George picks it up and starts looking through it. As he reads, his brows knit together.

Good sign or bad? I wonder.

'So, how did you get on with it?' asks Poppy.

'Er, not bad. A few tricky ones in there,' I say, severely down-playing how excruciating an exercise it was.

Tiggy and I started on Friday night – stupidly after we'd finished the first bottle of Tempranillo and before the Indian food arrived – and at first, it was a laugh.

'Favourite colour?' Tiggy asked.

'Mustard!' I declared.

'Favourite food?'

'Mustard!'

We fell about laughing and barely got through favourite song – Demi Lovato's 'Confident' (I know all the words) – and favourite movie – *Bridget Jones's Diary* (I can recite most scenes verbatim) – before dissolving into laughter so intense, we barely made any noise, just the occasional squeak. The poor delivery guy was totally bewildered when I opened the door to him, still laughing and with tears rolling down my face.

Saturday morning's hangover, however, cast a grim pall over the questionnaire and I spent the rest of the weekend treating it like the proper homework it was. I'd rather have written an article on the trials and tribulations of adolescence from the perspective of a short, chubby, red-headed bookworm (spoiler: that was me at fourteen).

'Excellent,' Poppy replies warmly.

Seemingly, I've pulled off 'confident professional on assignment' even though 'pathetic single in want of a baby daddy' may be closer to the truth. As I spent most of the weekend in deep retrospection, prompted by the behemoth George is now casually perusing, I suspect it may be.

'So, a quick update from our end,' Poppy continues. 'George and I have been working on a long list of potential matches, and once we've reviewed your questionnaire, we'll narrow that down to a shortlist. But, first, we need to know what you and Anjali have decided.'

'Decided?'

'Regarding how you'll approach the series of articles,' she replies.

George looks up from the questionnaire. 'The angle,' he adds.

'Ahh... Well, we haven't decided yet.'

The truth: after Anjali sprang Poppy and this (ridiculous) assignment on me Friday morning, I made a point of avoiding her for the rest of the day. Same again today. In fact, I spent several hours working from the coffee shop instead of in my office just to steer clear of her. I'm grasping onto a sliver of hope that she'll soon realise how unsuitable this concept is for *Nouveau Life*.

'Well, regardless of the angle, we're recommending that you write anonymously,' says George.

'Oh, really?' I look to Poppy, and she nods in agreement.

'That will allow you to be more candid in the articles, don't you think?' she asks. 'And it's more respectful to the potential matches if they remain anonymous too.'

The roaring ramps up. It also occurs to me that if I want to tell Poppy and George I'm onto Anjali and her obvious plan to marry me off, now would be the time. But would that be showing my hand too soon? Is there any advantage in keeping it to myself, at least for now? Without a clear answer either way, that's what I decide to do: keep mum.

'What do you think?' Poppy asks.

'Oh, yes, that makes sense. At the top of each article, we could state that the writer – and the subjects – have been anonymised to protect the guilty.'

Right as I say the word 'guilty', George says, 'Innocent,' and his eyes widen.

'I was only joking,' I say with a laugh.

He laughs along with me – though I imagine he's just being polite.

God, I really need to get this meeting back on track – or, on any track really. I've been on the back foot since I got here. I need to take charge and lay out how this will go. Otherwise, I'll be marching down the aisle, dressed in white, and married off to some suitable-on-paper bloke before I can say 'romance is dead'.

Poppy is watching me with an inscrutable look on her face. 'Greta, perhaps we should start again?'

Bloody hell, was she reading my mind?

She and George exchange a loaded glance, then she turns back to me. 'Look, we know this is an unusual assignment, and that you're not wholly comfortable with it.'

Understatement of the millennia.

'That said, we'd like to make it as painless – and as fun – as possible. For whatever reason, Anjali has her heart set on these articles and she thinks you're the perfect person to write them.'

The 'whatever reason' is that Anjali is playing matchmaker. She's obviously convinced that I'm sad and lonely and (very possibly) in need of a proper shag. That last part may be true, but I do *not* want my boss thinking of me that way – or spending *any* time pondering my nethers.

Poppy leaps out of her seat. 'Wait here for a sec,' she says, disappearing out the door.

'Is mustard really your favourite colour?' George asks, his mouth twitching at the corners.

I laugh. 'No, sorry, my bestie and I were having a laugh on Friday night, and I forgot to change it. Mustard is actually my *least* favourite colour. I'm always baffled when I see people *wearing* it. How about you?'

'Totes agree. It's right up there with camouflage and leopard print – or, god forbid, both at the same time.' He screws up his face in distaste, making me laugh again. 'I mean, just *why*?'

We snigger together and, for the first time since I arrived, I start to relax.

'Do you love working at *Nouveau*?' he asks leaning forward, his eyes locked on mine.

'I really do,' I reply.

'Ahh... professional goals,' he says with a sigh.

'Wait, really? Surely you love working here?' I ask, the journalist in me wading into the conversation. 'It must be extremely satisfying, helping people find love?'

'No, I do. I love it. But *Nouveau*... I mean, it's the mothership.'

For the first time, I take in his thoughtfully put-together, highly fashionable look. Periwinkle-blue, single-breasted blazer, sleeves rolled up to mid-forearm, revealing pink paisley lining, and a deeper-pink dress shirt with sky-blue collar and cuffs – also rolled up. I silently chastise myself for being so in my head I didn't realise I'm in the presence of a true *fashionisto*.

'Well,' I say brightly. His head cocks with interest. 'Now you have an in – to the mothership, I mean – and you're welcome any time.'

His eyebrows shoot up and his jaw drops. A moment later, he

breaks into a broad grin. 'You've just solidified your place as my number-one girl crush.'

'I didn't realise I was a contender.'

'Excuse me, with *that* ensemble' – he waves his hand in my direction like a warlock casting a spell – 'and *that* beat? Stun-ning. You being an editor at *Nouveau* is simply the icing on the cake,' he assures me.

I *did* take extra care with my appearance today, going with the look-great-feel-great tactic, which, until this meeting, had barely made a dent in my apprehension about Anjali's (misguided) plan. Thank goodness for George. His appreciation of the effort I've made is just the boost I need.

Right as he and I are basking in the glow of mutual admiration, Poppy returns with a portable whiteboard in tow. George pops out of his seat to help her get it through the door.

'Thanks,' she says to him, a little out of breath. 'We should have one of these in every meeting room,' she tells me. She's right – we have them in all the offices and meeting rooms at *Nouveau* – you never know when inspiration will spark a brainstorming session. 'But we're making do sharing this one.'

She manoeuvres it into place at the head of the table and takes a marker from the tray.

'Right,' she says, 'let's nut this out.'

An hour later, after Anita popped her head in with another offer of beverages and this time I said yes to a G&T, as did Poppy and George, we arrive at these concepts:

1. Matchmaker, make me a match – engaging a modern-day matchmaker

(Completely anonymised – not just me and all my potential matches, but the agency too.)

2. The dating pool – avoiding the shallows and swimming in the deep end

(Catchy title, but a little nebulous.)

3. Ten first dates – how to make a first date feel like the third

(I don't love this one – too close to the dreaded listicle.)

4. The best of both worlds – a career woman's guide to finding The One

(I don't love this one either – far too much pressure to create a definitive guide.)

Poppy steps back, her head at an angle as she regards our handiwork. George downs the rest of his G&T and crunches on an ice cube, then fishes for the lemon wedge with his fingers, and I sip mine, my editor's eyes roving the whiteboard over the rim of my glass.

'What do you reckon?' Poppy asks, turning to me.

'They'd all work,' I say. 'Though, that's me with my editorial hat on.'

'What about wearing your client-of-a-matchmaking-agency hat?'

I run my eyes over each item on our list again, really trying to imagine what it would feel like to be the subject of the ensuing articles.

'The first one... that's more of a behind-the-scenes take on the work you do, so...'

Although it's the easiest concept from my perspective, it's also the least personal, meaning readers may not engage with it as much as they would with the other, more vicarious, approaches. Hmm, that's me with my editorial hat on again.

I continue, grateful that both Poppy and George are giving me space to sift through my thoughts.

'I think two is too…'

'Out there?' Poppy offers.

'It's not really firmed up, is it?' I reply.

'Well, there are people who play a numbers game,' says George, snapping his fingers in quick succession. 'One date after the other, regardless of how wrong their dates might be for them, in the hopes that one of them might work out. I suppose this would be the opposite – more carefully curated dates, substance over volume.'

'I like that,' I say. George may have spent much of this meeting fangirling, but with one astute observation, he's proven his mettle as a matchmaker.

'What about number three?' asks Poppy. 'Too "women's magazine-y"?'

I laugh at that. 'How did you know?'

'A few reasons,' she says, 'not the least of which was your sour expression when I wrote it on the board.'

We all chuckle.

'Have you seen *How to Lose a Guy in Ten Days*?' I ask them.

'Seen it?' scoffs George. 'It's my second-favourite Kate Hudson romcom.'

'Only second favourite?' I tease.

'*Fool's Gold* was grossly underrated,' he replies earnestly.

'We're getting a little off track,' says Poppy before I can respond. 'I'm guessing you asked about *How to Lose a Guy* because the main character gets lumped with those awful how-to articles?'

I look between them, impressed. 'Are you all across famous –

and almost-famous – romcoms?' I ask with a laugh. Perhaps it's a job requirement.

'Yes,' they reply in unison.

I grin at them, delighted – even though they obviously missed my Kate Hudson/*Almost Famous* reference. And I'm sure the gin is playing its part, but I'm far less apprehensive about this assignment than when I arrived. I feel like I'm in good hands with Poppy and George.

'Okay, number three's off the table,' says Poppy, redirecting our conversation yet again. 'What about number four?'

I re-read it: *The best of both worlds – a career woman's guide to finding The One.*

'Bleh,' I say candidly. 'It sounds like something from *Cosmopolitan* circa 1985.'

'Well, then we have a concept,' says Poppy with a smile. 'Here's to the dating pool and avoiding the shallows.' She lifts her glass in a toast and I do the same, then we both take a sip.

'Oh, bugger,' says George. 'I'm totes dry.'

At that, I find myself laughing again. Perhaps this won't be so bad after all.

6

POPPY

'How do I look?' George does a spin, then looks at me expectantly.

'Like someone who will fit right in at *Nouveau*,' I reply – and I'm not just saying that. As he does every day, George looks a million dollars.

He beams immodestly, then scans my outfit. 'You too, Poppy. *Très* chic.'

'What, this old thing?' I quip, regarding my navy and turquoise wrap dress – Diana von Furstenberg-ish and quite the departure from my typical shift dress – and matching turquoise Lorenzos. 'Don't forget, I was once a fashion journalist,' I say, lifting my eyes to meet his.

'Oh, Poppy, this case is going to be brilliant fun!' He grins at me, gleeful.

But he needs to get this out of his system, because once we get to *Nouveau*, I want him on his very best behaviour – *and* focussed on our case. This isn't an excursion.

'Where are you two off to then?' asks Nasrin as she approaches. 'A wedding or something?'

It's not unusual for us to be invited to a client's wedding, but they're rarely on a Wednesday. Besides, we look chic but we're hardly in wedding attire.

'Today's Poppy's first day at *Nouveau Life* and I'm tagging along,' replies George. 'By invitation, of course,' he adds.

'*'Course* – you *definitely* didn't invite yourself,' she teases.

'You're just jealous,' says George knowingly.

'Well, yeah – obvs.' Nasrin breaks into a grin.

Something I've long admired about Nas: what you see is what you get. She's always upfront, never coy, and she won't blow smoke up your arse just to make you feel better about yourself (as my dinky-di dad would say). Her clients love Nasrin's special brand of pragmatic, no-nonsense matchmaking.

'Bring me back some goodies, eh?' she asks.

'Why do you think I brought that with me?' he asks, pointing to a small roller bag by his desk.

How did I miss that?

'George Michael Robertson,' I say, channelling my gran (no one messes with my gran), 'you are absolutely *not* taking that into *Nouveau*.' I prop my hands on my hips so he knows how serious I am (as in: totally).

'But—'

'No.'

He's about to protest a second time when a voice rings out across the office.

'Excuse me, sorry to interrupt, but are you three planning on joining us for the staff meeting?'

Oh, crap, it's Paloma. I am *never* late for staff meetings – I pride myself on being punctual.

'Coming!' we chorus, hustling through the door and pulling our chairs up to the large conference table.

'Poppy, let's start with you, shall we?' says Saskia with an amused half-smile.

Somewhat flustered – also very unlike me – it takes a second for my brain to switch into briefing mode. But then it does, and the words flow through me as if I were reading them from a teleprompter.

After the meeting, as I'm crossing to my desk, my phone rings. It's Olivia, the older of Tristan's cousins. I slide into my chair and answer.

'Hi, Olivia.'

'Hello, Poppy, how are you?' she asks cheerfully, as if she's just called for a chat. Only Olivia has never actually called me before – messaged, yes, but never a phone call.

'I'm good. How are you?'

'Very well, thank you.'

I can tell she's beating around the bush.

'So, what's up?' I prod.

'Umm...' The heavy sigh that follows immediately triggers my concern.

'Are you okay? Is Evie okay?' I ask rapid-fire.

'Yes, no, we're both fine. Well, I mean, it *is* Evie, but she's not hurt or in danger or anything. And now that I've got you, I don't know if I should say anything. Sorry, I shouldn't have called. But as soon as she told me, I thought of you because it's about this guy she's been dating.'

'Ah, okay. But you don't want to betray her trust?'

'Exactly,' she says with another sigh. 'Bloody *Tyler*.' She says his name the way most people say the word 'sewerage'. And it must be early days in their relationship, as Evie's never mentioned him before.

'It is a tricky one, other people's relationships.'

'I know,' she says. 'But do you think you could... you know, talk to her?'

'If I reach out to Evie out of the blue, there's every chance she might resent me for meddling – *and* you for telling me to.'

Giving romantic advice to family or close friends can be a minefield – besties included. There have been several times over the years when Shaz has been annoyed by my advice – even when she asked for it.

'Right, of course,' Olivia replies glumly.

'Look, you're coming over next weekend. See if you can talk her into confiding in me.'

'Will do.'

'I'm happy to help in any way I can, Olivia – just as long as it comes from Evie.'

'Thanks, Poppy. See you then.' She ends the call.

Now what's your deal, Tyler? I wonder. He'd better not be messing Evie about, but if his behaviour has prompted Olivia to make an *actual* phone call, that's not a good sign.

Greta

'Deep breaths, Greta,' I tell myself as I walk the short – and now familiar – path to the coffee shop. The Daily Grind has become my home away from... well, the office. The décor, the foliage... they soothe me. And a soothing atmosphere has become a necessity ever since I learnt about the Ever After Agency and Anjali's (mad) plan to match me and marry me off.

Yes, I, Greta Davies am *hiding*. From my job. That I love and am brilliant at.

They get my name right now, at least – the baristas, I mean, not the agency. Monday morning's coffee – and yesterday's – had

'GRETA' scrawled across the cups in neat block letters. Maybe Ewan said something to them.

Ewan.

Okay, it's not just the blond wood furnishing and pot plants that make me feel comfortable here, Ewan does too.

I wonder what work he does that he can hang about in a coffee shop, working on his laptop. Well, that's assuming he's here when I'm not. He may be like me – simply taking a daily breather from one of the dozens of workplaces within a two-minute walk.

Regardless of what Ewan does for work, he's becoming the biggest drawcard for The Daily Grind – and that speak volumes considering the calibre of their coffee.

He's just so easy to talk to, so *normal*. He also doesn't know I'm being forced to write a series of articles about dating, so when we talk, it's about anything else, like his spoodle (half cocker spaniel, half poodle), Remy.

We also talk about travel – mostly his, as I've been adding to my travel bucket list for years, but because I've focussed on my career, it remains largely unvisited – and books we've read – again, mostly books he's read, as my TBR list is as long as my bucket list. If the day ever comes that my career isn't as fulfilling as it is now, you'll find me holidaying somewhere exotic with a stack of books by my side.

Something especially fun we've started doing is hypothesising what different coffee orders say about the person who ordered them.

Yesterday, a bloke ordered English Breakfast tea – no milk – with a shot of espresso. Tea *and* coffee. Together. In the same cup! When the bloke behind the counter shouted the order to the barista, the barista did a double take. Half the people in the coffee shop did too.

Ewan and I decided he must work for MI6 and that his order

was a coded message. We even scoured the rest of the patrons, trying to work out who his contact might be, then fell about laughing when we came up short. Everyone else seemed too non-descript to be a spy – although, I suppose that's what they *want* you to think.

And who knew people watching could be so much fun? If The Daily Grind hadn't become a sort of sanctuary where I can spend an hour or two away from the office to decompress and collect my thoughts, I'd invite Bex to join me. Maybe she could write a *What Your Coffee Order Says About You* listicle.

I queue up to place my order, scanning for Ewan but, disappointingly, don't see him. I'll save him a seat just in case he shows.

When I collect my coffee from the counter, there it is again: 'GRETA'. By java, I think they've got it! Ha-ha. I make my way through the crowd, most of whom seem to be getting takeaways, and find a table at the back next to the window.

I sip my coffee – it's perfect – and watch the passers-by outside.

'Am I interrupting? You seem deep in thought.'

I look up, smiling. 'Hello, you.' Ewan raises his brows inquiringly, then flicks his eyes towards the chair opposite me. 'Please – sorry, yes, sit, *sit*.'

He does, chuckling.

'That came out like a command, didn't it?'

'That's *exactly* how I talk to Remy,' he says, his blue eyes twinkling. 'So, not working this morning?' he asks, indicating my still-closed laptop.

'I will. I've got a few decisions to make by the end of the day: articles for the—'

'Oh, for the next issue already?' he asks, interrupting.

'Actually, for the one after that.' I laugh gently at his shocked reaction. 'If I were still working in print, I'd already be planning the *December* issue.'

As expected, he gapes at me, clearly even more surprised. 'That's... Are you pulling my leg?'

'I promise I'm not. Magazines are meticulously planned in advance, even the fashion. Of course, hot topics always pop up unannounced – like news items and matches, hatches, and dispatches...'

His brows knit together, but it's obvious the moment he understands I mean marriages, births, and deaths. 'Ahh, yes.'

'Fortunately, being online affords us more freedom to cover those unexpected items than the print team has.'

'Was that a drawcard of being online – the freedom it brings?'

'Absolutely,' I say, omitting that I don't feel particularly 'free' now this assignment is hanging over my head.

'It sounds interesting,' he says, and I sense he means it. He raises his coffee cup in a faux toast and we both sip.

The coffee is delicious, but it's hard to enjoy it. Since the moment I woke up – and much of last night – I've been obsessing about Poppy Dean coming into the office today. I'm supposed to orient her and introduce her to the team. Then we'll get to the *real* reason she's coming in.

Today is when I find out who my first date is. To say I'm conflicted about it is a colossal understatement. What have I agreed to?

Poppy did offer for me to come into the agency for this part. Apparently, if I wanted, they would put together a slide show of the potential matches, then let me choose. But that felt... well, *icky*. I've avoided dating apps for a reason: I don't want to find someone as if I'm online shopping for shoes. No, swipe, no, swipe.

Not that I shop for shoes online.

No, if I'm doing this, I am placing everything in Poppy's hands. That way, when it all goes pear-shaped (as it is bound to do), I can tell Anjali that I tried, and we can shelve this assignment for good.

I realise I'm so deep in thought that conversation has stalled and now *Ewan's* watching out the window.

'Sorry. Bad company this morning,' I say, and his eyes return to me. 'I'm in my head.'

'That's all right. Can't expect you to be Graham Norton every day.'

'Graham Nort— Is it the outfit?' I say, looking down. 'Or the beard?' I run a hand along my jawline.

'You're funny, you know that?'

'Please tell my mum that. Her sense of humour is very... *German – so* dry. She doesn't find me remotely funny.'

'Well, she's wrong and I'll be sure to tell her if I ever meet her,' he says.

He takes another sip of his coffee, his gaze lingering on mine over the lid, and something actually pings inside me – that's the only way to describe it. It was a throw-away comment – much like mine about asking him to tell Mum I'm funny – but that *look*.

Is Ewan *flirting* with me?

Oh god, have I got to the point where I can no longer recognise if someone is flirting? Tiggy would know, of course, but she'd also laugh her arse off if I ever asked her about it.

He holds my gaze a little longer, then looks away. Hmm, it does *seem* like flirting. But we're friends. Just friends. He's a nice-looking bloke, I think anyone would agree – especially anyone with a crush on James McAvoy (seriously, it's uncanny). But *I* don't fancy him.

Before I can unpack any of this further, our MI6 agent appears.

'Ewan, look,' I stage whisper. 'Wait!' As he starts to turn his head, I grab his arm. 'Don't make it obvious.'

He shoots me an amused look, then makes a show of turning around so slowly, somewhere in the world, an entire glacier has formed by the time his back is to me.

The man gets to the front of the line and the bloke at the counter shouts, 'Earl Grey, no milk, shot of espresso.'

'Ooh, he's switching it up,' I say, still using my stage whisper.

'There's *definitely* a hidden meaning in that,' Ewan says over his shoulder, his lips barely moving.

I hold off as long as I can, but the laughter bubbles up inside me and I giggle. Ewan spins in his seat and we share the joke, our eyes locked.

Just then, my phone chimes with a message, breaking the spell. I check it and it's Bex:

They're here. I've shown them to your office. Getting tea sorted.

They? Poppy's early – *and* she's brought someone with her. Oh no! It's not my first date, is it? She wouldn't. Or would she?

'Er, so sorry, Ewan, but I've got to go!'

I quickly gather my things and head out the door, half-drunk coffee in hand and with the vague awareness that I've just been rude to my new friend. But I have something more pressing on my mind.

I'm going to *kill* Poppy Dean!

7

POPPY

'George, you seriously need to let this go.'

The case name 'Handsome and Greta' was vetoed by Paloma, and George hasn't stopped whingeing about it the entire way to *Nouveau*.

'But, Poppy—'

'No, no "but, Poppy". I don't particularly like case names based on fairy tales either. And didn't Hansel and Gretal get eaten by a witch or something?'

'They were *rescued*.'

'I genuinely don't care.'

He pouts. Wonderful, I'm sitting in a client's office with a grown-arse man who's sulking. Why did I bring him with me again?

'You're attached to the play on words, that's all,' I say, adopting a more soothing tone. Huffy sigh. 'Look, we're moments away from meeting the client. Can we please shelve this discussion?'

This alludes to me being willing to discuss it further, which I'm not. This is now 'The Greta Davies Case', which George will discover the next time he brings it up. He finally acquiesces to my plea and sits up straight, adjusting the sleeves of his sportscoat to show off his cufflinks: fluffy bumblebees which complement his bright-yellow shirt.

While we wait for Greta, I sip the tea that Bex brought us – it's not terrible but it's not good either. From my experience, the quality of tea relies heavily on the skills (or lack thereof) of the maker. Bex was also a little stand-offish with me, which surprised me considering we've worked together before.

'Poppy,' says an out-of-breath Greta as she bursts into her office. She stops short and looks between us. 'Oh, it's only you,' she says to George.

George and I look at each other, confused.

'Oh, thank god! Thank god!' Greta skirts around her desk, where she dumps her laptop and handbag, then sits heavily in her chair. She gulps from a takeaway coffee cup, tipping it up to finish it.

'Greta, is everything all right?' I ask.

'Yes,' she says, depositing the now-empty cup on her desk. 'I... I thought you were *him*,' she says, flapping a hand towards George.

'*Him?* Oh!' I exclaim. 'No, we wouldn't do that, Greta – spring a potential match on you without warning.'

'I realise that now, but when Bex sent the message...' She heaves out another sigh and sits back against the chair, making it rock back and forth.

George and I exchange glances again. His lips are pressed together so hard, they've all but disappeared. Greta is clearly on edge – it's a good thing she isn't meeting her match today (so to speak).

'That's on me, Greta. I should have told you that George was coming with me today. He's not staying – he just—'

'I just wanted to see the mothership,' he says, his tone hopeful. It's a weird thing to say but Greta responds positively.

'Of course you did,' she replies, breaking into a relieved smile. 'So, how about I show you both around before I introduce Poppy to the team?'

'Oh, yes, please.' George bounces in his chair like an excited toddler – I guess that means his disappointment about the case name has been put on the back burner.

Greta stands and comes around to our side of the desk. 'This way!' She leads us out of her office, George scampering after her and me following.

* * *

Greta

I don't know if I've ever been more relieved in my life. Okay, that might be a slight exaggeration, but an over-eager matchmaker who loves all things fashion is far better than meeting some random man I'm expected to fall madly in love with.

And a tour of *Nouveau*? The perfect procrastination tactic. The longer I can put off introducing Poppy to the team and orienting her as a (pseudo) new staff member, the longer I can put off the real reason she's here.

Ninety minutes later, I've taken them to all the floors of interest, including the studio where we watched ten minutes of a photoshoot, and now it's time for the *pièce de résistance*: The Wardrobe (capital letters intended).

'Oh. My. God,' says George breathlessly. He's like a child in a sweet shop.

If *Nouveau* is the mothership, The Wardrobe is the engine room.

I look about with fresh eyes. The Wardrobe really is remarkable and it's *enormous* – you could fit my entire flat in here four times over. There are dozens of aisles with racks of clothes on either side and all four walls are lined with floor-to-ceiling shelving. The Wardrobe showcases every aspect of fashion from shoes to bag to belts to jackets to trousers to dresses, and everything in between, and each season, everything but the museum pieces are rotated.

The mistress of this fashion wonderland is called Mimi and I spy her tiny form, dressed entirely in black à la Audrey Hepburn, way in the back, supervising a refresh of the nude shoe section, where three staff members buzz about her like worker bees doing her bidding. I have no doubt George would happily join them – he's even wearing bumblebee cufflinks today, I noticed earlier.

I wave for him and Poppy to follow me, which they do – George with a lolling tongue and eyes like saucers.

'Hello, ladies,' I say as we approach.

Mimi turns to me, her bright-red lips stretching into a smile. Even though I'm five-foot-two, she has to lift onto her toes to kiss me on the cheek.

'Hello, darling,' she says, her eyes drifting over my shoulder towards George and Poppy.

I make the introductions and George steps forward as if he's meeting royalty. Although, I suppose Mimi isn't far off – at least in fashion circles. She's been around almost as long as *Nouveau*, and even pre-dates editor-in-chief and international style icon, *the* Amelia Windsor.

'Oh, goodness,' says George – he looks as if he's about to curtsey. 'I cannot *believe* I'm meeting Mimi Prouse. I have adored you ever since I can remember.'

'Thank you.' I can tell Mimi's enchanted by him – she adores being adored.

'No, honestly, I mean it. I'm almost positive that my first word was "Mimi", not "Mama".'

Mimi tosses back her head and laughs heartily. 'Oh, Greta,' she says through her laughter. 'Where did you find this one? He's delightful. And so well dressed!' She runs an appraising eye over George's outfit.

'Oh my god,' says George, fanning his face with one hand. He looks to Poppy with a wide grin and shrugs his shoulders.

'Isn't he just?' I say, playing along to avoid explaining who George really is. 'Right, we should leave you to it.'

George utters a deflated 'boo'.

'Come on, George,' says Poppy, linking her arm through his.

'But come back and visit us properly sometime,' Mimi calls after him.

'Really?' he asks, spinning around.

'Of course!'

We make our goodbyes and when we're out of earshot, I say, 'You know, George, Mimi doesn't invite just anyone to come visit her.'

'I am literally going to die,' he replies, his hand pressed to his chest, and Poppy and I share an amused glance.

Once George left, still on cloud nine from his encounter with Mimi, I took Poppy to properly reacquaint her with Bex and meet the others in the *Nouveau Life* team.

Staff writer, Taj, who loves the idea for Poppy's advice column, peppered her with questions and made suggestions for its look and feel. Editorial assistant, Lisa, was warm and welcoming, asking Poppy about her articles in *Psychology Today*, an Australian publication she's written for in the past.

But Bex... well, ever since I briefed the team earlier in the week, she's made it clear she's not on board. This baffles me – she's worked with Poppy before, and the advice column concept is a strong fit for our vertical.

Maybe Bex senses how I'm feeling about *my* assignment, even though she doesn't know I'm the contributor – a decision Anjali made to help ensure my anonymity. We debated this aspect of the assignment – I don't like keeping things from my team – but Anjali believes this will give me the freedom to write candidly.

Regardless, I need to address this matter immediately. As Poppy's primary contact and the editor of the column, I need Bex to be fully invested or it won't succeed. I just hope Poppy hasn't picked up on Bex's reticence.

After the team meeting, Poppy and I head back to my office, and the roaring inside my head starts up again, increasing in volume the closer we get. When I close the door behind us, Poppy takes a seat in the chair across from mine, while a hurricane rages inside my head.

I take a seat *and* a steadying breath, then meet Poppy's eyes.

'Um...' she starts, 'have I done something to upset Bex?'

Part of me is relieved at not having to dive into the match-making discussion right away, but this topic is hardly any better.

'That's an astute question,' I reply, deflecting.

'It was pretty obvious,' she says with a wry smile. 'Do you think it's because of the Elle Bliss/Lorenzo article? Bex essentially had to re-write the entire thing, but I still shared the byline, remember? To sell my persona as a fashion journalist?'

The penny drops. 'Oh, of course. And was Bex looped in? That you're *not* actually a fashion journalist?' She reported to Anjali at the time, so I'm not sure how the assignment was handled. It suddenly occurs to me that Bex may know Poppy's true profession. *No, no, no.*

'I don't think so. Apparently, she was told it was a trial – that *Nouveau* was considering taking me on as a freelance contributor.'

I heave out a sigh.

'Are you okay? You're not, are you?' she asks, her understanding tone setting me at ease.

'No. It's just... this assignment and keeping it from my team... then the way Bex was with you just now...'

'You're also wondering if she knows I'm a matchmaker,' Poppy says, picking up on my additional concern. I don't even question how she determined that – just another example of my face broadcasting every thought and emotion.

'Yep, that too. *All* of it,' I reply.

'Look, I know we're supposed to get started on your assignment today, but if you want to leave it till next week, I can go smooth things out with Bex and start working on the column. Taj said you've already received quite a few reader queries.'

Poppy's right – there is work she can do on the column. We've opted for a soft launch, adding a thumbnail to the main page that invites readers to send us their romantic problems – just to see if there was any interest. We've had an excellent response so far, with dozens of queries pouring in.

But as tempting as Poppy's offer is, that would just be kicking this can (of worms) down the road.

'No, let's just get on with it.'

'That's the spirit,' she says, making me laugh. 'I really do want to make this as painless as possible for you,' she says. 'And, who knows, you might even have fun.'

I give her my we-both-know-that's-a-lie face, which makes *her* laugh.

'Okay, okay, maybe not rip-roaring fun, but aren't you at least curious?'

I sit back against my chair and take in her encouraging expression. 'You know, I haven't really thought about it like that. But now you've mentioned it... I suppose matchmaking is a rather interesting endeavour.'

'It is – from both sides.'

'Do you really think I could have fun with this?'

'Well, the alternative doesn't seem very appealing,' she says, the corners of her mouth twitching.

'Going on dates and having a miserable time?' I ask and we both chuckle.

'Exactly. But what if you go into this with an open mind? Think of it as a chance to meet nice, interesting people, explore some of London's hotspots... If you take that approach, then, yes, it could be quite fun. You also get to write anonymously, which gives you a lot of freedom.' There's that word again. 'Surely, that'll be enjoyable in its own way?' she concludes.

'How do you know the men are going to be nice and interesting?'

She grins. 'That's my job.'

'Right. I hadn't thought of that.'

'It's also why I had you complete the client questionnaire. No sense in setting you up with wildly unsuitable men if you're expected to explore the depths of modern dating, right?'

'Oh, good point,' I reply, realising she's just addressed my biggest suspicion about her methods. 'Even so, I'm not sure I remember how to do this. I haven't properly dated since, well...'

'Before the pandemic?'

'*Way* before the pandemic. Back then, I was listening to "Reputation" on repeat.' I don't mention that my favourite song from that album was 'King of My Heart', a song about being better off alone.

Poppy's eyes narrow and she shakes her head slightly.

'Taylor Swift,' I add to clarify.

'Ahh.'

'Not a Swiftie, then?' I ask.

'One of the few people on the planet who isn't.'

'I won't hold it against you.'

She smiles. 'Good. Now, now back to you,' she says, restoring me to the hotseat. 'Are you ready to meet your first match?'

I take a bracing breath. 'Why not?'

She reaches into her enormous handbag – a Lorenzo, like her heels – and takes out a folder. 'This,' she says, opening it and spinning it around so the contents face me, 'is Harrison.'

Harrison is a broad-shouldered, handsome man with thick, brown hair, russet-brown eyes, and the type of stubble that looks ruggedly sexy but probably requires constant grooming. The summary at the top of his biography states that he's forty, has never married, has no children, and loves to travel. He also teaches music at an inner-London school – a job he's passionate about – and is a part-time voice actor.

And the clincher, a direct quote from the man himself:

I genuinely want to find someone who'll be my best friend, my lover, and my partner.

He may just be the perfect man (on paper at least). Perhaps Poppy's right – this *could* be fun.

8

GRETA

'Yum-eee,' says Tiggy, ogling the photo of Harrison. 'He's a dish. If you don't like him, can I have him?'

I snatch it from her. 'He's a person, not a handbag. I'm not lending him out. Besides, you're already dating someone.'

'Not exclusively. And it's some-*ones*.'

I ignore her, my eyes perusing Harrison's face and lingering on his bottom lip, which is much fuller than the top one. Tiggy's right – he *is* a dish. Poppy's advice comes to mind, about having fun with all this.

'Well, he's proper fit, he is – Mountain Maaan,' she says, adopting a deep, booming voice.

'Mountain Man?' I ask.

Tiggy shrugs. 'I don't know – he looks like he chops down trees for fun. He does seem perfect for you – at least according to this.' She's not wrong; it's the exact thought I had earlier. 'So, *again*, no more complaining about this assignment.'

She stabs her straw into her G&T, making the ice clink against the sides, then sucks the rest of it noisily through the straw.

'Please don't say that. You're the only person who knows about it besides Anjali. And you're my bestie. Who else am I supposed to talk to?'

'Hear that? That distinction? Talk to – yes. Complain to – no.'

'And when everything goes pear-shaped?'

'What could possibly go pear-shaped with him?' She nods at the photo.

'Oh, I don't know. He could have bad breath or be a rubbish driver or—'

'Are we having another round?' she asks, cutting me off to save me from myself.

We're at my favourite bar for after-work drinks – Gin Palace – only mine's half undrunk because I've been reading Harrison's biography on repeat, fixating on the words 'wants to be a father', which appears on page two. It's a weighty – *and* enticing – addition to the short, snappy summary on the top of page one.

I eye Tiggy's empty glass. 'I'll happily stay for another, but only if you're having a proper cocktail and not just a G&T.'

'I like G&Ts.'

'So do I, but they do make specialty cocktails here, you know.'

'Are you doing that thing where you're a bossy cow because everything else feels out of control?'

I break into a grin. 'You're lucky we're best friends,' I say, shaking my head.

'No, *you're* lucky we're best friends,' she says, returning my serve with a winner.

I wave over the bartender and order Tiggy another G&T and a Convent for myself – a sweet, fizzy cocktail with a hint of ginger.

I take a sip of the cocktail in front of me, my gaze sliding back to the photo. I'm guessing that if Harrison works as a voice actor, he must have a deep, velvety voice to match those looks, something I'm especially drawn to.

An unbidden memory pops into my mind of Darren, the bloke

I dated throughout my final year of uni. He wasn't especially good-looking, but he was clever and funny and had the sexiest voice I'd ever heard. I would have married him had he asked. I'm glad he didn't, though. He was sleeping with two other girls at the same time he was dating me, something Tiggy discovered one night at a party across town.

I'd been so cross with her for telling me, which is ridiculous, of course. With a nudge from my mum, who was providing post-break-up sanctuary by ferrying toast and tea up to my childhood bedroom where I was wallowing, my rift with Tiggy didn't even last the weekend. By late Sunday afternoon, I was on the doorstep of her share flat, tail between my legs and bearing a bottle of her favourite plonk as an apology. Typical Tiggy, she called me a 'daft cow', hooked an arm around my neck in one of her I-am-so-much-taller-than-you hugs and invited me to share the wine while we bitched about Darren.

The realisation hits hard: Darren was my last serious boyfriend. I *can't* have been (practically) single for twelve whole years! I count back. Yep. Twelve years of the occasional date and the odd hook-up. And I mean 'odd' literally as well as figuratively, because there was a bloke called Miles who was visiting Tiggy's friend, Trav, from out of town and, foolishly, I thought it was a good idea to take him home after a very boozy night at the pub. I woke up the next morning and he'd stolen my towels. All of them, including the flannel. Maybe he was setting up house.

I've been in my head for minutes now and look over at Tiggy, who's scrolling Instagram.

'I'm not great company tonight, am I?'

She angles herself towards me. 'Eh,' she says with a shrug, 'you're fine. I do have a question for you, though.'

We're interrupted by our drinks arriving and we both thank the bartender.

'What?' I ask when we're alone again. I down the rest of my first cocktail and slide the empty glass away from me.

'Just...' Something in the tone of Tiggy's voice makes my head snap up. She meets my eye. 'What happens to the assignment if you and Harrison hit it off and fall madly in love?'

'Oh.' I know immediately what she means, and I'm surprised I didn't consider this before. *Bollocks!*

'And not just because of that,' she says, pointing to Harrison's biography. 'But because you're amazing and he'll adore you.'

'I, er... Well, thank you.'

''Course,' she says with a shrug. 'But you didn't answer my question. Do you have to keep dating blokes you're *not* in love with?'

'I hadn't thought of that. I have no bloody idea!' I wail.

Her brows lift and she presses her lips together, telegraphing something that resembles sympathy – or is that pity?

* * *

Poppy

'Hi, honeys, I'm home!' I call out. I dump my bag on the hallstand and step out of my heels. Even these, which are known for comfort, can be a bit much by the end of the day. I think I'll switch back to ballet flats or sneakers for the rest of the week.

'Tris?'

I know he's home – his keys are in the catchall on the hallstand – but he doesn't answer. He must be in the loo. We're a closed-loo-door couple, something that's supposed to keep the romance alive. Even if romance weren't a factor, I've never understood those couples who do their business in front of each other. Um, hello, *why*? Even Saffron prefers privacy when she uses her litterbox.

I wander further into the flat and am about to flop onto the sofa when there's a heavy knock at the front door. I rush over, only realising when I get there that this is a secure building. Who could that *be*? No one buzzed and no one was announced.

'Um, yes?' I say loudly to the solid door.

'Darling, it's me.'

I fling it open and there's Tristan, holding a wide-eyed Saffron. 'What the hell?'

He pushes past me, releasing her onto the lounge room rug, and I close the door.

'She ran out of the flat right as I got home,' he says breathlessly. 'And, of course, like an idiot, I ran after her without thinking to grab my keys. Then she got into the lift and the doors closed before I could stop them.'

'Oh my god, Saffron, you naughty girl!'

She ignores me, undaunted by my admonishment, and commences her ablutions in the middle of the floor, one leg raised and her little pink tongue dangerously close to her bum.

'She is such a little minx.' I turn back to Tristan, who's leaning against the breakfast bar, pale and clammy. 'Hey, she's okay. She couldn't have got far.'

'She got off the lift on seven. And while I was madly trying to find her, along with the entire concierge team, Maisie Stimpson had dressed her in doll's clothes and was about to have a tea party. Thank *god* I found her and that you were home when I did.'

I don't mention that the concierge team would have let him into the flat – they've done it for me when I've (stupidly) left without my keys.

Then my mind switches gears and the visual of Saffron wearing doll's clothes is too much. Laughter erupts uncontrollably and Tristan and I lock eyes. He starts laughing too and soon we're grasping onto each other, barely able to breathe.

When the laughter dwindles, I look across at Saffron. 'Oi, Saffron Dean Fellows,' I chide, using her full name. Her tiny tongue pauses mid-lick and she looks at me as if to say, *'What?'*

'I'll tell you what, missy. You're the most spoiled, most loved cat in the world. Don't you ever scare your papa like that again or we will *give* you to Maisie Stimpson and you will have to wear dolls' clothes every day for the rest of your life. Do you understand?'

She pauses for a micro-second, then goes back to licking the fur around her bum.

'Well, you told her,' says Tristan, setting us off again. I wipe tears from under my eyes with my forefingers, and my phone rings.

'No rest for the wicked,' Tristan quips.

I retrieve my phone from my handbag and see that it's Greta Davies. I mouth, 'I need to take this,' and Tristan mimes, 'Want a drink?' I nod and head over to the sofa where I make myself comfortable before answering.

'Hello, Greta. What can I do for you?'

'Poppy, I think we've made a terrible mistake.'

Greta

I'm so glad Poppy answered. I have no idea what I would have done if my call had gone to voicemail – probably left an incoherent message, babbling on about finding the love of my life in the midst of an important writing assignment and possibly losing my job.

All right, I *may* be catastrophising a little – it's unlikely my job is on the line – but there's certainly merit to my other concerns.

'Are you okay?' she asks. 'You sound really upset.'

'I'm not, no. I was out with my best friend tonight after work – Tiggy, she's called – and she asked this *one* question and now I can't see how this can possibly work – the dating... the writing assignment.'

I hate that my voice sounds all pitchy but if I'm going to wail to anyone about this, Poppy's the perfect person – she's part of the reason I'm in this situation *and* she's a trained psychologist.

'It must feel overwhelming.'

'Well, yes, it does,' I reply, calming slightly. Even just being *heard* offers some relief.

'That's completely understandable.'

'It is?'

'Absolutely. You're an accomplished professional, you excel at what you do, and you've been thrust into a situation where you'll be putting your private life out there for everyone to see. Even with the anonymity, it's still, at its core, *you*.'

In less than a minute, Poppy has pinpointed the root of my concern, and my heart rate begins to slow.

'Listen, why don't we discuss exactly what's troubling you and see where you land?' she offers.

'Are you sure? I know I've phoned you after hours.'

'That's what I'm here for,' she replies, though I seriously doubt Anjali engaged Poppy the Matchmaker to be my counsellor. Still, she's offered a friendly ear, so why not?

'And there's still time to back out if you're not 100 per cent comfortable with it,' she adds.

I don't tell her that when Anjali gets an idea in her head, she becomes single-minded. If I tell Anjali I'm not up to completing this assignment, she'd just find a way to convince me. But I may as well give Poppy the entire picture, which pre-dates Anjali's 'fairy godmothering'.

'I think it goes back to the day the vertical launched, when I started experiencing this intense rushing sound inside my head, like waves crashing on the shore. It was the first time I'd experienced anything like that.'

I pause, waiting for Poppy to interject, but she doesn't.

'Anyway, I let it slip to Anjali and she assured me it was part and parcel of launching such an enormous initiative – that she's experienced the same thing each time she's approached a significant milestone. She said it would go away and she was right. By the end of the day, when I knew the launch was a success, no waves crashing in my head.'

'That's good to hear. And Anjali *is* right: it's perfectly normal to have a physical reaction to the stress and excitement of launching *Nouveau Life*.'

'Right, but it came back – the noise.'

'And when was tha— Oh, when you got this assignment.'

'Exactly. And I know you said it might be fun and I'd love to believe that, but right now, trepidation is trumping gleeful anticipation,' I say, layering sarcasm over 'gleeful'.

I hear her murmur 'thanks' to someone and then she comes back to me. 'So, what was the question Tiggy asked you, the one that's got you out of sorts?'

'Well, we were talking about Harrison...' I pause, not sure how to explain, and Poppy leaps in with a follow-up question.

'Oh, is he not a good fit?'

'No, it's not that. He's almost *too* perfect. We have a lot in common, we want the same things out of life, I like how he expressed his desire to be in a relationship... That's why Tiggy's question threw me. She asked what would happen if I fell madly in love with him. I mean, I probably won't because—'

I stop myself before I lie to Poppy – and to myself. There is every chance I *could* fall in love with the handsome man who's passionate about teaching, wants to be a father, and (probably) has a very sexy voice.

'What I mean to say is... if I did fall in love with Harrison – or any of my dates – how do I complete this assignment? How do I keep dating half of London when my heart belongs to one person?'

Poppy is so quiet, I wonder if the call has dropped.

'That's an excellent question,' she says eventually.

It's hardly the answer I was hoping for, so I say the one thing I've been thinking about – and dreading – ever since I left the bar. 'Poppy, what do you think of me dating some *unsuitable* men?' She doesn't reply right away, and this time the silence is deafening. 'Poppy?'

'Sorry, I'm just thinking...'

'You see, that way I would have enough material for a series of articles before meeting... well...'

'Someone who might be your match,' she says, finishing my thought.

'Exactly. I know what you said before about why you had me complete the questionnaire – and really, with Harrison, you seem to have done a stellar job – but I feel that sticking with the original premise of the series... well, it puts me in a precarious situation.'

That's putting it mildly, I think. *Just tell her you know what's going on. Kill the series and go out with Harrison!* my mind bellows. Hah! If only...

But I don't have the courage to do that – namely because I'd have to confront Anjali about her plan and who knows what that would do to our relationship. But I'm also invested now. Tiggy was right. I have this startling realisation about the state of my love life and an *actual* matchmaker appears on my doorstep. I'd be bonkers not to take advantage.

'I can understand why you'd feel that way,' she says. 'How about you leave it with me and I'll confer with my colleagues?'

'Thank you, Poppy,' I say, both grateful and relieved she's taking my peculiar request seriously.

'Of course,' she says, and I can *hear* the smile in her voice. 'Your case is my number-one priority. We'll sort this out, I promise.'

We end the call and I nestle into the throw pillows on my sofa. My case may be Poppy's priority, but which version? Providing me with suitable fodder for my writing assignment or the version in which she's trying to find my perfect match?

I glance at Harrison's photo, which stares up at me from my coffee table. If Poppy's as good at her job as I suspect she is, there's every chance *he* could be my match.

This thought instantly ignites the roaring in my ears, but is that because Harrison might be The One or because he might not be?

9

POPPY

'Well, what do you think?' I ask George and Ursula. Going by their expressions – including a barely visible lift of Ursula's brows – they think I'm madder than a cut snake.

'Sorry, just to be clear, you want us to find *un*suitable dates for your client?' asks Ursula.

'Yes.'

'Poppy, I adore you – *really* – but have you gone completely mad?' George pipes in, verifying I was right.

'Not completely, no. Not when you consider the relevant factors.'

'Which are?' Ursula prods.

I need to be quick as the morning staff meeting starts in a few minutes. 'Well, first off, as confirmed by our conversation last night, I'd categorise our client as a hopeful romantic.'

'You mean hope*less*,' says George.

'I mean hope*ful*. Greta believes in love *and* she's ready to find it. I'm confident of that.'

'Then why would we want to match her with unsuitable men?' asks Ursula.

'Because she asked us to.'

'She *what*?' asks George incredulously.

'It was Greta's suggestion to date duds.'

'But that's not the writing assignment,' he says.

'Yes, I realise that, George, which brings me to the third consideration: Greta knows what we're up to – that the writing assignment is just a ruse to match her.'

'Are you certain?' Ursula asks.

'Positive. It was as much what she *didn't* say as what did. She also kept hedging as if she was about to blurt it out.'

'But *how*? How did she find out?' asks George.

'Because she's clever and she obviously connected all the dots. I did warn Anjali it was likely to happen.'

'So, why not just tell her boss that the jig is up? Or have Greta tell her?' Ursula asks.

'Because Greta doesn't know that I know she knows. If she did, I'm certain she would have brought it up last night. She's asking for a way to maintain her part of the ruse without revealing to me – or her boss – that she knows. *While* being open to falling in love.'

'But *why* doesn't she want her boss to know she knows?' asks George, his brow creased in confusion.

'Look, Greta's a pro. My best guess is that she wants to smash this assignment – it's good for the magazine, she loves writing articles... She'll also understand that Anjali's intentions are pure and maybe she's worried about damaging the dynamic of their relationship. Either way, we need to set Greta up with some duds. We can introduce her first real match afterwards.'

'Poppy, I'm going to need a headache tablet before I can decipher all that,' says Ursula drily.

'Just trust me – we need some duds. Can you help?'

Her lips purse slightly – the Ursula equivalent of dubiousness.

'If Saskia and Paloma sign off, I'll find you some from the reject pile.'

'Excellent.'

'Wait, we have a reject pile?' asks George.

She gives him a withering look, as if *he* should be relegated to the reject pile.

My eyes flick to the wall clock behind reception. 'Come on, staff meeting.'

As we make our way to the conference room, Ursula leans in. 'I suggest you let me explain what you're asking. You made about as much sense as one of those Australianisms you constantly spout.'

I wouldn't say I *constantly* spout Aussie-isms, but at least I've got Ursula on side.

* * *

'What about this bloke?' asks George as he slides a folder across the table.

'Give me the abridged version,' I reply, not lifting my gaze from the bio in front of me.

'There may as well be "misogynist" scrawled across the top of his file in giant, red letters.'

'Ah, that old chestnut.' Intrigued, I pull the folder towards me, and skim read. 'Oh, Michael – what a prince you are. He's definitely going on the list.'

'How many do we have so far?'

I look at my tablet. 'That makes five. We've got fifty-and-still-lives-with-his-mum, the guy who's playing the numbers game—'

'Sir Dates-A-Lot,' quips George.

'Hah, good one,' I say, glancing up to catch George's less-than-impressed expression.

'He clocks up nine dates a weekend, Poppy. If he hasn't found his someone by now, it's probably him, not them.'

I laugh. 'I was thinking the same thing. Right,' I say consulting the list again. 'There's also the part-time naturist and every-spare-moment-in-the-gym-and-won't-shut-up-about-it guy.'

'I don't know which one I'd rather date less. And where would you even *go* with a naturist? No shoes, no shirt, no *trousers*, no service.'

'Look at you with the snappy one-liners today.' George takes the compliment with a self-satisfied smile. 'And Mr Misogyny,' I add, typing in Michael's name.

George puts down the sheaf of papers he's holding. 'Are you sure you want to put Greta thought all this? I like her and these men are...' His face screws up as if he smells something foul.

'She asked us to. Besides, I gave her Harrison's bio and it took her less than a day to call me in a panic. And it's a valid concern, as there's every chance he's her match. And not just because we chose him and we're good – but it was the way she talked about him. If we do this, she gets to fulfil her end of the bargain without revealing to Anjali that—'

'That she *knows*... I *know*, Poppy. Blimey, this is like that episode of *Friends* when everyone finds out about Monica and Chandler.'

'Oh, I love that one,' I say.

'I *know*.'

We look at each other for a beat, then burst out laughing.

'Right,' I say a few moments later. 'Let's set up our client with some duds.'

Greta

I put the last biography back in the folder and close it, then rest my hand on top. I may have sent us down this path, but it's still a lot to take in.

Poppy and I are at The Daily Grind – our unofficial office for the duration of my assignment, as away from *Nouveau*, we can talk candidly about my writing assignment and everything it entails. Wary – and a little weary – I look across the table at her.

'What do you think?' she asks.

What do I think? I think I'm bonkers for agreeing to this assignment in the first place and even *more* bonkers for asking Poppy to set me up with men like these just so I don't have to admit to Anjali I know what she's up to. I also think I'm about ten seconds away from marching into her office and putting a stop to this ridiculous gambit.

Poppy cocks her head to one side and regards me with a half-smile. 'You can be honest with me, you know.'

Is she teasing me or alluding to the GREAT HAIRY SECRET I'm keeping from her and Anjali?

If it's the latter, can I trust Poppy with the entire truth? While I mull over this conundrum, she waits for me to say something, her kind smile fixed.

'Well, I think you've managed to find five reasons why women my age find dating so horrible,' I tell her, my eyes flicking to the folder. She chuckles and I join in despite myself. 'I know I asked you to do this, but we'll have to change the title of the series to "Dating Horrors of London". It was supposed to be about avoiding the shallows and dating in the deep end – having *meaningful* dates... And this is *so* far from the original concept...' I sigh. 'I'm being contrary, aren't I? Difficult, even.'

She presses her lips together as if she's stopping herself from revealing something. It's unnerving, especially as her eyes are still firmly locked onto mine.

'Can I ask you something, Greta?'

I nod, dread surging through me. I feel like I'm driving straight towards a cliff at full speed. But maybe Poppy has a parachute in her matchmaker bag of tricks.

'When we spoke a couple of nights ago – about Harrison – you seemed quite taken by him.'

'Well, yes, I suppose so. I mean, I'm just going by what's on the page, of course, but...'

I trail off again, my thought lingering in the air between us. I can't finish it because I'd be admitting that some biographical information and a photograph – one I can't stop looking at – has *affected* me. And crushing on someone I've never met is almost as pitiful as crushing on Luca for as long as I did.

'So,' says Poppy, pulling me from my self-deprecating thoughts, 'does that mean you're legitimately interested in finding love?'

And there it is: the dreaded question, the one that blares yet another person knows what's going on inside my head – *and* my heart. My best friend? Fine. But my boss? And now a professional matchmaker? Horrifying.

I may as well take out an advertisement on one of those billboards in Oxford Circus that says, 'I am thirty-five and single and it's only just occurred to me that I may have left it too late to find love and start a family!'

And if I do admit to the truth to Poppy, then what? Do I have to date these horrible men? Will Poppy still match me with Harrison?

Oh, to hell with it.

'Yes. Yes, I am interested in finding love.'

Poppy's face lights up with a wide smile. 'That's great news, Greta. Thanks for being so honest with me.'

It's a relief, speaking my truth – and to someone other than Tiggy. Possibly because Tiggy and I have very different perspectives on love – and life, come to think of it. Even though she's supportive, I don't think she truly understands that what began as a muted, niggling sensation a few weeks ago has taken root, is growing legs, and all other suitable idioms.

'So, now what?' I ask. 'Wait – you said this is great news? In what way?'

That enigmatic smile appears again. 'Because now I know our objective – the real one – what it is that *you* want.'

'You mean, instead of what Anjali wants for me?'

I clap my hand over my mouth. Having just told Poppy my deepest desire, *now* I've revealed I know there's a 'secret' plan afoot.

Poppy's response is to laugh, though I don't think it's *at* me. 'Sorry,' she says, 'but you should see your face right now.'

I drop my hand and sigh again. 'Cards on the table?'

She nods.

'I know Anjali only brought you into *Nouveau Life* for me – to help find me a partner. It's glaringly obvious.'

'I gathered you knew.'

'Really? Oh no! Do you think Anjali does?'

'At the moment, no. I think she's too excited to see that you've figured it out.'

'Well, there's that at least. Oh, Poppy, I'm *mortified*. Anjali – the woman I admire most in the world – thinks I'm such a sad case, she had to engage you.'

'Hey, I don't see it that way. She cares about you and she wants you to be happy. That's all this is.'

'I suppose,' I admit. 'That's the other reason I haven't said anything – I know she means well. Are you going to tell her that I know?'

As I await Poppy's reply, I suck in a deep breath and hold it. The thought of all this being out in the open is equal parts relief and humiliation, so I'm not sure which answer I want.

'I don't think we need to. At least, not right away.'

'Really? But I thought you'd— Actually, I don't know what I thought.'

'I meant it when I said your case was my top priority and I'll do everything in my power to make you a match – either with Harrison, or someone else.'

'And them?' I ask, grimacing at the folder.

'Well, if you don't want to reveal to Anjali that you're in the know...'

'Right.'

'How about this? You go out with two or three of these men,' she says, lightly tapping the folder, 'write about the dates, and once the series is established, we switch gears and you meet your real potential matches?'

'That sounds exhausting.'

'But doable?' she asks with raised brows.

'But doable, yes.'

'And look at it this way: there's a lot to be said for kissing frogs when you're dating. It helps narrow down what you want in a partner, especially the non-negotiables.'

'Such as *not* being a misogynist who essentially wants a housekeeper and thrice-weekly sex,' I say, referring to Michael.

Poppy laughs again. 'Exactly.'

'Poppy?'

'Mmm?'

'I am not going out with Michael. Not even a little bit.'

She smiles. 'Consider him struck from the list.'

I sit back against my chair and reach for my nearly empty coffee cup, taking a sip. My face screws up as I swallow – it's gone cold.

'Excuse me, are you Greta?' a young woman asks. She's wearing a forest-green apron with The Daily Grind's logo embroidered on it and is holding two takeaway cups.

'Er, yes, I am.'

'These are for you,' she says setting the cups on the table.

'But we didn't order these,' I say. I'm especially confused because there's no table service here.

She hooks a thumb over her shoulder. 'They're from him.' She turns and I follow her line of sight. Ewan is standing near the counter and smiling at me. I lift a hand to wave and he waves back.

'Enjoy,' says the young woman. Before I can thank her, she turns and goes back behind the counter.

'Do you know him?' asks Poppy.

'Er, yes.'

'Then invite him over,' she says, that familiar lilt of laughter in her voice.

I catch Ewan's eye and wave him over.

'Hello, you,' I say, my mouth stretching into an involuntary smile as he approaches.

'Hello.' We stare at each other for several seconds.

'Oh, sorry,' I say, realising, 'where are my manners? This is Poppy Dean, my... er, colleague. And this is Ewan— Actually, I don't know your last name.'

'Wilder,' he says to Poppy. 'And did I get your order correct?' he asks, motioning to the cup in front of Poppy. 'Strong tea, white, no sugar? That's what Harry behind the counter said.'

Poppy's eyes widen slightly and she shoots me a look, then her eyes swing back to Ewan. 'You have got that right and thank you, Ewan. That's very thoughtful.'

'A pleasure. I guessed you might be Greta's colleague. You seemed to be working quite hard and I thought you might like another round, so to speak.' Ewan seems shy suddenly – or perhaps embarrassed. It's hard to tell, as I don't know him that well. 'I've overstepped, haven't I?' He shakes his head. 'Or worse, *intruded.*'

'No, not at all,' says Poppy. 'And how do you two know each other?' she asks.

'From here, actually,' Ewan replies.

'How nice,' she says with a smile. Then she glances at her watch. 'So sorry, but I'll need to take this to go. Greta, I'll be in touch later so we can get started on our project.'

'Right, yes.' And then she's gone.

'I didn't mean to chase her off,' Ewan says as he watches Poppy leave.

'No, no, you didn't. We were done anyway.'

'Oh good,' he says, seeming relieved. 'So, an interesting project you're working on?' His eyes, filled with interest, land on the folder.

'Er, yes.'

Interesting, but also horrific, I think but don't say. 'Did you want to sit?'

I should probably be getting back to *Nouveau*, but what's another ten minutes away from the office? Especially when I need some respite after my meeting with Poppy.

'I'd love to, but I've got to get back to work myself,' he replies.

Oh.

'How about tomorrow? Ten-ish?'

'Perfect,' I say, my disappointment dissipating instantly.

Ewan flashes me a grin, then heads towards the counter just as the barista calls out his name.

10

POPPY

I'd intended to work at *Nouveau* this afternoon, finalising my content for the advice column, which is due on Bex's desk tomorrow. But there's something more pressing to attend to – a man called Ewan Wilder.

The way Greta's eyes lit up when she saw him and how they looked at each other during that conversation... There is definitely something between them. I wonder how long they've been meeting up at the coffee shop and – more importantly – if he might merit a place on Greta's list of potentials.

I take out my phone to call Marie Maillot, the agency's freelance investigator to see if she's working near Richmond. I could brief her over the phone, but if she can meet me at the agency in an hour, I'd prefer to do it in person. As always, she answers almost immediately.

Fifty minutes later, I walk into the agency and spot George at his desk. I owe him a trip to *Nouveau*, as he'd planned to meet me there later under the guise of taking me to happy hour – really, he just wanted to see Mimi and The Wardrobe. From the way he's slumped in his chair, I can tell he's still pouting.

'Hi, is Marie here yet?'

'In there,' he says, nodding towards one of the meeting rooms.

'Coming?' I ask.

He winces.

'She's not that scary, and you *are* my second on this case. Come on, put your big boy pants on.'

'Fine.' He stands, his lanky frame towering over me even though I'm five-six, and follows me into the meeting room.

'Marie!' I exclaim as I enter.

She looks up from her phone, an unlit cigarette dangling from her lips – one of her many quirks – and grunts her greeting. Marie is quite the character. I've said before that she looks like Lisbeth Salander, the girl with the dragon tattoo, right down to the black hair, heavy black eyeliner, and copious tattoos – only Marie's in her late sixties.

'Thanks for coming in,' I say, taking a seat. George sits next to me and eyes her warily across the table.

She removes the cigarette from her mouth and holds it aloft.

'Well, what else have I to do but jump every time you call?' she asks sardonically, her thick French accent adding an extra layer of disdain. Marie isn't a bad person, but I suspect she's suffered more than her share of fools during her lifetime and at some point, she decided enough was enough. George is terrified of her.

'I need you to look into someone for me,' I say, getting straight to the point, something I know she appreciates. No chit-chat for Marie.

'Ewan Wilder, approximately forty years old, works somewhere in the vicinity of 400 Strand, WC2, and he looks like this.' On my phone, I navigate to the photo I downloaded on the way here and show it to her.

'That is James McAvoy,' she says drily.

'Yes, I know. But believe me, there's a striking resemblance.'

Marie purses her lips and draws from the cigarette, then blows non-existent smoke into the air.

'Anything else?'

Having worked with her several times before, I know she's asking if I have any other information about Ewan, not if I need anything else.

'That's all I've got.'

'When?'

'As soon as possible.'

She nods. On occasion, Marie has found the information we've needed within a few hours but based on the little I've given her to go on, it will likely take longer than that.

'Give me a day, perhaps two,' she says and without saying good-bye, she leaves the meeting room.

'Don't you think Ewan Wilder sounds like the romantic hero from a Sandra Bullock movie?' asks George dreamily.

'Hah! I hadn't thought about that but now you've mentioned it, yes.'

'And does he *really* look like that?' he adds, peering at my phone.

'Yes, he does.'

George emits a guttural purr. 'I adore James McAvoy. *So* scrummy.'

'Hmm, *anyway*,' I say, getting back to the case, 'you should have seen them together, George.'

'Fireworks?'

'Less obvious than that, but definitely something, you know?'

George's eyes dance with excitement. 'Can you imagine if Mystery Man Ewan Wilder turns out to be the love of Greta's life?' he asks dramatically.

'Let's not get ahead of ourselves. We need to see what Marie digs up before we get too excited. He could be a serial killer for all we know.'

'God, you're so *dramatic*, Poppy,' he says, rolling his eyes without a trace of irony.

* * *

Greta

I'm in my office, attempting to edit an article for next month's issue, but I've now read the same sentence five times. Ordinarily, it would be a compelling read – the connection between what we eat, gut biome, and brain health – but my mind keeps drifting.

'Do you have a minute?' Bex is at the door.

'Yes, come on in,' I say, grateful for the reprieve – anything to distract me from the errant thoughts my monkey brain keeps tossing up.

'Have you seen Poppy's column?' she asks, perching on the edge of the chair opposite me. 'The draft she submitted?'

I haven't and Bex knows this, as *she's* the editor of the column. I can tell she's only asking to preface an issue.

'Is there something wrong?'

'I've just emailed it to you. Would you mind taking a look?'

I navigate to my emails and open the file, skim reading it to get the gist. 'Oh,' I say about halfway through.

'So it's not just me?' asks Bex.

I look up from my laptop. 'It's very dry, isn't it? Almost clinical.'

'Mmm-hmm. I'm not sure our readers need that much detail about pleasure receptors in the brain.'

'Are you able to... you know...?' I mime typing with both hands.

'Completely re-write it like I did the last time Poppy wrote for *Nouveau*?'

Ah, so *this* is why Bex was lukewarm about the column. She knew she'd probably have to do the heavy lifting to make it publishable. And as far as she knows, Poppy has legitimately been engaged by *Nouveau* as a contributor. She must be as confused as she is frustrated.

'I was going to say, "Work your magic".'

The corners of her mouth curve downwards, proving my suspicions.

'If you leave it with me, I could have a go?' I offer.

She blinks at me in surprise. 'Haven't you got enough on your plate?'

She's right, I'm already behind schedule for next month's issue, but I can't tell her why, so I wave her off. 'I'm happy to do it.'

Her eyes narrow. 'It's all right. I'll edit it. I just wanted to make sure I wasn't completely off base.'

'You were on base,' I say, eliciting a small smile at my play on words.

She gets up and starts to leave. 'You look especially gorge today, by the way,' she says.

'Oh, thank you,' I reply with a tight smile.

She sends another appraising look my way and leaves, and I slump against my chair. I'm meeting with the first of my 'Dating Horrors of London' dates tonight. Poppy set it up.

Teeming with nerves this morning, I took extra care with my appearance, even curling my hair with barrel tongs. But perhaps looking 'especially gorge' is the wrong approach when meeting someone I (almost definitely) won't like and (probably) will never see again.

Wonderful – the bloody roaring is back. I press my palms to my ears but that just makes it worse.

'Grets, have you got five?'

Perfect timing, Luca, I think with a metaphoric roll of my eyes.

He leans against the doorframe, hands in his trouser pockets, as if he's posing for one of his photoshoots. I once told Tiggy that his likeness should be carved out of marble and placed in a piazza somewhere, and she laughed at me for a full minute.

'Sure, what's up?' Even if I could concentrate on editing this article, constant interruptions aren't helping.

'Actually, it'll be more like twenty,' he says, feigning sheepishness.

I lace my fingers together and prop my elbows on the desk, looking at him expectantly.

'I'm in the middle of a photoshoot and I need you to come to the studio with me. Just a second set of eyes on something. I honestly can't decide, and my team are locked in a dead heat.'

'Wait, are you asking me to consult on a *fashion*-related matter?'

He pushes off the doorframe and swaggers into my office, bringing with him the scent of Italian sunshine that accompanies him wherever he goes. The scent stirs remnants of my crush, but I quash the flicker of attraction before it takes hold.

'Yes,' he says, his brow furrowed. 'Does that seem odd to you?'

'Just that you never have before,' I reply coolly.

'An egregious oversight on my part,' he says, throwing up his hands theatrically. He really does like to play into the Italian stereotype. 'You're as stylish as anyone else at *Nouveau* more so than many, as *you* have a certain *je ne sais quoi*. Like today. Look at you – just stunning.'

I can feel the heat rising in my cheeks. If he continues heaping praise on me – and looking at me like that – that flicker may turn into a roaring fire.

'*Do* you have time? I know you're mad busy, but your vote will be the decider. We're at three-all and it's one of the rare occasions in which I'm torn and can't make the call. Pretty please?'

Clocking his pleading look, I give my nethers a firm talking-to –

No, you don't want the sexy scoundrel! – and stretch my mouth into a professional smile. 'Happy to cast the deciding vote,' I say, standing and stepping out from behind my desk.

'Brilliant. You're a star, Grets.' He leads the way out of my office, turning towards the lifts. 'And after work – you, me, and cocktails. My treat as a thank you,' he tosses over his shoulder.

I fall into step beside him, realising that Luca has ostensibly asked me out – not on a date, as such, but it's rare we get together outside of work and if we do, it's never just the two of us. If this were several months ago, I would have cancelled on Marcus the fitness fanatic, then obsessed all afternoon about how to act around Luca and what to say to him.

Well, I'm no longer *that* Greta.

'Sorry, Luca, I can't tonight. I have a date,' I say with great delight.

There's a slight hitch in his stride and he gazes down at me, his expression showing a mix of disappointment and shock with a smidge of 'I'm impressed'. It's hard not to be insulted by the 'shock' part, but I do my best.

'So, *that's* why you look particularly glam today. Who's the lucky fellow then?'

We've stopped in front of the lifts and as much as I'd like to change the subject, there's no escaping Luca's brazen curiosity. I lift my chin and channel Poppy, giving Luca as enigmatic a smile as I can muster.

'Oh, you wouldn't know him,' I say with a slight shrug of one shoulder.

11

GRETA

I know instantly Marcus isn't for me: overbearing aftershave, too-tight dress shirt, and slicked back, eighties-banker-style hair. Definitely not my type.

We're at Dalla Terra, a restaurant in Covent Garden with an abundance of natural finishes: wooden floors, leather seats, and a bar made from granite tile and a single plank of highly polished wood. I've never been before, but I didn't want to meet Marcus someplace I frequent, taking dating advice from Tiggy: don't sully your favourite haunts with bad dates.

Her other advice: only ever commit to an hour and only stay longer if it's going well. With this in mind, I interrupt Marcus ordering a three-course dinner, saying I have a 'big day at work tomorrow' and time for just one drink.

His expression sours instantly at that. 'Right, okay. I wish I'd known,' he says with a pinched expression. He doesn't elaborate on what he would have done differently if he *had* known, so I smile politely then order a gin-based cocktail from the bartender.

'Vodka soda,' he adds gruffly. *Charming.*

The bartender starts making our drinks and Marcus takes this as a cue to launch into a monologue about his fitness regime. Even though Poppy warned me this might happen, it's still quite affronting – like a TED Talk but far less interesting. And it's obvious why Marcus' shirt doesn't fit properly – he spends two hours a day in the gym lifting weights. Who gets up at 4 a.m. every morning? To *exercise*?

When the bartender slides our drinks across the bar with a smile, I thank him. Marcus doesn't – he's *still* monologuing – or is it lecturing?

'It's all about discipline. The body is a temple and when we take care of it, it takes care of us.'

I nod along as if I've made *any* sense of that, and he continues – blathering on about intermittent fasting. Tuning out, I sip my cocktail in silence and start counting out the seconds in my head: *one-Mississippi, two-Mississippi...* Unfortunately, this does not make the time go faster. When Marcus looks away, lost in his own little world of the tenets of self-discipline, I glance at his smart watch. Eighteen minutes have passed. Eighteen!

I signal to the bartender to bring me another cocktail.

'You know, there are a lot of empty calories in that,' says Marcus, nodding towards my nearly empty glass. 'Soft drinks and fruit juice are essentially liquid sugar, and you know what they say: sugar is the new smoking.' His gaze momentarily lands on my waistline.

Wonderful, now he's fat-shaming me. What a total arse.

'Oh, I know. But as a reformed smoker, I'm betting on sugar being the lesser of two evils. And life's no fun without at least one vice, right?' I have no idea where that retort came from. I'm not usually so sassy. I've also never smoked a cigarette in my life.

Marcus blinks at me as if I've grown two heads.

'Right,' he says, his brow furrowing. From his expression, it's obvious he's grappling with what to say or do next. Perhaps he'll acknowledge this date is going terribly and make an excuse to leave. *I'd* leave right now if I weren't on assignment.

I finish my drink while he decides what to do next, girding myself for another instalment of 'This is How Much of a Wanker I Am', which I'm sure would be the title of his podcast if he had one. Actually, he probably does, he's so vain.

'Oh, shit,' he says abruptly. 'I've just remembered I'm supposed to drive my sister to the airport tonight.'

His performance so over the top, I need to stifle a laugh. And what a creative lie – I'm almost impressed!

He downs the rest of his drink in one gulp – I don't mention that he shouldn't finish it if he's *driving* – and stands, leans across to smack a dry kiss on my cheek, and says, 'Nice to meet you, Greta. We should do this again sometime.'

I watch him leave with great amusement and even a hint of satisfaction.

Date from hell number one: tick. And even though it only lasted twenty minutes, I'm sure I can get several paragraphs out of it.

The bartender arrives with my second cocktail, a Fizz 43, which is made with Liqueur 43 and ginger ale.

That's when I realise Marcus departed so suddenly, he's left me with the bill. While he *was* a self-obsessed, fat-shaming arse, I wouldn't peg him as a cheapskate. I'll give him the benefit of the doubt and assume he was just flustered by my shocking revelation that I used to *smoke*.

I chuckle to myself. There's something rather enjoyable about this dating-the-wrong-bloke endeavour.

Poppy did say this assignment could be fun – though she was referring to proper dating. I'll admit – at least to myself – I still have trepidation about that. The stakes are just so much higher. It's easy to dress up and play a part when I know I won't end up with any of these blokes.

I suppose this part of the assignment is essentially dating practice, bringing me to something else Poppy said about kissing frogs and how dating the wrong men will help me narrow down what I do and don't want in a partner.

'Please don't think I'm stalking you.'

The voice draws me away from my thoughts and I turn to discover Ewan standing next to my bar stool.

'Oh, hello, you,' I say, cheering up instantly. 'What are you doing here – besides not stalking me?'

'I met a friend for a drink after work, but his wife just called and he had to rush off – sick toddler.'

'Oh no. Poor little mite.'

'He's adorable – Oscar, he's called. Obsessed with trains. I'll call over tomorrow and take him something for his Thomas the Tank Engine collection.'

'Aww, how sweet. Sorry,' I say, realising he's still standing, 'did you want to join me?'

'Oh...'

'Only if you want to,' I hasten to add.

'I'd love to. It's just... I'm really *not* stalking you.'

I laugh. 'I know. And I'd love some company.'

I don't explain it's because I want to expunge 'Marcus' vibes from the atmosphere.

He climbs onto the stool next to mine.

'So, what brings you to one of my favourite spots in London?' he asks.

I cast my eyes about, properly taking in Dalla Terra's ambience. It's cosy – so cosy, I'm amazed I didn't see Ewan before he came over, but perhaps he and his friend were sitting outside on the terrace.

'It's lovely,' I say. 'And I just googled restaurants close to the office, so I—' Oops, I was about to reveal the *real* reason I chose this restaurant.

I shrug. 'I just wanted to try something new.'

'Well, you've made a good choice. Their duck ragu is to die for. I was just about to order and... Did you want to stay and have dinner with me?' he asks shyly.

My stomach rumbles loudly on cue, answering for me, and I laugh – from embarrassment more than anything else. Ewan joins in, but not mockingly, setting me at ease. I agree to join him, and we move to a table on the terrace near a topiary. When the waiter brings the menus, he seems to recognise Ewan and they share a brief but friendly exchange. Ewan must come here a lot.

'What looks good to you?' he asks, his eyes on the menu. I scan it, each menu item more tantalising than the last.

'Everything?'

He laughs. 'Well, yes. It's all delicious. I can suggest something if you like?'

I look up and meet his eye, realising the stark contrast between Marcus, who showed *zero* consideration for me during our brief date, and Ewan.

'That would be lovely.'

'Great,' he says with an enthusiastic smile. He goes back to the menu, a small furrow of concentration forming between his brows. 'And wine?' he asks, looking up again. 'They have an incredible cellar – not overblown... carefully curated... especially if you love Italian wine.'

I glance at my half-drunk cocktail. 'Well, I'm already nearly two drinks in...'

'So, just a glass then?' he asks without judgement. 'They'll bring it with our mains, if you like.'

'Perfect.'

I sit back, relaxed, as I watch Ewan navigate the menu and converse with the waiter about the specials. He orders focaccia and the burrata to share as our starters, the ragu for me, and the tagliatelle for him.

By the time the focaccia hits the table, bringing with it the heady scent of rosemary, I'm ravenous.

'After you,' he says, gesturing at the generous slab of bread.

I tear off a small piece and set it on my bread plate.

'It's so good,' he says, tearing off a much larger chunk. 'I have to remind myself every time not to fill up on it before the rest of the food arrives.'

I take a bite and stop myself from groaning in pleasure. We exchange smiles as we eat, which would ordinarily feel awkward, but doesn't.

'So,' I say, after I've swallowed. 'You know what I do for work. And I know I should have asked before but what about you? What do you do?'

An odd expression scuttles across his face but is gone in an instant.

'Sorry. It's a dull question, isn't it?' I say with a grimace.

'No, not at all. I work for myself but it's a reasonably new venture – that's why the hesitation. Sometimes I have to remind myself that I'm no longer a consultant at a multi-national. Probably because I worked in finance for years – since I finished uni, in fact. Most of my former colleagues think I'm mad, striking out on my own, doing something completely different.'

'The friend you were meeting... was he a colleague?'

'Yes. I suspect he was going to try and lure me back – it wouldn't be the first time.'

The burrata arrives and we pause our conversation to cut into it – I'm salivating as it oozes onto the plate – then slather generous portions onto grilled crostini.

'So, you're definitely not going back to finance then?' I ask. I take a bite with a satisfying crunch – it's heavenly.

He shakes his head. 'I've given myself a year out of the finance game. If all goes well...' He shrugs good-naturedly.

'And how far into the year are you?'

'Oh, about four weeks,' he says with a slightly apprehensive smile.

'Wow, so it really is early days.'

He nods.

'And so far?' I ask. I don't know many people who've drastically changed careers. Most people I know are like me, with their careers firmly locked in. Even Tiggy, who's a freelancer, has always been in the same field.

'So far, it's been brilliant,' he says, a thoughtful expression on his face. 'What about you? You seem to enjoy what you do.'

'I do. I absolutely love it. Well, mostly...' I say, alluding to my current writing assignment, which I do *not* love. Though it does have at least one silver lining – unexpectedly running into Ewan and being invited to dinner.

'And do you think you'll ever want to do something else?' he asks. 'Maybe write a novel or...' He leaves the rest of the thought unsaid.

'Maybe... I'm not sure about writing a novel – I've almost always written non-fiction – but I do miss the writing aspect of the job. I get to do so little of it now. When I started at *Nouveau*, I was staff writer – writing was my entire job. Now, as a managing editor, there's so much more I'm expected to do: marketing, reporting, far too many meetings... Even editing – my actual job title – only comprises about half of what I do.'

'That's always the way, though, isn't it? You can be in your dream job, but there are always some aspects that feel like a chore.'

It's odd that I've never thought about this in these terms before.

This is exactly how I feel about discussing *Nouveau Life*'s fiscal performance.

'That's an astute observation,' I say.

'Well, it's something I've been contemplating for some time. When the majority of my job started feeling like a chore, I knew I had to re-evaluate my career. Hence the change.'

'Actually,' I say with a laugh, 'now that I think about it, my boss, Anjali, constantly moans about doing the quarterly statements. "I'm an editor," she cries, "not a bloody accountant!".'

Ewan sniggers.

'I hope my new role doesn't get taken over by chores,' I say, voicing the thought as it pops into my head. 'At the moment, my plan is to work in magazines until it's time to retire – it's all I've ever wanted to do, and I absolutely love this industry. Though, what it will look like by then will be vastly different, I imagine. That actually excites me,' I add in a stage whisper.

'Well, you're already forging ahead with *Nouveau Life* – transitioning from print to digital,' he says. It highlights what a great listener he is and how much he remembers from our previous conversations – yet another contrast from Marcus the Monologuer.

'Thank you for recognising that,' I reply. 'I'm aware it's not for everyone, the digital side of publishing. Some of my colleagues are burying their heads in the sand, practically *clinging* to print.'

'Well, I can relate to that – not *print*, per se, but clinging to the more traditional modes and methods of a profession – *and* outdated definitions of success.'

'Yes!'

Ewan is not only a good conversationalist, he's so insightful. I also have a lot of admiration for him, leaving a high-powered job – and likely, a high-paying one – to follow his passion.

'So, what does Remy have to say about your change of careers?'

I ask, mentioning his dog. From Ewan's descriptions of his antics, he's very sweet – super affectionate – but also a little cheeky.

Ewan laughs. 'Remy likes having me around a lot more than when I worked in private equity. Less doggy daycare, more home time.'

'I'd like to meet him.'

It's only after the words are out of my mouth that I realise what I've said – and worse, what it *implies*.

'I'm sure he'd like that,' Ewan replies, not making too much of it.

Our mains arrive along with two glasses of wine, and conversation stalls as I take a bite of the ragu. It's so delicious, I can't restrain myself this time and I groan loudly.

'I told you,' he says, his eyes twinkling with a hint of self-satisfaction.

I swallow. 'Sorry, I'm not usually so vocal about my dinner.'

He laughs. 'No apologies needed. I'm sure the chef would love to hear you groaning with pleasure over the ragu. *I'm* certainly okay with it.'

As I take in his words, my mouth gaping open, the atmosphere around us crackles with energy – like the moment right before a flash of lightning. Ewan watches me intently and I can tell he senses it too.

I drop my eyes to my plate and busy myself by twirling pasta onto my fork. In all other ways, this feels like the start of a friendship, but that moment? That was something else.

'So, I hope you don't mind me asking...' he says, drawing my gaze again.

The moment of frisson has died, leaving me both relieved and disappointed – something to unpack later – and Ewan now seems to be hedging. After one aborted start, he says, 'That man you were with earlier at the bar...'

Oh no, he saw me with Marcus.

Think, Greta!

'Oh, just a work thing,' I say deflecting with a half-truth. 'Possible subject of an article I'm working on.'

Okay, that's enough information.

'About obsessions. For that man, it's fitness and exercise.'

Stop talking, Greta.

Marcus may have been an arse, but I shouldn't be spouting his business all over London. Although isn't that exactly what I'm expected to do by writing about him?

'I suppose it's like anything really,' Ewan replies, as if we're having a normal conversation and I'm *not* shouting at myself inside my head. 'Obsession, I mean. It's odd how often moderation gets a bad rap, how it gets labelled as "boring" and "safe". My obsession with work was… unsustainable. That's why I've given myself this year. My year of moderation…' he says with a head tilt.

I regard him thoughtfully. He really is an insightful person. And I sense there's some insecurity humming under the surface, perhaps him wondering if he's done the right thing with his venture.

I lift my wine glass. 'To your year of moderation,' I toast.

He smiles easily and clinks his glass against mine. 'To my year of moderation,' he echoes.

As we sip, we lock eyes over the rim of our glasses.

I'm so glad I ran into Ewan. It's nice to have a new friend.

12

POPPY

'Oh, you are just the sweetest, most beautiful kitty in the world.' Evie is lying on the floor petting an indifferent Saffron.

'Please don't tell her that,' I say dryly. 'She already has an ego the size of Buckingham Palace.'

'But she's so pretty! Aren't you just the prettiest?' she coos.

Saffron stares at me as if to say, 'See? I'm irresistible.'

'Evie always wanted a cat,' says Olivia, 'but Mummy said no so often...'

'I eventually stopped asking,' says Evie, finishing her sister's sentence. They're best friends as well as sisters and sometimes, it's like they share one brain.

'So,' says Tristan, who has endured a good fifteen minutes of three women talking outfits (mine) and hairstyles (Olivia's latest) and shoes (Evie's), 'you had something you wanted to discuss with us?'

Evie sits up and crosses her legs, then reaches for her glass of wine. 'You go, Liv,' she says to Olivia.

'Which topic?' asks Olivia.

'Surrendered pets, obvs. *Not* the other thing,' she replies, an edge to her voice.

I know right away from how quickly she shut her sister down that the 'other thing' is Tyler. Hopefully, we can circle back to him and his alleged wrongdoings later, just us girls.

Olivia regards her sister for a moment, her lips pursed, before turning to me and Tristan with a smile.

'We have a proposal. It's about the money you set aside from Grandad's inheritance.'

She's referring to the sum that Tristan earmarked for a charitable endeavour. I look over and meet his eye, and I can tell he's thrumming with excitement.

'Actually,' he says to them, 'I'm glad you've brought that up. I did write a cheque for the Avian Wildlife Trust of the Hebrides,' he adds, referring to his grandfather's favourite charity, 'but I've yet to put proper thought into anything else. What did you have in mind?'

Now the sisters exchange a look, with Evie sitting up even straighter and nodding encouragingly at Olivia.

'Well, as you probably know,' says Olivia, 'many families who adopted pets during the pandemic are now finding it difficult to keep them.'

'They've had to go back into work and school and the pets aren't coping being alone all day. And many people are finding pet ownership too expensive to sustain,' says Evie.

'This means shelters across Greater London – and the UK – are overrun with surrendered cats and dogs,' Olivia continues.

'Oh, are you thinking of opening a shelter?' asks Tristan.

'Well, at first we were, yes,' answers Olivia.

'But then we realised there's something else we can do, something that will have greater impact,' says Evie.

'Precisely. What we're proposing is to create a sort of scholarship programme, but for pet owners in need. If they're struggling financially to keep their pet, they can apply for a bursary from our not-for-profit,' Olivia explains.

'And, if their pet is suffering from separation anxiety while they're out of the house, they can ask for a subsidy for pet daycare or even a pet carer to come into the home,' adds Evie.

I look at Tristan, who's listening intently and beaming with pride.

Olivia reaches into her handbag and takes out a bound document. 'We've done our research, and we've put together this proposal.' She hands it to Tristan, who starts flipping through it, his eyes perusing each page.

'It's in two stages,' she says, 'with the first focusing on Greater London. And if we're successful, we can consider expanding to the rest of the UK.'

Tristan lingers on one page, his lips moving slightly as he reads.

'Read it later, Tris,' says Evie. 'It's just research and figures and projections.' She sighs and rolls her eyes as if she's a teenager and *not* the twenty-something co-founder of London's next not-for-profit.

'This looks fantastic,' he says, finally tearing his eyes from the proposal. He looks at them in turn. 'Very impressive. I'll look it over and we'll set up a meeting this coming week to talk it through, all right?'

'Thanks, Tristan,' says Olivia with a modest smile.

'I *knew* you'd like it,' says Evie, slightly smug. 'We totally smashed it.'

'Evie!' scolds Olivia playfully.

'What? It's a brilliant concept and we've worked bloody hard on that proposal,' she says. '*And* we'll both get to use our degrees, meaning Mummy will finally get off our backs about having proper jobs. "How long do you think you can backpack around the world sleeping on other people's sofas?"' she says, mimicking their mother. 'You see? Two birds, one stone,' she concludes.

I don't care for their mother, Lucinda, but I think if I had two daughters in their mid-twenties, one with an MBA and the other with a degree in social justice, I'd be encouraging them to (finally) start their careers as well.

'Not to mention, you'll be taking this off my desk,' says Tristan. 'Every time it comes to mind, I feel guilty that I haven't done anything about it.'

I pat him reassuringly on the leg – he's too hard on himself. He captures my hand in his and gives it a squeeze.

'So, now we've told you about our idea, we need your advice, Poppy. Well, *Evie* does.'

'Liv!' Evie hisses. She flicks her eyes towards Tristan, who takes the hint.

'I've got to crack on with preparing lunch anyway.' He gets up and makes a show of putting in his earbuds to give us privacy.

Evie watches him head into the kitchen and only when he dons an apron and opens the fridge does she turn back to me.

'Liv's been on at me about something,' she tells me.

'I've not been on at you – I just think you should talk it over with Poppy. She's a *professional*.'

'Evie?' I ask, pretending I had no idea this was coming. 'What's going on?'

She blows out so forcefully, her cheeks bulge. 'It's my boyfriend, Tyler... Look, never mind, it's silly really.'

'It's not silly, Evie. Just tell her.'

She bites her lower lip and reluctantly meets my eye, her countenance a stark contrast to the spunky person she was a few minutes ago.

'He's asked about an open relationship. He says he loves me, but he'd like us to see other people.'

'He wants to *sleep* with other people,' corrects Olivia, her voice brimming with judgement.

I adopt a poker face because there is no way I can say what I'm thinking.

'And how do you feel about that idea?' I ask evenly, now wearing two caps: matchmaker and (former) psychologist.

Evie shrugs, but it's obvious she's hurting.

'I don't know. I mean, I love Ty and I want him to be happy, but part of me thinks he's not as serious about us as I am.'

Her instincts are bang on. In fact, I'd wager that Tyler has already started seeing other people and is looking for a way to assuage his guilt with a retroactive 'agreement'.

'He doesn't deserve you,' says Olivia emphatically.

'How long have you been together?' I ask.

'Three and a half months.'

So, I was right; it hasn't been very long.

'Have you said "I love you" to each other?'

'I have. He just says, "Me too."'

I nod, wondering how best to couch my response. 'Are *you* interested in sleeping with other people?'

'Not really,' she replies sullenly. I get up from the sofa and drop down next to her on the floor, then take her hand. 'Oh, bollocks, is it that bad?' she asks.

'I can almost guarantee that Tyler is not your person,' I say.

'I told you, Evie,' says Olivia gently.

Evie expels a long breath then looks me in the eye. 'He's probably already sleeping around, isn't he?'

'Probably,' I reply.

'Bastard,' she whispers, tears welling up.

'Agreed.'

She smiles wanly.

'How about this? We pick a date, I kick Tristan out and you, me, and Olivia have a girls' night in?'

'Really?' she asks, swiping at a tear that's escaped.

'Sure. I can even invite Shaz and Lauren and Jacinda if you like. We can tell you our war stories.'

'War stories?' she asks, clearly confused.

'Our dating disasters,' I reply, thinking of Greta and how she's putting herself in the firing line for the greater good.

'Oh, okay. Thanks, Poppy.'

I draw her into a hug, which she returns, and Olivia leaps up and joins in.

'Should I be joining in?' Tristan calls loudly from the kitchen. He never realises how loudly he talks when his earbuds are in.

I untangle myself from the hug and call back, 'Secret women's business, Tris.'

'Gotcha. More wine then?'

'Yes, please, but I'll come and get it,' I reply.

'You're so lucky, Poppy,' says Evie softly. 'I want what you and Tristan have.'

'Well, step one is to give Tyler the Prick the flick,' I tell her, hoping the quip lands as intended.

To my relief, she bursts out laughing. 'Tyler the Prick gets the flick,' she says through her laughter. 'I love it.'

I'm glad I could be of help. Now she just has to follow through.

* * *

Greta

I'm flipping through the latest issue of *Panache* – something I do every month to stay abreast of what our closest competitor is publishing – and immediately after 'Trend Tracker' is a brand-new column that turns my blood to ice: Heart-to-Heart Hub, a romantic advice column by morning talk show regular, Lola Lovegrove, who has made a career of penning self-help books, mostly about romance.

I stare down at the page disbelievingly. 'What? But *how*?' I ask myself aloud.

I quickly scan each reader question, then Lola Lovegrove's advice. Not only is the concept eerily similar to Poppy's column, but so is the execution, right down to the format and tone. The only distinguishing feature is that Poppy is a psychologist, not a TV personality who purports to be an expert in all things romance.

'What *rotten* luck.'

I look up, checking the time on my laptop. The *Nouveau Life* staff meeting starts in eighteen minutes, but Anjali needs to see this. I scoop up the magazine and beeline to her office. I see through the glass wall that she's on the phone, but I slip inside and take a seat. She eyes me curiously and mouths, 'Everything all right?' I shake my head and she wraps up the call.

'What's happened?' she asks.

I open *Panache* to the offending page and slide it across her desk. 'It's this.'

I watch her face closely as she reads the page, her expression morphing from curious to unsettled to riled in moments.

'Well, fuck,' she says and I blink at her. This is only the second time I've heard her use that word. The first was when she slammed her fingers in her office door a few years back.

'We have to kill the column, don't we?'

'Yes. I can't see how we can publish it without looking like copycats.'

It goes without saying that although *Panache* is a competitor,

Nouveau is still considered the premier fashion magazine in the world. We don't *follow* trends – we *set* them.

'I thought so – it's disappointing, though.'

'It is,' she says, her gaze drifting.

It's obvious she's mulling something over and I wait for her to tell me what it is, but she doesn't. Then it hits me – Poppy's cover. She's only at *Nouveau Life* because of me – to play matchmaker. Without the column, there's no reason for Poppy to stick around. Anjali must be wondering how this will impact her (not-so-secret) plan.

Should I say something? Or would that reveal I'm aware of her true intentions? Then I come up with the perfect solution – one that will address Anjali's dilemma without divulging what I know.

'You know, Poppy and I have taken to meeting at The Daily Grind whenever we need to discuss the details of my assignment. We figured it's safer than meeting here and risking the team finding out *I'm* the contributor. We could just keep doing that instead of her coming into the office.'

Anjali meets my eye, the corners of her mouth twitching. 'How did you know that's what I was thinking about?'

I shrug. 'Just following the logical fallout of killing the column.'

She grins. 'Spoken like a true managing editor.'

I lift my chin, happily accepting the praise, then I catch sight of the clock on the wall over her shoulder. 'Oops – staff meeting. I'll let you know how it goes.'

* * *

The team has mixed reactions to my news, with Taj taking it the hardest – not surprising since they've always been the most invested in Poppy's column.

Lisa raises her hand, even though I've asked her a dozen times not to – we're not in school.

'Yes, Lisa?'

'Why can't we keep the column? Theirs is in the print format, not the digital,' she says, tapping on the page with her forefinger. 'Isn't that enough of a point of difference?'

Bex, who has been quiet until now, her lips pressed into a thin line and her brows knitted, lifts her gaze to reply. 'We can't,' she says quietly. 'We're *Nouveau* – we're leaders, not followers. They beat us to it – fair and square.'

'But that's just the thing...' says Taj. '*Is* it "fair and square"? Don't you think it's a little suspicious?'

'What is?' I ask.

I glance at Bex then Lisa but they're both staring at Taj.

'That *Panache* just *happens* to publish their column right as we're planning to launch ours. I mean, the timing is oddly coincidental, don't you think?'

'But their print issue would have been planned ages ago, just like *Nouveau*'s,' says Bex. 'It's just bad luck.'

'Or *Panache* only recently decided to print an advice column and appropriated space they'd set aside for news items.'

Taj's words hang in the air like a bad smell – because what if they're right?

And if they are, then how the hell did *Panache* get wind of our plans?

We stare at each other in silence for a few moments until Lisa says, 'Well, that's just shite, that is.'

13

POPPY

'Well, that's a bit of a bugger,' I mutter after I hang up from Greta.

'Everything all right?' asks George, his head popping up over the top of his monitor.

'*How* did you hear that?'

'I have excellent hearing,' he retorts, getting up and coming over. 'So, what's going on?'

'I've just been fired.'

'Fired?!' he exclaims, and several other heads pop up.

'Not from a case,' I tell the entire office. The other heads disappear.

'From what then?' asks George. 'Oh, from *Nouveau Life*?'

'They're scrapping the advice column. Something about *Panache* beating us to it.'

'Wait.' George rushes to his desk where he forages in his messenger bag. Triumphantly, he raises a rolled-up magazine above his head. 'Latest issue,' he explains. 'I haven't had a chance to read it yet.'

He comes back and leans against my desk as he thumbs

through the magazine, stopping about a quarter of the way through. He gasps, then shows me the page. 'Look!'

I scan it. 'Oh, bugger.'

'Is it the same as yours?' he asks.

'More or less,' I reply, thinking of the edits Bex sent over. When I saw how much of my original submission she'd changed, I had to remind myself I'm a matchmaker, not a writer – I shouldn't care that she didn't like my work. That took the sting off a bit.

'Wait,' says George, pulling me from my thoughts, 'what does it mean for your cover? If you're not *Nouveau Life*'s advice columnist, what are you? You can't keep showing up if they've sacked you.'

I sit back against my chair. 'To be honest, I don't think it's critical that I'm there. Greta and I have established a strong working relationship – *and* she knows the real reason Anjali brought me on. We can keep working closely together without me going into the office – we've already been meeting outside of *Nouveau*.'

'But *I* could still go visit Mimi in The Wardrobe, though, right?' he asks.

'George, the woman herself invited you to The Wardrobe, so you do you,' I reply.

'Oh, good point,' he replies, beaming with pleasure.

My laptop notifies me of an incoming email and I glance at the screen, seeing that it's from Marie.

'Ooh, this will be about Ewan Wilder,' I say.

George slots in behind me and reads over my shoulder.

'So, *that's* why... and of course, he's the... ah, yeah, that makes sense,' I say.

'You're talking in riddles,' says George, doing nothing to mask his annoyance. 'And what's The Daily Grind?' he asks.

'*That's* the coffee shop near *Nouveau*, the one where Greta introduced to me to Ewan. He's the owner.'

'*Oh*, I see. Does Greta know that?'

I shake my head. 'I don't think so – I reckon she would have mentioned it if she did. Look,' I say, pointing to the second paragraph of the email. 'He was in a long-term relationship but that ended nearly a year ago.'

'So, he's single,' says George, a hint of excitement in his voice.

'Yep, potential number two is single.'

'Wait, so you're officially adding him to the list?'

'He's definitely a contender, especially as Greta already knows him. But he's also less of a known quantity, so...'

'So Harrison Reid stays at number one?' he asks.

'*I* think so – based on his profile and the number of compatibility markers he shares with Greta. Don't you?'

'I do, yes. But we're sticking with the current plan, right – Greta goes out with Harrison but only *after* she dates the duds?'

'Well, obvs,' I say, rolling out my fave Britishism.

'Don't do that, Poppy,' he rebukes. 'With an Australian accent? Just... no.'

Well, I guess I've been told then.

* * *

Greta

'Hello, you,' I say to Ewan.

I'm sat at what's become 'my table', furthest from the door and tucked in the corner next to the floor-to-ceiling window – an excellent spot to watch the world go by any time my mind wanders, which is often these days.

For the past fifteen minutes, I've been pretending to work while pretending *not* to be scouring the coffee shop for Ewan (it's positively *teeming* this morning). It's silly really, my behaviour. We had a lovely time the other night and I should have asked for his contact details rather than hoping to run into him by happenstance.

'Hello,' he replies. '*Small* confession. I saw you come in, so I lined up to get you this.' He places a paper bag on the table.

'Oh, a mystery confection,' I say, eyeing the bag. 'How did you know that's my favourite?'

We share a smile.

'May I?' he asks, indicating the chair opposite me.

'Please.'

He sits and we regard each other for a moment.

'Aren't you going to open it?' he asks, his gaze dropping to the paper bag.

'Oh, sorry.'

I unfold the top of the bag and out wafts a delectable aroma, but when I look inside, I'm confused.

'Not the prettiest of pastries, but I assure you, they're delicious.'

I laugh. 'But what is it?'

'A cronut.'

'Now you're just making up words.'

He crosses his forefinger over his heart. 'I promise, they're a real thing. They've been taking America by storm for more than a decade.'

I tear open the bag, and the smell of cinnamon is like a slap to the face – a soft, delicious slap.

'Halvsies?' I ask. It smells incredible but there's no way I'm eating the whole thing by myself – it's *enormous*.

'Why not?' he replies.

He tears the pastry down the middle and we each take a half, then a bite.

'So,' he says after he swallows. 'How's your article going – the one about the bloke with all the muscles?'

A chunk of cronut goes down the wrong way and I cough and splutter.

'Are you all right?' Ewan asks, half standing and reaching around to pat me firmly on the back.

I hold up one hand to signal I am. 'Yes, you just took me by surprise.'

'I didn't mean to,' he says, concern etching his features. He sits down.

I should have been prepared for him to bring up my lie from the other night but, stupidly, I'm not, and we're quiet for a moment.

'So, have you seen our spy friend?' I ask, hoping to lighten the mood.

'Actually, yes,' he says, his face lighting up. 'He was in earlier – ordered his usual.'

'English breakfast with a shot of espresso?'

Ewan nods, grinning. 'I'm determined to find out what he's about. Maybe we should hire a private investigator or something.'

'Or follow him!' I suggest.

'Would you be any good at that, do you think?' he asks. 'Spy craft?'

'Looking like this?' I ask with faux incredulity.

I'm not sure why I said that. Now I sound like I'm up myself.

Ewan just laughs. 'You're right. An attractive redhead would probably stand out too much. It would need to be me. Less obvious.'

'Except the whole I'm-the-spitting-image-of-James-McAvoy thing.'

Oh, bollocks. I just keep digging myself in deeper. I eye my nearly empty coffee cup, wondering if it's been spiked with whisky or something.

But Ewan only laughs harder, which sets me at ease.

'What?' I ask with a laugh. 'That can't be the first time you've heard that, surely?'

He shakes his head. 'No, definitely not. In fact, my ex—'

His eyes widen and he stops talking. He may also have stopped breathing, because he's completely still, save for blinking.

'Sorry,' he says, recovering. 'I shouldn't have mentioned Sally— Well, shit, now I've done it again.'

'Hey,' I say gently. 'I don't mind.' Actually, I'm pleased he feels comfortable enough to mention her to me. 'And that's what friends do, right? Talk about their lives?' I add.

His expression sours slightly and his eyes drop to the table. There's another beat of silence, then he meets my eyes, giving me a forced smile.

'Quite right. So, as I was saying... Sally had this brilliant idea for my costume for a fancy-dress party.'

'Oh, you *didn't*?'

'I'm sorry to say, I did. Not the older Dr Xavier, the bald one, but the younger version, when he still had the use of his legs.'

'And his hair,' I add.

'Yes, and his hair. Nothing wrong with going bald, but I wasn't about to shave my head for a one-off event.'

'Well, it's such glorious hair,' I say.

Greta! Yet another instance of speaking without thinking.

Ewan smooths his hands over his head. 'Why, thank you.'

A longer silence descends – then we swap awkward smiles before speaking at the same time.

'So, you were say—'

'What are you up to—'

'You go ahead,' I say.

'I was just going to ask if you're free tomorrow night.'

'Oh,' I reply. I hadn't expected that.

'A friend of mine owns an art gallery over in Soho and there's a new exhibit opening. I thought we could grab a bite after work, then head over.'

'That sounds lovely,' I say.

It truly does, but Poppy has scheduled my second date-with-a-dud tomorrow night. Unfortunately, I've led with the wrong part of my reply and Ewan perks up.

'Except that I already have plans. I'm so sorry,' I add quickly.

'Interviewing another subject for your article?' he asks, his disappointment clear.

'Er, yes, actually,' I reply, sticking as close to the truth as I feel comfortable with.

He nods, his lips disappearing between his teeth. 'Well,' he says, donning a joyless smile, 'another time then. I should, er...' He hooks a thumb over his shoulder as he stands. 'See you next time,' he says.

Then he's gone and I'm left feeling rubbish with a mostly uneaten cronut.

* * *

I endured exactly thirty-eight minutes of my date with Aman before I dredged up the excuse Marcus used on me last week, and rushed off to take my non-existent sister to the airport.

It wasn't that, at fifty, he's considerably older than me, nor that he clearly doesn't care one iota about his appearance (or hygiene), nor that he's an IT specialist, who considers arts and humanities a waste of a university degree. It also wasn't that he doesn't read fiction because it's 'indulging in frivolity', nor that he would have voted for a certain tangerine-tinged ex-President were he an American.

Based on any of those traits alone – *or* combined, for that matter – I would have stayed longer, purely to get some juicy fodder for my article.

But Aman lives with his mother.

And not as in 'I live with Mum because her health is in decline and I'm there to take care of her'. Aman lives with his mother so *she* can take care of *him*. He even bragged about how she does all his washing and cooks for him every night. Or any night he's not on a date.

Once he dropped that into the conversation, I gaped at him open-mouthed for a good ten seconds, then trotted out the fake sister and got the hell out of there.

Where did Poppy even *find* him? He clearly has no intention of leaving his mother's house. Is he really looking for a partner or is he a sadist who enjoys torturing women with bad hygiene, questionable values, and insults?

As I head home (not to Gatwick with my fake sister), I think about Ewan's invitation to the gallery opening. I wish I *had* rescheduled the date with Aman and gone with him instead. It's probably not too late to show up, but I don't know where it is other than somewhere in Soho. And I can't ask Ewan because (stupidly) we haven't exchanged phone numbers yet.

I also need to crack on with my assignment. Anjali cornered me today, asking how I'm progressing. I gave her a vague response, but I could tell she's getting restless. And Anjali is not one to be fobbed off. She'll keep asking until I send her my first article, so tomorrow, I'm getting to work. And proper writing – not just scribbling down notes and half-baked ideas. Because the sooner I get through kissing the frogs, the sooner I get to meet my prince.

Blimey, if I keep on like this, I'll get a call from Disney asking for the rights to my life story for their next animated feature. *The Thirty-something Princess and the Frogs of London* coming to a cinema near you.

'Oh, Greta, you doughnut – or rather, *cronut*,' I say to myself with a chuckle.

14

GRETA

'Wait,' says Tiggy, her hand on my arm. We're standing on the doorstep of my family home about to have Sunday lunch with Mum, Dad, and Ru.

'What?'

'How much have you told them?'

'Told them?' I ask, confused.

'About the articles – your writing assignment.'

'Oh... Nothing.'

'But it's, like, always the first question your mum asks. "What are you working on, Greta?"'

'First, excellent impersonation as always...'

She dips her head, accepting the compliment.

'And second,' I say, starting to panic, 'you're just thinking of this now? We had the whole ride over here to come up with something.'

'I only just thought of it, and better now than when we're in there,' she says, jerking her head towards the door.

I have an idea. 'It's all right. I'll just use the lie I've been telling

Ewan,' I say, not liking how the word 'lie' feels, even if that's exactly what I've been doing.

'Who's Ewan?'

'The bloke from the coffee shop.' Confusion settles on her face. 'Surely I've mentioned him?' Her dubious expression indicates that (for some inexplicable reason) I have *not* mentioned Ewan to Tiggy. 'I promise I'll tell you lat—'

Out of the corner of my eye, I see Mum's face in the window beside the front door. She swings it open and looks at us, her head to one side.

'What are you doing? Why are you standing out here?'

I'm suddenly fourteen again and Tiggy and I have just been caught trying to sneak *back* into the house after a party Mum forbade me to attend.

'Hi, Mum – sorry,' I say, lifting onto my toes to kiss her cheek. The best way to defuse my mother is to shower her with affection.

'*Hallo, Liebling,*' she says, her sternness melting away.

'Hi, Mrs D. These are for you,' says Tiggy, handing over an enormous bunch of dahlias I picked up at the Sunday market this morning.

'Oh, Elizabeth, they are beautiful,' she says, her mouth curling into a smile. 'Come, come,' she says, shepherding us into the house.

'They're from *me*, Mum,' I say, but the moment has passed, and she calls upstairs to tell Dad and Ru that we've arrived, then goes back to the kitchen.

'You were only carrying them because I had this,' I whisper to Tiggy, holding up the two-bottle wine carrier.

She smirks at me with a shrug. Mum has always had a soft spot for Tiggy – and Mum's the only person who's allowed to call her Elizabeth.

My brother flies down the stairs and launches himself at me, winding me with his embrace. I pat his back feebly, waiting for him to release me.

When he does, he stands up straight, his chin lifted. 'I'm three inches taller than you now,' he says proudly.

'Pretty easy when she's only four-foot-ten,' Tiggy teases, and they share a conspiratorial laugh at my expense. 'Don't I get a hug?' she asks with a faux pout. She's known him since he was born – she's his Aunty Tiggy – but Ru has become slightly shy around her over the past few months. I suspect he's developed a crush, something she hasn't noticed and I've yet to share with her.

'Oh, er...' he mumbles.

They hug awkwardly and Tiggy shoots me a quizzical look over his shoulder. I'll have to remember to fill her in on the way home.

'Dolph!' calls Mum and he rolls his eyes at us and heads into the kitchen. I'm not sure I'm ready for teenaged-boy behaviour from my little brother.

'There's my favourite lassies,' says my dad in his distinctive brogue. He may be the last Scotsman on earth to still use the word 'lassie'.

'Hi, Dad,' I say as he takes the stairs a lot slower than Ru just did.

As has been happening with more regularity, I'm struck by the not-so-subtle impact of time on my dad. He's quite a bit older than Mum – seventy-two to her sixty – and he moves slower these days, with more care. Whenever I ask how he's doing, he launches into a litany of ailments, then concludes with, 'But getting older is better than the alternative, isn't it, love?'

When he reaches the bottom of the stairs, he gives me a tight squeeze, then moves onto Tiggy. 'Are you *still* growing, Tiggy?' he teases. This is a running joke between them from when she shot past his modest height of five-foot-six at age fifteen.

It reminds me, as it often does when we're here, that Tiggy's not just my best friend – she's essentially my sister. Growing up, she spent as many nights under this roof as her own, with the two of us sleeping in my single bed, head to toe, until we outgrew that arrangement and my parents bought me bunkbeds.

'Hi, Mr D,' she says, returning the hug with a warm smile. She's told me many times that she prefers my parents to hers. I do as well. Her dad is gruff and distant, and her mum is the most passive-aggressive person I've ever met – possibly *anyone's* ever met.

'So, what have you brought us then?' Dad asks, peering into the wine carrier.

'Same, same... rosé for Mum, red for us,' I say, handing it over.

Dad takes out the bottle of red. 'Ooh, I love Tempranillo. Good choice. Now, you girls go on through, and I'll open the wine and bring it in.'

Tiggy and I wander through the front room to the dining room and take our regular seats at the table. From the smells wafting in from the kitchen, I can tell Mum's making a traditional German feast: pork schnitzel, spaetzle (my favourite), and rotkraut.

Mum bustles in with the dahlias in a vase and sets it, pride of place, in the centre of the table. This will make conversation across the table near impossible, but I don't say anything. Margriet Davies has a certain way of doing things and there's no convincing her otherwise – and that's speaking from a lifetime of experience.

When Mum heads back into the kitchen, Tiggy pops out of her chair, pretending she's forging her way through brightly coloured jungle foliage.

'And here we have the thirty-five-year-old in her natural habitat, having returned to the familial home for the monthly family luncheon, where she will be grilled by the matriarch about every detail of her life,' she half whispers, impersonating David Attenborough.

'Hilarious. And here we have her completely bonkers best friend who has the maturity of a toddler,' I retort.

She sits down just as Dad arrives with the wine.

'Does Mum want any help, Dad?' I ask. 'I can take over from Ru.'

He gives me a we-both-know-that-isn't-going-to-happen look, then says, 'You and Tiggy are our guests, love.' He pours the wine, then goes back into the kitchen.

'So, are you going to tell me about Ewan?' Tiggy asks at full voice.

I lean hard to the left so I can see her around the dahlias and shush her sternly. 'Don't mention him here. You know what Mum can get like.'

Her mouth quirks.

'I mean it, *Elizabeth*.'

'Mean what?' says Mum, bearing a platter of schnitzel. I'm hoping food will distract Tiggy from opening cans of conversational worms – especially any mention of men.

I know Mum is proud of my professional accomplishments, but she's also started dropping extremely unsubtle 'hints'. She's worried I've waited too long to start a family or that I might be 'too picky'. And it's not lost on me that the more frequent these hints have become, the more I've been obsessing about meeting someone and falling in love.

Ru and Dad arrive with the rest of the food – a reprieve! – and we pass around platters and fill our plates, then eat between talking over each other as we share updates about our lives. So, a typical family lunch in the Davies household.

That is until Mum says, 'Now, Greta, you remember your father's friend, Ian?'

I wrack my brain for an Ian – *any* Ian – and no one comes to mind.

'Er...'

'You know, the *widower* – the one who lost his wife the year before last.'

As an aside, I don't like it when people use the word 'lost' to mean someone's loved one has died. Poor Ian didn't *lose* his wife – they weren't shopping in IKEA. He didn't misplace her amongst the dinglehoppers and snarfblatts. She passed away.

'Oh, yes, *Ian*,' I say, even though I have no idea who he is.

'Margie,' says Dad, laying his hand on hers. Is he really attempting to stop my mother from saying anything more – with his *hand*? Unsurprisingly, Mum does say more. SO. MUCH. MORE.

'Ian was around last week, and he mentioned it was time,' she says, giving me a penetrating look.

'Time?' I ask, suddenly feeling queasy.

'To find a new wife.'

Yep, she went exactly where I dreaded she would go.

'Oh, good for Ian,' I say lightly, hoping we can move onto *anything else*. Right now, I'd rather discuss the fact that I needed a bra from the age of ten while Tiggy – *and* most of the girls in my class – didn't develop breasts until their teens.

'And, very good for you too, Greta.'

'*Margie*.' But Dad's efforts to steer Mum away from this topic are futile.

Now patently ignoring Dad – *and* that I'm squirming in my seat – she launches into a lengthy monologue, detailing all the reasons Ian and I would be a 'good pairing', the first of which is that our age difference is not much more than hers and Dad's. This is a lie. Their age difference is twelve years and, as a solo immigrant to the UK, Mum was very mature for her age when they met. Ian is fifty-six. As in, more than twenty years older than me.

Mum concludes with, 'And he drives a brand-new Range Rover

– well, *nearly* new. It's last year's model, but still...' She raises her eyebrows at me as if I should be impressed.

Tiggy can't contain herself any longer and bursts out laughing.

Mum scowls at her and says, 'Elizabeth, being a widower is no laughing matter,' silencing her immediately.

She turns back to me and I can tell she's about to continue the onslaught – I need to say *something* before she invites Ian to join us for dessert.

'Mum,' I say firmly, 'I can't start seeing Ian.'

'And why not? I've *told* you, Greta: don't be so picky. Not at your age.'

'I'm not being picky, Mum. It's just... I'm already seeing someone.'

To her credit, Tiggy does *not* ask who. Though, when I glance her way and our eyes meet through the dahlias, hers are wide with astonishment.

'You are?' asks Mum, her eyes narrowing slightly. 'Since when?'

'It's fairly new, but he's wonderful, Mum.'

'Is he into gaming?' asks Ru. 'Will he play Minecraft with me?'

'When do we get to meet him?' asks Dad.

'What's he called?' asks Mum.

The questions overlap, overwhelming me, and there are too many bloody dahlias for me to telegraph 'Help' to Tiggy.

Somehow, she divines that I need it and says, 'He's called Harrison.'

As far as fake boyfriends go, I could do worse.

'Harrison. A good, solid name,' says Dad.

'But is he a gamer?' asks Ru.

Mum says nothing. She's too taken aback.

'It's very new, Mum, but he's lovely,' I say, going purely on what I've surmised from the information Poppy gave me.

'And he's a teacher,' says Tiggy.

'Yes, right,' I say. 'He teaches music in inner London. And he does voice-overs – you know, for advertisements and the like. And he—'

I'm dangerously close to rambling off the entirety of Harrison's biography when Mum interjects with, 'When do we get to meet him?'

Panicked, my eyes meet Tiggy's.

'Mrs D,' she says, 'they've just started going out. *I* haven't even met him yet.'

After this, I'm buying Tiggy whatever the hell she wants. An ice cream... a pony... a *car*.

Mum's lips stretch into a line and, miraculously, the corners of her mouth lift. 'This is wonderful news, Greta,' she says, patting me on the hand. Then, to really drive home her approval, she squeezes it.

Wonderful news...

Yes, Mum, it's bloody wonderful that you swallowed the lie I've fed you.

It's no wonder I instantly lose my appetite. For the rest of lunch, I barely hold up my end of the conversation, grateful for Tiggy entertaining the family with tales about contrary clients who say they want one thing but really want another. At one anecdote, about a client who described her preferred colour for the company logo as 'the colour smoked salmon takes on if it's been sitting out too long', Mum hoots with laughter.

When Tiggy and I climb into an Uber after lunch and I rest against the seat, relieved the ordeal is over, Tiggy starts singing 'It's Raining Men' under her breath.

'Oh, sod off,' I say, entirely over this whole thing.

Half cut on wine and the absurdity of the past two hours, she giggles beside me. 'Now, tell me about Ewan,' she says.

* * *

After I get home, I flop onto the sofa, emotionally wrung out. The (bloody) lies are mounting. Now I've told my family that Harrison and I are dating. Have I gone completely bonkers?

Speaking of Harrison...

I lean over and pick up his photo from the coffee table, my eyes tracing each detail of his face. His biography says he's tall – more than a foot taller than me – and I look over at the door to my bedroom, imagining him standing there. He's smiling at me, his eyes filled with lust and beckoning me to join him in the bedroom where he will have his way with me (and I will happily let him).

I cross to him and he takes my hand, pulling me to him so urgently, I collide with his formidable chest. He clasps me around the waist, his huge hands splaying on the small of my back, and leans down to kiss me. His mouth is warm and wet against mine, his lips hungry for me...

I shake my head to dislodge the scene from my mind. I'm not a heroine in a bloody romance novel!

It's also ridiculous that I'm obsessing about a man I've never met. I haven't done that since I was fourteen when I convinced myself that Chris Martin would dump Gwyneth Paltrow for *me*, if only he knew I existed.

'Greta, you total muppet. Next, you'll be ordering a pillow with Harrison's face on it.'

I eye the photo again – it's practically *taunting* me.

'Gah!'

I get up, taking the photo – and Harrison's biography – to my desk. I slip them into the top drawer and lock it. Then I take the key into the kitchen and standing on tiptoes, I slide it onto the highest shelf in the pantry. If I want to open that drawer, I'll have to get my step stool out of the loft and I *never* go up there – too many spiders.

This would be a brilliant tactic to stop me from staring at Harrison's photo and re-reading his biography, except that I've already committed everything to memory.

'Hang in there, Greta. Not long now and then you'll get to meet him for real,' I tell myself.

15

POPPY

'Thanks, Marie. And how long do you think it will take?' I ask, the phone pressed to my ear.

'Pfff, two or three days,' she says. I can imagine an accompanying shrug and the downward turn of her mouth. 'And the case name?'

'It's not for a case. This is for a family member. You can send the bill directly to me.'

'*D'accord.*'

The line goes silent, and I realise it's because she's ended the call. When I set my phone down, Tristan is standing in the doorway of our guest room (AKA Saffron's room).

'Working?' he asks.

'Just looking into that little worm, Tyler.'

Clearly intrigued, he comes in and sits on the bed. 'And Tyler is...?'

Evie confided in me, but Tristan is my husband, and everyone knows that spouses and partners are included in the inner sanctum when it comes to secrets.

'Evie's soon-to-be ex-boyfriend – well, *hopefully*, she gives Tyler the Prick the flick. From what she's told me, he's been cheating on her.'

'Ouch,' he says, recoiling.

'Yes.'

'So why engage Marie?' he asks.

'I want irrefutable proof – in case Evie wavers from her decision to break it off.'

'Is she likely to do that, do you think?'

'I'm not sure. Olivia says she hasn't done it yet, but that's understandable. I know how difficult it can be to leave a bad relationship, even when you know it's hurting you to stay,' I say, sorrow creeping into my voice.

Tristan reaches his arms out, and I stand and cross to him. He pulls me into his lap and hugs me as I rest my head against his. He knows all about Malcolm, a man I dated for more than two years, a man I thought I loved, but who was actually married the entire time.

'I've invited them over next Saturday night – Evie and Olivia. Jass is coming too, but Shaz and Lauren have plans.'

'Girls' night in?' he asks.

'Yep. Either to celebrate Evie's emancipation or continue coaxing her towards it. She deserves so much better, Tris.'

'Agreed. And I'm guessing I'm not invited to this girls' night in?' he asks, lightening the mood.

I lean back and regard him with a smile. 'You have guessed correctly, *Mr* Fellows,' I say, emphasising 'Mr'. 'You and Ravi should do something, since Jass will be here.'

'I'll give him a call.'

We watch each other for a moment, then I lean down and kiss him. It's a soft kiss to begin with, sweet and gentle, but being in Tristan's arms always ignites me and soon it becomes something else entirely.

Tristan's tongue parts my lips and touches mine as he pulls me closer, one hand reaching up to cradle the nape of my neck. He falls back onto the bed, taking me with him and our hands start roaming each other's bodies. He's tugging my top over my head when we're interrupted by my ringtone.

We stop and breathless, I look over my shoulder.

'You should answer that,' says Tristan, who knows I need to be on call for my clients.

I push off him and put my top back on as I cross to my antique secretary and pick up my phone. It's Greta. I take a deep breath to help slow my heart rate.

'Hi, Greta,' I say cheerily.

'Hi, Poppy, *so* sorry to bother you on a Sunday but do you have a few minutes?'

I glance at Tristan, who's now resting on his elbows, and mouth, 'I have to take this.'

He winks at me and leaves the room, closing the door behind him.

'All good,' I say. 'What can I do for you?'

* * *

The next morning, I call George over to my desk, telling him to bring his laptop. He rolls his chair over and sits, propping his laptop on his knees and looking at me expectantly.

'What is it? It's bad, isn't it?' he asks. 'Your face is all… pinched.'

'Greta's getting cold feet,' I reply, ignoring the comment about my face.

'How do you mean?'

'She's having a crisis of conscience. She's told Ewan she's writing a series of articles on obsessions, rather than dating, she hates Anjali not knowing that *she* knows the real objective for the writing assignment, and yesterday, she told her parents she's already dating Harrison. The only person in her life who knows the truth is her best friend, Tiggy, and, apparently, Greta's not as comfortable with lying as I am. She's reconsidering every aspect of the case.'

'First off,' he says, 'I'm going to need a spreadsheet to keep track of who knows what in this case.'

'Wanna get on that?' I quip.

'Er, no, thanks. And second, did she really say it like that, the part about lying?'

He's asking if she meant to insult me. In the business of match-making, we tend to use the term 'fibbing' instead of 'lying', even though we recognise they're the same thing and we're just playing semantics. Still, Greta wouldn't be the first person to mention their discomfort with 'fibbing' and I never take it as an insult if it comes up.

'She did, but I doubt she meant to offend me. I *do* think we need to help untangle some of the threads for her, though,' I add. 'Otherwise, she'll confess to Anjali she's in the know about her true intentions and tell her parents she and Harrison broke up before she's even met him.'

'But what if Harrison turns out to be her match?' he asks, aghast.

'Exactly. She shoots herself in the foot. "Hey, Mum and Dad, you know how I said I broke up with Harrison? Well, we're back together!".'

'You realise Harrison will need to be read in as well, right?' asks George.

'Oh, you're right. If Harrison *is* Greta's match, she's going to have to explain that she lied to her parents about when they started dating.'

'Mmm-hmm,' he replies.

We both think for a moment.

'How about—'

'What if—'

'You go,' I say.

'What if we convince her to stay the course by fast-tracking the kissing-frogs part of the case?' says George.

'But aren't we doing that already? She's had two of the four dates and she's meeting the part-time naturist on the weekend. I suppose we *could* squeeze in Sir Dates-A-Lot this week. What was his name?'

George's fingers fly over the keyboard of his laptop. 'Travis.'

'Right, Travis. If we can convince her to keep going with the current plan, she knocks off two more dates by the end of the week, writes some articles, which appeases Anjali, then we move Greta onto the next phase.'

'Meeting Harrison,' says George.

'Yep. Oh!' I point at his laptop. 'Can you just check…'

'Oh, good point.' His fingers fly again, and he angles the laptop towards me so I can see the screen. 'Still available,' he says, referring to Harrison's status in our system. Although, he may be using other services, and sometimes our potentials don't update us right away when they become unavailable.

'Are you all right?' he asks me, peering at me with concern.

'Yes. Just… there are a lot of moving parts with this case.'

'Poppy, remember: how do you eat an elephant?' he asks, raising something Ursula told us on a particularly tricky case we all worked on together.

'One bite at a time,' I answer.

'Precisely. Let's meet with Greta at *Nouveau* and—'

'George, I no longer work there. We're *not* going to *Nouveau*. If you want to see Mimi, just call her and set it up.'

'All right, *fair*. But we do need to meet with Greta.'

'Agreed, but I think I'd prefer to do it alone.'

I stare at the peace lily on my desk. How have I let this case get so complicated? Have I made a misstep somewhere? Great – now *I'm* having a crisis, only mine is a crisis of confidence.

'It'll work out, Poppy,' says George.

I look up and meet his eye, then break into a smile even though I don't feel like smiling. 'Thanks, George. One bite at a time, right?'

'Yes.'

He squeezes my shoulder, then rolls his chair back to his desk, and I call Greta to set up a meeting. It's time to get this case back on track.

* * *

Greta

As Poppy and I take a seat at my favourite table in The Daily Grind, tentacles of nervousness writhe through my abdomen. I know exactly why she's called this meeting – it's about my (latest) panicked phone call. I must be the neediest client she's ever had.

That is if I still am her client.

Despite everything I said to her on Sunday night, I woke up this morning feeling sick about the possibility of Poppy closing my case because I'm unable to handle the lying.

And when I examined why I felt sick, rather than relieved, it was because of Harrison – not just because I think he's handsome and 'good on paper'. What if he *is* The One?

'So, what should we discuss first?' I ask, pretending this is just like any other meeting. 'Your column? Or rather, your *former* column? I really am sorry we had to pull it.'

'Oh, that's all right,' she replies with a wave of her hand. 'Let's be honest, after the extensive revisions Bex had to make, it's fairly obvious I should keep my day job.'

I return her smile and take a sip of my coffee as I purposefully attempt to calm my nerves.

'I have been thinking about how to keep you on at *Nouveau Life*,' I continue. 'To maintain your cover, but I—'

'Sorry to interrupt,' she says, 'but if you're happy to keep meeting here, I don't think we need to fabricate another writing assignment.'

'Oh?' I ask, surprised. 'But... I'm confused – the first time we met, Anjali was adamant we needed a plausible guise for you to be at *Nouveau*.'

'I know and I understand your confusion. But, with you in the loop *and* my column being pulled... I think we can skip Poppy's Column 2.0, don't you? And if anyone from *Nouveau* sees us together, like here at the coffee shop, you can just tell them we've become friends.'

'So, another lie,' I say, bringing us back to Sunday's conversation and sending my abdomen into full-blown spasms. I shift in my seat and set my coffee down. I don't think I can stomach it now.

'Look, I understand that you're feeling overwhelmed by all the subterfuge. I imagine it's challenging, especially for such an honest person.'

'Well, yes,' I agree, somewhat relieved. 'A few days ago, after my date with Aman, I was all fired up. I was determined to write these bloody articles, put the bad dates behind me, and finally meet Harrison. And *then...*' I trail off, not wanting to work myself into too much of a lather – especially not here in what's become a sanctuary of sorts.

'Then you felt you had to lie to your family,' she says, completing my thought.

'Yes,' I reply softly. 'And now I'm not sure how to handle it – the guilt, the *confusion*... Poppy, I *really* don't want you close my case but I'm not sure how to—'

'Sorry – I know I'm interrupting again – but I'm not planning on closing your case. Not unless you ask me to.'

'Really? I... I worried that after I called you, you'd decide I'm not up the task and call it off.'

'Remember when I said your case was my number-one priority?'

'Yes,' I reply.

'I meant that. *You're* my client, Greta – not Anjali. I know how complicated this case has become and how much is being asked of you. I'm here to support you – to help you navigate the twists and turns and get everything back on track.'

'So you think I should just admit to Anjali I know what's going on?'

'That's entirely up to you,' she replies gently.

I breathe out noisily, now more confused than ever and – again – baulking at the thought of coming clean to Anjali. It would certainly simplify some of the machinations of this case but what impact would it have on our relationship? I find myself frowning at my coffee, and I look up at Poppy.

'I don't want to disappoint Anjali. She has such good intentions and we're *so* deep into the lie... Besides, as you said, kissing frogs is helpful, especially for someone like me who's practically a novice when it comes to love. *And* I've already drafted the first two articles. Poppy, they're *good* – they're really good – some of the best writing I've done in ages.'

Poppy chuckles. 'It sounds like you don't need my help getting back on track.'

'No, I do – or I *did*. It helps just talking to you.'

She smiles, then points to herself. 'Expert listener.'

'Now *that* would be a good article for *Nouveau* – the benefits of talking to a therapist.'

She raises her hands in surrender. 'Count me out. As of today, I'm retiring from all forms of journalism.'

'Well, back to me then,' I say, making her smile. 'So just two more bad dates, then I get to meet Harrison?'

'That's the plan. And George and I want to move the fourth date to this week.'

'Ooh, that means I could be meeting Harrison *soon*.'

'Yes.'

I bite my lip in anticipation, conjuring his handsome face in my mind. Ever since I imagined him in my flat – and what he would do to me in my flat – just the *thought* of Harrison has the power to flood my body with warmth. Those russet-brown eyes, those broad shoulders, that sexy stubble…

I've chastised myself innumerable times for crushing on a man I haven't met, but Harrison is Poppy's top pick and I trust her judgement implicitly. I have every reason to believe he will be everything I'm hoping for.

16

GRETA

'Babes, are you sure you have to go through with this?' asks Tiggy.

It's Wednesday night and she's stretched out on my sofa, intermittently stuffing crisps into her mouth between sips of wine.

'It's just two more dates. One bloke called Travis and the other called Ollie.'

She makes a face.

'What?'

'I've just never liked the name Travis.'

'It's not his fault his name's Travis. He might be a perfectly nice bloke.'

She rolls onto her side, leaning on her elbow, and rests her head in her hand. 'Isn't he supposed to be a dud?'

'That doesn't mean he's a bad person – just that he's not for me,' I reply, slightly defensive.

'What is *up* with you? Last week, you were all, "Only two more dud dates…" then Sunday, you were calling it off and now you're back to going on the dud dates. It's not like you to be so' – she flaps her hand in my direction – 'flip-floppy. You're also being defensive.'

'I'm sorry. It's just been mad these past few weeks. I'm all over the place.'

'No shit. I'm ten seconds from calling 999 and reporting a body snatching.'

'It's not that bad. It's just that once I really thought it through *and* talked it over with Poppy, I realised it's not such a big deal. It's just two more dates and then I get to meet Harrison.'

'And there's that. What if he's not what you're expecting? You've already told your mum and dad you're dating him.'

'To be accurate, *you* told them that.' She stares at me, clearly unimpressed by my semantics. 'Which I am very grateful for,' I add.

'I should think so. If it weren't for me, you'd be on a date with *Ian* tonight.'

'Ha-ha,' I reply sarcastically.

'And what about Ewan?' she asks, throwing me a scrutinising look.

'What's with the look? I told you, Ewan and I are *friends*.'

'Hah!' she scoffs.

'We are!'

'You see him nearly every day, you have these "lovely conversations"' – she waggles two fingers to denote air quotes – '*and* you described him as handsome,' she retorts.

Why did I tell her so much about Ewan on the way home from Mum and Dad's? Oh, that's right – because I didn't expect my *best friend* to weaponise something I told her in confidence.

'He *is* objectively handsome.'

'Ah-hah!'

'But that doesn't mean I fancy him.'

'Mm-hmm,' she murmurs, clearly unconvinced.

'Besides,' I continue, hoping to curb her insinuations. 'Harrison was handpicked for me and even if I *did* fancy Ewan – which I don't – it would be rude not to at least meet Harrison.'

'To who?'

'It's "whom" and to Harrison – *and* Poppy – *and* Anjali. A lot of work has gone into making this match.'

'Mm-hmm,' she replies again, her lips pursed with judgement.

She sits up suddenly and opens the drawer of my coffee table, taking out the notepad I keep in there in case inspiration strikes.

'What are you doing?'

'I'm making a list,' she says, finding a pen and clicking the end of it. 'Of all your men.'

'You hate lists,' I say dryly.

'That's how confusing this is. I'm being driven to list-making!'

'And they're not "my men",' I toss at her, but she ignores me and starts writing.

I don't know why she's bothering. I have no doubt Harrison is everything I'm searching for. Well, there's *some* doubt – *reasonable* doubt – but if I *don't* meet him, then I'll always wonder, 'What if?'

While I've been contemplating my match with Harrison – *again* – Tiggy has completed her list. She regards it thoughtfully.

'Can I see?' I ask, craning my neck.

She hands it over and I chuckle as I read down the page.

Marcus – fat-shaming arse – NO FUCKING WAY

Aman – lives with mum – NO FUCKING WAY

Travis – bad name – ???

Ollie – naturist (OMG) – ???

Ian – too old and (maybe) too sad

Harrison – love of Greta's life???

~~Luca – fit but not fit for purpose~~

Ewan – Greta's hot friend

'You put Luca on the list?' I ask.

'Yes, and I crossed him out.'

'Then why add him at all?'

'To remind you how far you've come.'

'And Ewan?' I ask.

'You tell me.'

'I *did* tell you. He's my *friend* – not my *hot* friend,' I say, stabbing the paper with my finger.

Is this one of those 'methinks the lady doth protest too much' situations? There *have* been a handful of moments over the past few weeks when I've wondered if Ewan has been flirting with me, but I've always dismissed them – in part, because I'm not the type of woman men typically flirt with. And maybe flirtation is a normal element of male–female friendships. Having never had one before, I'm completely in the dark!

Just like I am with dating.

I'm a thirty-five-year-old, professional woman who has dedicated so much of my life to my career, my social skills – including the ability to read signals from men who may or may not fancy me – are so underdeveloped, I should be fitted with romantic training wheels.

'Want to tell me what's going on in there?' asks Tiggy.

'What?' I've been so distracted traversing the landscape of my non-existent love life, I've dropped out of the conversation entirely. 'Sorry, I'm rubbish company tonight.'

'You are.' She holds up her phone. 'But at least I'm caught up on the fallout from the *Soulmates Unseen* reunion.'

Tiggy not only loves romcoms, she also watches all the reality dating shows – *and* scours socials for the 'hot takes'. Maybe I should start watching those shows – I'd probably learn something.

My mind lands back on Harrison and for the first time since

Poppy gave me his profile, I feel a twinge of trepidation – and not about the assignment itself, but about *him*.

'Tiggy, what if I've built him up so much in my mind, he turns out to be a disappointment?'

'Harrison?'

'Yep.'

She blows out a long breath. 'Babes, that's my biggest worry, out of everything else going on.'

'Oh.'

'I just don't want to see you get hurt. And this is bonkers. You're going on dates with duds and pining after a bloke you've never met... You're Greta Fucking Davies, don't forget – badass magazine editor, stylish woman about town, best friend extraordinaire – and this whole thing has your knickers in such a twist, your lady parts may never recover.'

I scrunch my nose at the last bit – Tiggy knows I hate it when she says 'lady parts'.

'Sorry,' she says, 'I meant your *vagina*.'

'Yeah, yeah, I get it.'

'Sorry for the tough love. Actually, no, I'm not, because I love you and I hate seeing you out of sorts.'

'I know. And thanks.'

She reaches over to pat my arm. 'Look at it this way: on the weekend, you get to date a bloke who likes to wander about in the nude and *then* you get to write about it. How many people can say that?'

We lock eyes, and she smirks, then starts sniggering, and I can't help but join in. Tiggy's right: this whole thing *is* bonkers. How on *earth* did I end up in this situation?

We laugh for a good solid minute, and I don't even care that we're both laughing *at* me. It's a wonderful release.

When the laughter fades away, I take huge, gulping breaths, then expel noisy sighs until my breathing steadies.

'Right,' I say, sitting up straight. 'Two dates this week, finish my bloody articles, and meet Harrison next week. I can do this.'

'Too bloody right,' says Tiggy. 'Raise your glass.'

I do.

'To Greta Fucking Davies,' she toasts.

'Ha!' I laugh, then we clink glasses and drink.

I'm bolstered by the reminder that I am in fact, Greta Fucking Davies, and with Poppy's advice and my bestie on my side, I can most definitely do this.

* * *

As I hypothesised to Tiggy, my next date, Travis, is not a bad person. But he's also not for me. I felt like I was on a speed date/job interview, with relentless questions being fired at me in rapid succession. I'm shocked he didn't have a clipboard.

As I near the Tube stop, casting my mind back over our one-hour date, sentences start forming in my head. This happens sometimes – the lightning strike of inspiration – and by the time I take a seat in a middle carriage, I have the opening paragraph of my next article mentally written. I take a small notebook from my handbag – a writer's must-have – and start scrawling before it disappears.

There was a sad desperation in his eyes as he peppered me with dozens of questions, one after the other. Would I be his person? As I answered each question in turn, the vibrating light of his anticipation dimmed ever so slightly until we were simply two strangers without anything else to say to each other. I made

my excuse and disappointment permeated the air around him as
if it were a pheromone discharged by his body.

It was impossible not to feel sympathy for him, but I could
tell he didn't want my sympathy. He wanted me to be THE ONE.

I re-read what I've written and make some additional notes, mostly about one of the biggest traps of modern dating: ping-ponging biographical questions at each other without ever achieving real depth in the conversation. Which, I just now realise, brings me back to the original concept for the series: swimming in the deep end of the dating pool.

But how does this fit in with 'Dating Horrors of London'? I think back to my date with Marcus the Arse – Marcarse? *He* certainly won't get any sympathy from me. I will lampoon him so severely, Taylor Swift could mine my article for lyrics.

It occurs to me that there are *two* angles here: dating horrors, featuring Marcarse and Aman, then one or more articles addressing the original concept and featuring an anonymised Travis.

It's unclear where Ollie will fit, but I may need more material, which would mean more dates with different men. Oh my god, am I *really* considering more dud dates?

I ponder this question all the way home.

* * *

Poppy

'All set for tonight?' Tristan asks. Evie, Olivia, and Jacinda are coming over for our girls' night in.

'Let's see… wine – check. Umm… I think that's everything.'

He laughs. 'And *dinner*?'

'Well, I've given the chef the night off, so we'll just order in.' He smiles, the corners of his whisky-coloured eyes crinkling with amusement. 'What about you? What are you and Ravi up to?'

'We'll also order in, I suppose, considering Jacinda will be here and Ravi has the culinary skills of... well, *you*...'

'Ha-ha.'

'And can I ask... a girls' night in? What does it entail exactly?'

'You know, we braid each other's hair, give ourselves facials, have a pillow fight...' He watches me in silence, his mouth twitching as he waits for the real answer. 'All right, we don't do any of that.'

'Imagine my surprise.'

'We'll just have dinner and drink wine, then spend the rest of the evening discussing Evie's love life—'

'Exposing Tyler for the cheating bastard he is,' Tristan interjects.

'Well, yes, that's part of it. Though, I'll need to tread lightly there. No one *wants* to hear their boyfriend is seeing at least three other women behind their back – even if they suspect it.'

'*Three?*'

'Yep. It took Marie less than twenty-four hours to unearth the first two and then she discovered a third.'

He frowns intensely, and a vein pulses along his jawline.

'Evie still intends to break up with him, right?'

'That's what tonight's about. Supporting Evie to make the best decision for her romantic future. Short of that, you and Ravi can go over to his place and rough him up. How does that sound?'

'You're teasing me.'

'Just a little. But it's sweet how much you care about Evie.'

'Yes, well, that's my job, as her older cousin.'

I scooch closer to Tristan and press my mouth to his. 'You're a good cousin, to both of them. And the not-for-profit is going to be amazing.'

He smiles, his expression softening. 'I really am so proud of them. And you're right, I think this venture will be quite something.' He stares off, his mind obviously having wandered. He blinks a couple of times and smiles at me again, then leans in for another kiss.

'Are you finished with work for the day?' he asks, his mouth mere inches from mine.

I nod. 'Yep. My brain is fried.'

'And how about your body?' he asks, raising his eyebrows at me. He reaches for me, his hand grasping my bum, and pulls me even closer. I feel the hardness of his erection against my hip.

'My body is *very* interested in what you have in mind, Mr Fellows.'

He chuckles as his lips graze my neck. 'Is that so, Ms Dean?'

I murmur, 'Uh-huh,' and my utterance transforms into a sigh of pleasure as Tristan begins to work his magic.

17

GRETA

'Hi, babes. I'm just on my way out the—'

'Can I come over?' I ask, talking over Tiggy.

'—door,' she finishes. 'Oh, you mean now?'

'Yes, now. I need to debrief – *desperately*.'

'I can't – I've got a client meeting.'

'On a Saturday afternoon?'

'The life of the freelancer.'

'Right.'

'I'm guessing this is a dating debrief?' she asks.

'Yes. I just spent the better part of two hours with Ollie – you know, the naturist. We have very little in common, so definitely not a match, which I expected, but he is a lovely, *lovely* person, Tiggy. There's no way I can write about him in *Nouveau Life*, even if I change his name. I mean, how many full-time vets and part-time naturists do *you* know from East Horsley?'

Tiggy's quiet for a moment, which is probably because I've been rabbiting on and she's waiting for me to take a breath.

'That *is* oddly specific,' she says eventually. 'Not sure how you'd disguise that – unless you made him a part-time vet and full-time naturist from Hertfordshire.' She laughs at her own joke.

'Hilarious,' I reply drolly.

'I always am,' she quips.

'Well,' I say, ignoring her self-congratulations, 'I suppose if you're not about, I'll just head home and watch *Bouquet Battle* or something.'

'Greta Lennox Davies!' she rebukes. 'It's a gorgeous day and if you go straight home to watch reality TV, I will—'

'Reschedule your client meeting and come to mine?'

'Nice try. Why don't you call the woman from the dating agency?'

'You know she's called Poppy and it's a *matchmaking* agency.'

'Whatevs! *Call Poppy*,' she says emphatically.

'It's the weekend.'

'You know what they say: a matchmaker never sleeps.'

'Can you hear my eyes rolling to the back of my head?' I ask.

'Message me with updates but I've got to go. Uber's here.'

'All right. Love you.'

'Love you back.'

She rings off, still sniggering, and I pop my phone in my bag and look about. It really is a stunning day: 25°C, puffy, white clouds in a cerulean sky, the vibrant green of the plane trees contrasting beautifully against the sky…

Tiggy's right. Being inside on a day like this *would* be criminal. No doubt Ollie would agree. He really was such a kind, gentle person. There's no way I'm writing about our picnic – one he'd thoughtfully assembled from his local farmers' market.

So, that leaves me with only two horror dates to write about – Marcus and Aman. Ugh, maybe I should gird my loins and agree to meet the misogynist – Michael – and make it a trio of articles.

As I make my way home, I decide I should stick to my previous declaration: I will not date Michael, not even a little bit. No article is worth *that*.

* * *

Poppy

'Wow,' I say as Jacinda heaves an inch-thick, leatherbound scrapbook onto the kitchen counter. 'What *is* that?'

'You said to bring my dating war stories...' She waves a hand over it like a gameshow host. '*This* is a history of every date I went on before I met Ravi.'

She and Ravi, who is Tristan's oldest friend, met through the agency before I started working there.

I open the scrapbook and on the first page are three selfie Polaroids of Jacinda around age fifteen. In each photo, she's with a different, awkward-looking boy and next to the photos are hand-written captions with the boy's name, age, and a brief biography, like Vihaan's:

19, likes video games and football

'Jass, this is...' I say, throwing her a quizzical look.

'I know, right? It started as a bit of a laugh, but...' She trails off, tilting her head from side to side, as if she's figuring how best to explain it.

'Remember I told you about my cousin, Aashvi?'

I nod – Aashvi was like an older sister to Jacinda growing up.

'Well, she gave it to me in secret along with the camera, suggesting I document all the blokes my parents set me up with in the hopes of matching me with my future husband.'

'Your future hus— But you're only, what? *Sixteen* here?' I ask, pointing to the first photo in horror.

'Well, *eighteen* – I was expected to focus solely on my studies until I finished school – but even eighteen felt too young. It was overwhelming for someone as naïve as me, and Aashvi must have seen that. Being older, she was already deep into the vortex. Anyway, *she* had a scrapbook – her way of coping with her parents' expectations – and thought I might want one too. It was our little secret – a fun way to maintain some control over the situation.'

'Oh-*kay*,' I say, trying to wrap my brain around this as I turn to the next page.

Jass once told me she approached Ever After because of the intense pressure from her parents to get married – *and* to a man of their choosing. But I never expected that their efforts began when Jacinda was still a *teenager*.

Jass peers over my shoulder as I turn more pages.

'When I was a bit older, I started including the blokes I dated that my parents didn't know about – like Kabir,' she says, pointing to a photo of an attractive young man with a beaming smile.

'And what does this denote?' I ask, tapping on the '5' next to his photo. 'Some kind of rating system?' I ask.

She laughs. 'No, that's the number of dates we went on.'

'*Oh*, yeah, that makes sense.' I scan the current page, then turn to the next one. 'So, not many of these guys made it past a first date,' I say, observing all the 1s.

'I did have a few longer-term boyfriends in my early-twenties – they're back here,' she says, turning to the middle of the scrapbook. 'But none of them would have been considered a suitable son-in-law.'

'Geez, I knew about the pressure from your parents, but this...'

'Mmm, I know.' She breaks into a grin. 'I've got some *brilliant* stories, though.' She flips through a couple more pages, then stops and points to an extremely handsome man called Avyaan. 'On our third date, we ran into his fiancée.'

'What?' I ask with a laugh.

She closes the scrapbook. 'I told you,' she says with raised eyebrows, 'brilliant stories – but let's wait till the girls get here. When are they due?'

I glance at the clock on the stove. 'Any minute, but then Evie's almost always late – it drives Olivia mad.'

'And has she dumped the boyfriend yet?'

'According to Olivia, no.'

'Well, then, we need to help her decide to dump him so she can find her *real* person. There's a new solicitor at work who might be a good fit for her – clever, funny, socially conscious…'

I regard Jacinda with a smirk. 'You sure you don't want to give up the law and come work for the agency?'

This isn't the first time Jacinda has actively nudged someone towards love. Earlier this year, she was the instigator of an intervention to move Shaz into Lauren's place while Lauren was on a work trip. All in the name of love – Jacinda is a closet romantic.

'Hah! Erm, no. I'd rather keep matchmaking as a hobby,' she says with a wink.

* * *

Greta

'Oh, were you just on your way out?' Bex is standing in the doorway to my office, her gaze landing on the handbag slung over my shoulder with my laptop peeking out.

'I was about to pop down to The Daily Grind to work on my assignment, but I'm happy to stick around if you need me. Is about next month's issue?'

She continues lingering, her expression pained.

'Bex?' I slide the handbag off my shoulder and set it on my desk. 'Why don't you come in and close the door?'

She does, reluctantly, and in moments, we're seated on opposite sides of my desk. She clearly has something to say but, for some reason, can't get the words out.

'You know you can tell me anything, right?' I say, trying to set her at ease, but she recoils with a sharp intake of breath. 'Wait,' I say, eyeing her closely, 'are you *leaving*?'

I can't think of any other piece of news she might share that would warrant her nervous behaviour.

'No! No, nothing like that. It's just...' She sighs.

'Bex, what is it?'

'Why wasn't I brought in on the decision to kill the advice column?' she asks, finally meeting my eye.

'Oh! Right, that,' I say, relieved she isn't resigning. 'Well, it all happened so quickly. I made the discovery, then immediately escalated the matter to Anjali... It was decided in minutes – we didn't really have time to bring you in.'

I don't add that it wouldn't have been her call if she'd disagreed with us, as that would just add salt to the wound – it's clear she's already doubting her role within the team hierarchy.

She scowls but remains silent.

'I thought you'd be pleased that we pulled the column. You weren't particularly happy with Poppy's submission and—'

'You didn't think it was any good either.'

'To be fair, it *did* need work, but setting that aside, it was obvious you were annoyed that we brought on Poppy in the first place.'

'Because you didn't even consult me!' she shouts.

I can tell the instant Bex realises she's been disrespectful. 'I'm so sorry – that was out of order. It's just...' She looks at her hands, which are clasped tightly in her lap. 'You didn't even *discuss* it with me,' she says quietly.

'Discuss what exactly?'

'*Any* of it,' she says, lifting her gaze. 'I'm supposed to be the assistant editor of *Nouveau Life* and you keep making decisions without me. If you'd consulted me about Poppy, I would have voiced my concerns. *I'm* the one who's worked with her before.'

I nod slowly as Bex's words register. I'm not sure what to say, because she's right. I was Anjali's assistant editor for years before the vertical – and she always consulted me on any major decisions that impacted the features department. Whereas, ever since *Nouveau Life* launched, I've been treating it as a solo gig, making unilateral decisions without conferring with my team. That's got to end – and now. I make a silent vow to do better by Bex and the team.

While I've been self-reproaching, Bex's eyes have glossed with tears. I quickly stand and slip around to the other side of the desk, where I crouch beside her. 'Bex, I'm so sorry. You're absolutely right. I've messed up – without question.'

'I know I'm only twenty-six, but I'm clever and hard-working and I deserved this promotion,' she says, still making her case even though I've already sided with her.

'You are absolutely right – and I promise that from now on, I will discuss all decisions with you, and we'll make them together, okay?'

She smiles and sniffles, dabbing under each eye with her fingertips. I reach for the box of tissues on my desk and she takes one.

After wiping her tears, she expels a long, slow breath, as if an enormous weight has been lifted from her chest. What a terrible boss I am for not realising what she was going through!

'Right.' She gets up, sniffles loudly, and tosses the used tissue away. 'I should let you get back to your writing,' she says, flashing me a warm smile, then heading to the door. 'And which assignment is this?' she asks, turning back. 'I wasn't aware you were working on anything.'

Mere seconds ago, I promised myself I'd do better by Bex and I'm about to break that promise already. 'Oh, it's just in the research stage, something Anjali wants me to look into. I'll let you know if anything eventuates – I promise.'

'Sounds good. Well, see ya.'

She goes and I lean against the desk, hating myself for the half-truth I've just told. How do I make amends for *that*?

Perhaps a latte and a leafy outlook will give me a fresh perspective. *And* if I happen to run into a certain friendly face at The Daily Grind, all the better!

18

GRETA

When I approach The Daily Grind, there's a line out the door – great for the owner of a new business in the centre of London, not so great for a person who's just admitted she messed up at work and wants to retreat to her favourite spot.

I join the queue, taking out my phone to mindlessly scroll through socials, like most of the people ahead of me. Only my mind can't cope with even this simple task. I can't believe I missed how discontented Bex has been. I really am a terrible boss. I adore Bex and she's right – she's clever and capable and I've been too focussed on other aspects of *Nouveau Life* to fully leverage her abilities and make her feel valued.

I know! Bex should edit my articles.

This would mean looping in yet *another* person on my so-called 'secret' assignment, but it's Bex. She's trustworthy – and what's one more person excavating the ruins of my love life?

I should ask Poppy to join us. If I want to show Bex I trust her unreservedly, she can learn the real reason we brought Poppy on. Hopefully, that will make amends and wipe the slate clean.

'Right, a plan of action,' I mutter to myself. Now knowing how to address my managerial misstep, I recommence the mindless scroll on my phone as I shuffle forward.

I'm watching a video of a cat who lives on a boat as I reach the head of the queue and when I look up to place my order, Ewan is there. Behind the counter. Wearing a forest-green apron with 'The Daily Grind' embroidered across the top.

My mouth falls open as my mind tries to interpret what I'm seeing.

'The usual?' he asks, flashing his signature lopsided smile.

'Er, yes – *please*,' I add as an afterthought.

He punches something into the register and when I hold my phone to the card reader to pay, I see '0.00' on the screen. I look up at Ewan, even more confused.

'On me,' he says with a wink.

'Oh, okay.'

This is the part where I'm supposed to step aside and let the next person order, but I'm rooted to the spot as if I'm in a horror movie and I've just spotted the scary man with the axe.

'Why don't you find a place to sit, and I'll bring it over,' Ewan prompts.

I nod and wander off, coming out of my stupor as I realise most people in the queue must have been getting takeaway. Nearly all the tables are free. I head to my favourite one, far from the caffeine fray, and sit facing the rest of the coffee shop.

That really is Ewan, and he really is serving behind the counter of The Daily Grind.

As I'm watching him, he switches places with one of the young men who works here and takes off his apron. He hovers near the espresso machine and when the barista pops the lid on a cup, he takes it from them, and heads towards me.

'Think, Greta. What are you going to say?' I ask myself out loud.

Ewan's eyes light up as he approaches, and I beam back at him.

'Good morning,' he says with a bright smile. He places my coffee on the table and slides into the chair opposite me.

'Good morning, Mr Coffee Man,' I say, immediately regretting it. Mr Coffee Man – what a *muppet*! You wouldn't know I make a living as a wordsmith.

Ewan chuckles good-naturedly and dips his chin, maintaining eye contact. 'I was going to tell you the night we had dinner, but then the conversation moved on and it never really came up again. Then I worried I'd left it too long and... well... Ta-da! I own The Daily Grind,' he says, his arms out wide.

Well, that explains why I didn't know sooner. And Ewan's positively radiating pride, as he should be, only the pride is underpinned with something else: an uncertainty in his eyes.

'It's totally fine – just unexpected is all. You're obviously making a success of it – there's a line out the door!' I say, hoping to make at least a dent in that uncertainty.

He chuckles and looks over his shoulder, then returns his gaze to me. 'My first time behind the counter today...' he says, shaking his head.

'Well, you did brilliantly. Although, please tell me you're not giving away free coffee to everyone.'

'Oh, no, only to people I like,' he says, imbuing the word 'like' with more meaning than I can unpack right now. I return the comment with a smile.

'So, what are you doing when you're not back there?' I say, indicating the counter.

'I spend most of the day in the office.' He nods towards a door tucked at the back of the coffee shop that, somehow, I've never noticed before. 'But there's no natural light in there, so I prefer working out here – especially when people I know come in.'

'And why a coffee shop?'

He bites his top lip and sucks in a breath through his teeth. 'If I tell you, will you promise not to tell a soul?'

'Of course I won't,' I say, suddenly serious.

He leans in and I do the same. After glancing left, then right, he says, 'I'm actually an MI6 agent and The Daily Grind is a front.'

I tut and sit back in my chair, pretending to glare at him. 'You had me going then.'

'I could tell,' he replies, sniggering.

'Is there a real reason or...?'

'It's going to sound wildly out of character.'

'I'm all ears,' I say.

'Well, I was with a mate at a pub, and I told him I was considering stepping away from my job for a year—'

'Is this the mate with the sick toddler?'

'Different mate – he doesn't work in finance – he's a teacher, actually... Anyway, we started "riffing", I guess is the best word, on the sorts of things I could do instead. And we ended up in this word association game and he said, "Whatever you answer to the next question – you have to do something related to that," or something similar.'

'And what was the next question?' I ask, literally on the edge of my seat as I inch closer, my eyes fixed on his.

'He asked, "What's the one thing – not a person, nothing essential, and nothing abstract – that you couldn't live without?"'

I blink at him, my mind instantly chewing on the question from my own perspective.

'You're trying to figure out what your "one thing" is, aren't you?'

I nod.

'Don't think about it too much – just say whatever comes to mind.'

'Reality competition shows,' I blurt. I clap my hand over my mouth. 'That's so ridiculous. I'm sorry. I could have said any number of things. Like magazines, for example!' I shake my head at myself and take a sip of my coffee.

'Ahh, but that's the thing – in your profession, magazines are essential.'

'I suppose so.'

'Which makes yours a perfect response.'

'Maybe...' I say, still feeling a little foolish. 'So what did *you* say?'

'Isn't it obvious?' he asks with a smile. 'I said, "Coffee".'

'*Oh*, of course.'

'And I thought, "Why not?". It was as far away from my profession as I could get, and I have a friend in commercial real estate and another in small business management... I called in some favours and bit the bullet and—'

'Other pertinent idioms.'

'And other pertinent idioms and' – he throws his hands out wide again – 'I'm the proud owner of a thriving coffee shop in Central London. Who knew?'

'I suspect that deep down, you knew it would take off.'

'I honestly didn't. These past months have been the steepest learning curve of my life.'

'But you've loved it.'

He grins. 'I have.'

'Oh, I've just realised... The Daily Grind... You named the coffee shop after what you were leaving behind.'

'That's it exactly.'

'Well, I love it – very clever.'

'Thank you,' he says, dipping his chin to accept the compliment. When he meets my eye again, his friendly smile warms me from the inside.

'Are you working on your article today?' he asks.

His question breaks the spell and I nose-dive back into reality.

Ewan's not the only one who hasn't been forthcoming about his work. And given my confrontation with Bex just now and the repercussions of keeping these things hidden, I'm wondering if I should confess to him about the real subject of my articles.

'Er, yes. I've got a couple of articles I need to polish – my boss is waiting on them.'

He squints at me curiously. Oh, bollocks, is he onto me, even without a confession?

'Are you *really* able to work in this environment?' he asks. 'What with the noise and everyone coming and going?'

'Oh!' I exclaim out of relief. He looks at me quizzically and I try to pass off my overreaction as 'normal' by adding, 'I get asked that *all* the time. I'm just fortunate really – I can work anywhere. I once wrote an entire article on my phone in the middle of Euston station while waiting for a delayed train.'

I'm rabbiting. Why am I rabbiting? Any moment now, I'll spout long, fluffy ears.

'Well, it's an impressive skill,' he says, regarding me thoughtfully.

'Thank you,' I reply. Only now I seem to have run out of things to say, which isn't all that surprising considering the number of words I packed into one thirty-second-long ramble.

Ewan starts to rise. 'Well, I should get back to it and leave you to your obsessions.'

'My obsess— right, yes.' So much for telling him the truth about my assignment but, just like he said earlier, the moment has passed.

'So, do you think you'll become a permanent fixture back there?' I ask, nodding towards the counter where there are still a dozen people in line. I'm keeping him from his work, but I don't want him to go just yet.

'I hope not,' he says with a laugh. 'My shop manager's already teeing up some interviews to hire more staff. I've also been thinking about adding—'

'Ewan!'

We both look in the direction of the voice – it's a woman and she's frantically waving him back to the counter. And no wonder. A large group has just entered and have bunched up near the door.

'Go, go,' I say. 'You can't keep coffee drinkers waiting – uncaffeinated people can turn rabid in an instant.' There, that was far wittier than the 'Mr Coffee Man' remark.

'See you soon?' he asks.

'Same time tomorrow!' I say cheerily.

'Excellent.' He goes but after a few steps, he turns back and points at me. 'And dinner this week. Let's make plans tomorrow.'

Before I can reply, he trots behind the counter and slips the apron on over his head.

He didn't even *ask* about dinner – it was more of 'this is what's going to happen' and I can't say I minded one bit.

* * *

Bex gazes back and forth between us with her lips parted, stupefied. I steal a glance at Anjali, who seems unperturbed by her reaction, then at Poppy, who appears tickled.

Eventually, Bex speaks. 'Wait, *what*?'

Anjali is the one to reply. 'It shouldn't be too much of an addition to your workload, seeing as it's a finite series that Greta's writing and we aim to space it out over multiple issues. Do you think you'll be able to take it on?'

'Oh, yes, absolutely,' Bex splutters, nodding eagerly.

Then she looks at me, clearly uncertain. 'So, you're really going on these dates?'

'Mmm-hmm.'

'With *actual* men?' she asks.

'Yes. That's why we brought Poppy in. She's a professional matchmaker.' This, of course, is an even bigger reveal than my assignment.

'She's a... she's a—' Bex stammers. She looks over at Poppy, who raises her hand in a small wave, and her eyes widen as her mouth stretches into a perfect 'O' of comprehension. Then she throws back her head and, one hand to her chest, starts cackling with laughter.

'*Bex*,' says Anjali firmly.

Bex stops immediately and clears her throat. 'I'm sorry, I just... That article about Elle Bliss and Lorenzo and then the advice column... It all makes sense now and I—'

It's comical how forcefully the second realisation lands. 'Oh my god. Did you match Elle Bliss and Lorenzo?' she asks, her voice shrill. 'You did, didn't you? God, that's so exciting. I want to hear *everything*.'

I catch Anjali's lips tightening with distaste, signalling that it's time to take this discussion anywhere other than her office.

'Let's head back to my office and discuss this further,' I say, standing and shepherding Bex and Poppy out into the hallway.

'Oh, and Greta,' says Anjali.

I pause in the doorway. 'Yes?'

'After Bex calms down, can you please have her edit your first article? I'd like it on my desk by noon tomorrow.'

'Of course,' I say, 'Actually, I've got two ready to submit.'

'Very good.' She smiles at me politely, then puts her reading glasses on and opens her laptop.

I leave, feeling like I've just been dismissed from the principal's office. It's not that Anjali seemed cross, but something was off about how we left things just now, which leaves me feeling unsettled.

I arrive at my office to find Bex bombarding Poppy with questions. I should have anticipated that she'd be ultra-curious about Poppy's job once she learnt the truth, but I need her focussed, not fangirling over the engagement of two fashion designers.

'Says you,' I rebuke myself softly. 'Several weeks ago, you were doing the exact same thing.'

'What was that?' Bex asks me.

'Nothing, never mind. Right, if you've finished interrogating Poppy, we need to get to work. Anjali wants to see the first two articles by lunchtime tomorrow. I'll email them to you now.'

'Oh, of course,' Bex says, popping out of her chair. 'And how do you prefer your feedback?' she asks. 'Tracked changes and comments, or I can send it in paragraph form, if you like?'

As Bex has never been my editor before, I understand her reticence in asking. This is a significant shift in our power dynamic.

'Tracked changes and comments is fine,' I reply.

'Perfect,' she says with a grin. 'And thank you again for this opportunity.'

'As you told me this morning, you've earned it.'

She beams, but then she glances at Poppy and her smile falls away. She not-so-subtly jerks her head towards the door, telegraphing that Poppy should leave.

'Poppy's staying for a bit,' I say.

'Ah, okay.' Bex gives me a terse smile and pulls the door closed after her.

'That went reasonably well,' says Poppy when Bex is gone.

Falling into my chair, I expel a heavy breath, then send her a wry smile. 'You have a very strange idea of "well",' I say.

'Was it your assistant editor behaving like a teen at a Taylor Swift concert or your boss sending us away as if she were a monarch weary of the peasants?'

'How did you— You're very astute about people's behaviour and relationships, you know.'

She shrugs immodestly.

'Anjali *was* a little taken aback by Bex,' I say, stifling a giggle.

'She physically recoiled,' retorts Poppy dryly.

I giggle. 'I suppose it's been a while since she was in the magazine trenches. If she only knew how younger colleagues behaved these days... They're effusive about *everything*; whereas I suspect Anjali entered adulthood fully formed, serious, and single-minded. That would certainly explain her meteoric rise in the world of magazines. And here's me – thirty-five and a massive Swiftie. I saw Taylor Swift twice last year – in the same week!'

'Impressive.'

'I know you don't like her.'

'I never said that,' she says with a shake of her head. 'I just... She's not my favourite.'

'Fair,' I concede.

'Can you imagine Anjali at a Taylor Swift concert?' she asks with a smirk.

'Don't laugh, but she took her eldest last year.'

'Anjali Bennett?' Poppy asks, incredulous. 'At a Taylor Swift concert?'

'Well, her son's a fan, *and* she said she went with an old school chum and her daughter. Saskia, I think – the mum, not the daughter.'

Poppy's eyes go wide, then she bursts out laughing.

'What? What's so funny?'

'Saskia...' she says through her laughter. She points to herself. 'She's *my* boss.'

'What?'

She nods. 'And she's just like Anjali – we call her "The Swan". Oh my god...' She flaps her hand in front of her face, barely getting out, 'Can you imagine?' Then she launches into a mime of a very posh woman at a pop concert, one who bops along to the music, but in an extremely reserved way, and instantly has me in hysterics.

I am *so* glad to be working with Poppy on this assignment – she's become a bit of a fairy-godmother. I wonder if we'll stay friends after it's over. *When it's over*, I think with a jolt. When I'm either matched or deemed unmatchable. And it's unclear which of those outcomes triggers the roaring inside my head.

19

POPPY

'And, Poppy, you have an update on the... Sorry, what's your case called again?' Saskia asks, consulting her planner.

'The Greta Davies case,' I reply, right as George leaps in with, 'Greta Expectations.'

I turn to George. 'That's pretty good,' I say quietly and he gives me a pleased-with-himself smile. And it only took him six tries to find a case name that didn't make me cringe – not that I'll mention that part.

'Greta Expectations,' I say to the rest of the team. Saskia's mouth twitches with amusement and Ursula nods approvingly. Beside me, George sits up taller, obviously proud that he has (finally) smashed the case name.

'Right, so, Greta has now been on four dates, two of which she will write about in her "Dating Horrors of London" series.'

'What about the other dates she went on?' asks Saskia.

'She's writing one into her deeper dive into dating in the modern age. And the fourth, Ollie, will be omitted entirely.'

'And why is that?' Ursula asks, her chin angled defensively.

Ursula prides herself in assembling the perfect list of potential matches for any client; maybe she feels similarly about providing a list of duds. How do I diplomatically tell her that Ollie wasn't *enough* of a dud?

'He wasn't a good fit,' I say. Ursula purses her lips and huffs noisily. I forge ahead. 'On a positive note, Greta can now draw a line under dating duds and move onto her first real potential, Harrison Reid.'

Freya, always the romantic, claps her hands together softly under her chin and, out of the corner of my eye, I see Ursula look my way. Hopefully, this news will appease her.

'Excellent,' says Saskia, 'and, Nasrin, how's your—'

There's a loud message notification and we all look around. It's an unspoken rule that we silence our phones for staff meetings, even though we all place our phones face up on the conference table in case an urgent call or message comes through.

'Apologies, everyone,' says Paloma in a rare moment of humility. She reads the message, the crease between her brows intensifying as her eyes scan the screen. She lifts her gaze and gets up from the table, taking her phone to the other end where she shows it to Saskia. Saskia grimaces, then they both look at me.

'Poppy, could you and George please see us after the staff meeting?' Saskia asks.

'In my office,' Paloma adds.

'Umm... sure.' I glance at George, whose eyes are as big as saucers, and an uneasy feeling settles into my stomach.

The meeting concludes with Nasrin's update, but I don't hear a word of it. I'm too busy trying to figure out what that message could have said to warrant an impromptu meeting.

Ten minutes later, George and I shuffle out of the conference room behind the others, but before we head to Paloma's office, we huddle.

'Do you have any idea what this is about?' he asks quietly.

'Nope.'

'Oh, hello, Poppy,' says a nearby voice. I look over and Anita is leading Anjali Bennett across the open-plan office.

What's she doing here? I wonder. I'm no longer posing as a contributor for *Nouveau Life*, so it must be about Greta's case. Have I missed something or made a mistake? Whatever it is, she doesn't look pleased.

'Isn't that...?' whispers George.

'Yep,' I whisper back. 'Hello, Anjali,' I say, faking a smile.

'Hello, lovely,' says Saskia, meeting Anjali at the door to Paloma's office. They exchange cheek kisses, then Saskia lets Anjali past. She looks at us, her expression inscrutable. 'Are you joining us?'

It's an instruction, not a question, and George and I hustle inside and get seated. Paloma introduces George and Anjali, then says. 'So, Anji, tell us a bit more about why you're here.'

I'd love to pretend this is a friendly catch-up between old school friends, rather than a meeting with a *V*-VIP client, but I'm a realist.

Anjali addresses me. 'Greta submitted her first two articles this morning...' she begins, her tone establishing that they weren't what she had expected. 'And I have concerns.'

A client with concerns is nothing new in matchmaking. We deal in matters of the heart, so the stakes are high – even when our actual client has engaged us on behalf of someone else, like in this instance. But being adept at managing client concerns is one thing; addressing them with my bosses looking on is another.

'So, that would be the articles about the fitness fanatic and the man who lives with his mum?' I ask.

The question seems to catch Anjali off-guard. 'Yes. So, you're *aware* that you set Greta up with inadequate matches?'

'I am.'

'But that's not what we agreed,' she says, her eyes narrowing to slits.

There's a beat of silence before Paloma and I speak at once.

'So, you didn't approve this, Anji?' she asks.

'It was a deliberate tactic,' I say.

Anjali looks between us. 'No, definitely not,' she says to Paloma. 'And what do you mean "deliberate"?' she asks me. 'You *deliberately* set Greta up on rubbish dates?'

'Yes,' I reply steadily.

'Poppy, when you asked for approval to set Greta up with unsuitable men, we assumed you had informed Anjali,' says Saskia.

She and Paloma may have assumed that, but they didn't mention it and I couldn't have informed Anjali even if they'd outright instructed me to. That would have been betraying Greta's trust; she didn't want Anjali to know she was onto her. She still doesn't, which leaves me in a precarious position, one that's compounded by three forty-something, highly powerful women staring me down.

'I understand how you may have reached that conclusion,' I say to Saskia. Turning my attention to Anjali, I say, 'But I assure you the primary objective remains the same. George and I are wholly committed to matching Greta with the perfect man for her.'

'Next on the list is Harrison and he's—'

'Have you read these articles?' Anjali asks me, interrupting George.

'I haven't, but Greta gave me a run-down on her unsuccessful dates.'

Anjali's lips press together. 'How many unsuitable men has she gone out with in the past few weeks?' she asks.

'Four,' I reply.

'I see.' She looks at George. 'And from what you're saying, fifth time's a charm? Is that it?'

'Oh, er...'

She comes back to me. 'I think you should read the articles, because it doesn't seem like they were written by someone who's keen to fall in love. It's quite the opposite.'

She takes out her phone and taps and scrolls. My eyes flick towards Paloma, but her expression gives nothing away.

'Here we are,' says Anjali. 'And I quote: "This may be my first proper date in some time but when did it become okay for a man to fat shame his date for her choice of beverage? I would rather eat shards of glass than endure spending another minute with someone like Marcel. I can't *believe* people actively choose to date when they could be at home rearranging their sock drawer." *End quote.*'

She lifts her gaze and pins me with a piercing look. Her displeasure is understandable. She engaged the agency for an HEA, likely not even considering the 'kissing frogs' part.

'Greta comes across as cynical, bordering on bitter,' she says. 'How on earth do you intend to help *this* Greta find love when she'd rather be eating shards of glass?'

'Poppy, perhaps if you explained your tactic to Anjali, so she can better understand?' says Saskia helpfully.

'I'd be happy to,' I say with a smile. I meet Anjali's eyes, knowing I can't throw Greta under the bus by revealing she knows about Anjali's plan, but I also need to offer a plausible explanation. Thankfully, something comes to me from the annals of my psychology practice.

'Sometimes, when a client is outwardly resistant to love,' I say, 'we need to provide them with a way of... well, essentially, saving face. The first of the four men we set Greta up with was Marcus – AKA Marcel. He was the worst of the unsuitable men, and our intention was for Greta to come away from that experience feeling vindicated. Dating is awful and trying to find love is a waste of time.

'Enter Aman, who doesn't fat shame her but – let's just say – has vastly different life goals from Greta. Greta continues to feel vindicated about her feelings towards dating, but there are diminishing returns on her self-satisfaction, as he simply isn't as awful as Marcus. Then she went out with Travis. I know for a fact that she's not including Travis in this series—'

'You mean, "Dating Horrors of London"?' Anjali interjects, a persistent edge in her voice.

'Yes – Travis isn't a bad person, just desperate to find love and Greta was empathetic to his situation; she's mentioned writing about him in a more in-depth, one-off article. Which leads us to Ollie – a lovely man, but for other reasons, not a good fit for Greta. She's not planning on writing about him at all.'

'I still don't see how this helps achieve our primary objective, to help Greta find love.'

'Because, over the course of these experiences, Greta is softening on the concept of dating. Each of these men gets her closer to what *we* know she wants, even if she isn't quite there yet herself.'

'Huh.' Anjali sits back against her chair, maintaining eye contact as thoughts play behind her eyes.

'What do you think, Anji?' asks Saskia.

I glance in her direction, then over at Paloma, who gives me a subtle nod.

Anjali shakes her head as if to clear her thoughts and adopts a chastened smile.

'I really don't know what to say... other than I'm sorry I doubted you, Poppy. You clearly know exactly what you're doing, and I just need to stand back and give you the space to do it.'

I smile at her, relieved that I've presented a plausible explanation for the dud dates *without* revealing it was Greta's idea.

'It's completely understandable that you'd be confused – *and* concerned. Especially after the issue with the advice column... It's been an intense few weeks.'

She huffs out a sigh. 'It has.' She looks to her friends. 'Soz, lovelies. I didn't mean to derail your morning.'

Paloma stands. 'It's all right. You're a valued client and were right to bring this to us.'

'*Ish* – I mean, who am I to question the methods of the best matchmaking agency in London?'

'Oh, Anji, now you're just sucking up,' says Saskia with a laugh, which shocks the hell out of me. Saskia *never* says anything like that.

'Right, well, I'd better let you get back to your day,' says Anjali, standing.

While Saskia walks Anjali out, Paloma joins me and George.

'You handled that very well, Poppy,' she says.

'Thanks.'

There was a time when I steered clear of Paloma, as I found her quite intimidating, but we worked closely on a case about six months ago and formed a solid professional bond. I gained a new appreciation for the talents she brings to the table, and she affords me the freedom to 'go off piste' – her words – when needed.

'I need a cappuccino,' blurts George as he beelines for the door.

'What?' I ask him, bemused.

He pauses in the doorway. 'I *could* go for a stiff drink – that was far too intense for an AM meeting – but as it's nowhere close to noon, I'll settle for a frothy coffee with extra chocolate,' he explains.

'Oh, if you're popping downstairs…' says Paloma with a cock of her head.

'Yes, yes, I know: a skinny flat white. Poppy? Cappuccino?'

'Yes, please, George – that'd be great.'

He leaves and Paloma skirts around her desk and sits in her high-backed chair, then logs onto her laptop. I linger, wondering if I need to explain anything further. Paloma is head of client relations and maybe I should fill her in about Greta and what she knows.

'Was there something else, Poppy?' asks Paloma without lifting her gaze.

'No, all good,' I reply, then I slip out of her office and head to my desk. I need to update Greta on Anjali's visit – *immediately*.

20

GRETA

I arrive at The Port House a little early, as the booking is in my name – *and* it's just good manners – but Ewan is already waiting by the door.

'Hello, you,' I say, taking in his freshly pressed dress shirt and jeans. He looks smart and not at all like he spent the day behind the counter at The Daily Grind.

He leans down and kisses my cheek. 'You look lovely,' he says, his eyes scanning my fitted wrap dress in periwinkle jersey. I grew up being told to shy away from pinks and purples – they clash with red hair, apparently – but that's just bollocks.

'You too. I mean, handso— nice. You look nice.'

He grins at me. 'Shall we?' he asks. Without waiting for a reply, he opens the door for me.

'Thank you,' I say.

We're greeted and seated and in less than a minute, have menus in our hands. 'I haven't been here before,' says Ewan, looking about. 'It feels quite authentic,' he says. 'Like they snatched it right out of Porto or even Barcelona.'

'You've ticked off so many destinations I still haven't been to,' I reply wistfully.

'Still plenty of time for exploring,' he says, his eyes twinkling at me, then lowering to the menu.

It's a nice sentiment, but where do travel and adventure fit in with continuing to advance my career and finding love and having a baby? Though a school friend of mine and Tiggy's – Rana – said something that has stuck with me ever since. She'd just had her first child and joined me and Tiggy for drinks after work, newborn in tow. When Tiggy and I made a big to-do about her being able to come out with us as a new mum, she'd replied matter-of-factly, 'Babies are portable.' And she and her husband travel avidly – *with* their three children – so maybe it is doable to meld travel and a young family.

'So,' I say, abandoning my rambling thoughts and shifting my attention to the menu. 'How about we choose one dish from each section?'

'Sounds like a good approach – and we may even have room for dessert,' he replies, with a double raise of his eyebrows. I *love* that Ewan's 'all-in' on ordering. 'And what about wine?' he asks, picking up the menu and scanning it.

'Can I defer to you?' I ask. 'You've actually been to Spain and Portugal, so definitely you've got a leg up on me.'

'If I do have an advantage, it will be a small one. Sally always —' He stops and sighs. 'And I've done it again. I don't know why I keep bringing her up to you.'

There's something in his tone that gives me pause. Why wouldn't he be able to talk about his ex with me? Perhaps if we were *dating*, but we're simply two foodie friends on a night out.

And then I remember Tiggy's list and the reference to Ewan as my 'hot friend'. He does look especially handsome tonight, but it's moot – I don't think of him that way. Besides, I'm just days away from my date with Harrison.

'It's fine – really,' I assure him. 'How long were you together?'

'Ten years.'

Ten years is a long time. If anything, this information makes me even more curious about her.

'And what does Sally do? For a living?'

'She was – rather, still is – a wine merchant – head buyer for a major chain here in the UK.'

My mouth falls open. 'Seriously?'

He laughs at my amazement. 'Mm-hmm. I'd say that 99 per cent of what I know about wine I learnt from her – or from someone she's connected with. Portugal… Spain… those were work trips for her and I would tag along. And to Italy, France, Germany… even Kakheti in Georgia. It's actually the birthplace of wine. At one winery, a monastery, we tasted their 1000th vintage.'

'Oh, wow – that's…' I say, leaving the thought unsaid. My wide eyes and shaking head say it all, really.

'I know.'

'And how was it, the wine?'

'Uh…'

I laugh. 'Not your favourite?'

'No, but a good experience.'

'And why did you two break up?' I ask, clearly catching him unawares.

'Oh, you don't want me to bore you with all that,' he says with an uneasy laugh. He returns to the wine menu, staring at it intently.

Right, so the subject of Sally is off the table, but I really don't understand why.

'Oh, I meant to tell you,' he says. 'I read *Nouveau Life* – well, a lot of it,' he says.

'Oh?'

He laughs. 'Not the demographic of your typical reader?'

'It's not that. We are hoping to appeal to a broader readership than *Nouveau* print... It's just... Well, thank you. I appreciate you showing an interest in my work.'

'Of course – you've shown an incredible interest in mine, especially the cronuts.'

'They are so good. *Why* are they so good?'

'Hmm, pastry, sugar, crème pat... who would have thought that'd be a winning combination?' he asks cheekily.

'You're teasing me.'

'Just a little bit,' he says, his lips curling up at the corners.

As his gaze drops again, I cast mine over Ewan. He really does look especially handsome tonight. I like him in blue – it brings out his eyes.

I focus back on the menu, suggesting several dishes. Ewan does the same and together, we assemble a delectable array. When our waiter comes back with sparkling water, Ewan orders, including a Grenache – or *Garnacha* as it appears on the menu – from Madrid. He promises it will be aromatic with a hint of pepper and spice.

We make small talk about how many restaurants there are in London – aren't we spoilt for choice? – until the waiter returns and we bear witness to the almost theatrical business of opening and pouring the wine.

When the waiter leaves us, Ewan lifts his tulip-shaped glass, the distinct garnet hue of the wine enticing, and holds it aloft. 'To new adventures,' he says.

I'm not sure exactly what he's referring to, but I appreciate the sentiment. Besides, isn't that what I've been embarking on recently? New adventures, both professionally *and* personally.

'To new adventures,' I echo. We clink glasses and drink, our eyes locked. 'It's delicious,' I say after I've swallowed.

'Mmm,' he agrees.

'I wish I had better vocabulary when it comes to wine.'

'Just say whatever popped into your head as you took that first sip.'

'It'll sound silly,' I say.

'Try it.'

'You're not going to let me off the hook, are you?'

'Absolutely not. I want to hear what that writer's brain of yours has to say.'

I laugh. 'Oh, so no pressure then. This is like that scene in *French Kiss* where Luc makes Kate describe the wine and she calls it "bold, yet lacking in pretention", then admits she's talking about herself.'

'I haven't seen it.'

'I've seen it enough for both of us, don't worry. My best friend, Tiggy, is *obsessed* with romcoms – movies, mostly.'

'Well, if *French Kiss* is about wine, I'd probably like it,' he says with a wink.

'Wine *is* featured – and there's this incredible scene set in the family's vineyard in France – that's the scene where he makes her describe the wine – but it's mostly about finding love in unexpected places.'

Unexpected places like the coffee shop near the office, Greta? I instantly dismiss the thought as ridiculous.

'Is that right?' asks Ewan, his mouth curving into a knowing smile. 'Then I'm *definitely* putting it on the list.'

Uncertain how to take that, I clear my throat and look away, then grab my wine glass and take another sip.

'Before you swallow, let it sit on your palate for a moment,' Ewan says softly. Mesmerised by his gentle command, I do. 'Now close your eyes.'

I do that too, remembering that Luc tells Kate the same thing in the movie.

'At the front of the palate,' he continues, 'you'll get the sweetness of the forest fruit. The acidity will hit the middle palate, on the sides. And it should feel quite smooth in your mouth.'

As he speaks, I take in his words, and they transform into descriptions as if by magic. I swallow and open my eyes to find him watching me.

'Now describe the wine,' he says. 'I promise I won't laugh.'

'That's not a good promise. What if I'm trying to be funny?'

'Describe the wine,' he prompts gently, 'while it's fresh in your mind.'

I inhale, the residual aroma of the wine flooding my senses. 'Okay, the first taste was strawberries, warmed by the sun on a summer's day, but then that transformed into cherries – like a cherry compote, even a hint of Kirsch. And there was also a tartness, like sour cherry, I guess...'

'And the texture?'

'Smooth,' I say with a nod, 'just like you said.'

'Any better words for the texture?' he encourages, and I scour my mental thesaurus.

'*Unctuous.*'

'Now *there's* a word,' he says with a mischievous smile.

Heat suddenly floods my cheeks, and I look away, sucking in a deep breath as the realisation lands with a thud. This isn't just witty banter between two foodie friends. Ewan is *flirting* – and *well*.

Oh god, I *cannot* unpack this right now. Not in the middle of dinner and not when I'm mere days away from meeting someone who could very well be my perfect match.

'See?' asks Ewan, evidently undaunted by my sudden silence. 'You described that wine brilliantly. An excellent use of your writerly skills, I'd say.'

'Thanks,' I mumble, barely able to get the word out.

But I can't just sit here struck dumb – time to change the subject!

'So,' I say brightly, 'how was day three working behind the counter?'

'Hopefully the last,' he says. 'We've got two new team members starting tomorrow and I've got an architect coming in on Friday to discuss my idea.'

'You're renovating already?'

'Born of necessity, I'm afraid – already a victim of my own success,' he says.

'Ah, yes, the duality of the blessing and the curse.'

'Precisely.'

'So, what are you thinking?'

'I'm *thinking* of adding a walk-up window where people can order takeaway coffee. That would free up space inside for customers who want to stay a while and enjoy the ambience. I'm assuming that's why you come every day?' he asks, flashing me a grin.

'Oh, absolutely. It's an oasis inside The Daily Grind – very *green*. I'm assuming you have a close mate who owns a garden centre and owed you a favour?'

He laughs, a warm, throaty sound that sends a shockwave rocketing through me. *Get a grip, Greta*, I chastise. *Harrison, Harrison, Harrison.*

'I was told there were too many plants.'

'By whom?'

His expression suddenly clouds, and I understand immediately – Sally.

'Oh, right.'

Sally certainly has a presence – like a spectre hovering over us. Their break-up must be reasonably fresh.

We're quiet, sipping our wine and looking about, and I'm relieved when the waiter reappears bearing several plates. He announces each dish as he places them on the table: *ensalada verde*, *gambas pil pil*, and *patatas bravas con aioli*.

The plates nearly fill the table and this is only half of what we've ordered. We move things around, playing a horizontal game of Tetris, only to have our efforts thwarted when he returns with three more plates: *Catalan canelones de espinacas*, *confitado de pato*, and two pieces of *tosta de salmon*.

We make more adjustments and now some of the plates are overlapping, sitting at angles so precarious that I'm struck by how ridiculous it was to order so much. I start to laugh.

'I think we could feed the entire population of Lichtenstein,' I say through my laughter.

'I'd say Luxembourg,' he retorts, making me laugh harder. 'Wait, what if we…' He takes our empty plates, the ones we're supposed to eat from, stacks them, then calls the waiter back and hands them to him. Turning back to me, he says, 'We can just eat straight from these,' indicating the plates and bowls brimming with food.

'Glad one of us has hospitality experience,' I say.

'Oh yes, my three days serving coffee have definitely saved the day – or, rather, the *night*,' he says with faux gravitas.

'See, you really are Mr Coffee Man,' I say, leaning into the silly thing I blurted out to him on Monday.

'By day, he provides a vital service to workers on the Strand,' Ewan says, playing along.

'By night, he rearranges the crockery, saving over-orderers from having to drag across a second table.'

'We're a bit daft,' he says affectionately.

'We are,' I agree, 'but also hilarious.'

'Well, that goes without saying.'

He tops up my wine, then we start eating, bites interspersed with exclamations of 'wow' and 'you've got to try this'. When we've made a decent effort on the array, but I can't possibly eat another thing, I sit back and dab my napkin at the corners of my mouth, then lay it in my lap.

'That was…' I shake my head and sigh contentedly, ignoring the niggling questions buzzing at the back of my mind. As I told myself earlier, now is not the time to delve into an analysis of my friendship with Ewan.

'It absolutely was,' he agrees. 'There's still a splash of wine left.'

'Oh, go on, then.' He pours the remainder of the bottle evenly between our two glasses. 'You mentioned Porto and Barcelona earlier… I've never been to either – did I say?'

'You alluded to it.'

'Right, so which should I visit first?'

'Which is my favourite?' he asks, touching his hand to his chest. He sucks his breath in through his teeth.

'Too difficult to choose?'

'It *is* a bit of a conundrum. I mean, Porto is… *breathtaking*. The Douro… it's as if the city was there first and the river carved its way right through the middle… And the buildings… There's this kaleidoscope of colour and textures and they're all piled up haphazardly, as if a child built the city out of Lego without any planning or forethought… And the terracotta roofs! They form this bright-orange blanket across the entire city. And if you ride the Gaia Gondola, which is on the southern bank of the river, or if you walk across the top of Luis I Bridge, you get to see all of it from on high. It truly is incredible.'

'So, Porto then?'

'Actually, I'd have to say Barcelona.'

'What?' I ask, laughing. 'After gushing like that about Porto?'

'I told you it was a conundrum. There's a wild kind of beauty to

Porto, but you see, I can't go past the carefully planned order of Barcelona. You've probably seen an aerial photograph of how the city blocks are laid out?' he asks, and I nod. 'Well, that. Plus, I love the architecture, especially in the Gothic Quarter. *And* the food. Oh god, the food.'

'What about the food in Portugal?'

He makes a face.

'Also not your favourite?'

'It's... Let's just say I prefer the food in Spain.'

'Ahh. And, tell me, if what you like about Barcelona is the order and how everything's laid out just so, how do you reconcile Gaudí's work? I mean, isn't that the opposite of order? I've only seen photos, of course, but Sagrada Família looks like a set of ancient candelabras all bunched together – and the candles have burnt down over and over again through the decades, but no one's ever cleaned up the melted wax.'

'That's... I've never heard it described that way before,' he says appreciatively. 'There's the writer coming out again.'

'You didn't answer my question,' I tease.

'Your quest— Oh, right. I suppose it's the juxtaposition,' he says, holding out both hands to illustrate. 'The order and the chaos together – the contrast...'

'A bit like people,' I say. 'I find that the ones I gravitate towards or am closest to are a mass of contradictions. Like my best friend, Tiggy – she's this chaotic person who lives whimsically and with verve, yet she's a graphic designer and her work has to be so precise – she's also very tech savvy and a total neat freak. So, like you said, the order and the chaos together – but in a person.'

'She sounds incredible.'

'She is,' I say, smiling fondly at the mention of my bestie.

'Only fitting really.'

'What is?'

'That a woman like you would have someone like Tiggy as a best friend,' he says.

Our eyes meet and his bore into mine and, once again, the mood between us shifts.

I have some *serious* unpacking to do after this.

21

GRETA

We step out into the cool, evening air and, as I'm now convinced we *are* on a date, I suddenly feel awkward. It's been easy to pretend we're simply two friends out for dinner while *actually eating* dinner, but this is the part of the evening where a goodnight kiss would typically occur.

Do I *want* to kiss Ewan? I stare at his mouth, the question looming large in my mind as the silence between us grows.

'Is everything all right?' he asks.

'Absolutely,' I lie and my response is so over-the-top enthusiastic, his lips part in surprise.

'Oh good. You just seem... Never mind,' he says with a smile. I note with disappointment that it doesn't reach his eyes, which in the dusk light are darker blue than usual. Even if I decided I *did* want to kiss Ewan, the mood between us is now decidedly *un*-datelike.

'Would you like me to walk you to Charing Cross station?' he offers.

'Oh... Thank you, but then you'd have to double back. I'll be fine,' I reply.

He nods. 'I had a lovely time tonight, Greta.'

'Me too,' I reply.

'We should have dinner again next week – I think it's my turn to choose, or perhaps we could try someplace neither of us have been, if you like?'

'I'd like that,' I say.

Then he leans down and presses his lips softly to my cheek. When he steps back, his cologne – one of Tom Ford's, I think – lingers in the air between us. He flashes me another smile and says, 'Goodnight, Greta. See you at The Daily Grind.'

'See you,' I say, then we head off in opposite directions, disappointment settling into the pit of my stomach like a lump of lead.

I did want to kiss Ewan.

* * *

'Bex, can you stay back for a moment,' I ask after the editorial meeting. Taj and Lisa leave, and Bex fixes me with an inquisitive smile.

'You did a great job editing "Dating Horrors",' I say when we're alone. As no one besides Bex and Anjali know it's *my* dating 'adventures' that are kicking off the series, we're aiming to maintain my anonymity indefinitely.

'Thanks,' she says with a glint in her eye. 'I'm so excited about the column. It's going to be brilliant – especially when we start incorporating reader contributions,' she adds, referring to her inspired idea to keep the series going. 'Terrific for online engagement.'

'You sound like a managing editor in the making,' I say proudly.

'Aww,' she says with a modest head tilt. 'That's the dream.'

I'm glad Bex and I got past our blip. I still have a lot to learn about being a boss, but I appreciate the lessons learnt from our recent conflict: be accountable, be transparent, and *trust*.

'Right, we should get back to our desks,' I say. 'There's still a bit to do before the end of the day.'

'Aren't you heading to the coffee shop this morning?' she asks as we walk towards my office.

I'm *not* going to the coffee shop because I'm steering clear of The Daily Grind until I can get my head around what's happening between me and Ewan. It's been two days since our dinner at The Port House and every moment outside of *Nouveau* has been spent unpacking what happened – mostly at the end of the evening. How the hell didn't I see it sooner – the shift in my friendship with Ewan to something potentially... well, *romantic*?

And I've got a date with Harrison tomorrow night.

Maybe it's not too late to ask Poppy to fit me with those romantic training wheels. I feel as if I'm careening off the path straight towards a giant tree.

'Er, no, not today,' I say lightly. 'Why do you ask?'

'I was going to be cheeky and ask you to bring me back a cronut, but I'll pop down myself. You want anything?'

'Er...'

She laughs. 'It's just a coffee, Greta,' she teases.

'Right. Sorry – I'm a little distracted,' I say.

'That's okay.'

'I just want the second issue to be even better than the first,' I add, outright lying. Not sure why I felt the need to say that. Nor am I happy with how easily they come to me now – the lies.

'Of *course* – me too. So... anything from the coffee shop?' Bex asks again.

'Oh, sorry!' I shake my head at myself. 'Thanks, but I'm all right.'

'Okay,' she says and with a baffled smile, she heads towards the lifts.

If I keep behaving like this, Tiggy won't be the only one calling 999 to report a body snatching.

I need advice from my matchmaker.

* * *

'This place is great,' says Poppy, sliding onto the barstool next to mine at Gin Palace.

'It's my favourite for after-work drinks,' I reply. 'I got here a little early to snap up seats at the bar. Otherwise…'

I look about, nodding towards the dozen or so patrons who are standing.

'Oh, good call. So, what do you recommend?' Poppy asks. She picks up the cocktail menu and scans it.

'This is a Royal Garden,' I reply, holding up my cocktail. 'Elderflower gin, prosecco…'

'Oh, yum.' When the bartender approaches, she says, 'I'll have the same as my friend, please.'

Friend. She could have said 'colleague' or 'client', but she called me her friend. I suppose the lines have become a little blurry over the past few weeks. Coincidentally, this is what I want to talk to her about – blurred lines.

We chit-chat about nothing of consequence while we wait for her cocktail and when it arrives, she holds up her glass.

'To "Dating Horrors of London",' she toasts.

'Cheers,' I reply.

Poppy takes a sip of her Royal Garden. 'Oh, that is good.' She licks her lips, then sets her glass down. 'Now, why are we having drinks on a Friday night?' she asks. 'I'm guessing it's not so you can show off your fave cocktail bar?'

'No,' I say with a smile. Poppy's always so forthright, something I especially value while I've been navigating my recent challenges.

'I'm in a bit of a pickle,' I tell her. She leans in, her eyes trained on mine, inviting me to say more. 'Do you remember Ewan, the man from the coffee near *Nouveau*?'

'I remember. What about him?'

'Well, first off, he actually *owns* The Daily Grind.' Predictably, she seems dumbfounded. 'I know, I felt the same way. But I went in on Monday and he was working there, which is how I found out. And because we see each other most days and have become quite friendly, I really thought it would have come up before. I don't think he was deliberately hiding it from me, but...'

'It's a little strange he didn't tell you but you're probably right that there's nothing nefarious in it.'

Bolstered by Poppy's understanding, I take a sip of my cocktail, then move onto the real reason I've asked to see her.

'And you know how I'm going out with Harrison tomorrow night?'

'I'm across that piece of information, yes,' she says with a wink.

'Right – of course you are. It's just... something's happened and...'

The smile falls from her face. 'Do you need me to postpone the date? Oh, you don't want me to cancel it, do you?' she asks, her concern obvious.

'I'm not sure.'

'Why don't you tell me what's happened? Are you having second thoughts now we're moving onto your real potential matches?'

'Sort of.'

'Is this "sort of" to do with Ewan?'

I nod and she watches me, patiently waiting for me to explain. I take a deep breath and launch into an account of the time Ewan and I have shared since we met, culminating in last night's dinner.

'And how did you leave things? You know, at the end of the… evening?' she asks, obviously skirting around the word 'date'.

'With a promise to do it again next week and a kiss on the cheek.'

'Describe the cheek kiss,' says Poppy. 'Was it a peck or softer, more considered?'

I think back to our goodbye outside The Port House – the internal battle, the kiss on the cheek, the disappointment as I walked to the Tube station alone…

The memory dissipates and my mind returns to the bar. I expel a loud breath, then meet Poppy's eye.

'That might just say it all,' she says.

'What might? And what is it saying?' I ask, already knowing the answer.

'The look on your face. Do you think you might have feelings for Ewan?'

I slip my forefinger into my mouth and nibble on the nail. Isn't this precisely why I asked to meet with Poppy, to get a second opinion? So why am I being coy? We both know what my answer is.

I drop my hand. 'I think so.'

'Okay. So now you're wondering if you should meet Harrison?'

'Yes. I mean, is it fair to Harrison when I already have feelings for Ewan – even if I'm not entirely sure what they are or what they mean?'

'Well, ordinarily, we only match a client with one person at a time and this is one of the reasons – to avoid situations where someone develops feelings for two people at once.'

'Is there a "but" coming? Please tell me there's a "but" coming.'

'But Ewan is already in your life, so…' She frowns slightly as if she's considering a conundrum.

'You don't know the answer?' I ask, panic rising.

'Matchmaking isn't an exact science,' she replies, 'but we have guidelines for a reason.'

'That makes sense,' I admit, my shoulders slumping. It may make sense but it's also disappointing. For the past month, I've been building up Harrison in my mind and I want to meet him.

'Hey, can you give me five minutes?' she asks, sliding off her stool. 'I want to call George and get his take on all this.'

A glimmer of hope!

'Of course! I'll be right here,' I say, flashing a smile. As soon as she leaves, I huff out another sigh and take a sip of my cocktail.

'Another?' asks the bartender, pointing to my nearly empty glass.

'Sure, why not?' If Poppy returns with good news, it'll be a celebratory drink. And if not, I can drown my sorrows.

Only, which news is which? Is the agency agreeing to let me go out with Harrison good news or bad?

'Oh, Greta, how did you get yourself into such a confounding situation?' I ask myself.

Poppy

'It's not like you to second-guess yourself, Poppy,' says George.

'No, I know, but I think Anjali showing up at the agency has made me a little gun-shy.'

It's only as I say this that I realise how much it rattled me to have my matchmaking methods questioned like that. I've gone to Saskia and Paloma for advice in the past – and there have been a handful of extreme situations in which I've sought their permission to implement a creative (i.e. *way*-outside-the-box) solution – but typically, I'm given full autonomy on my cases.

'Understandable,' he replies. 'But you *did* say Ewan was a potential match. I mean, we bumped him up to the number-two spot.'

'That's why I called you – to get a sense check.'

This is one of the main reasons we're always assigned a second – a lieutenant who can act as a sounding board and help us make sense of sticky situations.

'So, which way are you leaning?' he asks.

'That's the thing – in the five minutes since she brought it up, I've gone back and forth twice. Harrison is not going to stay single forever, and we don't want Greta stringing Ewan along if she and Harrison are a match. On the other hand, she met Ewan organically, which is always a plus, and based on her recount of last night, I'd say there's a strong chance they're a match.'

'Right. Hmm.'

I watch the traffic along the Strand as George and I silently chew on this dilemma.

'I suppose the big question is,' he says eventually, 'will Greta be able to set Harrison aside without meeting him? What if she always wonders, "What if"?'

George is right. I hadn't even considered that aspect.

'Then it could hinder her building a successful relationship with Ewan,' I reply.

'So, are we saying what I think we're saying?' asks George.

'We are. If we take Harrison off the table right now, it could backfire and I'm not prepared to take that risk. So, Greta gets one date with Harrison, then she must choose.'

'Only you have to make it a recommendation, rather than a mandate.'

'Yep.'

'Well, good luck, Poppy.'

'Thanks for being such a good second.'

'Of course! Oops, gotta go. My ride's here.'

He ends the call and now it's just me and an anxious client with two love interests. What could possibly go wrong?

22

GRETA

'*That's* the one,' says Tiggy, nodding vigorously from the bed. She's stretched out and munching on pickled onion Monster Munch. I can smell its pungent aroma from here.

'Are you sure?' I ask, turning this way and that in front of the mirror. 'You don't think it's too "business-y"?'

'I don't know. I lost interest after outfit number four.'

'Oi, no fair. I need your honest opinion.'

She props herself up and swings her legs over the edge of the bed. 'Okay, what are you going for exactly?'

'I don't know! That's why you're here.'

She gets up and crosses to the wardrobe, dusting her fingers off on her jeans. She points to outfit number one, a floaty, chiffon dress I wore to a wedding last summer. 'Too formal,' she declares.

'Right, okay. And what about this one?' I ask, looking down at the dress I'm wearing.

'Yep, too "business-y".'

I immediately unzip it and step out of it, then hang it up and return it to my wardrobe. 'And any of the others I've tried on?' I ask, hopeful.

Her eyes scan the array on the bed. 'Hmm. You want to look sexy and confident, but not like you're ready to skip off to the registry office after dinner.'

'Yes, exactly.'

'How about this?' she says, reaching into my wardrobe. She holds up a jumpsuit in black crepe with bell sleeves and wide legs. 'I've only ever seen you wear it once.'

'That's because I look ridiculous in it.'

'You absolutely do not.'

'Tiggy, I'm petite and curvy and petite, curvy girls should not wear jumpsuits,' I say.

She rolls her eyes. 'You're being daft – you'd never guess you work at a *fashion magazine*. You wear it with these,' she says, taking my highest heeled boots off the shoe rack, 'and cinch the waist with a belt.' She thrusts the boots at me. 'At least try it all on.'

I cross my arms across my chest.

'Humour me.'

Now I roll my eyes, but I do change.

'See?' I say, holding my arms out wide.

'All I see is a hot woman wearing a sexy-but-not-*too*-sexy outfit.'

I look back at the mirror, trying to see myself through Tiggy's eyes. 'My boobs look good,' I admit, running my fingers over the V-shaped neckline.

'Your boobs look amazing. *And* your waist. *And* your hips. I'm telling you: this is it. This is the one.'

'Five minutes ago, you didn't give a hoot what I wore.'

'I did give a hoot, honestly… It's just…'

She sits on the edge of the bed and looks up at me.

'What? Just say it.'

'Are you sure you should be going on this date?'

I flinch. 'What do you mean? I've had Harrison's bloody photo stuffed in a bloody drawer for weeks – just so I wouldn't stare at it for hours on end. Of course I'm going on this date!'

'Okay, okay.'

'Besides, Poppy said I should. And she's a professional matchmaker.'

'I said okay.'

'Why are you asking that anyway?'

'Babes, you haven't dated – properly, I mean – since *forever*. And now, in the space of a month, you've gone out with a who's-who of odd bods, have accidentally started dating your coffee-shop friend, and now you're going out with a man you've been obsessing about for *weeks*. Do you see why I'm concerned?'

'No, I don't,' I say, digging in my heels even though I *do* see. I've been worrying about the same thing.

'How about this: what if you've built Harrison up in your mind *so* much that he's a disappointment? Or worse, he's everything you've dreamt of and then you have to choose between him and Ewan?'

I haven't told Tiggy about Poppy's caveat to tonight's date. Out of respect to both men and the agency, I get this one evening with Harrison, then I have to choose. A knot twists in my stomach and I inhale deeply to breathe through it.

'Besides, I like Ewan for you,' she adds.

'What?' I ask, my thoughts swinging back to the conversation. 'You haven't even met him.'

She shrugs. 'Doesn't matter. I see how you are when you talk about him.'

'This isn't helping,' I say. 'Now you're just making me nervous – *more* nervous.'

'I don't mean to—' She sighs again. 'Okay, if you want to go on this date, I fully support that decision and I'll be here for you afterwards.'

'What, so you're going to sit in my flat all evening?'

'Greta! I mean *metaphorically*. God, you really are in a tizz.'

'I guess I am – sorry. Just... Am I doing the right thing?'

She laughs wryly. 'Look, I love you – you know I do – but that's exactly why I brought it up. I want you to consider this from every angle.'

'Mum says you only ever regret the things you *didn't* do,' I say quietly.

'Then that's your answer. Go on the date. We'll have brunch tomorrow – no, make that lunch because I plan on staying out *very* late,' she says with a waggle of her brows. 'And we'll debrief, okay?'

I nod, relief flooding my veins.

'And wear that. If he doesn't fancy you in that outfit, he's either not attracted to women or doesn't have a pulse.'

'Thanks, Tiggy.'

'Hey, I got you.' She glances at the clock. 'Bugger, I've got to go.'

'Hot date?' I ask.

'*Two* hot dates,' she replies.

'At the same time?' I ask, confused. She replies by waggling her eyebrows again.

'Oh, of course,' I say, realising she's off to have a threesome.

She stands, chuckling, and smacks a loud kiss onto my head.

'Not the hair,' I say, smoothing my deliberately messy up-do. Her cackling laughter follows her out of the flat.

* * *

Harrison is taller and even more handsome than I expected him to be. The Uber drops me off across the road from Le Mercury in Islington and he's already waiting outside. When I get out of the car, I take a moment to compose myself, while Harrison looks along the road in both directions, presumably for me.

It suddenly occurs to me that he may not know what I look like. I did provide a photo along with my client questionnaire, but I've never thought to ask how things work from a potential match's point of view. Was he given my biography, like I was given his?

'How much does he already know about me?' I mutter to myself. 'And what if he prefers tall, slender blondes?'

Though, if he did, I doubt Poppy would have matched him with *me*.

An older woman passes, catching me talking to myself. She gives me an odd look.

'Good evening,' I say, but she scurries away, shaking her head.

I glance back at Harrison and now he's looking across the road, right at me. He's squinting slightly as if he's trying to decide if I'm the person he's supposed to be meeting. *Or* he just witnessed me scaring away an elderly woman and he's plotting his escape.

'Hello!' I call out, lifting my hand in a wave. 'Harrison, it's me.' He doesn't react right away, so I wave my arm and shout, 'It's me – *Greta*.'

He waves, his smile faltering.

'Oh my god, you right bloody idiot,' I say through my teeth, which I realise too late probably reads as a grimace from thirty feet away. I step into the road, and the immediate blare of a horn stops me in my tracks. A car whizzes past so closely, I can see the white of the driver's horrified eyes, and I leap back onto the kerb.

'Are you all right?' Harrison calls.

I meet his eye with a fake smile. 'Smashing. Just forgot how to cross a road without getting run over,' I call back.

His deep laughter is audible from here, but my heart is still racing when I look both ways, then to the right a second time, and safely cross the road.

'Hi,' I say, a little breathless.

'Hello, Greta,' he says, flashing me a warm smile.

After only a handful of syllables, I'm already in love with his richly timbered voice. With those dulcet tones, he could easily be a *full*-time voice actor – none of this part-time nonsense.

He bends down to kiss my cheek, but I've stupidly stuck out my hand for a handshake and my hand collides with his chest – more specifically, his right nipple.

Good grief. Is it too late to go home and start this again?

'Sorry about that – touching your nipple,' I say. 'And saying "nipple" three seconds after I've met you,' I add, my mouth operating without permission.

He chuckles again, his russet-brown eyes alive with laughter. At least he finds me amusing.

'Shall we head in?' he asks, turning towards the entrance. 'And thanks again for coming out to Islington. Normally, I'd have suggested somewhere more central, but my private students had a recital this afternoon not far from here.'

'Oh, no problem at all. My best friend lives in Islington, so I'm a frequent visitor to this hood.'

I have never said the word 'hood' in my life. I am officially losing it.

'Have you been here before then?' he asks as he holds the door for me.

I cast my eyes about the cosy, French-style bistro; it has almost as much greenery as The Daily Grind, an unwelcome thought I dismiss immediately. It's also the type of place couples go for romantic dinners, so, no, Tiggy and I have never been. The Indian restaurant down the road? Absolutely! Our names are carved into our favourite table (JK, not really).

'First time,' I answer cheerily.

We're shown to a table by the window and when we're seated facing each other, my nerves kick into high gear. This is Harrison, the man whose face has been indelibly inked on my brain for almost a month now. He smiles, then his gaze drops to the menu, so I look at mine.

'It's my first time too,' he admits. 'My sister recommended it. Perfect for first dates, apparently. *Although…*' He says this in a way that makes me look up, and he meets my eye, his brow creased. 'How she knows that is a little baffling. She's been married for sixteen years.'

I doubt he's *actually* concerned his sister is stepping out on her spouse but just in case, I respond with, 'She probably googled it. You know, "Romantic restaurants, Islington".'

Romantic? Ugh. Presumptuous much?

Harrison appears unbothered by the 'romantic' part and laughs.

'You're right. Emily's so fixated on my love life – or lack of – she's probably mapped out a whole slew of perfect first-date locations across London.' He laughs again.

I inhale sharply and keep my gaze fixed on my menu.

His laughter stops abruptly.

'Oh… I didn't mean anything by that,' he says, frowning.

I nod, faking another smile, then swallow the enormous lump lodged in my throat. Which is ridiculous. I've only just met this man and the thought of him dating half of London shouldn't have this kind of impact on me. He's not *mine*.

'You're actually the *first* first date I've been on in ages,' he continues, 'which is why I'm cocking this up so spectacularly.'

I look up, my mouth falling open. He grimaces at his faux pas, adding a shrug, and we both start shaking with laughter.

'You are quite terrible at it,' I say as our laughter subsides. 'But at least you didn't nearly get run over crossing the road.'

'How do you know? I could have had a near-miss with a lorry before you were dropped off.'

'Did you?'

'No.'

'So, we're both rusty,' I say, realising what I'm admitting.

'Looks like it.'

The waiter comes over. 'Can I start you off with something to drink?' she asks.

Harrison and I both return to the menu. 'Wine?' he asks me.

'Wine... Er, yes...' I reply, quickly reading down the wine list. The waiter excuses herself to give us more time.

'To be honest, I'm rubbish at choosing wine,' says Harrison and (of course) I'm instantly reminded of Ewan, who isn't.

'Shall we go with the Pinot Grigio?' I ask, referring to the first bottle on the list.

'Perfect,' he replies, 'and dinner? What about the prix-fixe?' he asks. 'Though just two courses for me. I never eat dessert.'

Never? I think.

'Sounds good,' I lie, even though the dark chocolate tart would have gone down a treat. But there is no way I'm having dessert if he's not. I shift in my seat, hoping I've done a decent job of masking my disappointment – it's just a chocolate tart.

But what about all the desserts to come if you keep dating him? Bollocks, have I just set a no-dessert precedent?

Harrison catches the waiter's attention, and we order the wine, then give our choices for starters and mains. When we're alone again, I'm left wondering what to talk about.

'So, your students had a recital today?' I ask, latching onto something he said earlier.

'Uh, yes. The ones I teach outside of school. You know I'm a secondary school teacher, right?'

I nod.

'Well, my privates—' He stops himself, a blush rising from his neck. 'Wait, private *students*, not my privates... Oh god.' He runs a hand over the back of his neck. 'Can I start again – *without* putting my foot in my mouth?'

I giggle. 'You know, I gleaned from the context that "privates" meant private students and not your genitals. You did mention them when I got here. Oh! Not your genitals – your *students*!'

I start sniggering and his eyes light up with mirth.

'I knew what you meant,' he says, chuckling. 'I must be rubbing off on you already.'

'Rubbing off on me,' I say through breathless laughter and he joins in.

When the waiter returns with the wine, she clears her throat to get our attention, then show the bottle to Harrison, who tells her to show it to me, as I'm the one who chose it.

I check the label and agree it's the correct wine, even though I can't remember the name of the winery on the menu, then once she has poured a splash into my glass, I take a sip.

'Yummy,' I say without thinking.

The waiter smiles – I can only imagine what she's thinking – then pours two generous glasses and leaves.

'Yumminess being the primary characteristic of a Pinot Grigio,' I say, and Harrison grins.

'I like that you can laugh at yourself,' he says, regarding me closely.

'I find it's best to get in first before other people can.'

I have no idea why I said that – it makes me sound like I have low self-esteem, which I don't.

'Well, at least you aren't casually chatting about your penis on a date.'

'Harrison,' I say deadpan. 'I don't have a penis.'

This kicks us off again and when the laughter dwindles, we both reach for our wine and take a sip.

While our shared laughter has chased away my nerves, I'm left wondering, *Now what do we talk about?*

23

GRETA

Conversation does eventually start to flow, especially after Harrison tells me his sister put his profile up on a dating app without asking, which led to him being 'headhunted' by the Ever After Agency. I hadn't known that – how they find potential matches – and find it fascinating.

And following the unwritten tit-for-tat rule of conversation, over starters I recount my lunch at Mum and Dad's when Mum attempted to foist Ian, Dad's widower friend, on me as a potential partner.

We share another laugh, commiserating with each other about our well-meaning family members. Then we tell each other why we're still single.

Me: career-focussed and perhaps a little guarded after being cheated on by my only long-term boyfriend. Him: career-focussed and incredibly guarded after a several-year relationship that became routine and unfulfilling for both parties.

'So, here I am, forty, successful in my career, with a nice flat, good friends, and a solid social life, but firmly a bachelor,' he says.

'Did it feel like you simply lifted your head one day and that was the status quo – like it had crept up on you?' I ask. 'That's how it was for me.'

'Yes, except for the "lifting my head" part – that was just Emily sending me my username and password for Flutter.'

'I thought Flutter was for thirty-fives and under?'

'They recently raised the age cap to forty. Lucky me, huh?'

'Mmm,' I agree. 'And you haven't dated anyone from the app?' I ask. 'You mentioned before that I'm the first date you've had in a while.'

'No, I was too... well, scared, I guess. I mean, dating apps?' He shrugs. 'Not really my thing.'

This explains why he was still available to date me after weeks of being 'on hold' with the agency.

'And what about meeting me?' I ask. 'Not as scary?'

'Not as scary,' he admits. 'The people at the agency were really understanding. When I signed on, they promised I'd only be matched with one woman at a time – and they'd send me her profile and a photo – but that I wouldn't have to meet her if I didn't want to.'

And that answers my question about how much he knew about me before our date.

'What made you agree to meet me?' I ask.

'Are you fishing?' he teases.

'Of course!'

'Well, you're accomplished, we have similar life goals, and you're *very* pretty,' he states matter-of-factly.

'Oh, well, thank you.'

He sends a smile across the table, then sops up the sauce from his starter with a chunk of bread and pops it into his mouth.

But suddenly, I'm no longer hungry, and I set my fork on my plate. I'm not sure what I expected him to say. I also don't know why I feel disappointed by such a flattering description.

Maybe having my entire character – every attribute, hope, fear, and ability – reduced to three short statements – sorry, *two* statements, as the third was about my looks – is a reminder of how artificial this process is. How *super*ficial it is. Harrison has (likely unintentionally) turned me into a pull quote.

But isn't that what I've been doing with my 'Dating Horrors' subjects – and even with Harrison? Reducing them to the juiciest titbits?

Harrison Reed: tall, beefy, and handsome; voice like treacle being poured over granite; dedicated music teacher; eager to be a husband and father; loves to travel; and occasionally puts his foot in his mouth.

Most of that I got from reading a two-page biography, and other than his tendency to say inappropriate things (like I do), the rest I'd filled in with my imagination. And I've been anticipating this for so long, it never occurred to me that with everything we have in common, there could be a deal-breaker.

And never in a million *years* would I have guessed that the deal-breaker was my own romanticism. I don't just want to be in a relationship and have a baby with someone I share common interests with.

I want to fall in love. Head over heels in love.

And I certainly don't want someone perusing the details of my life like they're reading from a catalogue. No, I need to put an end to this whole affair (so to speak).

My appetite abandons me entirely and my stomach roils as I long for a time machine so I can jump ahead a couple of hours. I want to be snuggled in my bed, messaging Tiggy and hoping she'll reply between rounds of her threesome. Assuming there are 'rounds' in threesomes. I wouldn't know.

'So, what's on for the rest of the weekend, then?' Harrison asks as the waiter tops up our wine.

And so the rest of dinner goes: making small talk and me taking micro-sips of wine and picking at my food. Now I'm glad I *didn't* order dessert.

Less than an hour later, we're on the footpath waiting for my Uber to arrive. I offered to drop him off then continue home but (thankfully) he lives in Wood Green, which is in the opposite direction.

A Vauxhall Crossland pulls up outside the restaurant. 'This is me,' I say.

'It was really lovely to meet you, Greta.'

'Lovely to meet you too,' I say, smiling up at him. He leans down to kiss my cheek – a quick peck – and I climb into the car. I wave as the car drives off, and so does he, and then I rest heavily against the seat, realising that neither of us mentioned a second date.

'Nice dinner?' asks the driver.

'Er, yes, thanks,' I reply, hoping he's not chatty.

He doesn't say anything the rest of the ride home as I type out perhaps the longest message ever to Tiggy.

* * *

I am just about to leave my flat to meet Tiggy for lunch when my phone chimes with a message.

'Elizabeth, if you're cancelling on me...' I mutter, but it's Anjali:

Can you call me asap?

I've worked with Anjali for nearly twelve years, and she's only ever asked to speak to me on a Sunday once before. An unexpected development in a celebrity court case had been leaked, and it would have undermined an entire article that was due to go to print the following day. We rallied – re-writing, copy editing, and proofing the article – then dealt with the fallout from the production team, who were (very) cross about being called in on a Sunday. We barely made the deadline in the wee hours of the Monday morning.

I send off a short message to Tiggy telling her I'll be late and call Anjali.

'Greta, thanks for calling straight away,' she answers.

'What's going on? Are you okay?'

'I'm all right, yes, but I've just learnt something rather disturbing.'

It must be to do with *Nouveau*. She's not calling to share gossip about her nanny.

'Do you remember my friend, Fenella? I think you met her when we ran into you at Covent Garden that time,' she says.

I have a vague recollection, but we only exchanged a few words. 'I think so.'

'Well, I met her for breakfast this morning – our ritual on the last Sunday of the month – and she relayed something that her friend, Adele, told her about *her* friend who works at *Panache*.'

'Oh-*kay*,' I say, mentally cataloguing the who's-who of this story.

'And if what I've heard is true, *Panache* is going live tomorrow with a new blog on their website, and guess what it's called?' She doesn't give me time to guess, immediately supplying the answer. '"Disasters of Dating".'

'*What?*'

'That's exactly how I responded. Now, Fenny only knew to raise it with me because... Well, confession time – she's my best friend and I tell her everything, so she knows all about our plans for *Nouveau Life*,' she says, her contrition obvious. 'Such a shame.

Fenny was very much looking forward to the launch of your new column.'

'Wait, what do you mean *was* looking forward to?'

'Well, we can't go live with it now.'

'Why not? We've been working on this for weeks. Does it really matter if *Panache* has something similar on their website? *Nouveau Life* is a full vertical – not just a blog.'

'Greta, I think you're missing the real issue.'

'Which is?'

'Don't you think it's uncanny that they published an advice column in their last print issue right as we were about to introduce one to our online magazine and now they're launching a blog with the same premise as your column?'

I clap a hand over my mouth as the realisation lands.

'We have a mole,' I say, breathless.

'It seems that we do, yes.'

'So, what now?'

'Well, I've called Amelia—'

'Amelia Windsor?'

'How many Amelias do you know at *Nouveau*?' Anjali replies, her tone slightly terse.

'Right, and what did she say?'

'She'd like to meet with us this afternoon – at the office.'

My stomach clenches and that bloody roaring in my ears makes a comeback. Being called into the office on a weekend is rare and always a cause for concern. Being called in to meet with AMELIA WINDSOR is terrifying. What if she blames me for the leak? What if she thinks *I'm* the leak?

'Greta? Are you there?'

'I'm here,' I reply sullenly.

'Good. Be in the boardroom at two-thirty. Just you.'

'Just me as in…?'

'No one else in the *Nouveau Life* team.'

'You think it's someone on my team?' I screech, my mind conjuring Bex, Taj, and Lisa, who I personally selected.

'We don't know, and until we do...'

'Right. I understand.' But I *don't* understand. This whole thing must be a huge misunderstanding – or just a coincidence. *Two* coincidences. In a row. Hmm, not likely.

'See you there. And Greta? No matter what, I trust you implicitly and I will have your back, all right?'

At least there's that. 'Thanks. I'll see you at two-thirty.'

When the call ends, I sit with my phone in my hands, feeling powerless.

A month ago, I was riding high, smashing it professionally with my own vertical. I was also happily single – okay, that's bollocks, but at least I wasn't consumed by dating, desperate to land the perfect man. Perfect for *me*, that is. By most metrics, *Harrison* is the perfect man, and no one is more astonished than me that I didn't lock in plans for a second date.

'But there's "perfect on paper" and then there's reality,' I tell myself.

My phone chimes again, reminding me I need to tell Tiggy I can't meet her for lunch. Hopefully, she hasn't left already. I head back to the sofa and retrieve my phone. It is a message from Tiggy and I call her immediately.

'Hey. Sorry, but I won't be able to make lunch,' she says.

'Well, I was just about to cancel on you, so... Out of interest, why can't you make it?'

She laughs her throaty laugh and someone giggles in the background.

'Oh,' I say. 'You're still out.' This makes me wonder if she's read my message from last night. I navigate to it, seeing it was delivered but remains unread.

'Um, yeah,' she says. 'But how 'bout I pop over later, for dinner? We can order takeaway and you can tell me all about your date with Mountain Man.'

'Sure, sounds good,' I say – though I have no idea if an all-hands-on-deck-including-OH-MY-GOD-Amelia-Windsor meeting will run long.

The giggling gets louder. 'Apple, give me a sec,' says Tiggy to the giggler. 'Sorry, babes. Gotta go.'

The call ends abruptly.

If I were remotely attracted to my best friend – and her to me – I can only imagine the sexual adventures I'd be a part of.

I glance at the clock. I have just over an hour before I need to leave, but I should probably change out of my lunch outfit into something more work appropriate.

I head to my bedroom and stare at my open wardrobe. What the hell do I wear to a meeting with my boss and *her* boss to determine how to handle a mole sharing our secrets with a competitor?

My ringtone shakes me from my thoughts, and I dash back to the lounge room and grab it from its spot on the sofa.

'Hello?'

'Hi, Greta, it's Poppy.'

'Oh. Hi.'

'Am I calling at a bad time?'

'Er, no,' I lie as I think of the multitude of reasons I don't have the time – or the mental space – to speak to her right now.

'Oh, good. I was just wondering how it went last night – with Harrison.'

I heave out a frustrated sigh before I can temper my response, and Poppy laughs.

'That good, huh?' she asks.

'I'm sorry. It's just... Heh...'

'Was that a laugh?' she asks.

'Sort of... Oh, Poppy, *so* much has happened since I spoke to you last. And the date with Harrison is the least of it.'

'What's going on?' she asks, her tone serious.

I explain about the suspected mole at *Nouveau* and the possible implications.

'I might be able to help with that,' she says when I finish.

'How?'

'Our agency has this primo investigator – total gun. If anyone can track down the leak, she can. And as this issue is case-adjacent, I can probably secure her services through the agency. I'd have to run it past my bosses, of course, but do you want me to try?'

'Er... maybe? I'm not sure Anjali will agree – this is really a *Nouveau* matter.'

'Leave it with me,' she says cryptically.

'Okay,' I say, feeling unable refuse Poppy's offer. Fingers crossed it all works out.

I turn and lean against the back of the sofa, catching my breath.

This is the strangest Sunday morning I've ever had – well, second strangest. There was that Sunday that Tiggy and I missed the 5 a.m. ferry off Phangan Island in Thailand after the Full Moon Party and ended up onboard a Greek billionaire's yacht.

The memory brings a smile to my face, a reminder that I used to be a lot more fun than I am now.

24

POPPY

Several calls later – made *and* received – Marie is officially on the case, and I have permission to accompany her to the *Nouveau* meeting. I'm having to abandon my Sunday-picnic-in-the-park plans with Tristan (boo), but he sends me off with a kiss and a wave of Saffron's (indifferent) paw.

Outside our building, I only wait a minute or two before the town car pulls up and I slide into the backseat.

'Hi, Carl,' I say to the driver as I buckle my seatbelt.

'Hello, Ms Dean.'

'Are we picking up Ms Maillot or is she meeting us there?' I ask.

'Paul's collecting her, and we'll meet them there.'

'Great, thanks.' It was sheer luck that Marie is in London today – *and* available this afternoon. No wonder the agency pays her the big bucks – she's ostensibly at our beck and call.

When we pull up at *Nouveau* on the Strand a short while later, Marie is waiting outside dressed, as always, in head-to-toe black leather despite the warm weather, and drawing deeply from a cigarette – lit this time. As I approach, she takes a final drag then puts it out with the heel of her boot and reaches down for the butt so she can toss it in the nearest bin. She may be a chain smoker, but at least she doesn't litter.

She gives me her typical perfunctory greeting and we head towards the main doors, having been told a security guard is expecting us and will let us in.

'Poppy!' I turn around and Greta is running towards us.

'Hi, Greta,' I say as she joins us, a little out of breath. 'This is Marie Maillot, the agency's investigator. Marie, our client, Greta Davies.'

'*Allô.*'

'Hello.'

'I've already briefed Marie,' I tell Greta, 'and if you like, I'm happy to make the introductions when we get inside.'

'Right, yes,' she says, but even though her breathing has steadied, she's clearly still flustered.

Greta, who's known to the security guard, leads us into the building and in the lift, I hear her muttering to herself, some kind of affirmation. By the time we reach the correct floor, she's added bouncing on her toes to her repertoire of nerves.

Just outside the lift, as the doors close behind us, I gently take her arm.

'Hey, are you okay?' I ask.

She shakes her head. 'Nope, far from it. *Nouveau Life* is about to implode and that's probably my fault. And if it *was* me who let the fox into the henhouse, I'll likely get the sack. I'm also dating half of London, but *no one* is a match, including my perfect-on-paper crush – isn't that an interesting twist? And for some reason, I decided to dress for a normal workday when clearly this day is anything but normal and everyone else is dressed—' She stops herself and glances at me in my T-shirt and jeans, then Marie. 'Well, not like *this*,' she says, indicating her business attire.

She stares at the floor, breathing noisily through her nose. I cannot let her go in there like this.

'Marie, could you give us a minute?' I ask.

Marie shrugs and wanders towards a large window that overlooks an atrium. She takes out a cigarette and sucks on it, even though it's unlit.

Satisfied she can't hear us, I turn back to Greta.

'No matter what's revealed or what the solution to this problem is, you've got this, okay? You're smart and capable, *and* you've brought a secret weapon.' I jerk my head in Marie's direction. 'Like I said on the phone, if anyone can weed out the mole, it's Marie. Okay?'

Greta's cheeks puff out as she exhales a long breath. 'Okay.'

'Just remember, you are Greta Davies and you've got this.'

She breaks into a smile.

Now, my pep talks are good, but this is a complete one-eighty.

'What?' I ask. 'Did I say something funny?'

'Just... Tiggy said something similar to me recently. Only *she* said, "You're Greta Fucking Davies," and then she called me a badass magazine editor.'

'Well, she's right. You *are* Greta Fucking Davies *and* a badass magazine editor. So, let's get in there and figure this out.'

She nods, and with her head high, she walks towards a large glass-walled conference room. I call for Marie, who trots over, and we follow Greta into the lion's den. I may have given her a pep talk just now, but I'm expecting this could be brutal.

Greta

Oh my god, there she is. Amelia Windsor. Do not fangirl. Do not fangirl. Do not fangirl.

And in a weird and wonderful twist of fate, she's also wearing a shift dress, and I send a silent thank you to my previous self. I'm just about to introduce myself to Amelia Windsor (*always* her full name inside my head), when she looks up from her phone and her mouth falls open.

'Marie Maillot, you scamp. I didn't know *you* were the renowned investigator.'

Marie half coughs, half cackles as Amelia Windsor stands and crosses to Marie, where they exchange four cheek kisses.

'Let me look at you,' says Amelia Windsor.

'How can you see *anything*?' barks Marie in a strong French accent. She snatches the signature dark sunglasses off Amelia Windsor's head, eliciting a girlish laugh I'd wager no one at *Nouveau* has ever heard. 'That's better,' she says, giving Amelia Windsor the side-eye. 'How do you still look this good when I look like an old leather saddle? We're the same age!'

Amelia Windsor waves her off. 'Oh, you. First, I wear these day and night,' she says, taking her glasses back and letting them dangle from her fingers. 'And you look terrific. Very chic. You always did march to the beat of your own drum,' she says, appraisingly.

Marie cackles again and Poppy, who is standing next to me, pokes me in the arm. I meet her eye and she gives me a can-you-believe-it? look. No, Poppy, I can't, and when I look over at Anjali she's clearly as bamboozled as we are. She shrugs at me with a mystified smile.

'Right, everyone,' says Amelia Windsor, 'I suppose we should get started.'

'Er, yes,' says Anjali, taking back control of the meeting. 'First, thank you, everyone, for giving up your Sunday afternoons.' She gestures for us to sit, which we do, then she introduces Poppy to Amelia Windsor, mentioning that she works for the Ever After Agency as a matchmaker and has come onboard as a consultant.

'You look familiar,' she says to Poppy, her infamous icy tone returning. 'Were you at the Lorenzo show in Paris?'

She eyes Poppy coolly before sliding her sunglasses back into place.

'Yes. I was there with—'

'Elle Bliss,' says Amelia Windsor. 'I remember.'

It's unclear whether this is a positive memory or not, but I watch the exchange fascinated, Amelia Windsor's reputation for having a laser-sharp memory and never forgetting a face playing out before my eyes.

Note to self: do not cross Amelia Windsor.

Like cocking up by hiring a mole into your team, Greta?

I gulp.

Then Anjali launches into the details of our dilemma and, as I'm across all this, my mind wanders, trawling through that bizarre exchange between Marie and Amelia Windsor.

Questions. I have so many questions! If they're the same age, are they school friends? If so, was Marie in London for school or was Amelia Windsor in France? And how old is 'the same age'? Marie looks like she could be Keith Richards' older sister, whereas Amelia Windsor looks like a *very* well-preserved sixty-something. Maybe she made a pact with the Devil or something – that would certainly explain her reputation. I once heard a fashion assistant call her 'Medusa' – well, an *ex*-fashion assistant. They were sacked shortly after.

'*Greta?*'

'Oh, er, yes?'

Bollocks. Anjali has just thrown to me, and I wasn't listening. I *am* going to get the sack.

'I was just saying that you'd like us to consider proceeding with "Dating Horrors of London". Would you care to talk Amelia through that?' she says, giving me a lifeline.

'Oh, absolutely.'

Fortunately, I can speak off-the-cuff about *Nouveau Life* at length, a by-product of having lived and breathed it for so long. I explain the concept of the column, including our plans to add readers' anonymised contributions, and Amelia Windsor nods along as she listens.

I conclude with, 'So, even though *Panache* has likely stolen the general concept, I'd still like to launch it tomorrow. I think they'd be hard-pressed to replicate our exact angle, as there's no way they have a professional matchmaker on the team, particularly one of Poppy's calibre.'

Greta Fucking Davies, badass editor at your service!

While I pat myself on the back for staving off a panic attack and proving my professional mettle, Amelia Windsor leans across to confer quietly with Anjali.

Bollocks, is that a good sign or bad?

Anjali nods and says, 'Understood,' and Amelia Windsor settles back in her chair and addresses me.

'I appreciate Ms Dean's – as you put it – "calibre" as a consultant...'

I perk up.

'*But...*'

Oh no, a premature perk-up.

'Based on what I've heard, I don't think the horrible dating column is *Nouveau*. Let *Panache* publish trite rubbish like that and see where it gets them.'

I'm not keen on her depiction of my column, but there is no way I'd ever challenge *Amelia Windsor*.

'We're dropping it,' she says definitively.

'All right,' I reply, fighting off disappointment. I may have baulked at the assignment initially, but it's evolved so much over the past month and now I'm invested.

'*Panache* has always been a grasping poor cousin to *Nouveau*,' she continues, 'and no doubt, they'll shoot themselves in the foot with their little *blog*.' She says the word 'blog' as if she's referring to a venereal disease.

'Anji' – Wait, she calls Anjali *Anji*? – 'I'm actually surprised you agreed to publish the horrible dating column in the first place.'

Anjali gives her a contrite smile, her mouth pulled into a taut line. She didn't even know I was writing the column until I was two articles in, but she takes the rebuke without laying the blame on me.

'Now, Marie, you're going to find this mole for us.'

I note this is a statement, not a question.

'*Mais, oui. Ça sera facile.*'

'Good. Right,' says Amelia Windsor, casting her eyes around the table and standing, 'if that's all, I'll get back to my garden party. I've kept my guests waiting long enough.'

OH. MY. GOD. She was hosting a garden party! That she hasn't sacked me on the spot is a bloody miracle.

After four more cheek kisses for Marie, Amelia Windsor leaves the boardroom, her phone pressed to her ear. 'I'm ready to leave,' she says, presumably to her driver.

By unspoken agreement, no one says a word until the lift doors close behind her. Then we all – well, except Marie – emit a collective sigh of relief.

'*How* do you know Amelia Windsor?' Poppy asks.

'School,' Marie replies, giving no additional information.

'And you didn't think to mention it *before*? You knew we were meeting with her,' she chides.

Marie shrugs, sucking on an unlit cigarette as if she hasn't a care in the world.

'Marie,' says Anjali, 'to get you started on your investigation, I've prepared this.' She slides a manilla folder across the table and Marie opens in, her eyes scanning the first page.

'What's that?' I ask.

'Just some thoughts on who might want to derail *Nouveau Life*. I've included everyone in your team.'

'Right, of course. Wait – you said *included*? Is there someone else you're thinking of?' I ask, grasping at the hope that it's *not* a member of my team.

'A couple of people came to mind – colleagues who might consider you a riva—'

'Who is Ivy Jones?' asks Marie, interrupting, and my head snaps in her direction of its own accord.

'Ivy?'

'As I was saying...' Anjali continues, and I look back at her. 'You *may* have a rival or two.'

'But not Ivy – she and I get along just fine.'

'But she also wanted to lead her own vertical and got knocked back.'

'Well, yes, because Ivy's so-called idea wasn't even remotely *Nouveau*. It was essentially *The Daily Sun* only more tabloid-y.'

Anjali looks at me as if I've just made her point for her.

'Oh,' I say, realising I have. And then I recall the strange exchange with Ivy on the day of the launch.

Could she really be the mole? She works in beauty, which is in a completely different division of *Nouveau*, but she'd be privy to enough information about *Nouveau Life* to do some serious damage if she wanted to.

'*Alors*,' says Marie, closing the folder and placing her palm on top. 'I will have something for you in the next day or two.'

'That soon?' asks Anjali, which is exactly what I was about to ask.

'*Oui*,' she replies – as if it's a stupid question.

When I catch Poppy's eye, she's smirking knowingly. She must be used to Marie's quirky and arrogant ways.

'All right,' says Anjali, 'with Marie working on outing the mole and Amelia's decision about the "Dating Horrors" column, we have a strategy. Greta, you'll need to sort pulling the column and the reader submission portal this afternoon.'

'Of course. I'll do that before I leave.'

'And Poppy, any chance I can coax you into the office first thing tomorrow morning? I have another matter I'd like to discuss with you.'

'Sure.'

The 'other matter' is me and my love life, which sends my already fragile stomach into spasms. Anjali still doesn't know what I know about her 'secret' plan. I try to catch Poppy's eye again, but I'm unable to, and after they've said their goodbyes, I'm left alone to pull the plug on my column.

Tiggy had better be up for a lengthy debrief session tonight. So much of my life has gone to shit in the past twenty-four hours, she's going to get an earful.

25

POPPY

'Hello, darling, welcome home,' says Tristan from the sofa. 'I'd get up to greet you but...' He points at Saffron, who's snuggled up on his chest. In his other hand, he's holding his book at an odd angle so he can read it over her fluffy face.

'Saffron, get off Tristan so he can greet me properly.'

One eye opens a sliver, then closes again. She doesn't care – *I'm* convinced *she's* convinced that *they're* married and I'm just the interloper who feeds her.

I offload my handbag and keys on the hallstand then cross the combined kitchen–dining–lounge room to plant a kiss on Tristan's lips. I scratch the top of Saffron's head. She's purring, which has nothing to do with me and everything to do with who she's sitting on.

'So, how was it?' Tristan asks, inverting his open book on his stomach, spine up. Shaz would be appalled if he ever treated any of her books like that – though, he doesn't exactly read romcoms.

I flop onto the sofa opposite him and stretch out, toeing off my ballet flats and rolling my ankles. 'It could have been a lot worse. Though, they're pulling the column Greta's been working on.'

'Another column?'

'Yep. And this is the one she and I invented as a cover.'

'A cover for...?' he asks without judgement. As always, Tristan is privy to the ins and outs of my case, but with this one, there are so many intricacies and layers of deception, it's no wonder he needs me to clarify.

'That she doesn't know her boss – that's the V-VIP – hired me to match her.'

'Which she did? The boss?'

'Which she did, yes. *And* which Greta figured out almost immediately, but she doesn't want her boss to know because that might make her – Greta's boss – feel bad about wanting to match her – Greta – in the first place. And tomorrow, I have to spin the loss of this second column *and* the fact that I still haven't matched Greta – because Greta has more or less kiboshed potential number one – so she doesn't close the case. The boss, not Greta.'

He scrubs a hand over his face.

'I've lost you,' I say.

'Just a bit. I make million-pound trades that are less complicated than that.'

'How about I *don't* explain it a second time and you join me in the bath instead?'

He raises his brows, his lips curling into a sexy smile. 'Sorry, Saffy,' he says as he lifts her off his chest and puts her on the floor. She mewls in protest, but he ignores her and rushes off to the en suite to fill the tub.

'Sometimes it's not all about you, Saffy,' I say.

At that, she turns and, with a swish of her tail, struts out of the room.

* * *

Greta

'I need a holiday,' I groan to Tiggy. I'm stretched out on the sofa with an arm flung over my eyes like the heroine from a silent movie. 'Today was...' I sigh, leaving the sentence unfinished because today was a lot of things and none of them were enjoyable. 'I just can't *believe* we're dropping my column – right after I became invested in it. I was sure it would be a hit.'

She doesn't respond.

'Are you even listening?'

I lift my arm and look about, but Tiggy's not even here. 'Tiggy?' I call.

'I'm in the loo,' she replies, her voice muffled by the bathroom door.

I raise myself onto my elbows. 'How long have I been talking to myself?' I yell.

'Dunno,' she shouts back. 'No more than usual.'

I snigger. 'Probably time to stop moaning, anyway,' I tell myself.

Tiggy returns, wiping her wet palms down the front of her jeans, leaving damp patches. 'I'm starving. Can we order in?'

'Course. Order what you like but don't go mad – I'm not really hungry.' I resume my silent-movie-star position on the sofa while Tiggy orders us dinner.

'Right, that's sorted,' she says. 'Now back to you. It's shit you've spent weeks pining over a bloke you don't actually fancy. And the work stuff... Well, there was no way you could have seen a mole coming, so that's shit too. I mean, what kind of person would deliberately sabotage your online mag? What a cockwomble! Or cockwomblette – I suppose the jury's still out.'

'Exactly.'

'That's another reason I love working solo: no cockwomblery from co-workers!' she declares. Ordinarily, I'd laugh at her silliness, but I don't have it in me, and she must realise. 'I really am sorry – it's proper shit. All of it.'

'Thanks,' I say. I roll onto my side and prop my head on my hand.

'Does it actually help me saying that?'

'That everything's gone to shit?'

She nods.

'A little. I'm just feeling sorry for myself. I *really* thought Harrison was going to be a good fit, you know?'

'Okay, we're back on the bloke.'

'Sorry, jumping around a bit – my mouth following my brain.'

'Sooo... now that *you're* not going to date Harrison, can *I*—'

'No!'

She cackles with laughter. 'I was just having a laugh, you muppet. You've started wallowing, which is becoming extremely boring.'

I snigger despite myself. 'What did you order, by the way?'

'I thought you weren't hungry.'

'Humour me.'

'Pizza.'

'Hmm. Actually, that sounds g—' My phone interrupts me with a notification of an incoming message. Tiggy scoops it up from the other end of the coffee table and tosses it to me. 'Ow,' I say, rubbing my boob where it landed.

'Oops.' She grimaces at me. 'Sorry.'

Still rubbing my boob, I check my phone and immediately sit up, staring at the screen.

'Ooh, is it Harrison?' she asks, sitting up and craning her neck to see.

I shake my head. 'No – Ewan.'

I read the message.

Hope you've had a lovely weekend. Fancy dinner tomorrow or Tuesday?

'What? What does it say? And why are you grinning?'

'I think I might have a date.'

'Gimme.' She wags her fingers at me, and I pass the phone to her like a civilised person, instead of lobbing it across my lounge room.

'Seems pretty straightforward to me. He's asked you out and you like him.'

Tiggy's evaluation of my situation elicits a pressing question: is *Ewan* the reason I didn't feel a spark with Harrison last night?

I conjure a mental picture of him: his blue eyes that twinkle when he's making a joke... his wavy, brown hair with the slight cowlick in the front... his cheeky smile, which lights up his whole face... how he smelled when he kissed my cheek, all *sexy*.

And he *is* sexy, I realise with a jolt – maybe not in an obvious way, like Harrison, which – ironically – had little effect on me when I actually *met* him. But definitely sexy. And clever and funny and thoughtful.

Most of all, I think of how I feel when I'm with him, how he makes me laugh, how much I look forward to seeing him at The Daily Grind, and how easily we can fill a whole evening just talking, eating, and laughing...

'Oh my god, you're right. I'm such an idiot.'

Tiggy gets up from the floor and heads into the kitchen. 'You're not an idiot, except for when you don't realise that I'm *always* right. Can I open some wine?' she asks rhetorically.

While Tiggy opens a bottle of red she took from the wine rack, I stare at the message. Tomorrow night might not be a good idea considering how tomorrow could play out at *Nouveau*. There's every chance I'll want to head straight home, install myself on the sofa with the remote control, and watch repeats of *Britain's Best Bakers* while munching on a block of Monty Bojangles – or maybe even a box.

But Tuesday... Even if everything is still pandemonium at work, at least that gives me forty-eight hours to get my head straight about Ewan.

'Hello?' Tiggy's standing beside me, holding out a glass of wine. She shoves it in my direction and the wine nearly sloshes over the rim.

I take it. 'Thanks.'

'Have you replied?'

'Not yet.'

'Penning the perfect response?'

'I'm thinking.'

She adopts a higher-pitched voice. 'Dear Coffee Shop Bloke—'

'*Ewan*,' I say, mildly annoyed.

'Dear Ewan the Coffee Shop Bloke,' she continues, reminding me that I did call him 'Mr Coffee Man' – *to his face* – which looking back on makes me cringe. 'It has only just occurred to me that—'

'Could you not?'

She immediately drops the persona. 'Yeah, course.'

'You don't think I'm merely awarding myself a consolation prize, do you?'

'You mean because it didn't go as you hoped last night?'

I nod.

She takes a sip of her wine, donning her contemplation face. 'I don't think so. You were keen on Ewan before you met Harrison.'

At that, I'm all ears. 'How do you mean?'

She opens the drawer under the coffee table and takes out the list she wrote – the 'All Your Men' list.

'Because of this,' she says, sliding it across the table with so much force, it falls to the floor in a flutter of pages.

'Will you *stop* tossing things about?' I ask, leaning down to retrieve it from the floor. Tiggy may be the clumsiest, bull-in-a-china-shop person I know.

I set the notepad on my lap and read through the list again. Only the last two names are of any consequence, especially now my column's been killed: Harrison and Ewan.

'Can you please hand me a pen?' She does and I draw a line through 'Harrison'.

'So, it's official then?' she asks.

'*This* doesn't make it official,' I say, tapping on the page with the pen, 'but telling Poppy does. Harrison is no longer a potential match.'

'I'm sure he'll make someone a wonderful husband,' Tiggy says dryly.

'Yes, someone *else*,' I say, my eyes fixed firmly on 'Ewan – Greta's hot friend'.

'Have you heard from him?'

I'm only half listening. 'Who?'

'*Harrison*.'

'We exchanged messages this morning – we're on the same page. "Nice to meet you but..." Why?'

'Just curious. Also, you haven't replied to Ewan yet.'

'Oh, shit!' I reach for my phone and cradle it in my lap. 'So, what do I say?'

Tiggy shakes her head at me and lifts her gaze to the ceiling as she sighs wearily.

'Okay, it's fine. I've got it.'

Dinner Tuesday sounds just woederful.

I hold it up to show Tiggy. 'How about this?'

'Well, you spelled "wonderful" – *wo*ederful? That doesn't bode well – and it's also kind of... meh.'

I correct the spelling. 'Okay, what then?'

'How about something less Jane Austen?'

'All right...'

I type:

I'd love to have dinner with you. Tuesday?

'This?'

'*Love?* You'd *love* to have dinner with him? Gimme.' She wags her fingers at me again and I hand over the phone.

'I'm trusting you...' I warn, not wholly trusting her.

Tiggy grins – full-on Cheshire-cat grin – and I instantly regret giving her my phone. She takes a slug of wine, then puts down the glass so she can type with two thumbs, her head tilting from side to side as she composes what must be the longest message in the history of the world.

'There. And send...'

'Oh god.' Now I take a slug of wine. That pizza had better arrive soon or I'll be drunk before I know it, which, piled on top of frazzled, could get ugly.

'Want me to read it to you?' she asks, her mouth twitching with delight.

'Go on then.' I settle back against the sofa, steeling myself for the lengthy Cyrano de Bergerac-style message my bestie has just sent to my... my what? Friend? Barista? Friendly barista? Hot friend?

Tiggy reads, adopting a tone and pitch that I could only describe as 'very Greta'.

'Hey, nice to hear from you. Weekend "okay" but something

came up at work. I'll tell you about it at dinner on Tues. Let me know where and when and I'll see you there. Smiley face.'

Simple. Friendly. Keen, but not *too* keen.

'Oh, that's... For some reason, I thought you'd be all...' I try to come up with something, but my mind stalls and I shrug instead, making Tiggy laugh.

'You really do *not* have game, babes. What did you think I was going to say? "You – me – storeroom at the coffee shop NOW"?'

'No! But seriously, it's perfect. Thank y—'

I'm interrupted by the chime of another incoming message. Tiggy tosses back the phone.

'*Please* stop throwing my phone. Grrr,' I tell her, baring my teeth.

She shrugs off the reproach and I read the message:

Perfect. Will let you know. Looking forward to it. Maybe see you at TDG tomorrow? Xx

'Oh, wow. He sent a kiss – well, *two* actually.' I show her my phone for the umpteenth time tonight, and she bursts out laughing. 'What?'

'A reminder that you're thirty-five, not fifteen.'

'Oi, that's not very—'

But I don't get another word out, as the buzzer to my flat sounds, and Tiggy leaps up, shouting, 'Pizza's here!'

26

GRETA

The roaring inside my head is back – but it's unclear if it's just nerves or nerves plus a hangover. It's probably the latter, as 'roaring' brought along his friend 'pounding headache'. I blame Tiggy, which is juvenile of me, but she's the one who opened the second bottle of wine. And even though we finished a large pizza between us, we also finished that second bottle.

What was it she said last night? Something about being thirty-five and not a teenager? Though she was talking about my love life, not being able to drink as much as I once did without suffering the repercussions.

I've arrived at *Nouveau* very early, wearing more make-up than usual (to disguise the sins of last night) and wishing it was acceptable for me to wear sunglasses inside, à la Amelia Windsor.

It's strange being here when it's so quiet, which is doing nothing to ease my nerves. To take my mind off... well, *everything*, I log into my laptop and scroll through emails, deleting, filing, and typing out quick responses. There's nothing of consequence until I get to the most recent email, timestamped 7.01 a.m., which is four minutes ago, from Marie Maillot with the subject line: The Mole.

'What? How did she find them so quick—?'

I don't finish the word, as I'm overcome by a wave of nausea. I gulp in a breath to stave it off, but saliva floods my mouth and there's nothing more I can do but reach for the bin and retch into it. When my stomach eventually stops spasming, I wipe my face with a tissue. And only when I'm convinced I won't be sick again, do I set down the bin and look at my laptop screen.

I open the email, immediately seeing that Marie has copied in Poppy and Anjali. Before I discover who's been sabotaging *Nouveau Life*, I lift my gaze and take a series of steeling breaths. I'm placing bets on Ivy Jones. Ever since Anjali raised her as a suspect yesterday, I've been remembering instances of her being sarcastic or rude or condescending, even though I have *several* years' more experience than her at the magazine.

Eventually, I'm ready to read the email – well, as ready as I'll ever be. I scroll through the explanation of Marie's methods, searching the dense email for a name. When my eyes land on it, I cannot believe what I'm seeing.

'It can't be...' I gasp. But it says it right there in the email.

Rebecca Lovell

Bex. Bex is the mole, the one who's been sharing our ideas – or *IP* – with *Panache*.

The nausea threatens again, but knowing is marginally better than not knowing and I'm able to breathe through it.

I go back to the start of the email and read every word – *twice*. Somehow, in less than twenty-four hours, Marie has uncovered call logs and an email chain that irrefutably links Bex to an editor at *Panache* – an unsavoury woman I know only by reputation. Stupidly, Bex was using her work-issued phone and *Nouveau* email address – I don't want to know how Marie got access to those records. She's attached several documents, one of which is the contents of the emails, something I suppose I'll have to read at some point, but *after* I speak to Anjali.

Bex. I can't believe it. She's been my right-hand woman since I selected her as *Nouveau Life*'s assistant editor *months* ago. She's been with me every step of the way. We've even been to bloody brunch together and I rarely see my colleagues outside of work!

My phone rings, startling me, and I dig it out of my handbag. It's Anjali.

'Hi,' I answer, my breathy voice betraying my maelstrom of emotions.

'So, you've seen it then?'

'Yes. I can't believe it.'

'Nor me. I *hired* her,' she says.

'So did I in a way, hand-picking her for *Nouveau Life*.'

'We've both been duped.'

'I hadn't thought of it like that,' I say sullenly. 'The betrayal, it compounds it, doesn't it?'

'Absolutely! I wish it *had* been Ivy – much easier on us, if anything.'

I don't mention that I'd had the same thought – there's no point.

'Look,' she continues, 'I'm heading in early – can you meet me at the office in half an hour?'

'I'm already here.'

'Oh. Well, I'll see you soon then.'

She ends the call abruptly and my phone rings again before I've even put it down. It's Poppy this time.

'Hey, I was just checking emails over brekkie. Did you see it?'

'Yes.'

'Are you okay?'

'I'm... I'm *blindsided*, Poppy.'

'I can imagine. I'm really sorry, Greta. Let me know if there's anything I can do. I'm coming in later to meet with Anjali, and I'll pop by your office afterwards, okay?'

The reminder that Poppy and Anjali are meeting to discuss my love life cuts through the mental noise about Bex.

'On that,' I say. 'What are you going to tell Anjali? About me, I mean.'

'Just that I'm still on the case – *your* case – and I'm hopeful we'll find you a match.'

'Is that the truth?' I ask.

She doesn't reply right away, which sends yet another round of spasms through my gut.

'Well, that depends,' she says eventually.

'On what?'

'On you. Do you want me to keep the case open, or fall on my sword with Anjali and close it, leaving you to your own devices?' She must be alluding to me pursuing things with Ewan. 'I'll do whatever you want, Greta. You're my real client. But I should probably tell you about potential match number two before you make a final decision.'

The agency's 'one match at a time' guideline comes to mind, now more pertinent than ever as I think of Ewan. Just last night, I was exchanging butterfly-inducing messages with him, *and* we have a date tomorrow night. It's not fair to him – or me – to maintain the façade with Anjali, especially when Poppy's prepared to admit she didn't find me a match.

Still… I should hear about the second potential match – if only for due diligence and to close the loop for good.

'All right, quickly tell me about him,' I say with a sigh.

'The broad strokes are: he's forty-one, has his own business – which is a recent career change, but has *really* taken off. He's a foodie and loves travel. He's been single for about a year, but is amicable with his ex, and he lives in Central London with his dog.'

'Oh, well, I did ask you to make it quick.'

'Does any of that sound familiar?' Poppy asks, and something in her tone ignites an all-over tingling sensation.

'And what's his name?' I ask slowly, the tingling intensifying as excitement bubbles up inside me. Because I'm pretty sure I already know the answer.

'Ewan Wilder.'

I was right! But now I'm also baffled. 'Wait, what? How? And when did—?'

Poppy laughs.

'Did Ewan sign up with the Ever After Agency?'

'Nooo,' she replies.

'Then how is he on the list?'

'Because I'm good at what I do,' she replies simply.

'I don't understand.'

'Well, when I met him, I saw there was something between you, so I had Marie do a little digging to make sure he was unattached and a decent human being and—'

'Wait – you had Marie investigate him?' I ask, my voice high and screechy.

'It was due diligence, Greta. We vet all our potential matches.'

'Sorry, of course you do.'

'But the rest was all you. I just paid attention to what you were telling me – *and* what you weren't. If it didn't work with Harrison, my next step was to nudge you towards Ewan.'

I chuckle – mostly at myself. First Tiggy, then Poppy... did *everyone* know how I felt about Ewan before I did?

'We've actually got dinner plans tomorrow night,' I say, an unbidden smile breaking across my face.

'Great! See, you didn't even need the nudge, and at least there's *something* positive amongst all this sh—' She stops herself.

'Shit,' I supply, making her laugh again. 'It's okay to call it that. This situation is a heaping pile of shit.' Saying that, the gravity of what Bex has done lands with full force. 'Oh, Poppy, I honestly can't believe it's Bex.'

'I know,' she says, her tone suddenly sobered. 'I'm really sorry. I imagine you'll be confronting her this morning?'

'I'm not sure. Anjali's on her way in now and I suppose we'll work out what to do together.'

'I hope it goes as well as it can.'

'Thanks, Poppy.'

After the call, I rest heavily against the back of my office chair, staring at the wall and reflecting on the swings and roundabouts of my current life. I *am* eager to see where things can go with Ewan, but right now, that's completely overshadowed by the dread of having to confront – and sack – Bex.

When Anjali first mentioned we had a mole – was that really only yesterday? – it seemed preposterous that it was someone in my own team. Of course, I'd extrapolated from there, imagining that if it was, I'd be held accountable. I pause at the thought. What if that's the case? What if my head's on the chopping block too?

I glance at the clock on my laptop screen. Anjali will be here soon. 'Should I pre-emptively offer my resignation?' I ask myself. 'But what if she accepts it?' *Oh god.*

My phone chimes with a message notification, a reprieve from my worrisome thoughts:

I hope you have a lovely day. Let me know if you're coming to TDG and I'll save your favourite table for you. Xx

Despite everything, it brings a smile to my face. I reply:

Thanks. Bit of a sticky situation here this morning. Not sure I'll make it.

Three dancing dots, then:

Sorry to hear that. Will let you know about tomorrow night.

Thanks. *smiley face*

At least I have dinner with Ewan to look forward to.

I should probably head to Anjali's office so I'm there when she arrives. I close my laptop and tuck it under my arm, then cast my eyes about my office. If the absolute worst does happen, this could be my last day at *Nouveau*. Even though that's not likely – I *hope* it isn't – tears prick my eyes. I've given so much of myself to this magazine, and I have so much more I want to do here.

Oh, Bex, what have you done?

* * *

Bex looks small and frightened when Anjali outlines what we've discovered.

We're in the boardroom with me, Anjali, and Amelia Windsor (sans sunglasses) on one side of the large table and Bex on the other, visibly on the verge of tears. I fight the urge to run around and give her a hug.

'Well, what do you have to say for yourself?' barks Amelia Windsor.

Bex bursts into tears, burying her face in her hands, and I have to grip my chair with both hands so I don't leap up to administer that hug. I glance to my left at Anjali, and she meets my eye, shaking her head slowly. We're both feeling it – disappointment as well as betrayal. We trusted her, we *believed* in her.

'Tears are not appropriate,' Amelia Windsor continues. 'You're only crying because you got caught.'

Bex lifts her tear-stained face. 'No, I...' she stammers.

'You what?'

'I just... It was a mistake.'

'A *mistake*?' asks Amelia Windsor, loading the word with incredulity and scorn.

Bex nods, her lower lip quivering, then looks right at me.

'I'm so sorry, Greta. I was out with a friend of mine who works at *Panache*. Well, we're sort of friends – I don't really see her much these days. Anyway, we were at a bar, and I'd had a few drinks and it was stupid of me, but I wanted to show off to her, so I bragged about our advice column. At the time, I didn't think anything of it. Actually, I completely forgot about it, but the next day, her editor called me and said she might have a spot for me on her team – and not as an assistant editor but as an *editor*, which was really flattering. And then she put me on the spot and asked if I had any ideas I could bring to *Panache* and the only thing that came to mind was "Disasters of Dating". It all just snowballed from there.'

Bex punctuates her rambling monologue with a loud sob, which echoes throughout the room, bounces off the glass wall, and reverberates in my ears, making me even more unsettled.

She betrayed us for a job at *Panache*? One that probably never existed in the first place, if my knowledge of the editor in question is any indication. She isn't known for her professional ethics.

Looking past Bex, I see a group of onlookers outside the conference room, boldly staring at us through the glass. I suppose it was a misstep to conduct this meeting where everyone could watch it play out, but perhaps it was a deliberate move by (the terrifying) Amelia Windsor. At least Taj and Lisa work on a different floor.

Anjali notices the onlookers too. She rises, strides around the desk, throws open the door, and bellows, 'Back to work, everyone!' like an angry school principal. I've never heard her shout like that, but it's only the third most alarming aspect of this meeting after Bex's sobbing and Amelia Windsor's callous interrogation techniques.

There's a chance *I'll* be in that hotseat after Bex is dismissed and I gulp, swallowing the lump in my throat.

'Rebecca,' says Amelia Windsor evenly, and to her credit, Bex meets her eye. 'Your paltry excuse may have explained the *first* indiscretion on your part, but not the second. You actively entertained being poached by a competitor to the detriment of *Nouveau*.'

Bex licks her lips. 'I'm so, *so* sorry. It just all got away from me.'

'So, this has nothing to do with your resentment over Poppy Dean being brought on?' Amelia Windsor asks pointedly.

My head snaps towards her. This is new information to me – it must have been in the emails Bex exchanged with *Panache*. Which means Amelia Windsor has read them, something I couldn't bring myself to do. No wonder she's called the Thatcher of the magazine world – iron fist indeed.

'You have nothing to say about that?'

Bex is frowning now, the frightened girl giving way to something harder, angrier. 'It was a stupid decision to bring back that hack. She can't write and it made *so* much extra work for me. Stupid advice column.'

My jaw drops open, but I quickly recover. 'You should have said something,' I say.

'I *did* say something and you didn't care,' she retorts, lobbing the accusation with enough venom to fell an ox.

'That's... that's...' I splutter, but Amelia Windsor lifts her dainty hand in my direction, signalling that I should be silent. I close my mouth, looking at Bex through fresh – and very hurt – eyes.

'Rebecca, you are terminated, effective immediately,' Amelia Windsor says.

'I'll just get my things then,' she replies, standing.

'You will do no such thing. Your systems access has been revoked and your belongings removed and packed up. They will be sent to your residence.' She lifts her gaze and signals for two security guards – who I've only just noticed standing outside the door – to enter. 'These gentlemen will escort you out.'

Bex looks to me – clearly flabbergasted – and her bluster instantly evaporates. Tears gloss her eyes, but I steel myself against them. She is no longer my right-hand woman and she's no longer my protégé. She's just a young woman who made an egregious professional error, one she didn't own up to until she was confronted with it, and one she may never recover from.

She drops her gaze and slowly crosses to where the security guards are waiting, and they march her out of *Nouveau*.

'Is it too early for a dram of whisky?' asks Amelia Windsor. 'You look like you could use one – you both do.'

'Thank you for handling that, Amelia.'

'I'd say it's my pleasure, but I hate this part of the job.' This staggers me considering what I've just witnessed, which must be apparent, because her mouth quirks when she glances in my direction. Then she puts her sunglasses on and stands. 'Good luck with your second issue, Greta. I have no doubt it will be as well-received as the first.'

And then she's gone.

'God,' says Anjali. 'I *could* actually go for a whisky.' She checks her watch. 'I can't believe it's only just gone nine.'

'Mmm,' I murmur, still not having recovered.

'You going to be all right?' she asks, eyeing me intently.

I nod. 'I think so. Part of me was worried I'd get the sack too.'

'*What?* Hardly. I don't know what we'd do without you. Besides, no matter what Bex said, none of this was your fault. This was all her.'

'Thanks.'

Anjali sends me a tight-lipped smile. 'Right, back to work, I suppose.'

She leads us out of the boardroom, and we take the lift, then head to our respective offices. When I arrive at mine, there's a take-away coffee cup and a paper bag on the desk, and on the bag is written:

I hope your morning improves. See you soon. E xx

'It already has,' I say, inhaling the delicious aroma of the cronut. I take a sip of the still-warm coffee, sit in my chair, and mentally prepare myself to break the news to Taj and Lisa.

27

POPPY

'It sounds brutal,' I say to Anjali after she finishes recounting what happened to Bex.

'I can't remember a worse situation – at work, I mean. I do have a wayward sister who's caused havoc in my family for years,' she responds wryly.

'We can meet another time if you like – about the case?'

'No, now is fine. It's not like this day can get any worse.'

'Actually, I've got good news,' I say.

She narrows her eyes at me, clearly perplexed. 'All right, now I'm intrigued.'

Without revealing that Greta's in the know about Anjali's true intentions – or Ewan's identity – I outline the status of the case: namely, that Greta is dating someone she met organically and it seems to be progressing well.

'So, you see, we have every reason to be hopeful,' I say.

She side-eyes me curiously, the left corner of her mouth lifting slightly. 'But that's not cricket, surely? Greta met this man outside of our arrangement.'

It's interesting that she's calling this case 'an arrangement' and not 'sneakily forcing my employee to go on dates until she falls in love'. Like many people, Anjali seems comfortable rationalising her behaviour – likely because she has good intentions.

'I'm not taking credit for the introduction, no, but I have had him fully vetted, and I've been coaching Greta extensively on how to navigate her feelings.'

'Oh, I'm not questioning your professionalism,' she says, backpedalling. 'It's just, by engaging you…'

She trails off, but I think I understand what's she's getting at. I'll need to tread lightly. She's my bosses' close friend and I can't have Anjali thinking she's been short-changed – even if Saskia and Paloma will refuse her attempts to pay for our services.

'I'm hopeful of this match,' I say, 'and I promise to support Greta in any way I can.'

'And if it doesn't work out with this other man?'

'Then I'd suggest closing the case.'

'Oh.'

'I can see that surprises you, but I've got to know Greta quite well over the past month and even if this man is not her person, I can assure you she's much more attuned to what she wants from a relationship than she was when we started. I think we need to let her find her own way.'

Anjali smiles. 'Thank you – for being honest with me and for being such a good support to Greta.'

'Of course, that's my job.'

'Well, yes, but… I *mean* it, Poppy. Thank you for looking after Greta.'

'It's been a pleasure. Greta may be my client but she's also a top chick.'

Anjali grins. 'She is indeed.'

* * *

Greta

Despite how the day started, including the onerous task of explaining everything to Taj and Lisa *and* seeing Taj through a bout of tears so intense, I considered sending them home, by the time I log out of my laptop and leave *Nouveau*, it has drastically turned around.

Poppy was the bearer of good news when she stopped by earlier – Anjali's up to speed *and* pleased – and the response to the second issue of *Nouveau Life* has exceeded last month's, with more site hits, reader comments, and engagement on social media.

Even Taj recovered. They came to me this afternoon with a proposal outlining how we can distribute Bex's responsibilities between them, Lisa, and me until we hire a new team member. So, I think I've just found my new assistant editor.

And as exhausted as I am, my mind is abuzz with the triumphs of the day and the possibilities of the future. The last thing I can imagine doing is going home – I'll end up bouncing off the walls. I send a message to Tiggy, asking her to meet me at the Gin Palace, and ride the lift to the ground floor.

By the time I step outside the building, she's replied that she'll see me there and I head off on foot. On the way, I receive another message and, hoping it's from Ewan with details of our date, I open it right away. But it's not Ewan, it's Mum:

> *Ich habe die neueste Ausgabe geliebt. Ich bin so stolz auf dich, mein Liebling. Du bist so clever!*

Aww, it's Mum congratulating me on the issue and telling me how proud she is.

Tears spring to my eyes. It's *so* sweet of her to message me. *Nouveau Life* is not exactly pitched at my mum's demographic, but it means the world to me that she reads it. She's always read my work – every last thing I've ever written. And her pride in my work means the world to me.

I type a quick reply, one I can manage one-handed:

Danke Mama xx

As I'm basking in the glow of her pride, she sends a second message:

Wann lernen wir endlich Harrison kennen?

Oh god, now she wants to know when they're meeting Harrison. Fuck! How did I forget the enormous lie I told my family? And why did I tell it in the first place?

'Because you've been living on an emotional rollercoaster for the past month, and can barely tell your arse from your elbow,' I mutter to myself.

I shove my phone back in my handbag and accelerate my pace – I need a cocktail and *now*.

I show the message to Tiggy the moment she arrives at the Gin Palace, making her bellow with laughter.

'I don't even need to read German to find that funny,' she says.

'Oi, you're not being helpful. And technically, *you* told them I was seeing Harrison.'

'Don't put this on me. You were all flustered and flailing about,' she says, flapping her hand to demonstrate. 'And what other name was I supposed to give?'

It's a fair question. Giving the name of a real person, one who I'd been matched with, was probably better than making someone up entirely.

'No, you're right.'

'So, what are you going to tell her?'

'That it didn't work out?'

'And how will you explain Ewan?'

'What do you mean, *explain* Ewan?'

'Hi, Mum, hi, Dad, meet the bloke I haven't told you about yet because I lied about dating a bloke called Harrison.'

Shit, she's right about that too!

'Gah!'

'You need to tell her *something* – you know how she gets when you don't reply right away. She'll have the coppers knocking down your door for a welfare check if you don't message back soon.'

I puff out my cheeks and type a reply to my mum, hating myself for perpetuating the lie:

Will let you know. Xxxxx

Tiggy glances at my near-empty glass and signals for the bartender to bring me another drink, but I wave him off with, 'I'm okay for now, thanks.'

'You invite me out for a drink and you literally meant *one* drink?' she asks.

I cover a yawn with my hand; the weight of the day – and last night's sleeplessness – has caught up with me.

'I'll try not to be insulted by the yawn,' she says dryly.

'I'm sorry for being rubbish company. I can rally,' I say, vigorously patting my cheeks to perk myself up. 'Tell me about your day.'

Tiggy rolls her eyes.

'Please? I'm all ears, I promise.'

She runs through her typical digest of clients who've changed their minds mid-project and concludes with, 'And I'm seeing Apple again later.'

'Apple? *Oh*, the one from the threesome!'

'Could you say that louder, please? I don't think the people on the Strand heard you.'

'Sorry.'

'And yes, her.'

'Wow, a date with a hook-up...' I say, feigning amazement.

'A second hook-up with a hook-up,' she clarifies.

I yawn again. 'I'm too shattered to banter.' I slip off my stool and signal to the bartender to bring the bill. 'My shout.'

'Uh, yeah. You drag me all the way into Central London for one drink, you're buying.'

'You came from Holborn,' I say, giving her a pointed look.

She shrugs, tipping back her head to down the last of her drink, and I tap my phone to pay our bill. We leave the bar together, parting ways on the footpath with a hug and a promise that I'll fill her in on my date with Ewan the moment it's over.

I won't, though. She can wait until at *least* Wednesday – especially if it turns into an overnighter.

* * *

Tuesday vanishes in a blur of meetings. I didn't even make it down to The Daily Grind, so I was thrilled when my coffee-of-choice and another cronut showed up mid-morning. Although that may have had something to do with the text I sent Ewan:

Help! Drowning in meetings and having withdrawals.

As an aside, something they don't tell you when you're starting out in your career: the further you move up in the hierarchy, the more meetings you're required to attend.

Before *Nouveau Life* launched, Anjali once mentioned she had twenty-seven hours of meetings on her calendar that week. *Twenty-seven*. At the time, I'd wondered when she was expected to get her work done. Now, I realise that 'work' – AKA editing an online magazine – is what I do between attending meetings and handling crises.

I just need to make sure the chore of attending meetings doesn't take over what I love about being an editor.

But it all went well. By the end of the workday, HR had posted a job listing for an editorial assistant – I've moved Taj into Bex's spot and am giving Lisa a chance to flex her (promising) writing skills as our new staff writer – and I've thoroughly reviewed the numbers for the second issue. The short version: they're great and *Nouveau*'s finance team is delighted.

I even chaired an editorial meeting in which we – and by 'we', I mean the three of us left after Bex's departure – have tweaked what's included in next month's issue and reviewed our plans for future issues. Overall, I have a welcome sense of 'it's going to be all right'.

Now I'm standing in front of my wardrobe deciding what to wear on my date with Ewan.

I'm already showered – one of those 'everything' showers, in which I slathered, lathered, and scrubbed every part of my body, top to bottom, and denuded myself of hair in the applicable regions. I've dried my hair in loose waves, leaving it down and skimming my shoulders, and for my make-up, I've gone with NARS blush in 'orgasm', a smoky eye, and a glossy nude lip.

I look hot and I smell great.

And it may be presumptuous of me to have undergone my entire pre-sex-date routine – one I haven't completed for so long, I've forgotten the last time it happened – but worse would be *not* anticipating the possibility of sex, being asked back to Ewan's, and *not* have undergone my entire pre-sex-date routine.

He hasn't told me exactly where we're going – just to meet him at the end of the Golden Jubilee Bridge closest to Embankment Tube station, with the promise that there won't be 'too much walking'.

This could mean a number of things. All I know for sure is that we're going to dinner and when I looked up the location online, I found a dozen restaurants within a stone's throw, including McDonald's, which made me giggle. Imagine if we ended up there! Though I am partial to their French fries.

I flick through my wardrobe a second time, settling on navy linen, straight-leg trousers from the Bliss Designs petite collection and a polka-dot silk, sleeveless blouse. The look will go perfectly with my glittery Lorenzo heels.

I dress, then snap a photo for Tiggy, and send it to her with the caption:

Well?

She replies almost immediately, making me laugh out loud:

Scorching hot *flame emoji*

Another message arrives almost immediately following and I expect it to be Tiggy, weighing in with a GIF, but it's Ewan:

Can't wait to see you. Xxx

'I can't wait to see you either, Ewan,' I say as I slip the essentials – lipstick, phone, and keys, plus a travel-sized toothbrush, a teeny tube of moisturiser, and a clean pair of knickers (don't judge me) – into a navy clutch, then head off on date number three (sort of) with potential number two.

28

GRETA

As I climb the stairs to our meeting point on the Golden Jubilee Bridge, my nerves ratchet up. The whole journey here, I've been mentally replaying my friendship with Ewan, wondering again at which point it shifted towards something romantic.

I think it might have been that first night when we met up by accident – his friend having to rush off and the gym fanatic fabricating a sister who needed a ride to the airport. There was that moment between us over dinner – a romantic spark.

I dismissed it in the moment, just like I have every time it's occurred since, being too far up my own arse to see what was right in front of me.

But I do see now. I see it as if there's a giant flashing sign blaring, 'Greta, you muppet – it was Ewan you wanted all along!'

And that's what makes me nervous.

What if I've completely misread everything, and Ewan doesn't feel the same way? I'm hardly an expert in reading romantic signals. Maybe he *was* just being friendly. And now that I've realised I have feelings for him, what if he only wants to be friends?

Oh god, is this how proper dating works?

With Darren, we just sort of fell into a relationship. We never discussed being exclusive – which in hindsight, we should have because I obviously needed to spell out to him that sleeping with other women is a no-no when you have a serious girlfriend.

And now...?

What I've learnt over the past month is that I'm a total novice in this area, constantly confused and full of doubt. *How* are people doing this as part of their normal, everyday lives?

'Because normal people simply date and fall in love, and your situation is *anything* but simple,' I mutter to myself.

I don't have time to ponder this conundrum further because when I look up, Ewan is waiting at the top of the stairs, and my heart elbows my head out of the way, shouting, 'There he is!'

We exchange grins and when I reach him, he gently clasps my arm to pull me close for a soft cheek kiss. He's wearing that lovely cologne again – the one with spicy sandalwood notes. It's divine.

'Hello. You look beautiful,' he says, his eyes taking in my outfit, then meeting mine. A thousand butterflies launch inside me, fluttering about, and I have to nudge myself to reply.

'So do you – handsome, I mean.' And he does, having chosen a dress shirt in the exact shade of blue as his eyes. He smiles at me, tilting his head in modest shyness, then slides his hand down my arm and clasps mine.

I never knew that holding someone's hand could be so... so... *sexy*. The tingles racing about my body are compounded when he laces our fingers together.

Even I know this is a good sign that Ewan feels the same way I do.

'Now those are rather gorgeous shoes,' he says, 'but we do need to walk across the bridge and a little further. I'm not going to need to carry you, am I?' he teases.

We both look down and I point one toe and move my ankle from side to side to show off the shoe. 'These are Lorenzos, so, no,' I say, and our eyes meet again. 'The most comfortable sexy shoes on the planet.'

'Excellent. This way,' he says, and we cross the bridge towards South Bank.

* * *

'So, have I managed to find someplace you've never been before?' asks Ewan as we're being seated.

He has! We're at The Archduke, which is cleverly integrated into the arch under the bridge, its architecture and design a mix of industrial and 'high-end pub'.

'Was that your goal?' I ask with a laugh.

'I wanted to return the favour,' he says. '*And* impress you. The food here is fantastic, by the way – *and* they have a comprehensive cocktail menu. I know you like your cocktails,' he adds right as the waiter hands me the bar menu.

'Thank you,' I say to him.

'Now we do have to be somewhere else at a quarter to nine,' says Ewan mysteriously, 'but that leaves us plenty of time to have a drink and eat dinner. It's nearby, so no need to rush.'

'You're not going to tell me where we're going?' I ask.

'Better if it's a surprise,' he replies, winking.

With a smile, I look back at the menu, hoping it's not obvious to Ewan that I'm catching my breath. Between the cologne and the way that blue shirt accentuates his eyes – *and* the thoughtful plans – this is already the best date I've been on since... well, *ever*.

We decide on cocktails – a Negroni for me and something called a Mezcalita for Ewan, which is made with tequila – as well as steaks (what The Archduke is famous for) and wine to have with dinner.

Like last time we went to dinner, I defer to Ewan to order the wine, and he selects an Argentinian Malbec. No doubt it will have the one wine characteristic I'm confident of: yumminess. Though, Ewan won't let me get away with that – not after that whole 'close your eyes' episode when we were at The Port House. *Note to self: pay extra special attention when the wine is served.*

'Congratulations on the latest issue, by the way,' he says after the waiter takes our order.

'Oh, you enjoyed it? And, yes, I *am* blatantly fishing for a compliment.'

'A well-deserved compliment. It really was an interesting read. I especially liked the article on professions of the future, how the traditional nine-to-five model is diminishing – fascinating.'

'*Thank* you. And I can see why that would have resonated.' I regard him closely. 'You know, I have so much admiration for you – how you stepped away from corporate life and did something completely different, something you're passionate about,' I say.

I realise as soon as the words are out of my mouth how unguarded that was, but isn't that what this evening's about, letting down my guard and diving into this date wholeheartedly?

'Oh, that's...' He looks down, his slight embarrassment evident, which is endearing. 'Thank you. So far, so good – even though most people in my life think I'm just "going through a phase" – a midlife crisis of sorts – and soon I'll "come to my senses" and go scampering back to my old job.'

'Who says that? I want names,' I say, making him laugh.

'Let's see, there's my parents, my brother, his wife...'

'God, that makes what you did even more impressive. Is anyone on your side?' I ask.

'Well... *you* are.'

He holds my gaze, then reaches for my hand across the table. My breath hitches as I slide my hand into his and he looks intensely into my eyes.

'Thank you for telling me that – about admiring me. You have no idea how much I battle self-doubt on a daily basis. Even though The Daily Grind is a success – by any metric – I still keep questioning what the hell I'm doing. I mean, I was that bloke at uni who was laser-focussed on my studies and my career. I knew exactly what I wanted to do, who I wanted to work for, and I landed my dream job right out of the gate. But recently, only just this year, I had this epiphany – sorry, that sounds naff...'

'No, not at all. So, what was the catalyst?'

'Well...' He inhales a deep breath. 'Sally never wanted children and I thought she would change her mind about that. She didn't and it all came to a head one day – we'd been to this christening for our friends' daughter and... Never mind, you don't need to hear the gory details, but we talked it through and realised we would be better off as friends.'

'That's... That must have been really difficult,' I say, though a teeny part of me is rejoicing at the discovery that Ewan wants children.

'It was,' he replies, 'but that was nearly a year ago and I think we're in a good place now.'

It seems like he doesn't want to say anything more on the subject, and while I don't mind him *mentioning* Sally, I'm glad we're not going to keep talking about her.

Our cocktails arrive and after the waiter sets them down, Ewan raises his and meets my eye. 'To Greta, for being kind and understanding and a good listener.'

We lock eyes and I raise my glass. 'To Ewan, who is brave and funny and very generous, especially with baked goods.'

He breaks into a smile, and we clink our glasses together and drink. I swallow, then lick my lips. 'That is an excellent Negroni,' I say.

'This is good too.' He sets his glass on the table. 'So, back to *Nouveau Life*,' he says. 'I looked for your article – the one about obsessive behaviour – but I couldn't find it. When's it being published?'

Well, bollocks. I'd forgotten about that lie.

I quickly recover, dodging the question with a half-truth. 'Actually, that got pulled. Part of the fallout from the situation at work I mentioned.'

'Did you want to talk about it? I wasn't going to bring it up, but I'd be happy to listen if you want to tell me what happened.'

'That's kind, but it's messy – *very*.'

'I can handle messy,' he says.

I take a moment, feeling the weight of his seemingly simple statement. Because isn't that what we all need at times? Someone close to us who can handle the messy parts?

'Okay,' I say, accepting his offer to listen. 'We discovered that my assistant editor was feeding *Nouveau Life* IP to a competitor.'

'Oh no,' he says, recoiling in horror.

'Yes. That's about how I responded when I found out. Anyway, yesterday we sacked her, and it was... it was shit, actually,' I say with a droll smile.

'I can only imagine. Were you close? Professionally?'

'I chose her especially for the role. And yes, we were close. Or I thought we were. That's what hurt most – the betrayal.'

'I'm so sorry.'

I shake my head to dislodge all thoughts of Bex and smile at him brightly. 'Anyway... enough of all that. Tell me something fun. Tell me what Remy's been up to – or how about our MI6 agent?'

'Our MI6— *Oh*, the English-breakfast-plus-a-shot-of-espresso bloke.'

'Has he been back?' I ask. 'With everything going on, it feels like ages since I was at The Daily Grind. I've missed out on all the action.'

Ewan grins. 'Actually, he came in again yesterday.'

'And?' I ask with a laugh.

'*And* I overheard him telling another patron why he orders coffee and tea together.'

'You did not! Way to bury the lead!'

'Sorry,' he says, raising his hands in contrition. 'I'd planned to tell you, but the moment I saw you on the bridge, I was so taken aback by how gorgeous you looked, every other thought flew out of my head.'

The compliment sends a shockwave of joy surging through me. I'm more lit up inside than London on Bonfire Night.

'Well, in that case, I forgive you,' I say with my best flirtatious smile.

His mouth quirks. 'How magnanimous of you.'

'I am nothing if not magnanimous.'

He pauses, his expression becoming earnest. 'I think it's a good sign that we can tease each other, don't you?' he asks.

'I think so too. And I *enjoy* teasing you,' I say with a head tilt.

His eyebrows shoot towards his hairline, and he smirks knowingly.

'Oh god, I didn't mean that to come across as *sexual*. Not that I *don't* want anything sexu— Bollocks. Shut up, Greta!'

His smirk widens into a grin and we both burst out laughing.

'So,' he says as our laughter dies away, 'just to clarify: you *are* amenable to something sexual happening between us?'

'Oh my god.' I grab the top of my head with both hands,

pulling my chin onto my chest while Ewan chuckles away. 'Please stop laughing at me,' I say.

I feel a gentle tug on my forearms. 'Hey...' I drop my hands and lift my gaze. 'I promise I'm not laughing *at* you.'

I stare at him disbelievingly.

'Well, I was, but it definitely wasn't malicious. On the contrary, I am delighted to learn that you—'

'Stop!' I say, dissolving into laughter again. 'You win! I fancy you, all right?'

'That is more than all right,' he says wearing a cat-that-got-the-cream smile, 'because I thought you were gorgeous the very first moment I saw you.'

'You did?'

'I absolutely did.'

We fall silent, an intense look passing between us. I really wish we hadn't ordered steak *and* sides *and* a bottle of wine. All I want is to abandon dinner and head back to mine – or Ewan's – I really don't care.

'The ribeye and the sirloin,' says our waiter, placing our plates in front of us. His not-so-perfect timing breaks the spell, and Ewan and I both make a show of oohing and ahhing over our steaks. 'I'll be back with your sides,' says our waiter.

'So!' I say, pretending as if we didn't just engage in a sexually charged bout of staring, 'the MI6 agent – what's the story behind the coffee–tea combo?'

'I'll tell you, but I should preface by saying it's hugely disappointing and has nothing whatsoever to do with spy craft.'

'Maybe you should make something up then.'

He laughs.

'No, don't – I want to know the real reason.'

'Okay, but don't say I didn't warn you.'

I prop my chin on my hand to show him he has my full attention.

'So, one morning...' he begins, as if he's about to regale a richly layered tale, 'he was making coffee for his sister and tea for himself, and he absent-mindedly added the second shot of espresso to the wrong mug. He didn't realise until he drank his tea that it had coffee in it, and he liked the result.'

'You're right. I need you to make something up.'

'I *told* you.'

'You did.' I sit back and pick up my knife and fork. 'So, tell me what Remy's been up to instead – it's gotta be more exciting than *that*.'

Our sides arrive – mashed potatoes, mushrooms, and green beans – and we serve portions onto our plates.

'He's doing well. He's made a new friend at doggy daycare – a female poodle called Coco. Apparently, they spend all their time together – they even share a bed.'

'Oh, that's adorbs,' I say with a laugh.

'He'd like to meet you, you know.'

'Oh, he told you that, did he?'

'Probably just to shut me up – apparently, I talk about you all the time.'

'You're flattering me.'

'Is it working?' he asks.

'I'm not mad at it.' We exchange another charged smile. 'So, are you really not telling me where we're going after this?'

'I'm really not telling you. Besides, it will become *extremely* obvious almost as soon as we leave The Archduke.'

'Hmm, okay...'

'Just let it be a surprise...' he teases with a grin.

'*Fine*,' I say with a pretend pout.

'The wine, sir,' says our waiter. 'Apologies for the delay.'

Now, I don't mind our waiter – he's polite and he's reasonably good at his job, even if he did bring the wine after the food – but his timing is atrocious. 'Bugger off!' I want to tell him. 'Can't you see this lovely man is trying to seduce me?'

Trying? Who am I trying to kid? Ewan very much had me at 'hello'.

29

GRETA

'Are we going on the London Eye?' I exclaim. We're walking hand in hand along Belvedere Road and, just as Ewan said earlier, it comes into view almost immediately.

He laughs. 'I told you would be obvious – and yes.'

'That's lovely.'

'Have you been on it before? I don't want to assume – a lot of Londoners haven't.'

'Only once – not long after Ru was born. I would have been about twelve or thirteen. I loved it – I felt like I could see forever. What about you?'

'My second time too – but I was in my twenties last time. A uni mate came down from Edinburgh and he wanted to ride it – I wouldn't have bothered otherwise.'

'But that's the way, isn't it? It's so easy to get caught up in the day-to-day that you never take the time to explore your own city.'

'Exactly. You know what we should do? Have a day out, the two of us, and explore London as if we've only just arrived.'

'I'd love that,' I say. Then he lifts my hand – the one he's holding – and presses his lips to it, his gaze holding mine.

It is the single sexiest thing a man has ever done to me. Okay, that might not be entirely true, but nothing else comes to mind and heat is *flooding* my body. I'm guessing Ewan's already booked tickets for the London Eye – otherwise, I'd be ordering an Uber and inviting him back to mine.

We're quiet as we walk the rest of the way and when we arrive, Ewan shows the attendant the booking on his phone, and we're whisked away to priority boarding.

Has he booked us a private pod? That's so… *romantic*.

We're next in the short queue and a young woman in uniform introduces herself as Catriona, our host. We step into the pod and on the seat in the centre are a bottle of champagne and a box of chocolates – this just keeps getting better – but, surprisingly, Catriona boards the pod with us.

As the doors close behind us, she makes short work of opening the champagne and while she pours two glasses, I turn to Ewan.

'This is gorgeous,' I whisper. 'You're spoiling me – thank you so much.'

'You're welcome. It seemed like you've had a hard time over the past few days and—'

'But you didn't even know what had happened. I just said that there was a sticky situation at work…'

'I made an educated guess that you were playing it down, making it seem less difficult than it was.'

'That was a good guess.'

He shrugs. 'Besides,' he says, tucking my hair behind my left ear and trailing the back of his fingers down my cheek, 'I wanted this night to be special.'

My breath hitches. 'Well, you've definitely succeeded,' I manage to say.

'Madam, sir,' says Catriona. We turn towards her, and she

hands us brimming champagne flutes then steps back, giving us as much privacy as is possible in the confined space.

Ewan ushers me to the other side of the pod and we face the window. The sun has nearly set, the sky above us an inky blue, and a smattering of low clouds hang above the horizon, alight in an array of pinks and purples. Along the Thames, lights from landmarks dance on the surface of the water. Parliament House is particularly beautiful, spilling its golden light onto the Thames, with Big Ben standing proudly, a striking beacon.

I wander over to the other side of the pod, Ewan trailing close behind, and this view is just as beautiful as the southern-facing view. Be still, my heart, I love this city.

'What should we toast to?' asks Ewan.

I look up at him, my eyes roving the features of his handsome face. 'To London – a beautiful city that I too often take for granted,' I say.

'I like that,' he replies, gently touching his flute to mine. We sip and it is *delicious*.

As we climb higher and the view changes, we chat – nothing too serious or too flirty, as I'm hyper aware that there's another person with us. Catriona tops us up when our glasses are nearing empty, but as discreet as she is, I can't shake the uncomfortable thought of her watching us together.

When she tops us up a second time – I am going to be *drunk* by the time we leave the pod – she offers to take our photo.

'Oh,' I say, amazed I hadn't thought of it myself. 'That would be lovely.'

Ewan and I both give her our phones and we pose for several photos, his arm around me, his hand resting on my waist and pulling me towards him. When the mini photoshoot is over and he steps away to retrieve our phones, I want to haul him back to me and kiss him – *hard*.

I don't, though. I'm not sure I want our first kiss to be in front of Catriona.

The thirty-minute ride comes to an end and, as predicted, I'm giddy from the champagne. Leaving the unopened box of chocolates, we step onto the platform and Ewan takes my hand. Oh, bollocks, we're still moving.

Yes, Greta, the London Eye doesn't stop to let off tipsy women.

Of course, I instantly lose my footing and stumble, but Ewan's got me. He clasps my hand tighter and steadies me.

'Are you all right?' he says once we've cleared the platform.

'I'm all right – a little embarrassed.'

'No need to be – it's just me,' he says softly.

It's just me.

And there it is – another seemingly simple statement that's loaded with so much more.

Because Ewan has gone from the bloke at the coffee shop who I made small talk with to a friend and dinner companion to this man – this lovely, sexy man – I'm on a date with. And yes, it's early days – this is just the beginning of us – or at least I hope it is – but I still feel foolish for not having seen it until recently.

At least I see it now.

And – to my utter joy – he seems to feel the same way.

These thoughts fly through my mind in seconds. He's watching me intently – like I'm watching him – and I couldn't say who moves first, but suddenly his hands are resting on the small of my back and mine have snaked around his neck, my clutch dangling from one hand.

Our faces mere inches from each other's, we pause, me looking up at him, him down at me, our breath mingling and our lips parted.

'You are so gorgeous,' he whispers.

And I can't wait a moment longer. I stand on my tiptoes and press my mouth to his.

He embraces me tightly, his fingers digging into the fabric of my trousers, and I tighten my arms around his neck. The kiss is firm, both of us wanting it, wanting each other, and his mouth moves against mine with a sureness I find so incredibly sexy, my whole body is alight. His tongue slips into my mouth, the tip touching mine. When it withdraws, I bite down gently on his lower lip, feeling his mouth stretch into a smile.

Then the kiss deepens and I am lost in the sensations of him – the taste, the smell, the feel of his body against mine, his hands on my back just above my bum, his fingers now splayed.

This is the best kiss of my life.

Eventually, the kiss ends – I was vaguely aware of a passer-by telling us to get a room – and we pull apart, both breathless and grinning.

'You know, that may just be the best kiss I've ever had,' he says, and I swat him in the chest. 'Ow, what was that for?' he asks with a laugh.

'I was thinking the exact same thing.'

He side-eyes me. 'You're not going to get violent every time I say what you're thinking, are you?'

'Not *every* time.'

He places a dainty kiss on the end of my nose, which is sweet, but I prefer the other kind of kiss. Then he lifts one hand to rub the back of his neck the way blokes do sometimes when they're mulling something over or are worried.

'What's on your mind?' I ask, hoping he'll say something like, 'Shagging you senseless.'

'You know how Remy wants to meet you?' he asks, suddenly shy.

'I do, yes.'

'What if that was tonight?'

Yes, yes, yes, yes, yes!

Inside, I'm doing a happy dance – and *never* have I appreciated my foresight more.

'I would love to meet Remy tonight,' I reply, maintaining the pretence.

He grins again.

'I can't stop grinning,' he says, shaking his head.

'I don't mind.'

'I'll get us an Uber.' He takes out his phone and taps away and I watch him closely.

I am going home with Ewan! I AM GOING HOME WITH EWAN AND HE MAKES ME FEEL ALL WARM AND GLOWING INSI—

'Excuse me, sorry to bother you,' a woman says to Ewan. I hadn't even noticed her approaching, being in my own little bubble of Ewan-ness.

He lifts his brows inquisitively.

'Would you mind signing this, please? I just *loved* you in *Atonement*.' She shoves a Tesco receipt and a pen at him and – to his credit (another thing to add to the Ewan-is-wonderful list) – he takes it from her. 'To Meryl, please – that's me,' she says with a slightly embarrassed smile.

A few feet away, a man, who I presume is her husband, rolls his eyes. 'Sorry to bother you, mate,' he says.

'It's no bother at all,' he replies. He leans down to rest the receipt on his thigh and writes:

To Meryl,
   Very nice to meet you.
   James McAvoy
   xxxx

He hands it back to her and she's beaming. 'Thank you. You have a lovely night now.'

They leave, the woman glancing back over her shoulder at Ewan – twice – and he turns to me, his mouth open and his hands held out. 'What? Just? Happened?'

'You were lovely – you gave her a story to dine out on for the rest of her life.'

'Can you imagine if she'd asked for a photo? Someone would have burst her bubble as soon as they clapped eyes on me.'

'Hardly. I told you, it's remarkable how alike you are.'

He barks out a laugh. 'Anyway, we should go. Uber will be arriving soon,' he says, pointing to where he's dropped the pin.

As we walk towards it, I say, 'She was adorable. She even told us to have a nice night.'

'I think you'll find she said, "*lovely* night," and I have every intention of making it that and more.'

I make a show of fanning my face. 'Phoof. That Uber driver better not be worried about getting a ticket,' I quip.

'If they do, I'll pay for it.'

30

GRETA

Waking up in Ewan's bed the next morning, just as the warm glow of the sun peeks through a tiny gap in the curtains, my mind teems with memories from last night – each one more swoon-worthy than the last.

I have never known sex to be like that, especially the first time with someone.

I sigh quietly, basking in the sensations of my still-thrumming body, which was taken to the brink and back – *twice*.

'Good morning,' Ewan murmurs in my ear. He snuggles closer, big spoon to my little one, and starts kissing my neck. I close my eyes as his lips send shivers down my spine. His hand slides onto my waist, pulling me to him, and I reach for it as my eyes flutter open.

That's when I realise there's a dog watching us.

'Um, Ewan?'

'Mmm?' He keeps kissing my neck until I gently nudge him in the stomach. 'What's up?'

'Look.'

He lifts himself up and peers over my head.

'Remy, *out*!' he bellows.

Remy makes a whiny doggy noise that sounds like 'aww', which makes me giggle, then trots off, his claws clacking on the wooden floorboards.

'At least he didn't see anything,' I say, sitting up. 'Unless he was watching us last night.'

Ewan presses his palms into his eyes. 'Oh god – hopefully not.' He drops his hands and looks at me. 'I'm sorry – I should have been paying more attention.'

'I'd say your attention was exactly in the right place.'

'Is that so?' he asks, the left corner of his mouth curling up.

I lean over and press my mouth to his. 'That is so.' My eyes flick to his bedside table where his phone shows the time, and I groan.

'Are you going to love me then leave me?' he asks, wriggling closer and sliding his hand up my back.

'I don't want to,' I say, relaxing into his embrace.

I'm *so* tempted to call in sick, but what would I say? 'Hello, this is Greta Davies. Can you please tell Anjali that I'm having lots of lovely sex and don't want to get out of bed?' I'm sure that would go down a treat, especially as we're still in crisis-management mode – albeit at the tail end, but it's a terrible time to skive off work.

'But I have to,' I say.

'I could call in on your behalf. Tell a fantastical lie about why you can't possibly come into work today.'

The word 'lie' feels like a pinprick to my heart. After last night – and this morning – I'm 99 per cent certain Ewan and I are embarking on a relationship. I ignore the irritating reminder that I haven't been truthful with him about my writing assignment – but no need to bring it up now that it's behind me.

'What's going on in that head of yours?' he asks.

'Oh, just trying to figure out if I need to shoot home quickly or if I can leave from here.'

Greta! Yet another lie! Though a pertinent one. I glance at the time again and do a quick series of calculations. If I leave directly from here in the next fifteen minutes, I *should* make it into *Nouveau* before nine.

'Last chance – I am fully prepared to call your boss and tell them you're on doggy daycare duty.'

I chuckle. 'I already adore Remy, but I wouldn't want to stay here without you.'

'Oh, no, in this scenario I'm calling in sick too. I can do that, you know, being the owner.'

'Tempting...'

He cups my cheek with one hand and leans closer to kiss me. Oh, I could *so* lie here in this bed all day, just talking and...

'Nope!' I say, abruptly sitting upright.

Ewan responds with surprised laughter. 'Hopefully that wasn't an indictment of my kissing skills. I'm a little rusty, but...'

'Definitely not that,' I say, flinging back the covers and climbing out of bed. 'But if I stay in this bed a moment longer, I will be late, and the repercussions will be... let's just say, *unpleasant*.' I begin scouting the room for my clutch and my clothes when it suddenly occurs to me that I'm completely naked, something I haven't been in front of a man for ages.

I glance back to the bed where Ewan has propped his head up on two pillows and is watching me with a lusty expression on his face. I can conclusively say I've never had a lover who's looked at me like that.

I stand still, cocking one hip and placing a hand on the other, meeting his eye with newfound confidence.

'You are so sexy, you know that?' he growls, and it takes all my willpower not to launch myself onto the bed and call in with that paltry excuse he fabricated.

'Why, thank you, Mr Wilder. I could say the same about you.'

We hold each other's gaze for a while longer and I am serious danger of my nethers erupting into flames.

'Right!' I say, snapping out of my sex-themed trance. 'Shower!'

With Ewan accommodating all my (non-sexual) needs – a shower, a coffee, a cronut for the Tube, a kiss goodbye, and a promise to call later – I arrive at *Nouveau* twenty minutes before my first meeting. That's just enough time to steal into The Wardrobe and raid their make-up stash.

I'm applying some cream blush when Mimi comes to stand behind me, meeting my eye in the mirror.

'Hi, Mimi.'

'Hello,' she says with a smirk. 'I haven't seen you in here before – like this... to... er...' She draws a circle around her face with the forefinger.

'To make myself up because I spent the night somewhere else?' I proffer.

She's shocked for a moment, but then she cackles with laughter. 'Oh, to be that young again,' she says with a sigh.

She wanders off towards her desk, but her words echo in my ear. For weeks now, I've been telling myself that the biological clock is ticking, and that I may have left it too late to fall in love and start a family.

Now I'm seeing Ewan – wonderful, funny, kind, sexy Ewan – and the life I want seems within reach for the first time.

And I *am* still young – relatively speaking. If I live as long as my Oma, who's still as bright as a button aged ninety-six, I'm barely a third of the way through my life.

'So stop being such a drama queen about ageing,' I tell myself in the mirror.

I select a mini mascara from the vast array and do my lashes, then regard myself. My hair has this sexy, mussed-up vibe and my make-up – hastily applied from samples – will do. Ewan even ironed my clothes while I was in the shower – darling man.

I stand and regard myself in the mirror.

'Greta Fucking Davies, badass editor and recently shagged woman, at your service.'

* * *

Poppy

I arrive home on Wednesday evening to find Evie sitting at the breakfast bar, sobbing. Tristan meets my eye, panicked and telegraphing 'Help' with his eyes.

I dump my belongings on the hallstand and cross to her.

'Evie, what's wrong?' I ask, wrapping her up in a hug.

'I'm sorry to show up unannounced but Liv's away and I didn't know what else to do.'

It's a good thing I speak 'sobbing woman' fluently – if I didn't, that would have been totally unintelligible. I look to Tristan, who shrugs at me.

I hold Evie, letting her have a good cry while rubbing her back. When her sobs start to diminish, I release her. Tristan's had the forethought to place a box of tissues on the kitchen counter and I snatch up a handful and offer them to Evie.

'Thank you,' she says, taking them, but her nose is blocked and it comes out 'dankoo'.

'Would you like something to drink? A cup of tea?' I've always found tea to be the perfect panacea when everything feels too much.

She blinks at me, her lashes still wet. 'Can I have wine?' she whines.

Tristan quickly goes to the fridge and takes out a bottle of

Chardonnay, pours a glass, and slides it across the counter to Evie. She takes it and downs a big glug.

'And water, I reckon, Tris.' He nods and comes back with a highball brimming with water. 'Drink that, Evie,' I say, pointing to the water, 'then let's go sit in the lounge and you can tell me what's happened.'

She complies, much like a woeful child would. Shortly after, she and I are installed on one of our sofas, each with a glass of wine, Evie facing me, sitting cross-legged. Tristan brings over the tissues, then signals he's going into the bedroom.

'Right, so, what's going on?'

'It's Tyler...' she wails.

I'd figured as much – that little weasel. I thought it might take more than a pep talk and a girls' night in to exorcise him from Evie's life. I don't rush her, though, letting her tell me the latest development in her own time.

She sets down the wine glass and grabs a handful of tissues to blow her nose, then inhales deeply.

'Okay, so, Liv and I have this group of friends, see? Because we're only eighteen months apart and we've always been close, we know a lot of the same people, and now we're both living back in London... Well, we're part of the same friendship group and we see everyone all the time – parties, dinners out, weekends away...'

She's setting the stage so, again, I don't rush her.

'Anyway...' More tears spring up and she breathes through them, then licks her lips. 'Our so-called friend, *Delia*, well, it turns out *she's* the one Tyler's been sleeping with. Besides me, I mean.'

'Oh, Evie, that's awful. I'm so sorry.' Of course, I don't raise that I know of at least *two* other women Tyler is sleeping with (the little shit).

Evie sniffs, watching her hands as she fidgets with a wad of soggy tissues.

'How did you find out?' I ask.

'She *told* me. She did it under the guise of "caring about our friendship" and "being transparent because we're so close",' she says sarcastically. 'So close, you're bonking my boyfriend, you utter... utter...'

'Cow,' I supply.

She coughs out a laugh and looks up. 'I was going to say something else but "cow" will do, I suppose.'

'Well, I can understand why you're so upset. There's no excusing that behaviour – from either of them.' I phrase my next question carefully, as it could trigger another bout of tears. 'Evie, how have you handled things with Tyler – since he asked to see other people?'

'What do you mean?'

'Have you broken it off with him entirely or...?'

Her lips disappear between her teeth and she shakes her head. 'No,' she replies, her voice small and childlike. 'I've still been seeing him. This is my fault, isn't it?'

'*No*, not at all. Two people you trusted, *cared* about, went behind your back. The onus is on them.'

What I don't tell her is that I have no doubt Tyler considered Evie staying with him as permission to 'see other people' – 'I brought it up, she's still dating me, she must be okay with it...' Voilà – arsehole logic.

Evie expels a long, ragged sigh. 'I've been trying to concentrate on my work all afternoon – you know, keep my mind off things, but...'

She shakes her head and reaches for the wine again. She takes a sip, then cradles the glass in her hands.

'Can I ask, how close are you with the cow?'

This makes her smile. 'I don't really know the answer to that. We've been friends since school – we came up together. I *thought* we were close, but now... God, she even spent a summer with us once in Italy – I'd forgotten about that.'

It strikes me sometimes that I've married into old money – the kind of people who use 'summer' as a verb. Even if Tristan hadn't inherited his grandfather's fortune, the Fellows family would be considered wealthy by any standards.

I set the thought aside and focus back on Evie.

'Would you like to hear what I think?'

She nods vigorously.

'Do you remember our conversation when you first told me about Tyler's request?'

'Yes. And I know what you're going to say.'

'What am I going to say?'

'That he's not my person.'

'He is definitely not your person. And I can understand that you hoped to change his mind – even sacrificing what you wanted to suit him – but you deserve so much more. You are kind and generous and loving. You have a beautiful heart and the Tylers of the world don't deserve someone like you. They only deserve cows.'

She laughs – a lovely sound, especially considering the situation – and runs the back of her hand under her nose.

'I also promise you this: even though it will hurt for some time, that will fade.'

'Time heals all wounds,' she says.

'It's a cliché, but a lot of clichés are true. This one is.'

'I really miss Grandad,' she says, throwing a non sequitur into the conversation – though, I'm used to those. When I was a psychologist, a lot of my patients would make statements out of the blue. And they were often the truest, most self-aware things my patients would say.

'I know you do,' I say, reaching for Evie's hand, wad of tissues and all. 'And I know Tristan and Olivia do as well. I wish I got to meet him.'

'He would have loved you,' she says, meeting my eye with a smile.

Tears fill *my* eyes now. I'm so grateful to have Evie and her sister in my life – to be part of the Fellows family, as well as my own. Granted, it includes Helen, my mother-in-law, but in small doses, she's bearable. *Very* small doses.

We both wipe away our tears and I sit up straighter, pinning Evie with a look. 'Right, so what are we going to do about the cow?'

'Delia?'

'Mmm-hmm. Is the friendship group aware of what's going on between her and Tyler?'

'Umm... I'm not sure.'

'Well, maybe they need to be,' I say.

'How do I do that?'

'How do *we* do that?' I reply, reaching for her hand again and squeezing it. She smiles through her tears. 'You know, I have certain resources at my disposal...' I say with a wicked smirk.

'You sound like that dad in that movie,' she says with a laugh.

'*Taken*?' I ask.

'That's the one. He has a set of special skills or something...'

'Well, I can promise there'll be no weapons – other than the truth.'

She rolls her eyes.

'Too cheesy?'

'A bit.'

'How about this: who is the biggest gossip in your friendship group?'

'Bella,' she replies instantly.

'Well, then, I suggest you set up a coffee date with Bella – or whatever you young people do these days...' I tease.

She sniggers. 'You're like, what? Ten years older than me?'

'Thereabouts – closer to thirteen – but I'm an old soul.' This self-deprecation is for entertainment purposes only – to make Evie laugh, which she does. I don't actually *feel* old, especially as I'm only thirty-seven.

'Anyway,' I say, getting us back on track, 'meet up with Bella and tell her your sob story. Lay it on as thick as you can. That will get the word out. And then you will see who your true friends are.'

'And justice will be served,' she declares.

'Says the woman with a degree in social justice,' I reply, and she grins proudly. 'And I'd say it's very likely. So, does that make you feel a bit better about things?'

'So much better. Thank you, Poppy. You know, Liv and I think of you like a big sister. We just love you.'

'Oh, I... Thank you for saying that.' My tears make another appearance right as Tristan does.

'I thought— Oh no. Now *you're* crying, darling,' he says, looking helpless.

'My fault,' says Evie. 'Just telling Poppy how much Liv and I love her.'

'Oh, well, of course,' he says, crossing to the sofa. He leans down and kisses the top of my head. 'She's very lovable. You both are.' He smacks a kiss on Evie's head then strides off to the kitchen. 'Right, so am I making us dinner?'

'Yes, please,' we chorus from the sofa. Saffron must have heard the word 'dinner' because she wanders in from her room and Evie leaps off the sofa to play with her.

As I watch them, sipping my wine, I consider that 'set of special skills' I have at my disposal – namely, the agency's vast resources. I could make Tyler's life a living misery. He's just lucky I'm not Liam Neeson.

31

GRETA

I hover in the doorway to Anjali's office, waiting for her to finish a phone call. She waves me in with a smile, then mouths, 'Just wrapping up,' as she points to the phone.

I slide into the chair opposite her right as her smile falls away and she says, 'I mustn't have made myself clear – I'm not *asking*, Jerome. Amelia was explicit... *Yes*, this is coming directly from Amelia. Mmm-hmm, I thought as much. Look, I have to go – a colleague's just stepped in.' She ends the call with a shake of her head and without saying goodbye.

All these years working with Anjali and in the past few days, I've witnessed a different side to her entirely. Maybe it's me being promoted to managing editor that has fostered the shift in our relationship from (awed) subordinate and boss to something closer to peers. She did just refer to me as her colleague.

'So, Jerome...?' I ask.

'Ugh...' she groans. 'He's new – based out of New York. He's come over from *Torque Talk*.' I make a face. 'I know,' she says, rubbing between her brows. 'He's not my hire – the son of one of

Amelia's friends, apparently. But you don't need to bother with all that. What's up?'

'I was just about to pop down to The Daily Grind – did you want me to bring you back a coffee?'

Her expression shifts from annoyance to bemusement. 'That sounds innocent enough,' she says cryptically.

'Innoce— What do you mean? I only offered to get you a coffee.'

She places her elbows on her desk, steepling her fingers and resting her chin on top.

'What?' I ask again. 'Now you're making me feel self-conscious.'

'This doesn't have anything to do with a certain bloke who frequents the coffee shop, does it? The one who reminds me of that handsome Scottish actor?'

Oh no. *What* did Poppy tell Anjali? I didn't explicitly ask her not to mention Ewan to Anjali, but I'd hoped she wouldn't. And the possibility that she did feels like a betrayal.

Although, Anjali is Poppy's real client in this case, so maybe her loyalties are to Anjali, despite everything's she's told me about being her top priority.

I feel like I'm going to be ill. I spy a bin next to Anjali's desk and wonder if I'll be able to reach it in time. And now she's chuckling! *What* is going on?

'Soz, I shouldn't laugh, Greta, but your face right now. Oh, I'm being wicked, aren't I?'

Yes! She is! Give her a hooked nose and paint her green and she'd be Elphaba.

'You want to know how I know about him, the bloke from the coffee shop?' she asks, waggling her eyebrows at me.

I swallow the enormous lump lodged in my throat. 'Sure,' I say, my voice scratchy and tight.

'I saw you together – on Tuesday night.'

Well, *that's* not what I expected.

Then the full force of what she said starts to land. Tuesday night I was at the London Eye with Ewan – where we had our first kiss – a passionate, not-suitable-for-work kiss. Oh my god! Did Anjali see me kissing Ewan after the London Eye? My jaw drops in horror, and I may actually be the first person to die from embarrassment. At the very least, I'm about to vomit all over Anjali's lovely office.

I only came in to ask if she wanted a sodding coffee!

'Er…' I clear my throat. 'So, where did you see us exactly?' I ask, braving the possibility of an even *more* mortifying revelation.

'Gordon and I were at The Archduke – for dinner. It's one of our haunts.'

'OOOHHH!' It's comical how long I draw out that sound, making Anjali laugh again.

'What did you think I was talking about? Never mind – I probably don't want to know, do I?'

'Definitely not,' I reply succinctly, recovering from the single most horrifying moment of my life in record time.

'Anyway… two plus two and all that… I only realised after you'd gone that he was the bloke from the coffee shop.'

'Ewan.'

She snaps her fingers and points at me. 'That's right.' Then she tuts at herself. 'As if you'd get that wrong – soz. So, he's the mystery man you're dating?'

I nod, realising that Poppy *didn't* betray my trust, after all.

'Well, bravo, Greta Davies!'

With part-relief and part-pride, I grin and somewhere in the back of my mind, I recognise the multitude of twists and turns that this (bizarre) conversation has taken. In the entire time I've known

Anjali, this is the most personal conversation we've ever had – and that includes the one in which I confessed how much I wanted to fall in love and start a family.

'Honestly, I'm thrilled for you,' she continues. 'And he's a good bloke? Not like any of those...' She struggles to find the word. 'Those *men* you dated for the articles?'

'He's lovely. It's early days, of course, but...'

'No, no, I understand. But you let me know when it's not-so-early days. As I said, The Archduke is a favourite haunt of ours, and we could all go for dinner sometime.'

I'm taking this offer with a grain of salt. Anjali's still my boss and going on a double date with her and Gordon... It's hard to imagine.

'Right, so I should probably...' She gestures towards her laptop, meaning she should get back to work, and I pop out of my seat, grateful to be excused.

'Of course. And where did we land on coffee?' I ask. 'Yea or nay?'

'Oh, definitely yea. And one of those fancy croissant/doughnut thingamajigs, if you don't mind.'

'Cronuts.'

'Is that what they're called?'

'Mmm-hmm.'

'How clever.'

Anjali's phone rings and I leave her to answer it. On the way out of her office, it occurs to me that I didn't tell her about Ewan owning The Daily Grind. I'll fill her in when I get back.

* * *

It's even busier than usual, but Ewan isn't working behind the counter today; he must be in his windowless office. I queue up, doing multiple sweeps of The Daily Grind when I spy him – not Ewan, but the bloke who's *not* an MI6 agent. He's cosied up at my favourite table talking to a woman who has her back to me.

As I progress in the queue, I watch them – well, *him*, as all I can tell about her is that she makes him laugh – a lot – and that he seems keen on her, nodding along as she talks and smiling across the table.

Oh, they might be on a date!

I wonder if this is what life will be like now – I'm embroiled in a romance, so I'll see the signs of romance everywhere I go.

There's a gentle touch on my shoulder and I turn. This time it's him! *The* him.

'Hi,' says Ewan.

'Hi.' It's unclear what the done thing is regarding kissing in a busy coffee shop – especially when one of you owns it. We settle on smiling at each other.

'Perfect timing,' he says. 'There's someone I want you to meet – a friend of mine. We're over in the corner, so join us when you've got your coffee.'

'Great,' I reply, even though I've promised a coffee to Anjali and staying will mean it'll be cold by the time I get back. I suppose I could heat it up in the staff kitchen – it's only a long black.

Eventually, I have my order and I cast my eyes about for Ewan. In the furthest corner, away from the window, he's standing next to a table and talking to someone I can't see. I approach.

'Ewan?' I say, and he turns with a bright smile.

'Greta, I want you to meet an old mate of mine. He's just come in to say hello.'

When he steps aside, there's a seismic shift in the universe. I gasp, nearly dropping the cardboard tray of coffee and cronuts.

'Harrison?'

'Greta?' he asks, clearly confused.

'Wait, have you two met?' asks Ewan.

We all look at each other, our eyes darting about in confusion and (for me) horror. This is far worse than thinking Anjali might have seen me kissing Ewan by the London Eye.

And after a pause so pregnant it could birth quadruplets, Harrison says the worst thing he could possibly say in this situation. 'Yes, we had a date over the weekend.'

'A date?' Ewan barely gets the words out.

'Yes...' Harrison must finally realise what he's said. 'Oh, wait... *you're* the woman Ewan's been telling me about.'

I gulp, reaching for any words that might make this situation better. But none come to mind, and I'm left gawping like a proverbial fish out of water, my mouth working but no sounds coming out.

'Greta? You're dating my friend?'

'No!' I say vehemently, finally finding my voice.

'Mate, it was one date,' says Harrison reassuringly. 'It didn't work out – we're not seeing each other again.'

He's clearly trying to make it better, but from the look on Ewan's face, he isn't.

'You're— But how did you two *meet*?'

'Through a matchmaking agency,' Harrison replies.

Gah! Harrison, you're not helping.

'A matchmaking ag— What are you talking about?' Ewan asks Harrison, incredulous. He turns to me. 'What is he talking about?'

'Technically, we did meet through an agency, but it was for an assignment – a writing assignment,' I say, fudging the truth a little.

'What?' they ask in unison.

Bollocks, why did I say that?

'You went out with me for a writing assignment?' asks Harrison.

Ewan shakes his head in disbelief. 'Greta... I don't... *What*? I thought you were writing about obsessions?'

'I wish you'd told me,' says Harrison, interrupting Ewan, but I'm not listening to him. I'm focussed on Ewan, who looks like he's on the verge of tears – furious ones.

'Ewan, I'm sorry. Please let me—'

He holds up his hand, his gaze fixed on the floor. 'This is a lot to take in right now and I... I need to go.'

And before I know what's happening or how to stop it, he's made his way through the crowded coffee shop – stopping briefly at the counter to talk to an employee – then stepped out onto the Strand.

'Oh god. What just happened?' I whisper to myself.

Harrison glowers at me. 'I had no idea you were the woman from the coffee shop.' I meet his eye. 'Or that you were dating my friend when you went out with me – *or* that you only did that to *write* about me,' he says, an angry edge to his voice.

'I wasn't— I didn't—'

Only I was, and I did... Well, to borrow a phrase from Anjali, *ish*.

'Please let me explain,' I say, sliding into the chair opposite him.

He sighs and signals for me to go ahead.

'I promise, I had no idea Ewan felt the way he did until very recently – this week, in fact. I thought we were spending time together as friends. But then, when I realised... I discovered *I* had feelings for *him*. And you were lovely and all, but us not fancying each other – that was mutual, right? I mean, we messaged each other...'

'No, you're right – I'll give you that. But what's this writing assignment?'

Every second I spend here explaining my actions to Harrison is a second I'm not going after Ewan. But he's also an old friend of Ewan's and if there's any chance I can fix this, then I need to make nice with Harrison.

I also need to avoid spinning any further lies because those will just keep following me. I've become a duplicitous little liar and it's time to stop!

'All right, look, I *was* assigned to go on dates by my editor,' I say. 'But most of them were—'

'Most? How many dates was this?'

'Including you – five.'

'Five!'

'You're making it sound like I was traipsing about with half of London. Four of the dates were with unsuitable matches – on purpose!'

'You've lost me.'

'It was part of the assignment,' I explain, but I'm losing patience.

'And me?'

'There was every chance you could have been a match, but if you were... Just keep in mind I had no idea how Ewan felt about me at the time.'

He regards me sceptically.

'He didn't even tell you my name. Do you think he was openly declaring his feelings to me, but I was what – just ignoring him so I could go on *one date* with you? I mean, you're a catch – granted – but...'

My words finally sink in and he snorts out a laugh, the tension between us evaporating instantly.

'No, you're right. Ewan does play things close to his chest – especially since he and Sally... Oh, sorry,' he says, shifting uncomfortably in his chair.

'What is it about you two and thinking that mentioning his ex is so criminal? Ewan's in his early forties. Most people in their early forties have an ex. *You* do.'

Only when I say that do I realise Harrison must know Sally.

'Fair,' he concedes. 'God, can you imagine if we *had* been a fit? It would have been a bloody awkward conversation when I asked Ewan to be my best man.'

'What? You're *that* close?'

He nods. 'Best mates at uni – we met before I switched from commerce to teaching. Look, he'd kill me if he knew I was telling you this, but he's been talking about you for weeks. He's really keen on you, Greta.'

'Well, good! It took me some time to realise, but I feel the same way. Actually, going out with you helped me see it.'

'Um, thank you?'

'You know what I mean,' I say, and we exchange smiles. 'Can I just ask... He talked about me for weeks, but he never told you my name?'

'He said he didn't want to jinx things.'

'Jinx thi–– Something to unpack another time, perhaps. Look, I really want to... you know, go after him.'

'Oh! Yes, go, *go*!' he practically shouts.

'I will, but... are *we* all right? I promise, I won't be writing about our date.'

'Well, *good*, and yes, we're all right.'

That's one thing off my mind, but I still have a lukewarm coffee and a pastry to deliver. I also have no idea where Ewan would go. 'I could just go to his,' I mutter under my breath.

'He probably wouldn't head home – not right away,' says Harrison, who must have heard me. 'He tends to walk when he's upset, sometimes for hours.'

'Oh, okay. Thank you.'

We stand and he gives me a hug, which with our height

discrepancy is like a giant engulfing a pixie. With a wan smile, I collect my tray of coffee and cronuts.

'Bye,' I say.

'Bye, Greta, and good luck.'

I head back to the office to ask Anjali for the afternoon off. I need to find potential number two and ask him to be my number one.

32

GRETA

'Oh, you *are* in a pickle,' says Anjali, describing my predicament perfectly. She takes a sip of her coffee, then frowns and puts it down. With the urgency, I didn't have time to reheat it. 'So, what are you going to do?' she asks.

All I've told her is that Ewan and one of my agency dates know each other, and I've given a truncated recap of the scene in The Daily Grind. But if I'm owning up to all my lies and secrets, I need to own up to the secret I've been keeping from Anjali.

I take a deep breath. 'Before I ask for the afternoon off so I can sort this out,' I say. 'Sorry – I meant to come to that later.'

'You can have the afternoon off, Greta,' she says, which I appreciate but am also a little surprised by, unless... Of *course*! Anjali is as committed to my relationship with Ewan – such that it is – as I am. 'But there was something else?' she prompts.

'Yes. And thank you – for the time off.' I'm stalling. 'Anjali,' I say with a sigh, 'I know the real reason you brought Poppy on and gave me that assignment.'

There, I've said it.

She sits back, clearly taken off-guard. 'Did Poppy tell you? She wasn't supposed to say anything.'

'No, I worked it out. And then I asked Poppy not to tell you I knew, because I *so* appreciated the thought behind your scheme— Oh, er...' Calling it a 'scheme' may not be the most flattering characterisation of what Anjali did. 'Your *plan*.'

She waves her hand. 'Don't worry, it was a scheme of sorts. I told myself it was for a noble cause, wanting you to be happy, but... Greta, I think I owe you an apology.'

'An apology?' Well, this is unexpected.

'Yes. Almost immediately, I started having doubts that I'd done the right thing. I even said something to Poppy the first time she and I met – about it being patronising of me to assume I knew what was best for you.'

'No, that's— It wasn't patronising.'

'You're being very forgiving. But in hindsight, I think it was, and I'm sorry. And you were *such* a good sport, going on all those awful dates...'

'Well, a few of them were awful, but a couple of the men I met were lovely – including Ewan's friend – just not for me. And, as Poppy says, there's merit in kissing some frogs to help narrow down what you want in a relationship. And I hadn't been near a pond in *years* before I met Poppy! Sorry, I really flogged that metaphor, didn't I?'

'Or "frogged" it,' she says with a cheeky smile.

'Oh no,' I groan.

'That bad?'

'Is there such a thing as "mum jokes"?'

'My children would tell you there is. They don't think I'm funny at all. But back to you,' she says, serious again.

My stomach does a flip. It's all very well masking my true feelings with humour, but the real reason behind this conversation makes me ill.

'How are you going to sort things out with Ewan?' she presses when I don't say anything.

'First, I need him to respond to my messages. I've already sent two and nothing.'

'Can I see?'

I hesitate, then quickly decide I need all the help I can get – especially as Tiggy's leading a design workshop all day for her biggest client and is unreachable. I unlock my phone and hand it to Anjali so she can read the two messages I sent on my way back to *Nouveau*:

I am so sorry. Please let me explain. Can I meet you?

I'll come to you. Just let me know where. Xxx

'Well?' I ask.

Anjali frowns slightly and purses her lips – her thinking face.

'There you are, Grets!'

At hearing my name, I twist in my chair. Luca. Leaning against the doorframe.

'Sorry, Luca, not now. We're in crisis mode here,' says Anjali. Talking about 'fudging the truth' – she's made it sound like a work crisis.

'Oh. Anything I can help with?' he asks, stepping into Anjali's office.

'No,' we say together.

'But thank you,' Anjali adds, smiling at him sweetly.

'Was it urgent?' I ask. 'What you wanted me for?'

'Er, no,' he replies. 'Just wanted to show you how that spread turned out – the one you helped me with a couple of weeks back.'

'I'll be sure to come and find you, then,' I say. 'But it won't be till tomorrow.'

Luca's eyebrows jump an inch. He isn't used to being fobbed off, especially by someone who crushed on him for years. Maybe now he'll get the message.

'Right. Er, thanks. I'll just...' He gives us a lipless smile, then leaves.

'That was... intriguing,' says Anjali. When I turn back to her, she's eyeing me curiously.

'Oh, it was just one of his fashion shoots – I helped him with a decision.'

'I don't mean Luca. I mean you. You're *actually* over him, aren't you?'

'Oh, 100 per cent. Ever since he made a play for Tiggy, then got all stroppy when she turned him down.'

Anjali mouth falls open in surprise. 'I had no idea. I thought you'd just grown tired of him. Anyway, Luca's a darling, but he's never deserved you. Too much of a cad.'

'That's exactly what Tiggy said,' I reply. I still can't believe I wasted so much time on him.

'Right,' says Anjali, 'getting back to you and Ewan. What do we do next?'

'We?'

'Look, I got you into this mess in the first place – if it weren't for my meddling, you'd be loved up with Ewan by now – and all your own doing. So, I'm going to help. Oh!' she exclaims. 'We should call Poppy. She'll know what to do.'

'I don't know why I didn't think of that before.'

'Tell her we can come to her. I'll clear my schedule.'

'You don't have to—'

'Greta, please. Let me help – as my apology.'

'Okay.' I leave Anjali's office and head towards my own, my thoughts returning to Ewan. His face when he discovered I'd gone out with Harrison... My stomach flips again at the memory and by the time I reach my office, I'm in full panic mode.

What if he can't get past what I've done and everything I've kept from him? What if meeting with Poppy is moot and he's already decided to move on?

'Well, you've at least got to try, Greta,' I tell myself.

* * *

Poppy

As soon as they arrive, I lead Anjali and Greta to Paloma's office where she and George are waiting.

When she called earlier, Greta told me that she and Anjali spoke at length, and now everyone knows everything. So that's one less thing to worry about.

They also seem to be on good terms, meaning their relationship has withstood the circuitous fibbing this case has required. That doesn't always happen. Even with Tristan, our relationship was tainted by duplicity. We got past it, him being angry after he discovered an intricate 'fib' I'd told, but it wasn't pretty.

We get situated on the sofas in Paloma's office, with me seated next to Greta, angled towards her. Almost immediately, her everything's-all-right façade falls away.

This shift in countenance is understandable. This morning, she was riding the high of a new relationship, then the situation took an unanticipated – and alarming – turn.

'First things first,' I say to her gently. 'Have you heard from Ewan since you called?'

She nods slowly, her brow furrowed. Right, so even though she's heard from him, it's not good.

'I have, but he said he needs some time to think,' she replies, her voice tight. 'At least a few days.'

'And how do you feel about that?' I ask.

She begins to breathe noisily through her nose as she stares at the coffee table between the sofas. 'I feel... stupid and guilty and...'

'Hey.' I reach across to place my hand on her arm. 'You're not stupid.'

Anjali echoes the sentiment with a reassuring pat on Greta's hand.

'Then why didn't I see it sooner?' she asks, lifting her gaze. 'I wouldn't have gone out with Harrison and—'

'Greta, hang on,' I interject before she spirals. 'You've only known Ewan for just over a month now and from what you've told me, friendship was foremost on your mind. He didn't tell you otherwise, so you can't be blamed for not guessing what was in his head.'

'Or his heart,' chimes in George.

'Exactly,' I concur.

'I suppose,' she mumbles gloomily.

'And you know, many solid romantic relationships are founded on friendship,' I say, thinking of Tristan again. We may have started out as client/agent, but that quickly evolved into friendship, then something more.

'Mine is,' offers Anjali. 'I don't know that I would have fancied Gordon if we hadn't been friends first. We met through mutual friends and the more time we spent together, the more I appreciated his wit and good humour, his intelligence... And one day, I realised I found him wildly attractive. That's when I knew I had to be with him.'

'Apparently, my husband fancied me for over a *year* before he confessed his feelings,' adds Paloma. 'Before that, I just thought of him as my work husband. Sometimes people find it difficult to reveal how they feel. It's definitely not on you that you were unaware of Ewan's feelings – even if there were signs.'

'Were there signs, do you think?' asks George. 'In retrospect?'

'In retrospect, yes,' Greta replies. 'But I'm such a novice at all this, I didn't *see* them.' She stops, obviously checking herself.

'No, that's entirely true. I did notice him flirting with me a few times, but I told myself it was my imagination, or that it was just part of our budding friendship. I'm realising, only as I say this, that it was more likely because Ewan having feelings for me didn't fit in with the narrative I'd created in my head – that *Harrison* was my perfect match.'

This is highly astute of Greta to realise – very self-aware – but she's winding herself up again.

'That's also understandable,' I tell her. 'Emotions are complex, and every person brings their own experiences and hopes and fears to a relationship.'

'So, not knowing right away that I fancied him?' she asks me.

'Not guilty,' I reply.

She expels a sigh. 'But I did lie to him – about the articles and going on dates. I need to be honest with him about that – if he ever talks to me again.'

'He will,' says George assuredly.

'Most *likely*,' I add, shooting him a look. There *is* a chance Ewan could walk away from Greta entirely, slim though it may be, and we shouldn't peddle false hope.

'Almost definitely,' he clarifies.

'Wait,' says Anjali and we all look to her. 'What if I explained to Ewan that I gave you the assignment – that you were just following orders?'

Uh, yeah, no, I think. I can tell Anjali wants to take responsibility for her part in this, but I don't think her suggestion is the way to go. 'That might be a little...' I look to Paloma for help.

'It's inappropriate, Anji,' she tells her.

'Of course. Too "here's a note from my mummy",' Anjali replies.

'Precisely,' Paloma replies, and I'm glad we've curtailed that potential detour before it gained traction.

'But what *do* I do?' Greta asks Paloma. 'Do I just... message him again in a few days and hope he'll talk to me? What if he won't?'

Greta raising the what-if-Ewan-wants-to-call-it-quits? question again is valid.

'Well...' Paloma looks to me.

'We'll cross that bridge if we come to it. But, in the meantime, Ewan needs to know exactly what happened *and* how you feel about him, so he can make an informed decision.'

'You mean decide whether he wants to be with me,' she states simply.

'Yes.'

We're all quiet for a moment, then Greta lifts her head and sits up straighter. 'I think I have something.' She quickly looks at us in turn. 'I'm a writer, aren't I? I should write to him.'

'Oh, I love that,' says George, and Greta breaks into a smile.

'A stellar idea,' says Anjali.

'And writing to him... I'll be telling him how I feel, but still giving him space, right?' Greta asks me.

'Exactly,' I reply.

Paloma gets up and goes to her desk, returning with a notepad and pen. Greta takes it and starts scribbling hurriedly while we all watch. I look up and catch Paloma's eye with a questioning shrug. She mouths, 'We should go,' which is a generous offer considering this is her office.

'Why don't the rest of us give you some privacy,' I say, prompting the others to leave.

Greta barely looks up, mumbling her thanks and the rest of us leave the office. Now, we wait…

33

GRETA

This may be the most important piece of writing of my life. No, forget 'may be' – it is. Because the thought of losing Ewan for good, when we've only just embarked on a romantic relationship, makes me feel ill. This *has* to work.

I'm vaguely aware that the others left a while back and when I lift my head to check the time, nearly an hour has passed. I quickly read over my letter, satisfied with my first draft.

But it will need to be perfect.

I tear off the pages I've filled and put them into my handbag, then leave the pad and pen on Paloma's desk. When I open the door to the open-plan office, it's humming with activity. I spy Poppy at her desk reading something on her laptop and make my way over.

'Hello.'

'Oh, hi,' she says with a warm smile. 'How'd you go?'

'Good, I think. A start anyway. I should probably head back to work, though, see out the day. I've got some résumés to look through.'

'Will you be able to concentrate?' she asks.

'I think so – now we have a plan and I've got my thoughts down. I still need to revise it, of course – and I want to run it past Tiggy…'

'Always a good idea to get your bestie's point of view,' she replies. 'Mine's still a psychologist; she's never shy about giving her advice – solicited or not.'

We share a laugh. 'Tiggy and I are nothing alike, but I think that helps, her having a unique perspective on things.'

'Absolutely.'

'I'll go – I don't want to keep you any longer than necessary.'

'Oh, I'm just helping vet some potentials. You're my *client*, Greta. You're still my number-one priority until the case is officially closed.'

I don't ask what will determine that. Other than me ending up with Ewan, I don't want to even *consider* what would constitute 'case closed'.

'Thank you,' I say instead. 'I suppose that makes me your client-*ish*.'

'There you go,' she says with a grin. She leans closer and lowers her voice. 'She does say that a lot.'

'Anjali?'

'Yeah.'

'You get used to it.'

I'm dawdling, but I know it's because I feel safe here – in the agency, with Poppy. And once I step outside, I'm on my own.

Yes, I have a whole slew of people supporting me from the sidelines, but it's solely up to me to deliver – literally, as I'll be the one dropping off my letter to Ewan's – and I need to do this on my own.

'Well, bye, Poppy. I'll keep you updated.'

She reaches up and lightly clasps my forearm. 'You've got this, Greta. And I'm here if you need me – any time of day. I'll even go over there with you to deliver it if you like.'

It's a generous offer, but I meant what I told myself just now. I need to do this on my own.

'Thanks, Poppy.'

And with that, I head out into the sunshine to catch the Tube back to *Nouveau*.

* * *

I watch Tiggy closely as she reads, clocking every nuanced twitch, brow furrow, and utterance. She reads the letter three times, back to back, before she looks up.

'It's good.'

'Really?' I ask with a relieved sigh.

'Really. I've read everything you've ever written, remember, and this,' she says, holding up the pages, 'is top tier. It does need to be cleaned up a bit...'

'Of course, it's only the first draft but... Will it work, do you think?'

'Well, I've never actually met the bloke, so it's hard to say...'

'No, I know, I know.' I leap up and go to the kitchen, where I swing open the fridge and study the contents.

'I will say this,' Tiggy says, having followed me. She gently reaches around me to close the fridge and I peer up at her. 'It's not just good, it's *beautiful*.'

'It is? I mean, that's what I was aiming for.'

'Well, you've succeeded.'

I exhale a sigh of relief.

'And if he doesn't fall instantly in love with you after reading it, he has no soul.'

This makes me laugh. Though, it could be nervous laughter, as I've been a wreck since I left the office. I was fine throwing myself into work – editing an article by one of our contributors, advising

Lisa on a pull quote, *and* even during a quick impromptu meeting with finance. But once I stepped outside the office...

All I could think of, all I could *picture*, was Ewan's expression when Harrison told him about our date.

'What?' asks Tiggy. 'You've got a strange look on your face.'

'I can't believe it's still today.'

'Huh?'

'It was only this morning that I went to The Daily Grind to see Ewan... Then everything exploded. Or *im*ploded.'

'It's been a day, that's for sure,' she commiserates.

'It's been a *fortnight* in a day,' I retort. 'This morning feels like it happened ages ago. Do you think he's home yet?' I ask, changing the subject.

Tiggy gently takes me by both shoulders. 'Again, I've never met Ewan. I have no idea if he'd be home yet.'

'Right, of course – sorry.'

She drops her hands and I move past her and go back to the lounge.

'So, when are you planning on taking it to him?'

I flop onto the sofa while Tiggy leans against the breakfast bar.

'I keep going back and forth,' I say. 'It still needs polish, as you said, but I could do that first thing in the morning – let it marinade overnight and approach it with fresh eyes. I also haven't decided if I want to place it in Ewan's hands or somehow leave it in his mail-box. Tomorrow night, maybe.'

'I'll go with you if you like? To drop it off.'

'I thought you had a date.'

'Babes, my "dates" are hook-ups and none of them mean a thing next to you.'

'Thanks, Tiggy, but I don't know. I keep going back and forth. Poppy offered too, but I think I need to go alone – in case he *is* home. Maybe he'll talk to me.'

'Whatever you decide.' She yawns loudly and I look up from the coffee table, which I've caught myself staring at – again. God, I really am inside my head. My eyes flick towards the clock: 8.08 p.m.

'Have you eaten? I've just realised, I didn't have dinner – or lunch. I'm hungry. Are you hungry?'

She crosses to me, her hand extended. 'Hello, Tiggy Marsh. I don't believe we've met.'

'Hilarious,' I say, swatting her hand away. 'So that's a yes, then.'

She flops down next to me. 'If you're buying, that's always a yes.'

* * *

The early-morning Uber ride to Ewan's is an out-of-body experience.

The streets of London are a surreal blur, yet punctuated with these distinctive details that leap out at me. A red postbox, gleaming as if freshly polished. The faded paint of a yellow box junction on the road, still doing its job of keeping an intersection clear. A sixty-something woman wearing a red vest on a corner selling *The Big Issue* to commuters, smiling at passers-by. A huddle of smokers outside a BeanVibes (the sad bastards – both for the smoking and drinking sub-par coffee). Shopkeepers sweeping the footpaths outside their shops, stopping to chat to each other. Shiny back doors of terrace houses flanked by topiaries. Double-decker buses 'merging' into traffic. The meandering Thames dotted with barges.

I notice these details with a proud interest. They encompass London. They *are* London.

I love this city.

I've toyed with the idea of an overseas stint – an adult gap year, or two – but I suspect that even if it eventuates, I'd be happy to return to London. It's home.

And as true as they may be, these thoughts are also an effective distraction from my building nerves – make that panic. Because I am about to lay my heart bare.

The car pulls up outside Ewan's at 7.32 a.m. and I take a deep, bracing breath.

I've had less than five hours of fitful sleep, and have been up since four, revising my letter. I've shown up straight from the shower wearing leggings and a long-sleeved T-shirt, with my hair tucked behind my ears and no make-up.

I am as ready as I will ever be to face the man who may or may not be – but I really hope is – the love of my life.

By bedtime last night, I'd decided to leave the letter at Ewan's while he was at work, then message him to say, 'Check your mailbox!' But in the wee hours of this morning, as I climbed out of bed, exhausted but wired, I knew I had to deliver it in person.

Ewan deserves that.

I deserve that.

'Thank you,' I say to the driver as we arrive.

I climb out and look up at Ewan's building. My stomach is doing gymnastics, but I don't waver. I walk up the short flight of steps and press the buzzer to his flat. There's a security camera on the console and I know that as soon as he answers, he'll be able to see me.

Three rings, and nothing.

Bollocks. His shop manager usually opens The Daily Grind, but maybe he went in early.

'Yes? Oh, hi,' he says, his voice falling off the cliff of disappointment. He must have answered before he realised it was me.

'Hi,' I say.

Remy barks twice in the background. 'Shush, Remy,' he says.

It's strange not being able to see him but knowing he can see me. I take a bracing breath.

Be brave, Greta, I will myself.

'I know you asked for some time, but... I wrote you something,' I say, holding up an envelope. 'I just wanted to drop it off.'

He doesn't respond so I keep talking. 'I understand if it's too late but I...' My breath hitches and tears flood my eyes. Maybe it wasn't a good idea showing up sleep-deprived and desperate.

'Sorry,' I continue, talking to the silence. There's a loud beep and then absolute silence, and it takes me a moment to realise we've been cut off.

'Fuck!' I stab in the number of Ewan's flat a second time. It rings and rings and then the three loud beeps sound again. 'Fuckety fuck fuck!' I shout *right* as a well-dressed, elderly woman exits the building, giving me a look that would turn me to stone if this were a Greek myth.

'Sorry, madam,' I say feebly. 'Ahhh, fuck,' I whisper to myself.

'Greta?'

It's him.

He's half in, half out of the building's front door wearing an oversized Take That T-shirt and tracksuit bottoms.

'Hi,' I say, dragging my eyes from the T-shirt to his face. 'Robbie or Gary?' I ask.

'Sorry?'

I drop my gaze to the T-shirt, then he realises. 'Oh, uh, neither. My mum was a Mark Owen fan, so...'

'Ewan, I'm so, *so* sorry.'

'I understand.'

'You do?'

'Well, no, actually. It's just what you say, isn't it?'

We look at each other, the silence taking form, and my eyes rove the features of his face, memorising it in case I never see him again. Oh god – he owns the coffee shop half a block from *Nouveau*. What if I run into him by accident, just going about my day?

Be brave, Greta, my mind whispers again.

'I brought you this,' I say, holding out the envelope. 'I wrote it. For you.'

He takes it and a microscopic part of me rejoices.

He looks at it, turning it over in his hands. 'Thanks,' he says quietly.

'You don't have to read it now…'

'I wasn't…'

Our voices fall away.

'I should go. I've got work,' I say, ignoring that I didn't ask my driver to wait and now I'm stranded.

'Yeah, me too.'

'Can't keep the caffeine addicts waiting,' I say. I smile, even though on the amusement scale, that was barely a one out of ten.

'Right.' He holds up the envelope. 'Thanks for this.'

'You're welcome.'

'Bye, Greta.'

And then he's gone, the door to the building closing behind him, and I'm left standing on a doorstep in Central London, wondering if that's it.

Ewan,

It's a funny thing, the moment you realise something's missing.

You can have the fullest life – the career you've always dreamt of, close family ties, a best friend who's like a sister, colleagues you adore. You can live in the most beautiful city in *the world, have a wardrobe full of clothes, and a lovely flat with a leafy aspect.*

You can have all these things – all these people in your life – and one day, it occurs to you that you also want to be in love.

And not just the romcom version of love with its Sunday breakfasts at the dining table, sun streaming in the window, or playful visits to Portobello Market to try on silly hats and laugh at each other, or all the other parts of a romcom movie montage.

You want real love.

You want difficult conversations about ex-partners, and not-so-perfect love scenes where noses crash as you kiss, but the connection – physical and emotional – is real. You want to learn about each other gradually, conversing about trivial anecdotes that make you laugh, and big ideas that form the foundation of who you are.

You want the anticipation of seeing them, the warmth of being in their presence, the delight of making them laugh, the assuredness that you will be there when they need you – because when you love someone, it's never a case of 'if' but 'when'.

You want to grow together and explore – the world and life and all its possibilities – and perhaps one day create a family, first of two – or three, if there's a beloved pet – then having a child, maybe two.

You want to lay yourself bare and say, 'This is me. I'm kind and generous and selfish and vain. I'm clever and sometimes stupid and driven but also stuck and needing a nudge. I am awake to the wonders of this world but blind to what is in front of me.

I'm me – flawed, imperfect, but open and willing and wanting.

Wanting you.

If you will have me.

If you will let me explain.

If you will consider forgiving me.'

You want to say all these things when you're on the brink of falling in love with someone and have behaved badly.

You want to be given a second chance because you're so unbelievably sorry – for not being truthful, for failing to see what you had, for being swept up by a construct of what you thought you wanted…

You want to say all this and be forgiven and start again with, 'Hi, I'm Greta. So nice to meet you…' and with hope in your heart, see where it can go.

I'm so sorry, Ewan. Please can we start again?

Love,

Greta x

34

GRETA

Yes, I am showing up to work in leggings and a T-shirt, sans make-up and sporting a hair-don't rather than a hairdo.

I arrive before most people, but the few that are in the office give me odd looks as I pass. Roger from accounting says, 'Hi, Greta,' so cheerfully, it's clear he's overcompensating for my appearance.

I don't care.

When I get to my office, I proceed with my usual routine – log onto my laptop, check my calendar for the day, read emails... I could definitely go for a coffee, but the thought of showing up at The Daily Grind sours my already fragile stomach.

'Focus on work, Greta.' It's the sole reason I'm here, after all – to distract myself.

I could have called in sick – Anjali would have been okay with it – but what would I *do* all day? Lie about my flat, moaning? I doubt even bingeing old seasons of *Britain's Best Bakers* would be enough to distract me.

As I trawl through my inbox, an email subject line catches my eye: 'APOLOGY', written in all caps. It's from an unknown email address, one that doesn't include even part of a person's name, making it impossible to identify who it's from.

'Oh no, what if it's Ewan?' I whisper.

We've never exchanged email addresses – no need as we've always messaged each other – so it *could* be from him.

APOLOGY

Maybe he's responding to *my* apology. Maybe *he's* apologising, although I don't know what for. My heart starts hammering and my breath becomes raspy and shallow. An email. If he wanted to accept my apology and start again, wouldn't he ask to meet in person?

An email can't be good.

My mouse pointer hovers directly over it, but I can't make myself click on it.

Instead, I slam my laptop shut and dig my phone out of my handbag to make a call.

'It is literally the crack of dawn,' says a sleepy Tiggy.

'You're too old to use the word "literally" non-literally,' I quip, and she chuckles.

'What's up?' she asks. I hear the rustle of bed clothes – though with Tiggy, they could be hers or someone else's.

'I need you to get dressed and come to *Nouveau*.'

'Now?'

'Yes, right now. Immediately, if not sooner.'

She groans.

'Where are you? Are you at home?' I ask, doing a quick calculation. Even if she left her flat in the next five minutes, she still wouldn't be here inside an hour.

'Nope,' she says, raising my hopes about her getting here sooner.

'Are you close, then?' I prod. Can she not sense the urgency in my voice?

'I'm in Soho.' I hear a muffled voice, then a loud yawn, then, 'Be there in thirty.' Even from Soho, that's optimistic, but I'll take it.

'Thank you, Tig.'

'Wait, why am I coming?' she asks.

'I dropped off the letter and now there's an email in my inbox from an unknown sender titled "Apology". I can't read it without you here. What if it's Ewan telling me it's over – for good?'

'Be there as soon as I can.'

I set down my phone.

'Now what?' I ask myself. I don't want to continue reading my emails – it will be torturous staying away from 'APOLOGY' – and I can't just sit here for the next half an hour. I'll go bonkers.

I may not want to step foot in The Daily Grind, but this is the middle of London and you can't swing a dead cat without hitting a coffee shop. I grab my handbag and head out, turning right as I exit the building instead of left, and walking purposefully towards the nearest coffee shop in the opposite direction to Ewan's.

It's a BeanVibes but I don't care – as emotionally spent as I am, I may be beyond caring about anything ever again.

I queue up, place my order, and hover near the pickup station. It's ready in record time and I take a sip as I step onto the Strand. The coffee is bitter and burnt and the milk is scalding – perfect penance for me cocking up what could have been exactly what I wanted.

I'm outside of *Nouveau*, about to turn into the building, when a voice stops me in my tracks.

'Greta.'

I look towards the voice and it's Ewan.

'Hi,' he says.

'Hi,' I say back.

'I'm glad you're here,' he says cryptically. 'I thought you might head home but then, your office is closer, so I tried here first and… Here you are.'

'Here I am,' I say numbly.

Showing up at Ewan's flat this morning was a surreal experience, but him standing before me outside *Nouveau*, still wearing his Take That T-shirt, takes 'surreal' to the next level. It feels like time is standing still, but the ground below us is moving.

'You cheating on me?' he asks with a half-smile.

'*What?*' I reply, mortified. 'No, I—'

'Sorry,' he says, holding up his hand in conciliation. 'Poor joke. I was talking about the coffee.' His eyes flick to my hand where 'BeanVibes' is stamped in garish letters on the side of the cup.

'Oh, right. It's rubbish.'

'Well, yeah.'

We hold each other's gaze for a moment, then I look away. It must have gone 8.30 a.m. by now and we're standing in a thoroughfare, people streaming past us as they head into the building. This is not the place to have a conversation – *this* conversation.

'I read your letter,' he says, retrieving it from his back pocket.

'I know.'

'You know? How?'

'Your email.'

He shakes his head, his eyes narrowing in confusion. 'I didn't… I haven't sent an email.'

'Oh.' Now I'm confused.

'What email?' he asks.

'It… it doesn't matter.'

We're quiet again. Someone jostles me as they walk past, and I have an idea about where we can go.

'Come with me,' I say.

I walk into the building, skirting past the bank of lifts and heading through a glass door into the atrium. It's as tall as the building and filled with towering palms in enormous pots. I cross to a stone bench and sit. I didn't check to see that Ewan was following me, but he was. He perches on the other end of the bench, facing me.

'We were at the part where you said you read my letter.'

'Right, yes...' He appears to be gathering his thoughts, which is fair considering I've just relocated us and probably interrupted his thought process. 'Well, first off, it was... it was beautifully written.'

We exchange brief smiles.

'It was also honest and *real*... But, Greta, there's an aspect I'm not comfortable with – your apology.'

'Oh.' I drop my gaze, fixating on the granite tiles, how perfectly they're laid. I try to gulp in air and swallow at the same time, which makes me choke on my saliva and induces a violent coughing fit. Ewan stands to reach around and pat me on the back – just like he did when I nearly choked on a cronut at The Daily Grind.

'All right?' he asks when the coughing abates.

I nod my reply, still unable to look at him. If he's not comfortable with my apology, then I have my answer. We're over before we even began.

I also need to find a new coffee shop.

'Can I explain?' he asks, sitting again.

'Of course.'

'The reason your apology doesn't sit well with me is that this – this situation, our misunderstanding – wasn't just your fault. I share in the blame – in fact, I own most of it.'

'What?' I meet his eye and he's watching me intently.

Only now do I notice that his (beautiful) blue eyes are rimmed with red and showing the signs of a sleepless night. Mine must look similar, but I haven't looked in a mirror this morning to know for sure.

He inches towards me and picks up my hand, running his

thumb along the back. 'I should have told you how I felt, rather than playing things so close to my chest.'

The dense mass of fear and sadness lodged in the pit of my stomach starts to dissolve, replaced with something warmer and lighter – hope, perhaps.

Is he saying what I think he's saying?

'Especially after that first night,' he continues, 'when we ran into each other at Dalla Terra. I was already smitten by then, just from your visits to The Daily Grind, and I should have just... *told* you.'

'Smitten?' I ask, teasing him.

'A smitten kitten,' he says with a smile. Serious again, he squeezes my hand. 'You know, coming here, I had this whole speech planned – well, it was kind of all over the place – much like what I'm saying now. The poor Uber driver – not to mention *Remy*...'

'Remy?'

'I tried it out on him first. He was really cross with me for walking out on you yesterday.'

'He's wise beyond his dog years,' I say, making a feeble joke.

Ewan smiles gently, then looks deep into my eyes.

'Greta, I'm really sorry. It's been over ten years since I dated someone new and I clearly have no idea what the fuck I'm doing.'

'That's not tr—'

'It *is* true. Beyond being good company, I keep mess—'

'*Exceptionally* good company,' I interject.

'That's kind. You're kind.'

'And selfish and vain,' I remind him, quoting my letter.

'Everyone is at least a little bit selfish. No one is purely altruistic. Besides, I like that side of you.'

'Selfishness?'

'*Or* we call it drive and determination and *independence*. Those are traits I value, that I *want* in a partner.'

'Okay,' I reply softly, my mind latching onto the meaning behind his words. Ewan wants me. Suddenly, it feels as if my heart has sprouted wings and is about to burst from my chest and take flight.

He runs his thumb along the back of my hand again, his eyes boring into mine. 'So, will you accept my apology? For not telling you how I was feeling – and sooner?'

'That depends.'

His face falls, his disappointment evident.

'On,' I say, hurrying to expound, 'whether you're willing to tell me now.'

'Tell you— Ahh,' he says, breaking into a smile. 'Well, as previously mentioned, I'm smitten.' He leans closer. 'I also really want to see where this can go, Greta. I can picture a future with you *so* clearly. I think we'd have a wonderful life together – whatever it brings.'

'Even bizarre writing assignments?'

'As long as they don't require you to date other men.'

'I'm sorry I lied to you about what I was writing.'

'I know.' He inhales a deep breath. 'Just tell me, did you fall for any of those men – even a little bit?'

'*No.* Just the opposite.'

'Really? By all accounts, Harrison's a dreamboat.'

'Dreamboat? Where are you getting these words? Do you have a time machine or something? Are you frequenting the 1960s?'

'I'm not sure what the latest lingo is. I'm older than you, remember.'

'By six years!'

He shrugs, clearly unbothered by my teasing.

'And no – to the question about Harrison. Not even the tiniest spark. In fact, it was after my date with him that I realised how I felt about you.' I clock his expression and ask, 'Why does that surprise you? You're a catch too, you know.'

He dips his head in modesty. 'Thank you.' He meets my gaze again. 'So, we're really going to give this another go? And before you answer, keep in mind that Remy will murder me in my sleep if I don't get a second chance with you.'

'Well, we can't have that. And yes, we really are going to give this another go.'

'Then I'm going to kiss you now.'

We reach for each other, our lips meeting in a fervent kiss. One of his hands rest firmly on the back of my neck, the other around my waist, both pulling me closer as the kiss deepens. My hands close into fists as I grab the back of his T-shirt and lean into him.

It feels very much like a reunion, even though we were apart for less than a day.

Silly us. So much misunderstanding and hurt because we weren't open and honest with each other.

A loud voice echoes through the atrium, breaking the spell of the kiss.

'*There* you are!'

Ewan and I leap apart, panting slightly, and I look for Tiggy. She's standing just inside the door to the atrium, her hands on her hips and her eyebrows raised like an exasperated mum from an American sitcom.

'Hi, Tiggy,' I say.

She strolls over, her eyes narrowing at me. 'I went up to your office, but *obviously* you weren't there. I ended up having to ask the security guard out the front if they'd seen you.'

'Sorry.'

'Hi,' she says. 'I'm guessing you're Ewan.'

He recovers from the mini stupor induced by Tiggy's intrusion and jumps up, holding out his hand. 'Hi, lovely to meet you. I've heard lots of good things about you.'

It's the perfect thing to say, disarming Tiggy instantly. 'Yeah, me too – about you. Apparently, you have a very cute dog.'

She smirks and Ewan laughs.

'So, you two have made up then?' she asks, looking between us.

'Yes,' we say in unison. We look at each other and grin, and Ewan wraps an arm around my shoulder and kisses my cheek.

'Excellent – so the email…?'

'Oh, right, the email,' I say. 'I completely forgot.' I look to Ewan. 'I got this random email this morning from an address I didn't recognise, and I thought it might have been you. That's why I called Tiggy. I wasn't brave enough to read it by myself.'

'Ahh,' he says. 'That explains what you said before.'

'So, who's it from then?' asks Tiggy pointedly.

I open my handbag and take out my phone, then navigate to my work email, which I've buried three folders deep to avoid getting in the habit of checking it when I'm not at work.

I scroll, then tap on the email.

'It's from Bex,' I say softly.

'That little—'

'Wait,' I say, cutting Tiggy off.

The email is short and apologetic, and Bex takes full responsibility for her actions. The last line says:

I'm so sorry. I hope one day you can forgive me.
Bex

'She's apologised,' I say, holding up my phone. 'I mean, I won't be hiring her back or anything, but I can put this behind me now.' I heave out a hefty sigh. 'God, I'm—'

'Exhausted?' suggests Tiggy.

'Famished,' I say. I turn to Ewan. 'Are you hungry?'

'Starving. Skipped breakfast this morning to come here.' He looks to Tiggy. 'Do you want to have breakfast with us? I know a really good coffee shop, just down the road,' he says, waggling his eyebrows.

'Thanks, but heeding this one's cry for help meant I haven't even showered yet. I'm gonna head home.'

'Another time then,' says Ewan.

'For sure. I definitely want to be there when you meet Mrs D.'

'Mrs D— Oh, your mum?' he says to me. 'Should I be worried?'

'No,' I say, right as Tiggy says, 'Yes.' She cackles with laughter.

'I'm off.' She reaches down and hugs me. 'So happy for you, babes,' she whispers. She steps back. 'See ya, Ewan.' She pats him on his arm and leaves.

'Well, now you've met my best friend.'

'She's...'

'She's a lot, but she is one of the best people I know.'

'You're one of the best people *I* know,' he says, scooping me into his arms. I don't answer him because it's impossible to talk when you're being kissed.

EPILOGUE

GRETA

Three weeks later

'I'm nervous. Why am I nervous? I'm a grown-arse man.'

I lace my fingers with Ewan's and lean closer. 'They will *love* you.'

'Yeah, relax,' says Tiggy. 'They're lovely people. Plus, you brought wine *and* flowers *and* a dog. Something for everyone. You're golden.'

Ewan huffs out a short, sharp breath.

'Ready?' I ask.

'Nope, not even cl—'

He doesn't get to finish the word because the door swings open and Mum's frowning at us. 'Why do you always stand out here instead of knocking? Come, come.'

She herds us inside but with four of us *and* Remy, it's crowded in the entry.

'*Hallo*,' says Mum to Ewan, 'you must be Harrison.'

'Mum!'

How can she have made such an egregious error? The day after

Ewan and I sorted things out, I told her and Dad – *and* Ru – everything that had happened, including my 'fibs'. She *knows* this isn't Harrison.

A beat later, Mum bursts out laughing. 'I am joking. Just joking, Greta. Always so serious,' she says to Ewan. 'Doesn't take after me. Germans are very funny people.'

'Oh god,' I mutter.

'She's in fine form,' says Tiggy low in my ear.

'Ewan,' she says deliberately. 'So nice to meet you. I'm Margie.'

'Hello, Margie. And this is Remy.'

Remy, who has been perfectly behaved so far, looks up at the sound of his name.

'Oh, *Liebling*... What a good boy you are.' She reaches down to scratch under his chin, while I try not to be insulted that Mum's just given him the endearment she uses for me.

'And we brought you these,' says Ewan. He holds out the flowers and Mum pretends to have only just noticed them.

'Oh, how lovely.' She gives me a loaded look over the enormous bouquet.

'Hello, everyone,' says Dad, coming downstairs. 'We've got quite the gathering this afternoon.'

'Hi, Dad.'

'Hello, lass.' He gives me a hug.

And now I'm about to introduce the two most important men in my life – deep breath, Greta.

'Dad, this is Ewan.'

'Lovely to meet you, Ewan.'

Dad gives Ewan a warm smile, his eyes creased at the corners, and they shake hands. Witnessing this exchange sends a ripple of joyful tingles through me, like a goose walked over my grave, only far more pleasant.

Ewan is meeting my family.

'Ooh, looks like you brought a good one there, Tiggy,' says Dad, eyeing the red wine she's carrying.

'I can't take credit,' she says, handing it to him.

'Er, I chose that for us – it's a favourite of mine,' says Ewan modestly. 'From Piedmont – in Italy.'

'Ewan knows a lot about wine, Dad,' I say. I can tell Ewan's still nervous, but I'm hoping this will help set him at ease.

Dad looks up from the bottle. 'Do you now? Well, you'll fit in brilliantly here,' he says, clapping a hand on Ewan's shoulder.

My heart might explode with how much I love my dad right now.

'Now, you two go on through,' he says to me and Ewan. 'Tiggy, you give me a hand with the wine.'

'Sure thing, Mr D.'

'And your brother's on his way,' he says to me. 'He was at a friend's house this morning.'

'Thanks, Dad.'

Tiggy follows Dad into the kitchen, carrying a bottle of rosé for Mum, and I take Ewan and Remy into the front room. Remy finds a corner and flops down, resting his chin on his paws – adorbs.

As Ewan looks around, I see the room through fresh eyes.

It probably looks like millions of other front rooms around England, only it's steeped in our family history – including the photos of me and my family sitting on the fireplace mantle. Of course, Ewan spies them immediately and beelines to the other side of the room. I follow. He's quiet as he inspects the family gallery, leaning in to look closer at some of the photos and smiling, especially at the ones of me on my own.

'You were a sweet little girl.'

'Hah!' I laugh. 'I was a little terror at times. Mostly when Dad was in charge. With Mum... Let's just say she was way scarier than Dad. I'm sorry she called you Harrison, by the way.'

He turns back to me.

'It's fine. Just her sense of humour. And he is one of my closest friends – it's not an insult or anything.'

'I forget that sometimes.'

'You know, we *will* have to see him eventually,' he says.

I suck air in through my teeth and he laughs.

'It can't possibly induce the same degree of squidgy bum that coming here did.'

I step closer. 'They already adore you,' I say.

'Still early, yet.'

We exchange smiles and I stand on my tiptoes to kiss him.

'Eww, gross!'

Ewan and I spring apart. What is it with the people in my life catching us kissing?

'Hello, Ru,' I say to my brother as Ewan clears his throat. 'This is Ewan.'

'Hi,' says Ru from the doorway.

'Well, come in and say hi properly.'

Ru comes into the front room but it's clear he's not sure what to do. Ewan takes the lead and holds out his hand. 'Hi, Ru, pleased to meet you.'

Ru steps up and shakes Ewan's hand and I couldn't have scripted this moment better myself. Ru may still be a child, but by shaking hands, Ewan has treated him like a young man.

He's scoring points all around!

'Greta said you have a dog,' says Ru.

'Yep. Remy,' Ewan calls and Remy leaps up and trots over.

'Heya, Remy.' Like Mum, Ru is a dog lover. 'Can I take him out the back?' he asks Ewan. 'I've got a tennis ball I can throw for him.'

'Only if you want him to love you forever,' Ewan answers, feigning seriousness.

Ru's face erupts into a wide smile. 'Wicked! Come on, Remy.'

He and Remy bound out of the room, and it would be hard to pick which one has more energy.

'And that's all of them,' I say. 'Not bad, Wilder. You've properly managed to charm my entire family in' – I check the clock on the mantle – 'eight minutes.'

'And how long did it take me to charm *you*?' he asks, capturing me around the waist.

'Oh, you had me at, "Excuse me, I think this is your coffee".'

'Oh yes, famously romantic words.' He regards me thoughtfully. 'I like your family.'

I grin, and he steps closer, slipping his hands around my waist where they nestle on the small of my back. As happens every time he holds me like this, my whole body thrums with electricity.

Ewan looks deep into my eyes, his face drawing nearer. 'But I *love* you,' he says, his voice low and raspy.

My mouth falls open but no words come and, with a soft chuckle, he kisses me. Blissful beyond anything I could ever have imagined, I throw my arms around his neck and kiss him back.

ACKNOWLEDGEMENTS

All my heroines have amazing best friends – the friend who is always in their corner, has their back, and is there for them no matter what.

This book is dedicated to *my* best friend, Lindsey – my sister from another mister. Linds, I love you – thank you for being one of my biggest champions, for making me laugh with daily memes, for being there through thick and thin, and for always giving me a place I can call 'home', just because you're there.

As always, a huge thank you to my incredible editor, Emily Yau, who has, with her insightful feedback helped elevate my writing and my storytelling. With this book, Emily challenged me to break some writerly habits, dig deep, and ramp up the romance, and I think we achieved that together.

Thank you also to the rest of the Boldwood team for your ongoing support, and the care you take with publishing my books. I am so pleased I got to meet (most of) you in person in London back in May.

To my agent, Lina Langlee, thank you, thank you, thank you. Our 11th book together in only 5 years! I greatly appreciate your unwavering support and guidance, which makes the tricky times easier to navigate and the successes even sweeter. Here's to the next 11 books and beyond!

And a special thanks to Caro Clarke, who stepped into Lina's shoes earlier this year, giving me feedback on my pre-submission draft.

I am so grateful to fellow authors Carmen Radtke, who reviewed the German, ensuring Greta's mum, Margie, was saying what I intended, and Ritu Bhathal, who lent her creativity, making the scene with Poppy, Jacinda, and the dating history scrapbook feel authentic, as well as funny. Thank you, as always, to my brother-in-law, Mark Penrose, for taking time to edit my mediocre French. Marie is such a fun character to write, and your help in bringing her to life is much appreciated.

To my author besties, Nina, Andie, and Fi, I can't begin to explain how much I love and appreciate you all. Thank you for your frank advice, your bolstering support, for making me laugh, for championing my success, and picking me up when I stumble. I am *thrilled* that I get to see you all in person this year. Mwah!

To Ben, my love, your generosity in giving me the space and time to write, and in supporting me to achieve my writerly dreams feels boundless. I couldn't do this without you and even if I could, I wouldn't want to.

Thank you to my beautiful family and dear friends for believing in me, celebrating with me, and shouting to all and sundry about my books. Thank you also to my fellow author friends – your support and friendship are sustenance for my heart and mind.

A big thank you to all the booklovers who have embraced my stories. I so appreciate that you love my books as much as I do, and I love hearing from you.

I hope you enjoyed *The One That I Want*. See you soon for Book 4 in the Ever After Agency series...

Sandy xxx

ABOUT THE AUTHOR

Sandy Barker is a bestselling author of destination romance. She's lived in the UK, the US and Australia, and has travelled extensively across six continents, with many of her travel adventures finding homes in her books.

Sign up to Sandy Barker's mailing list for news, competitions and updates on future books.

Visit Sandy's website: https://sandybarker.com/

Follow Sandy on social media here:

facebook.com/sandybarkerauthor

x.com/sandybarker

instagram.com/sandybarkerauthor

bookbub.com/profile/sandy-barker

ALSO BY SANDY BARKER

The Ever After Agency Series

Match Me If You Can

Shout Out to My Ex

The One That I Want

WHERE ALL YOUR ROMANCE
DREAMS COME TRUE!

THE HOME OF BESTSELLING
ROMANCE AND WOMEN'S
FICTION

 WARNING:
MAY CONTAIN SPICE

SIGN UP TO OUR
NEWSLETTER

https://bit.ly/Lovenotesnews

Boldwood

Boldwood Books is an award-winning fiction publishing company seeking out the best stories from around the world.

Find out more at www.boldwoodbooks.com

Join our reader community for brilliant books, competitions and offers!

Follow us
@BoldwoodBooks
@TheBoldBookClub

Sign up to our weekly deals newsletter

https://bit.ly/BoldwoodBNewsletter

Printed in Great Britain
by Amazon